Meet Me

At the River

Buddy Holly

A Novel By

Bob Lapham

ISBN: 1-4107-4626-7 (e-book)
ISBN: 1-4107-4625-9 (Paperback)
ISBN: 1-4107-4624-0 (Dust Jacket)

This book is printed on acid free paper.

Library of Congress Control Number: 2003092502

Printed in the United States of America
Bloomington, IN

1stBooks - rev. 06/03/03

To Mary

For all the things you are…
…My lover stands on golden sands

Other books by Bob Lapham:

**Twenty Years of Life Begins at Forty—The
Story of a Unique Golf Tournament (1973)**

**What Made Wyatt Urp—The Life and Times
Of Toad Leon…a biography (2001)**

The Wild Blue…And Family Too *By Buster
Bridges, as Told to Bob Lapham* **(2003)**

Cover design and author's photo by John Mark Lapham

1. Prologue

February 19, 1984:

Twilight is settling over Houston, Texas. Outside Soundmasters Recording Studio, Treb Maple is leaning against the family automobile. He is exhausted. As a reluctantly resurrected member of the late 1950s pop vocal trio The Picks, three decades removed from the last time they had done anything like this, he has just completed a weekend of almost-nonstop rehearsal and recording. The trio over-dubbed their voices to nine obscure Buddy Holly recordings. The tapings were done for potential release by MCA, which had provided the original master tapes.

"Are you all right, Daddy?" his daughter asks, as Treb's wife, Louise, talks to John Pickering. John now acts as leader of The Picks. He has worked out a deal with MCA, which at this time owns rights to all Holly and Crickets recordings. It was John who brought his brother, Bill, Treb and him together again, this time at producer-engineer A.V. Mittelstedt's Soundmasters. John, a geologist in the oil business who never got over what almost had been for The Picks, hopes this weekend signals new life for the trio. At least so far as Holly is concerned.

"Daddy, are you all right?" Gale asks again.

"Huh?"

"Your hands are shaking. And you're sweating here in the dead of winter. I never saw that before. I'll drive back to Austin."

"Thanks, hon. I don't think I'm up to it."

"This is gonna be big. Big! I promise you that," John is telling Louise as Treb crawls into the back seat of the '83 Monte Carlo.

"I hope you're right," Louise says. "Treb didn't want to do this, you know."

"Yeah. Don't understand his thinking. We've been shoved under the rug for almost thirty years, getting laughed at if we were *ever* stupid enough to tell anybody that Buddy's using our vocal backup arrangements on almost all the early Crickets' songs. Our voices too." John's demeanor takes on a comic Napoleonic flair. "Now, the *world* will know the truth!"

"Money speaks louder than words," Louise mumbles.

"There's gonna be that too," Pickering replies, slipping into a Southeast Texas twang and grinning big. "Lots of it. Y'all drive carefully. I'll be in touch."

"Um-hum. Hope you're right," she says, climbing into the front seat and buckling up as Gale starts the engine. "We could use a little of that stuff."

"Mother, make sure I don't miss the Highway 290 sign," Gale says, pulling out of the parking lot and waving to John.

"OK…Hey! You all right back there?"

"Huh?" Treb replies, suddenly shaken from his exhausted state.

"I guess he is."

They drive in silence for a couple minutes. Then Treb responds to his racing mind.

"Wonder if we've done the right thing?"

"You talking to us?"

"No, Lou. Just wondering if Buddy would've approved of what we just did to his songs."

"I'm sure I have no idea. I just hope this Picks stuff is out of your system now. For good," she says, taking a pack of Virginia Slims from her purse and pushing in the car's lighter.

"I figure he would like our arrangements. He sure did before. These old Decca songs were dead and quickly buried in '56. They weren't going to go *anyplace* without us, that's for sure."

"I hate to tell you this, Treb," Louise says, in her patented, matter-of-fact put-down monotone, "but they're not going any place now, either."

"I liked them, Daddy."

"Thanks, Gale. Me, I haven't made my mind up yet," Treb says, shifting to get a little more comfortable as he lies in the back seat. His eyes close. Immediately he shudders, blinking in the semi-darkness. He is certain he can see Buddy Holly sitting on some sort of wooden arm chair, unsmiling as he stares straight ahead, seemingly oblivious to Treb Maple, as well as to his own apparent little corner of the hereafter.

Treb fends off encroaching sleep, surprised to see the rock 'n' roll figure unchanged in his wide-awake vision and wondering for a minute or two if he should initiate conversation.

"Well, what do *you* think?" Treb finally mumbles, figuring this is all the result of hyper-exhaustion. "I'll be up there, or where ever, pretty soon, you know. Doubt that we will travel in the same celestial circles. But I've got to know. Me, I'm kind of uncomfortable with the whole thing. John sure is excited though. I guess you noticed poor ol' Bill wasn't much help."

Silence, except for the turn indicator as Gale guides the Monte Carlo onto the Austin highway. The deceased rock 'n' roller, now so lifelike Treb can almost reach out and touch him, never changes expressions.

"C'mon Buddy. You never said three words at a time to me when you were alive. Thanks to the Picks, your scrawny butt got saved, musically speaking."

Louise looks back, over the seat. Treb's eyes are still open.

"What? I didn't hear you," she says.

"I'm talking to Buddy," he whines, immediately regretting his candor with his wife, who is always painfully pragmatic.

"Holly? Sure, you are! Be sure to tell him I always liked Elvis better. A *lot* better."

Treb concentrates on the matter at hand, deciding that if this is a valid vision, he can communicate on something closer to a spiritual level.

"Aw, Buddy," his mind relates. "Just nod or shake or something. Did we do right by you this weekend? If we didn't, at least cut me a little slack. We damn well did OK back there in Clovis, late summer of 1957. You've never talked to me about *that*. Sure. You did John and Bill. But *me*? The guy who doubled your voice range? *Nada!* You never liked me, that's for sure. You made that pretty friggin' plain. And here I am, acting like I'm drunk outta my gourd, talking to a ghost!"

Suddenly, Treb is excited to see the vision shift ever so slightly. He can't see Buddy's lips move, but he hears, as plain as the whirring Chevrolet differential just below him.

"It doesn't matter anymore…"

"You mean, after all these years, you're gonna answer me in *song titles!?*

Nothing. So Treb shuts his eyes and yawns.

Do I care? That'll be the day! Rave on, fella! he thinks, then laughs aloud. *Oh boy! Now he's got* me *doing it!*

"That's all right" he mumbles, as Louise looks over the seat. "I'm dog tired. Dead dog tired. I figure there's a mighty good chance we'll talk soon, if I can ever corner your stuck-up soul's twat sometime."

Treb is really feeling sorry for himself now. The old recording sessions at Norman Petty's studio in Clovis, New Mexico used to take their toll on him, both physically and mentally. But nothing like what he's just been through at Soundmasters.

"So, get ready to meet me at the river, Buddy Holly."

"What?" Louise Maple asks. But her husband has fallen into the deepest sleep he's ever experienced.

"Your father is in la-la land," she tells her daughter, taking a drag on her cigarette.

1. Brain Storm in a Tornado

Almost 15 years later.

Brad Poole leaned back from his Unisys and watched the computer screen flicker as his story began to close. He followed the Word 98 commands and smiled as he saw a few of the phrases he had just written zip into cyberspace, or where ever newspaper verbiage went these days. The drama department at Crescent University, one of three schools of higher learning in this small West Texas city, was staging "Waiting for Godot." It had been in his own undergraduate days at Texas Tech almost 20 years earlier since he had last seen the play.

Didn't understand it then, he thought, and I doubt I'll do any better when I review this attempt. He always thought if he ever did fathom the philosophical fantasy, he'd hate the thing.

Can't do that though, he thought, sighing aloud. As the recently settled-in new arts and entertainment editor, one didn't hate the stuff the three local universities put on their stages. Or, for that matter, in their art galleries. Or in their concert venues. One simply learned to write around the bow-wows, finding something—sometimes stretching for *anything*—nice to say.

Godot, he figured, was an enigma of similar proportions for actors and directors on the collegiate level. But someone somewhere with clout had christened the play as masterful. That blessing had become a given quantity. To stand against it was setting oneself up for ridicule by the Society for Pseudo Pucker-Asses, as he called them.

"So much for the old A&E beat," he sighed, making sure *godot1108* was saved in the Sunday features basket. One in the newspaper business, unless his beat was as investigative reporter, realized that jobs were few and far between. Compromising newspapers were cutting their own jugulars, Brad often thought, but who knew how long the corpse would kick? With the overhead the print medium has, you'd figure cable news would've buried them by now. But there was something about curling up with your Sunday newspaper that made the world seem more understandable, even if banking on their weekday editorial pages, papers by all rights should've gone out with the 1990s.

But they didn't, thanks mainly to kowtowing to insert advertising that was proving more manageable and a whole lot cheaper for chain and franchise businesses. Now the newspaper's nemesis, the local television stations, was suffering through its *own* survival struggles.

I'm committed, he thought. I've got two daughters who will come into college age pretty soon. I'm not trained to do anything else. So I'd better

1

stay with the lousy pay and hope the corpse doesn't quit kicking before I get the girls educated and curl up with my 401-K.

He stared across the newsroom at the large picture window that looked out across Walnut Street, a floor below. It was the only visual connection to the outside world on the *American-Telegram's* entire second floor, most of which was taken by the editorial department. The window was a popular venue when it rained—always a big event in West Texas—or when there was a parade below on Walnut. Or when somebody wanted to appear deep in thought for his or her next sentence, when in reality he or she was simply copping a quick daydream.

Brad's problem was, the sports department lay between him and the window. Uncomfortable recognition occurred when he daydreamed, only to finally focus on another self-conscious pair of eyes. Sports was his old beat, and it hadn't been too long since those six desks were a battleground for the very survival of *his* career. Never mind that his professional status now languished in his one-man bailiwick of play and movie reviews, concert openings, painters' and sculptors' interviews, and features on the latest high school-age garage band or—more often than not—young Loretta Lynn or George Strait wannabees seeking to emerge from the swamps of local nothingness into more acceptable obscurity.

Brad self-consciously smiled as he realized it had happened again. His glazed-over eyes focused on those of Chris Stemple's, who likewise gave a sheepish grin and nod before looking away. Stemple was sports desk man at the *American-Telegram.*

The phone rang. Brad reached across the keyboard and picked up.

"Bradley Poole, entertainment," he said, mechanically.

"Brad. Tornado here. You got a minute?"

Poole sat upright and planted both feet on the floor, in spite of the caller being downstairs, out of sight in the publisher's sprawling, ornate office. Even just the audio presence of Mr. Big at the *American-Telegram* was enough to make Brad come to attention. Not only did the 64-year-old kingpin own at least 15 percent of the paper's parent company, B.A. "Tornado" Thornton had been an important friend when Poole returned to the old hometown and its newspaper four years earlier.

"Uh, yessir!" Brad replied. "Whats up?"

"Why don't you come downstairs? I've got an idea to try out on you."

"Well, sure. Right now? I can be downstairs in two minutes."

"That would be just fine."

Some around town said Brad's losing battle with his sports department would've spelled doom, at least with this paper, had it not been for Thornton, even though he probably never said one word in Poole's defense. Thornton was a display advertising and circulation guy, tending to let editorial run its own ship. But the editor's and managing editor's fear of Tornado's potential wrath kept them thinking twice on each and every major decision. Forget that their publisher was a hands-off boss when it came to what went into the oft-criticized daily publication. They knew to run two conservative editorials to every liberal. And if they didn't know it as fact, they suspected that Tornado Thornton really, *really* liked Bradley Poole.

Thornton had married into and re-sculpted a business that was now publicly owned, a member of a chain that stretched into 20 medium sized cities' papers and two TV stations in three states. Tornado (nobody knew where he got his nickname, and nobody seemed to want to find out badly enough to ask around) was worth a cool $10 million in cash, and $90 million more on paper.

"GO RIGHT in, Brad," Gloria, Thornton's secretary said. "He's expecting you."

"Sit down, sit down, Brad," the publisher bellowed, keeping his seat and leaving his feet propped up on his massive mahogany desk.

"Thank you, sir."

"How about a drink?"

"I'm OK," Brad said, fearful of sounding condescending if he brought up the fact that it was 11:30 a.m.

"Aw, c'mon. A beer? Mixed drink? I'm gonna have a gin and tonic."

"Well, if you had some wine…"

"Gloria, whip me up the usual and bring Brad a glass of wine," Tornado hollered through the open door. "What flavor, Brad"

"A little white wine. Maybe a chardonnay?"

"Bring Poole a woosie chardonnay." He turned and smiled at his visitor. "So, how're things on the new desk?"

"OK. I'm enjoying the change of pace," Brad replied, mindful that it had been almost six months since he was almost fired.

"I've read your stuff. You'd think you were trained in the arts, rather than the jock circuit," Thornton said, before taking on a serious look. "It was *your* decision, wasn't it? I thought you were handling that bunch of sports guys real well. But if you wanted a change…"

Brad knew that Thornton knew, but he decided on the spot not to rock this little canoe. If the big boss wanted to go fishing for tales on others, it didn't seem wise to bait *that* hook. The publisher was probably just wanting to show his stuff, and woe be it to Brad to force his hand and make trouble for anyone else.

Which he could do, all right. In spades. But what good would come of that? A little revenge, maybe? Not worth the price. They might want him to go back to sports, and that's something Brad Poole has discovered he *never* wants to do.

"Really, it worked out for the best," Brad said. "I'm two years shy of forty, and sports has become a young person's deal. Too many angry parents, too many night football and basketball games, too many sports to cover now, with Title IX. Call me a coward. When A&E was offered, I took it."

Thornton smiled, pulled out what had to be a Cuban cigar and lit up. He arched his eyebrows into an unmistakable invitation.

"No thanks," Brad said, as Gloria came in with their drinks, then slipped from the huge office without a word and closed the door.

"Guess you're wondering why I really got you down here," Thornton said, blowing the sweet-smelling smoke away from Brad.

"I'm just enjoying the visit," Brad replied pleasantly. He always wondered if Tornado knew that he knew about the night Thornton's life changed so dramatically. The publisher started out as a poor boy from the Rio Grande Valley. He came to West Texas to go to school, met Vivian Young at the local college they attended, and then ran from the rich co-ed until she caught him.

That had been one night at Union Baptist Church, in the next-to-back pew. Viv spent most of the sermon whispering excitedly to Tornado how they should just hurry up and get married. How his business major would please her daddy to no end. Charles Young was an equal partner with two brothers named Best, and their Best-Young newspapers were small gold mines. When they added television in the late 1950s, they hit the mother lode.

Sitting right behind the young couple that fateful night was Brad's late mother, Gladys, and her best friend, Faye Anderson. When Brad came home to be the sports editor at the *American-Telegram,* Gladys had told of listening to the animated whispers of the two in front of them, how Viv actually asked Tornado to marry her.

"Gee, Viv, I don't know," he had responded. "I don't fit in with your family…"

"Yes you do!"

"No, I'm hard-scrabble poor. Your daddy…"

"Daddy will *never* do anything to disappoint me. But he will want you to go to work for him…"

"Oh, I don't know about that, Viv."

"It'll work out, believe me. Say yes," the young woman pleaded, casting a look at the two fortyish women behind her when she realized her whisper had become quite audible, while the eavesdroppers quickly looked down at their hymnals as the sermon ended. "Please!"

At that moment, more than just Brad's mother and her friend could hear Thompson whisper through clinched teeth, "Later, sweetheart! *Later!*"

Well, Tornado did the smart thing and asked for Viv's hand just two weeks after that. It would become an elegant engagement and finish as the society wedding of the year. Even Senator LBJ and Lady Bird attended, with Speaker of the House Sam Rayburn in tow.

"BRAD, YOU ever hear of Treb Maple?" Thornton asked, slamming Poole's mental notebook shut.

"Pardon?"

"Trebor Maple. Guy I knew down in the Valley, when he was assistant pro at the Inn and Country Club."

"Oh, sure. The guy who won a senior event a couple seasons ago, his first time out, and then disappeared."

"Not only won his first, but was the oldest guy to ever win a pro tournament, senior or otherwise. He was 67."

"Oh yeah. He became big news when he walked off the course the next week, leading by something like half a dozen shots through more than two rounds..."

"Actually, four shots," Thornton interrupted. "So you do remember?"

"I'm trying to recall the details," Poole said, wondering where this was going. He knew Maple had a falling out with the PGA, that he had brushed the tour officials aside and had disappeared.

"Wasn't it something about a fight?" he asked the publisher.

"Not with fists. Words. Pretty heated stuff. They really crucified the guy. I knew him at Brownsville High, even though he was two years ahead of me. Wild as a March hare. Drank tequila and Oso Negro. That's the cheap gin and vodka brand we could buy across the river in Matamoros. Treb drank the stuff like it was water. But could he hit a golf ball! Good players usually managed to beat him pretty easily. But nobody had a solid swing like Treb Maple.

"What I'd like to know is, what happened to him? Where is he now? Why did he vanish? I'd like to break the story, maybe win an APME award next year with a series. Chase him down and get the scoop."

"Sounds interesting, One of the guys in sports would like that assignment," Poole said, suddenly wondering where this interview was going. Especially since Tornado Thornton was famous for seldom suggesting story ideas to his twin towers of yes-men, Scott Campbell the editor, and Tom Richards, the managing editor.

"I've got a different angle than sports," Thornton replied. "And no, I haven't talked to Campbell and Tom about it, either. I got this idea, and it may blow up in my face. So I want to do it on the sly. I want you to track Treb down. I do know on good authority that he lives in Las Vegas, but there's no listing. I think he gives lessons at some club or public course. There're a bunch, but for a veteran newspaper guy like you, this ought to be a piece of cake. At least to find him. Last I heard, he had become a social dropout. Has his buddies like Don Cherry out there, plays and teaches some golf, and plays poker."

Poole sat silent for a few seconds, wondering how to phrase his response. "And do the story?" he finally replied. "Sir, it does sound like it has possibilities. But where does entertainment come into play?"

"Maple should be an interesting guy to write about, though probably not easy for someone to get to open up. That's what makes it such a great story idea. At least," Thompson added, smiling through a cloud of Cuban cigar smoke, "I *think* it's a great idea.

"See," he continued, after pausing to line up his ideas, "Maple was in entertainment one time. Sort of. Like Cherry, he wanted to be a singer. Like Cherry, he got a big break. I think it had to do with Buddy Holly. He sang on his records, with three or four other guys. What was that group?"

"The Crickets."

"Sure. That's what it was. The Crickets. They were big when I was in high school, two or so years after Treb left Brownsville. Then Buddy got big as a solo artist, as I recall. Then he died in a plane crash."

"Uh, Mr. Thornton—"

"Ah-ah now. Call me Tornado."

"Uh, Tornado, I've read about Holly, since he's a Texas rock 'n' roll icon. I don't remember *anything* about Treb Maple, the golfer, ever being a Cricket."

"I know he had a connection there somewhere, Brad. I remember in Brownsville, when I'd go back during summers when I was in college, people talked about it for a year or two. Then after Holly died, his songs sort of disappeared. And so did the stories connecting him to Treb. By the way, did you know Kris Kristofferson grew up in Brownsville?"

"No, Mr...Nope, Tornado, I didn't. Maybe he would be a good—"

"Nah. Been done to death. Country music song writer, movie actor, and one of the 'Outlaws' along with Willie Nelson, Johnny Cash and Waylon Jennings—"

"Now, *there's* a story. Waylon used to be with Holly. Before Jennings died, I remember reading interviews about how he gave up his seat on Buddy's ill-fated plane to another singer. Let's see...um, right! The Big Bopper. Richie Valens died in the plane crash, too, because both he and Buddy got bio-flicks out of it. Holly was re-discovered in the 1970s.

Probably ranks second only to Elvis in the list of influential rock 'n' roll pioneers. We could do Kris remembers Waylon—"

Tornado Thornton held up his hand in a halting motion.

"No, again no news value. I really think there's something about Treb Maple that would be good reading. The poor guy failed at everything he ever tried. He might've been a big singing star, you know. He didn't do squat in golf until he was in his mid-sixties, when he won that seniors tournament out west somewhere—"

"And then walked away from *that* little brush with fame! I kind of see where you're going with this now, sir. Not much of a local connection, but statewide, yes. I can't understand why someone hasn't tried to sniff it out before."

Thornton smiled, and hissed. "Because Treb's a *loser!*" Then he settled back in his leather office chair, took a drag from his cigar and blew a perfect smoke ring, while he put his feet back on his desk. "Only, maybe we can make him a winner one more time. And," he added in a stage whisper, while slipping his feet under the desk and leaning on his elbows, "we get the APME award next spring for best series. Hey! You might even get a *book* outta this. If you play your cards right with this crackpot, he might know where lots of bodies are buried. Lots, besides Buddy Holly, who we all know is buried in Lubbock."

"So, what's next?" Brad said, shifting himself in his chair.

"I want you to ask around, real low-profile like, with some of your connections," Thornton replied. "I don't want your pals upstairs to know. Loose lips sink ships. I don't relish the *Fort Worth Star-Telegram* or the *Dallas Morning News* getting wind of this. They might shoot us out of the saddle."

Thornton shifted back to his regular posture of feet on the desk and eyes focusing on an idea. "I'll explain to our own editor and ME what we're cooking up, and swear their rusty rumps to secrecy. Here's the deal. You'll be taking some advance vacation time, if anyone asks. We'll square that later. Probably have to wait until next year, since I think you've already vacationed out this one. Hey!" the publisher added, as if a brain light bulb suddenly went on. "That girlfriend of yours—pretty little thing, God bless her. What's her name?"

"Amanda Scott."

"Oh yes. Amanda. Why don't you ask *her* to go with you? Make it look like a real holiday in Sin City," the publisher said, then adding with a sly grin, "get you some good lovin'."

"I don't know, sir. Mandy's sort of straight-laced."

"Nonsense! She was hanging onto you like a schoolgirl two Sundays ago, at the company party. She's in *love*, son!"

Poole smiled, but bristled inside. Where does this old fart get off sticking his nose in my business? "Still, I don't think—"

"Give it a try, Brad. All on me. I'll pay you 30 cents a mile to drive to Midland and back. Leave your car at the airport. You can fly direct to Vegas on Southwest. Viv and I used to stay downtown at the Fifth Jack. I still know people there. I can get you all a high-roller's room, with most meals covered. And," Thornton added with a twinkle in his eye, "you won't have to be out any of your own money. You can establish an account of, say, twenty thousand in action after you check in. Better still, I'll set that up ahead of time. Then, every so often, you and Amanda place a few bets on the blackjack tables, or shoot a little craps. You don't *really* gamble, do you Brad?"

"Oh, I play a little poker every now and then..."

"That's out. At least on *my* money. You buy the chips, and keep up with your losses. Play blackjack or shoot craps, and let the little lady pull on some slots. All I ask is space it out, and keep the losses to a couple grand. That'll satisfy the Fifth Jack people. Winnings over that you can keep. But when you get close to two housand in the red, haul ass away from the tables. That action, with the casino underlings and lower office employees *assuming* you will be betting upwards of twenty thousand during your stay, should cover you with the casino's hotel and restaurant for two weeks, if it takes that long to get Maple to open up. Hell, play a dollar slot now and then. You two go to some shows. Have some fun. I'll spring for any other expenses, like a rental car, when you get back. But concentrate on Treb Maple. I *do* expect a story for my seed money. You're probably gonna lose my two thousand—the maximum, I remind you in the *most* emphatic way— and I'll be responsible for getting the eighteen-thousand dollars back."

"Look, Mr. Thorn—ah, Tornado—why don't I just go out there and see what I can dig up? As I said, I don't think Mandy will want to go."

"OK. You be the judge. But I want you to stay at the Fifth Jack. They owe me. Big time! And I'd love your young woman—bless her—to go with you. The way she handles her, uh, affliction, well it's damn commendable. And if she was along and you ran into someone from here, who knows someone at the paper, they wouldn't think anything of what you're doing in Vegas."

"I'll ask her, Sir," Brad finally responded.

"And you're all set for the story?"

"That part sounds real interesting. Yes."`

"Good man!" I'll do the arrangements myself, just in case, after you tell me it's for two, or just one. I figure you'll know if the story will make by a week. But take more time if you think it will help."

Brad stood and reached across the desk, taking his publisher's outstretched hand. "I'll go over and feel Mandy out about this."

"Fine, son. Get back to me."

AFTER CHECKING his voice mail upstairs, Brad went out the back way and crossed the alley separating Walnut Street from Peach. Mandy's little cards and book store was on the corner of Peach and Second, whereas the paper took the entire block from first to second, Walnut to Peach.

Leave it to Mandy, the queen of quaint, Brad thought to himself, as he heard the familiar tinkle of the bell above the store's entrance. A beautiful, very slender, curly-haired brunette looked up from a customer and gave Brad a quick five-fingered wave with her right hand. Mandy had taken over the store from her grandmother, with whom she lived. She stocked mostly paperbacks and major magazines. Brad scouted the best-seller rack while Mandy, ever locked into what had to be the sweetest smile this side of heaven, listened to a matronly customer.

"Amanda, is it possible for you to order me some back editions of Danielle Steele?"

"Of course, Mrs. Schroeder. It wouldn't take too long."

"Are you able to get large print? My eyes are becoming worse by the week."

"Sure! And just because I don't stock them, I can order hardcover if you prefer."

"I just love this woman's way with a story. Don't you, Amanda?"

"She's quite good, only not my style. But Danielle Steele has been very, very popular for years."

Brad picked up what appeared to be a spy thriller he'd never heard of and, turning his face away from the two women, winced. That's my gal, he thought to himself. She couldn't tell even an innocent little white lie.

"I don't know why I'm just now taking the plunge," Mrs. Schroeder sighed, before chuckling. "I'd never have guessed I'd become a candidate for romance novels. I just got hooked on all those TV versions. My, my. That Danielle can really write. How she can come up with all those different stories, year after year, every summer and Christmas, and even Easter sometimes, is beyond me She's just like clockwork."

More like a cash register than a clock, Brad idly thought. Probably doesn't hurt to have a sweat shop, albeit a well-paid sweat shop, of researchers in your corner. Maybe even some fledgling authors penning a little dialogue now and then.

"But I don't know that, do I?" Poole mumbled as he replaced the paperback in its "Number Eight" holder.

Both women looked up. "Did you say something to us, young man?" the older woman inquired as the beautiful face of Amanda Scott's turned a little pink.

"Pardon me, M'am," Brad said. "Just talking to myself. I, uh, didn't even hear what you all were talking about."

"Danielle Steele."

"Danielle? Great writer. I read her stuff sometimes."

"*You,* sir?"

"Sure. Her novels are real page-turners," he said, quickly looking away from the dagger-stare Mandy was giving him.

"YOU DON'T read Danielle Steele!" Mandy chided, after her customer had rung the little bell on her way out.

"How do you know?" Brad teased, watching the beauty, at 25 much-younger than he, rattle her way one-handed through the computer keyboard in her own unique but highly proficient way.

"You don't. I just know!"

"Well, if I could sell like her, I'd wear a bonnet down Peach Street at high noon. All the way to the bank. Is Thelma coming in pretty soon?"

"Grandmother? I haven't heard otherwise." She deepened the beautiful, glowing smile she always wore. "You want some lunch?"

"You read my mind, as usual. You want to step across the street to Gordo's?"

"OK. If you'll go to church with me tonight. That way, we can trade out dinners."

Brad sighed. "I'm sure yours comes with a Wednesday night Bible lesson."

"Oh, it's not so bad," she said, as she flashed her smile at a man who rang the entrance bell and headed for the Hallmark Cards section.

She was right. Her Presbyterian friends were nice, without literally hog-tying a guy into signing up. Since his divorce, Brad had been courted by Baptists, Methodists and Church of Christ acquaintances to attend their singles Sunday school classes. Just one or two of those outings made him sure their styles wouldn't take.

In fact, he had eyed the pretty Amanda Scott even before he and Betty split, and his ex-wife had gone back to San Antonio with their two daughters.

Mandy had no airs about her. Just an unmistakably honest genuineness. A question here and an inquiry there had told him that she was 13 years his junior. Minus one there. He also found that she didn't date much, but when she did, it was usually with guys in their early thirties. Even a forty-plus or two. But no one for very long, Brad had discovered. That had been a plus. Doubly so now, since he had been going with her for three months, only recently becoming a serious item with her. What a night *that* had been! Amazingly, they both recovered.

He smiled, unable to resist thinking that this was a plus that cancelled all minuses. And why. At least, so far. Truth was, he was falling in love with this girl, and had told her so. After, he was surprised to have experienced, she had told him the same thing.

A relationship? Definitely! Marriage? He had sworn off buying another ticket on *that* leaky boat. But if anyone could change his mind, it would be Mandy Scott.

"Hope the anniversary evening is a good one," he heard her tell the man who had just bought a card and was waving at her as he exited, just as the familiar figure of Thelma Walker was entering.

"Hi Brad," the handsome woman in her early seventies greeted.

"Hello, Thelma. Just in time. I'm taking our girl across the street for a sub."

"You want us to bring you something, Grandmother?" Mandy asked, as she slipped on a sweater to guard against the brisk November north wind."

"I'm fine, dear. You two take your time."

AFTER THEY crossed Second, they entered the former square block of mall space now divided into small and medium-sized offices for attorneys, accountants—even a recording studio—and a smattering of the precious few independent producers still active in the dried-up West Texas oil patch.

"You're the quiet one!" Mandy teased as they steered a course for the indoor sidewalk café put together to resemble one in Italy. "What're you thinking about?"

"You noticed? Tell you in a minute."

"Now you've got my curiosity up," she replied.

They ordered subs, he a pepperoni and she a veggie, and carried ice tea and chips to a table at the far end, away from the other seating.

"Well?" she asked, as he scooted a wrought iron chair beneath her shapely, if not a bit slender, hips.

"Well, something has come up," he replied taking his seat and reaching for her right hand.

"Sounds ominous."

"No, actually it's pretty neat. At least one way of looking at it."

There was a pause, then Brad continued.

"Ever been to Las Vegas?"

"What?"

"Vegas."

Mandy smiled. "Didn't I ever tell you that I'd never been out of the state of Texas?"

He vaguely recalled that she might've mentioned it some time ago. But so much had happened recently in their budding relationship, he had all but forgotten.

"Rhetorical query, I guess," he responded, wondering how best to ease her toward an invitation to the world of interstate travel. "The thing is, I have to be in Nevada on business, probably within a week or so."

"How long will you be gone?" Mandy asked, looking as sad as she could through those luscious brown eyes, without crying. An ultimate and shattering situation Brad had known only once before.

"A week. Possibly two. But there is an upside, if you'll consider. You're invited."

Mandy stared across the table. Her eyes narrowed.

"Sounds like a proposition to me," she finally said, slowly and rather coolly. "Are you taking the past two weeks a little for granted?"

"No, no, nothing like that..."

"Hey Brad, come and get it," the hulking proprietor, chief cook, cashier and bottle washer hollered."

"Nothing like that, Mandy," Brad repeated, standing. "Hold that thought—and please, your tongue—for a minute or two."

"Nine ninety-five, counting the chips, tea and sales tax," the man said, smiling. "Amanda, she looks ravishing, as usual. No?"

Brad smiled. "She does, doesn't she?"

"Just a leetle sad. Or bothered, maybe? More than when you two lovebirds came in. Hey! You haven't hurt our girl, have you? You weel have to answer to Gordo, if you make her sad. Remember that! I have connections," the big man said with false bravado. "I know people, you know. From the old country."

"Are you Italian this week, Gordo? Or Mexican?"

"Both," he replied with a toothy grin. "The bad kind, both ways."

Brad picked up the sandwiches. "I'll remember that."

When he got back to the table, Amanda was deep in thought. As he sat and parceled out their lunch, she looked up.

"Brad—"

"Now, before you say no, think about it. You know Thelma will hold down the fort. You know we will have some fun. And you *know* you can trust me."

"Sure, I can." She smiled as she saw Brad's demeanor droop. "Oh, come on! I'm not blaming you for what's been happening. If there's someone I don't trust, it's me. Not you."

Brad had to think about how exasperating this conversation was getting, given the age in which they were living. He decided to take another tack.

"Here's the deal,' he said, drawing imaginary doodles on the marble tabletop. Then he proceeded to lay out the entire plan as Tornado Thornton had to him, scarcely an hour earlier.

"This close to Christmas, I'll bet Siegfried and Roy will be at the Mirage. Maybe Tony Bennett will be appearing—"

Mandy had to grin, elfishly. "Tony Bennett is dangerous. We found that out 15 nights ago...remember?"

"You're counting days? I'm impressed. Anyway, We can take in some shows. You can learn to gamble just a *little*. Jesus has such a grip on your soul—"

"Brad!?"

"OK, for one reason or another, I'd give a thousand to one odds that nothing could get you hooked. And I promise I'll get Tornado to make sure our room has *two* beds. In fact, the way he talked, we may even have a high-roller's suite. Any hanky-panky will be instigated by you, my dear. Yes, I will respond gingerly. Quickly. Passionately! But I will not make the first move. I promise. If I'm lying, may they cut off..." *Damn!* He thought. "...cut off my expense account that will whisk us away to where we shall show the world how to enjoy Las Vegas without compromise."

Amanda laughed. "You really *want* this to happen, don't you?" She reached across the table and picked up his hand. "I'll think about it. OK?"

"That's all I ask. Only, uh, I need to know by tomorrow. And would you keep smiling, please? Gordo thinks I'm giving you a hard time, and he's threatening me with Mafioso-style hurts if I don't cut it out."

"I'll decide this afternoon, after I talk to Grandmother," Mandy replied as they stood to leave. "But you smart guy! You probably know I want it to happen."

When his heart frittered away a beat, Brad felt just like a college freshman hustling a date to a dance.

"Hey Gordo," Mandy whispered as they walked past the counter. "Forgive him, OK? He's a kid at heart."

"You justa tell me if he's ever *not* a gentleman," the big man replied with a whoop. "*He* knows whata I can do to him."

As the pair left the sidewalk café area, a man Gordo had not seen before walked to the counter.

"That girl is quite pretty," he said.

"You gotta that right," Gordo replied, eyeing the man carefully.

"In fact, she's drop-dead beautiful."

"Um-hum."

"But...but..."

"Yes?" Gordo interrupted, warily.

"She's, uh, she's missing her left hand. And most of her arm, up to the elbow."

Gordo smiled. "Oh? I hadn't noticed. None of us do, once we get ta know Mandy."

The stranger smiled as he pondered the lunch menu. "I can understand that."

2. A Very Special Young Woman

Amanda Scott was backing out of the driveway when Brad drove up to her grandmother's house on Palm Avenue. She smiled, waved and stuck her head out as he motored down his driver's side window.

"Gone to the drug store. Be back in half an hour," she called out. "Grandmother forgot to call in her prescription, so I'll have to wait for it. Go on in. She's waiting for you. I'll hurry. Bye."

Brad waved, smiled and parked his four-year-old Dodge Stratus in front, beside the walk leading up to the two-story, 60-year-old frame and brick house Amanda shared with Thelma Walker. He strolled slowly up the concrete walkway, wishing he had known their date would begin later.

He and Mandy had attended her church the evening before, then she had told Brad she "probably" would be going with him to Las Vegas.

"I just want to tell Grandmother first. OK?" she had conditioned.

"Hey, Mandy, you're a big girl," Brad had said with some irritation, then regretting that he sounded like someone on the threshold of middle age whining to his younger sweetheart who had taken control away from him.

"I just want to tell her what I'm planning, Brad. I want her to feel like she has some say. I mean, she raised me. I still live with her, and run the business that she built from the ground. Do you mind terribly?"

"Of course not. I just want you to go to Nevada with me," he had grumbled. Damn! It was just so natural a thing for Mandy to want to do, so nineteen-fifties-ish, but so foreign to what was happening now. Certainly for people in their mid-twenties.

By late afternoon, just a couple hours earlier, she had called Brad and green-lighted the ticketing and reservation process. Brad then turned it over to Gloria, Tornado Thornton's secretary. In short order, they were set for departure in five days.

"I handled the airline," Gloria had conveyed. "Mr. Thornton called the Fifth Jack. You got the suite, the best they have, you lucky dog you! Take me next time! Oh yes. The boss wondered if you'd had time to do any advance legwork on Treb Maple."

He had told her Monday would be reserved for that. Michelle, the young weddings and anniversaries writer in Lifestyle, was tabbed to be his temporary replacement by the obviously none-too-thrilled managing editor, Tom Richards. Brad would wrap up his Sunday advances tomorrow, catch the only movie worth reviewing in the early afternoon, then spend the rest of Friday showing Michelle the ropes.

He had found the young writer and former summer intern beyond excitement at the challenge and opportunity.

"And you'll be gone *how* long?" she had gushed.

"A week. Maybe two."

"Ooohh. Make it *two*. Everybody *knows* you have the best beat here. Let me borrow it for as long as you can."

"I'll do my best," Brad had responded, smiling.

NOW, HE was at Thelma Walker's door, wondering what the next half-hour's conversation would be like. Dumb feeling, he chided himself.

"Brad! C'mon in! I did a stupid thing and forgot to call in my Tamoxifen prescription. I had to borrow Mandy for a while. Hope I'm not spoiling your evening."

"Not at all. We were going over to Gap Springs for some catfish. We've got plenty of time."

Well, well...WELL!" the attractive senior citizen clucked, motioning Brad to sit opposite her in the lounger. "Mandy told me all about your trip. Sounds exciting!"

"I think it'll be a fun time, especially since Mandy insists she's never been out of the state."

Brad hated to admit it to himself, but he coveted a quick subject change, and thinking about beauty in reference to Mandy's grandmother seemed to present one. "It's hard to believe she's been a non-traveler. And never has flown. Doesn't she ever want to go to—where is it, Miami?—to visit her mother?"

Thelma was what Brad would describe as a good ol' girl. She had survived breast cancer without a mastectomy, and was in her fourth year of remission. One more year on Tamoxifen and the doctor said she'd pretty well be in like Ms. Flynn. Or, so Mandy had told him. He figured she was paraphrasing her grandmother on that diagnosis.

Looks were in Mandy's genes. Thelma was still a pretty woman in spite of being close to seventy. She had the figure of a fashion model, and wore jeans and a man's shirt quite well for someone her age. He'd never met Mandy's mother. But he had seen photos, and Mary Katherine Walker Collins Gerard Arnaz left nothing on the table, so far as beauty was concerned.

Thelma shook her head. "Not Miami, but close enough. Coral Gables. No, she and her mother aren't real close. Mary Katherine comes through here one or two times a year. Often forgets to call on Mandy's birthday. Used to send her Christmas presents now and then. Mandy never seemed to let it get her down, when M.K. forgot. She used to make excuses for her mom, back when she was little.

"M.K. That's what *she* calls her, too. Mandy *always* remembers her mom on special days. It breaks my heart sometimes. But Mandy is so unflappable. I don't worry too much about their relationship, or lack thereof."

"Too bad," Brad mumbled, wondering if now would be a good time to pump Thelma about some mysterious family history the young woman with whom he was falling in love had steadfastly kept from him.

But no such luck.

"About Las Vegas," the older woman said. "Where are you staying? As if I'd be able to relate to it, since I've never been there and never intend to go. Not to detract from your trip, understand."

"Of course not. We're staying at a hotel called The Fifth Jack. And Thelma, I want you to understand my boss has sprung for a two-bedroom suite."

She smiled. "You don't have to explain anything to me, Brad. I love that little girl more than I ever could my very own. I can read her like a book, as if I had to. She beats me to the punch, telling me *everything* that goes on in her precious life."

Brad felt his cheeks heat up. A change-of-subject move now would be transparent. He figured his goose was cooked.

"*Usually* everything. She began talking about you around a month or so ago. Never had before, like that, with any other beau that she might've been seeing. They used to line up outside my door, the young ones, but she refused to get serious with any of them. Then, by her senior year in high school, she was into dating college boys who went to our church. They didn't fare any better. I felt so sorry for the promising ones, who would bring her back after the second or third date, get that hang-dog look on their faces, and never be seen again. She experimented with older types for a while. They'd usually call, young ones and older, but what little I'd overhear, Mandy politely but firmly would give them that old let's-just-be-friends' speech, or something close to it. She never meant to hurt anyone, though that little grandgirl of mine has broken many a heart. I know. Some of them tried to move back into rotation through me.

"But I'm talking out of school here."

"No, no. I mean, if you don't mind. Mandy can sidestep a question about family or boyfriends or...or her arm like she was dancing around a diamondback. I sure didn't want to cause friction between us. But I was understandably curious. As matters, uh, progressed between us, I figured I'd get to know things when the getting-to-know time was right. Go on. I mean, if you're not uncomfortable."

Thelma flashed that magical Walker-Scott smile again, the one she could turn off and on; about the same one her granddaughter wore virtually all the time. Brad had laughed to himself quite a bit lately, wondering if that endearing look was worn by Mandy when she slept.

They had made love, all right. Whoa! What a night *that* had been, the first time! But they hadn't slept together, in the literal sense. What a stupid way to describe sexual intercourse, anyway, he mused, as he noticed Thelma gathering her own thoughts. You sleep, you sleep. You screw, you screw. You make passionate, even exotic love as he and Mandy had, twice more since that very awkward maiden—in every sense of the phrase—voyage, and you share a special kind of love. To his credit as a word merchant, he thought, he had never broached the trite phrase, "We slept together," or "I slept with so-and-so."

"You're smiling, Brad."

"Huh? Oh, sorry. Where were we, Thelma?"

"You were thinking about Mandy. Right?"

"Uh, right. I do a lot of that these days, actually."

"Not surprising. So, what is it you'd like to know about our girl, that she won't come right out and offer? I know what she might *not* like me to talk about. I also know what she might be hesitant to tell you, only she wouldn't care if I talked to you about parts of her past that sort of simply lie there, right under the surface of that sweet demeanor of hers. Things about people she has found a way to control, to not think about."

"Through her religion."

"That's right. Her religion. A relationship with God through Jesus that is so special, it's indescribable. Me, I'm a Christian. I pray sometimes. I go to the same Presbyterian church that Mandy does. I consider myself a good person. A caring person. But my walk with God is light years short of Mandy's. Hers is natural. Close to perfection. So genuine…"

The ringing phone prompted a pause in the conversation, and not a moment too soon, Brad figured. This was *not* what he wanted to discuss with Thelma Walker.

"Oh hi, hon," Thelma spoke into the 1970s-style rotary desk phone. She mouthed the words, *It's Mandy.* "Um-hum. Um-hum. Nope. I don't want generic, if there actually is such a thing. Tamoxifen. The original. C'mon home. I can skip a day, and pick it up tomorrow…Oh, I hate for you to do that. Brad's here. You all are going out to eat…Well, OK. We're having a grand talk. No, I'm not into that, silly! We're just visiting. All right. See you then."

Thelma sighed, replaced the phone in its cradle, and returned to the sofa opposite Brad in the lounger. "Amanda says they ran short of Tamoxifen. Wanted to know if she should ask them to substitute generic. I've gone through four years and four months with this stuff sometimes playing havoc with my insides. But the tiny, pencil-eraser sized cancer they took out hasn't come back. So I'm sticking with it. Mandy said they were sending someone across town to borrow four pills, and then fill the monthly supply when theirs comes in. Mandy said it'll take another half hour or so. Care for some tea? Coffee? A Coke?"

Brad shook his head.

"Now, where were we," Thelma mused. "Oh yes. Religion. I'm going to take a wild guess and figure you don't want to stay on *that* subject for long."

"If you don't mind," Brad mumbled.

"Mandy said she considered you a work in progress."

"Thelma, I have to be honest. That's a pretty optimistic assessment on her part. At least for now."

"Let's leave it there, shall we? What else can I tell you?"

"You know, I never have asked her exactly how she lost her arm. Except once. Not that it matters. I hardly ever notice it."

"Nor anyone else, once they get to know her. I'm sure you've seen that. What did she say when you asked her how she lost her left hand, and the arm just below the elbow?"

"That it was an accident in a car her father was driving, when she was five."

Thelma paused. "In a way, that's correct. Do...do you want me to tell you the whole story? Mandy has opened the door to it, but I'll wager she'd never go beyond that on her own. Besides, I probably know more than she does anyway."

"Well, I *am* curious, all right. That is, if you're sure she wouldn't care if I heard it from you."

"I don't think she would, or feel that I was being disloyal," Thelma said, shifting in her chair. How cute, Brad thought. This little old lady is sitting on her socked feet, just like she was in a college dorm. "She'd like you to know, I think, and this way she wouldn't have to tell you herself."

She sighed. "It's not a pretty story, Brad. But Mandy has adjusted to it well, I think. Or, actually, I *know!* I've tried several times during the past fifteen or so years to talk to her about it, to see if *she* wants to discuss that night, and how much she remembers of it. But she always waves me off. 'I'm OK with all that now, Grandmother,' or something to that effect."

She shifted in her chair again.

"I take it that Mandy hasn't told you much about her mother, either," she said, matter-of-factly, watching Brad eye her intently as he shook his head.

19

"Just that she moved away when her father died, and wound up in Florida. She told me, without my asking, that you and her mother decided it would be best if Mandy stayed here, with you."

"No. *I* decided. And I didn't get much argument from my daughter, either," Thelma replied, defiantly.

"We had Mary Katherine fairly early, and everything we did bringing her up with no brothers or sisters seemed to be wrong. I don't know what happened or how it did, or when, but by her teenage years, Ed—you knew he was my late husband—Ed and I had a daughter who was totally self-centered. She married almost right out of high school, to Peter Scott, a boy whom she met in her freshman year in college here. He was from Waco. They lived with us, and they fought all the time. I mean, it was sheer *misery* to listen to her ride that poor little guy, dusk to dawn to dark, about how he didn't have enough money to treat her properly, how he didn't show her enough respect. He just wasn't good enough for Mary Katherine.

"Ed and I suffered through it so much. Then she started drinking along with her husband, who had come into her life with a pretty solid collegiate fraternity alcoholic background.

"Soon she was pregnant. They would *really* get after it then. Ed finally put his foot down, if you could call it that. He said they ought to have their own place, finish college and then maybe things would get better. He rented a garage apartment for them, as far across town as he could.

"Mandy was born, and what a beautiful baby! Since we had ducked out on their domestic life, day to day, we had no way of knowing what was going on with them. I think we liked it that way. Neither of us really felt the fighting had ended, but if we didn't hear it or see it very much, we didn't worry. However, we should have."

THELMA PAUSED. "Mary Katherine quit college after her sophomore year. Just as well. She was majoring in speech and dramatics, and planned on becoming a professional actress." Thelma gave a rather pathetic laugh. "My daughter could've had a great career of playing Maggie the Cat," she said with a smirk. "But I don't know how many revivals of *Cat On a Hot Tin Roof* one could expect to play in a career. Anyway, Peter got a business degree and took a job with First National Bank."

"Here?" Brad asked.

"Yep," Thelma sighed. "They stayed in town. Actually, I was glad, since I could see Mandy regularly. And sort of look after her. Anyway, the years passed. Mary Katherine couldn't hide her discomfort at becoming a stay-at-home mom. When the little theater troupe would stage a play she particularly liked, she'd audition for it and always get the lead, or whichever role she went after, from the ingenue in *Sabrina Fair* to heavier fare, such as Annie in *The Miracle Worker.* My daughter was good. No question about that. And she was beautiful.

"Peter, meanwhile, was not going much of anywhere at the bank. So he signed on with an independent insurance agent. Meanwhile, he tried to keep up with Mary Katherine's specialized needs. He really did try. But she wanted so much, not the least of which was to 'get out of this hick West Texas town,' as she loved to say, in my presence.

"By the time Mandy was five, Ed and I were real worried. Mary Katherine and Mandy would come here to sleep over, at least one night every two or three weeks. Then it happened."

"The accident?" Brad asked.

Thelma nodded. "M.K. stormed into this very room with Mandy in tow. She was a bit drunker than usual. Then here comes Pete, bombed out of his mind. Ed played referee while I grabbed Mandy and headed upstairs with her. But we couldn't get far enough away. They were easy to hear. Mandy sat there, those big eyes filled with tears. I could've shot *both* her parents, on the spot!

"Finally I heard Pete holler, 'OK, this is it. I'm gone. And I am pretty sure I won't survive the night…one way or another. All I ask, please, is that you let your folks raise our daughter.' 'Good riddance!' M.K. half-screamed, half-hissed, tacking on a pet name she frequently called Peter during their brawls, a name I could never repeat, but will never forget. 'And don't you worry about MY daughter. *I* will make sure she gets what *she* needs. *And* wants! Something you will never be able to handle!'"

"Well, before I could grab her, Mandy was out of the bedroom and down the stairs in a shot. I stood at the top, looking down, as my drunken daughter, then Ed, grabbed for her. Both missed. M.K. cried out, 'Honey, he's no good. Let him go!' and then shut up, stunned when that tiny little girl turned and gave her mother the only hateful look I've ever seen come across that gloriously beautiful face. Real hate. I think it did something to M.K. I *know* it did me; another something I'll never forget."

"Wow!" was all Brad could utter, before Thelma continued.

"Mandy screamed for her daddy, and in an instant I, perhaps all of us, realized for the first time how much her father meant to her. It seems that this fragile little bird had never taken sides in the wars between her idiot parents. But she was now. She ran to Pete. By this time Ed and I were through the front door, past where M.K sat on her knees, stunned. 'Honey, go back!' Pete wept through his stupor, giving her a hug. 'Always remember your daddy loved you more than anything in this life.' He got up, staggered to his car, and after a couple of false starts, somehow got the engine going."

Thelma began weeping softly, then continued. "'Please Daddy! Stay!' Mandy begged, crying while grabbing for the open door just as Pete slammed it. She screamed. So did I."

Thelma paused, wiped her eyes, then continued softly. "Pete didn't hear, or it didn't register. He slammed the door again, and took off, dragging his little girl along for at least fifteen feet. He sped off into the night, probably never realizing what he'd done to his little girl, who lay in a heap in our street."

"My God!" Brad mumbled.

"We spent the evening in the emergency room. You want a real capper to this nightmare from hell? About two hours later, the cops followed an ambulance crew through the ER entrance. A body lay under a bloody sheet. It was Pete. He had driven his car at a high speed into a median, bounced airborne for a good seventy-five feet, and slammed into a concrete divider. One of the policemen recognized Ed, and told him. Ed came and told us. M.K. fainted. I collapsed in a chair and didn't move for what seemed like hours. Thank God Mandy was heavily sedated.

"Prostheses, back twenty years not being what they are today, weren't ruled a viable option for Mandy. Then years later, she said she had grown used to her arm being what it was."

"How in hell did she ever survive all that?" Brad quickly responded.

"Well, certainly not in hell," Thelma replied, with both of them immediately feeling guilty about what they'd just said. Thelma smiled, and held up her hand. "That's OK, Brad. I know you didn't mean it. Well, our girl spent a couple of years in pretty sad shape, not the least of that time when her mother pulled out within a month and headed for Hollywood. After three years taking booze and whatever else that cruddy city has lying around, she married some clown named Coop Collins. He was an actor who never made the third page of credits for a film or TV show. She didn't either, for that matter. They were married just long enough to drop in and introduce Mandy to her new step-dad. I'll never forget when they drove up in a five-year-old Cadillac. Ed, God bless 'im, pulled M.K. aside and told her in no uncertain terms that they could get back on I-20 and go to Dallas or back to L.A., if there was one peep out of either of them that would upset Mandy.

"Didn't matter. They stayed thirty-six hours, and we never saw Coop Collins again. Nor M.K. either, at least for several years. Finally, a couple in our bridge club who'd been to Miami said they'd run across our daughter at some club in the Little Havana district, dancing topless. Lousy excuses for friends! They couldn't wait to tell us that. Said they weren't sure they'd recognized M.K. at first, but tracked her down after the club closed and she remembered them. 'Tell my mom hello,' they said M.K. told them. 'And my little girl too.' Of course, Mandy never heard anything about *that*, even though by now she was in middle school. Shortly after this evening of bridge, maybe a month, Ed keeled over with a heart attack and died."

"I can imagine why," Brad muttered.

"Not out of sadness. He was past all that. Mandy had changed our lives so dramatically, no other human being could ever dull our delight at sharing hers. Not even our own daughter and the horrible messes she had got herself into.

"Mary Katherine has seldom been back since then. She got hitched to some guy in Miami named Girard, whom we never met. That lasted maybe six months. Then she married a slick-looking Cuban American named Oscar Arnaz. M.K. says he's supposed to be a distant kin to Desi. Wouldn't know about that. Oscar has a little ponytail, and doesn't say much. But he apparently has money, and that's all M.K. cares about. I have no idea how he makes it. But nothing would shock me. They come through here a couple times a year, en route to Las Vegas, coincidentally. Have no idea why they don't fly. He shows not the least bit of interest in Mandy, which is all right by her, I'll bet. She doesn't show *anything* one way or another, though."

"Thelma, if you don't mind my saying so, you sell yourself short. You have to be some kind of special person to have brought a little girl through that physical and, in particular, emotional maelstrom, and helped her become the special person she is."

Thelma shook her head. "Not my doing, Brad. Not long after the incident that cost her her arm and her pitiful excuse of a weak-kneed father, the minister in our church—"

"Central Presbyterian?"

"Yes. Will Pearce. He shepherded her through the first couple of weeks. Then our associate pastor, a fellow named Stew Clifford, was a champion of no small stature to that granddaughter of ours, off and on for two years. Ed was great for her too. But Stew was a rock. He's now a missionary in Romania. Anyway, by the age of eight, Mandy had turned to her church with a passion you just cannot believe. It crushed her when Stew moved on, but they remained pen pals. She was an avowed Christian by twelve, and hasn't looked back since. Me, I was always a lukewarm Presbyterian, neither hot nor cold, and spewable, as my Savior would say. But you can't stay that way around Mandy. She doesn't preach Jesus to you. Doesn't have to. Jesus *lives* in her, in a very special way."

She paused, then added, "Keep that in mind, Brad Poole."

He just smiled, uncomfortably.

"Now, about this project you'll be working on in Las Vegas..."

23

JUST THEN, Mandy burst through the front door. "Sorry folks. It's been a strange night, back and forth across town while pharmacists tried to straighten out their mess."

"Hon, I'm so sorry. It's my fault—"

"No apologies necessary. It gave me a chance to visit with a couple of people I ran into. What've you guys been talking about the past hour and a half?" she said, eyeing with suspicion Brad's somber look and the trace of tears on her grandmother's cheeks.

"I'm pumping Brad about your trip. Sounds exciting. What's this about Buddy Holly?"

Brad recovered his composure after the horror story he'd just heard. "Well, this fellow Treb Maple has a connection to back when they were at Texas Tech, or at least Maple was."

"Buddy Holly was close to my favorite, after Elvis and Carl Perkins," Thelma said.

"Anyway, Maple later became a club golf pro. Took him almost half a century, but he finally made a competitive splash. Then he just vanished. Mr. Thornton wants me to track him down. As an ex-sportswriter turned entertainment scribe, he thinks we can get a series that will scoop everybody with a human interest angle."

"Sounds interesting," Thelma said. "And promising."

"The thing is, I understand this Maple is sort of a recluse. Won't talk to the press anymore. Thornton wants me to try, though. At least, we'll get a paid trip out of this. All Mandy has to do is pull a few handles. Mandy, you still want to go get something to eat?"

She shook her curly head. "Uh-uh. I'll whip up something for us here."

"Count me out," Thelma said with a yawn. "It's upstairs for me, and a coin toss to see whether Jay Leno or David Letterman gets to put me to sleep."

3. The Sports Staff from Hell

Late Monday morning, Brad Poole decided to chase a little background on Mr. Trebor Maple, the object of his concentrated attention the next couple of weeks.

Brad had made sure Michelle of Lifestyle was up to speed on knowing what would be happening around town the coming seven to fourteen days. *Noises Off,* the British backstage farce, was opening Thursday at Crescent University's brand new performing arts center. Good show. But Brad had seen it three times, as produced by three different venues—the most recent only six months ago as one of his first plays to cover on his new beat. Next week, the little theater troupe would present its annual musical, this time reprising Lloyd-Webber's and Rice's *Joseph and the Amazing Technicolor Dream Coat.* He sort of hated to miss that one, which would have been a first for him, outside of Donny Osmond's less than spectacular version on television.

Michelle was ready, however.

"You remember the Drake Museum will preview that 20th Century Russian art exhibition Friday after next," Brad said, reaching for the folder his public relations connection at the museum had provided. "It's pretty good stuff, though a little brooding since it comes from the post-Revolution to post-World War II period. Heavily weighted to the Communist line. Lots of smiling factory workers and farmers. But Russian art work always has possibilities."

"Any dominant style?" Michelle asked, which made Brad uncomfortable, since paintings were his short suit. He liked impressionism and, in particular, early Van Gogh. But he couldn't tell you why.

"To be honest, damned if I know, hon," he admitted. "Brandi's stuff is OK, for canned PR material. See if you can pin her down for next Sunday's cover. There are color slides in the folder, so you should have good art to go with your advance."

Michelle gathered up the material, plus some movie press kits for openings due in the near future. "Brad, you don't know how *great* this is going to be! I can't thank you enough!"

"You'll do fine, Michelle. Just have fun."

She scampered off, and Brad opened his computer file that contained phone numbers for his sources. The Associated Press' statewide office in Dallas had a 1-800 connection, but he wanted to chat with his pal, Denne Cochran, on a straight line. He got past AP's switchboard, then heard the older man's familiar voice.

"Cochran, sports."

"Hey, Denne. Brad here."

"Poole? You hound dog you. What're you up to? Been missing talking to you regularly. And seeing you in the press box at Texas Stadium. Boy, aren't those Cowboys stinking up the place these days!"

"Yeah. It was fun. I've got a new beat now."

"So I hear. You wanna tell me what happened? Let me guess first. Bart and Will, with some McKnight thrown in."

"That's the short answer, all right. But I've got a job, at least. And no offense to the great Denne Cochran, but I am *so* glad to be out of sports. I don't want to bitch too much about the screwing I had to take. They might make me go back."

"So what happened?"

Brad sighed audibly into the phone, which he cradled on his shoulder while he scanned his three-day backlog of e-mails reminding him of upcoming arts and entertainment events, correcting an obscure *who-cares?* misstated fact from his mid-week column five days before that bitched about a blown date in yesterday's A&E Marquee bits and pieces section, and attacking his stupidity for giving a film a one-star rating instead of three, "which anyone with an appreciation of *film noir* the director was re-inventing would recognize as deserving."

"Long answer necessary, Denne. I'll tell you sometime. Since you're an Aggie, it involves last spring's A&M intrasquad game we all went to. And the most beautifully orchestrated Shakespearean back-stabbing you could ever hope to see."

"Et tu, Brute?"

"You said it, pal. If the twin towers of *American-Telegram* editorial dictates would've had their way, I'd have been sent packing. But a war between the churches, plus the fact that Tornado Thornton likes me and my work, again plus knew and liked my mother, all saved my hide. If," Brad continued, with a sardonic laugh, "holding down this one-man beat at a 50,000-circulation rag could be construed as rescuing my rump."

"Religious conflict? The Aggies' spring training game, following our most excellent media golf tournament? Tornado and *your* mother? Hey, Buddy. You got my appetite for dirt whetted!"

"Later. I won't leave out a gory detail. I promise. Except don't get the wrong idea about my late mother and Tornado, a good twenty years her junior."

"OK. You win. I've been perusing our computer archives while we talked—"

"That trick of the trade must be inherent for us print media types," Brad said.

"Comes in handy, huh? Anyway, I've got a lot of dated stuff about Maple, but it's things you have already called up, probably. Any inside scoop, like why he walked into and quickly out of the Senior PGA, doesn't get to the meat of what must be a story. I remember I tried to get the tale from the horse's mouth and assigned Mike to do a piece."

"Freeman?"

"Yeah. Maple wouldn't talk to him. As I recall, we got a lot of nothing from the players. Most never got a chance to know Maple. Some bad-mouthed him, most of which we decided not to use, since he wouldn't defend himself. He *was* a colorful interview for those couple of brief and shinning weeks, wasn't he? What're you up to? Doing a feature?"

Cochran had become a good friend, but Brad didn't want to take the chance of scaring any ducks off *this* pond and spoil a puzzlingly close relationship with his publisher.

"Just sort of musing about a story angle. I think Maple might've lived here, during his old club pro days. As an assistant to Morgan out at the club. Might make a piece. Probably won't."

"So, you moonlighting on your old beat now?"

"Sports? Nah. There seems to have been an angle to rock 'n roll with this guy. But like I say, it's pretty remote. I may just have to spike it."

"Before you do, call Freeman in Fort Worth. I noticed in the archives that he covered the tournament Maple won in Utah. He could remember some stuff that might keep the story idea at least on the back burner."

"OK. Thanks for your time."

"By the way," Cochran said, "How're Betty and the girls?"

"All right. Last time I heard. I try to call the girls every week. But I don't get off to San Antonio but once every month or six weeks. Betty has nothing to say to me, really. And I can't blame her."

"Man," Denne Cochran said softly and slowly, "I never thought you guys would split. Do you...do you still play cards?"

Brad smiled. "Not like I used to. Fortunately."

"I've got to be at Texas Stadium for a press conference in forty-five minutes," Cochran said. "It's been fun. Sure do miss you at the Cowboys' games."

"Me too. Later."

As he hung up, the thought of poker, Vegas and twenty-thousand bucks in his pocket, or at least seemingly so to a casino, oozed into Brad Poole's thinking, like the first rays of a day's sunlight cutting through the dark of pre-dawn.

He smiled. Tornado Thornton was saving a buck or several hundred on expenses. He hadn't said so, but Brad figured he'd be turning over a couple of ten-thousand-dollar money orders made out by Thornton to the Fifth

Jack, most likely to the attention of one of Tornado's buddies in the casino's front office. The books would show twenty thousand in stakes, but Brad figured that the contact at the casino would make sure the daily chit-sheet would note a limit of a couple thousand. Brad would come home with the minimum of an eighteen-thousand dollar casino money order made out to Tornado. Brad and Mandy would sleep and dine like royalty for a couple of weeks, maybe even get lucky on the tables or at the slots, and pay for their shows on the side.

He smiled. Fat chance, he thought. I wonder if the pit bosses who log your action do so at the hold-em table?

Brad looked up Mike Freeman's number at the AP desk in Fort Worth and dialed. Forget it, he told himself. No poker. And not in Vegas, for sure.

"MIKE FREEMAN," the familiar voice spoke through Brad's earpiece.

"Mike-o. It's Brad."

"Poole, you sorry excuse for a golfer! What're you doin'?"

"Seeing movies, snoring through college plays, acting like I know an old master from Andy Warhol, and reviewing orchestral concerts while wondering why an oboe always gets to start things off."

"Sounds the A, buddy boy. Sounds the A."

"So I have since found out," Brad replied with a laugh.

"Hey! How's that beautiful wife of yours?"

"Uh, we got a divorce, Mike. About a year ago."

"Oops! I didn't know. Did I?"

"You just forgot, probably."

"Well, I have to admit that two years ago, at the Aggie spring game, she wasn't acting like the happy camper we had got used to knowing and loving. What happened, if you don't mind my asking?"

"She drank a lot, and I drank a lot. We got through that somehow, though I wonder if our little girls will ever get over it. I'll be honest. I got burned a couple of times playing cards."

"You? *Burned?* By whom? Texas Dolly? Man, I'd have backed you in a minute in the World Series of Poker. You've been in *my* pocket enough times."

"Guess I wasn't as good as I thought I was," Brad replied, giving a stock answer that he still refused to believe. "At least, her father got that idea, when he had to cover me not once, but twice. About twenty grand's worth, total."

"Whoa!" Freeman replied with a whistle. "You get Dear Old Dad on your case, watch out!"

"That wasn't the main reason. Betty and I had gotten tired of each other a long time ago. No hanky-panky. At least on my part. Or at least, nothing real serious. A marriage just blew up, in spite of two great children who came out of it. The money I had to crawl for, to get a couple of busted oil men from Midland off my back, was only the fuse."

"I missed the spring game last March, so I guess that's why I didn't know any of this," Mike said. "You did go, didn't you?"

"Yep. We tried to play 'Talk Crazy,' but it wasn't the same without you."

"As well it should! It was *my* game! Denne said it was a super outing as always. Golf was great. Food at the football dorm was five stars. Nobody cared about the game."

"That's about it. Skip puts on a great show, in these days of disappearing junkets. It changed my life, that's for sure!"

"In what way?"

Brad sighed, then after a couple of attempts at changing the subject, finally gave his friend a spiel pretty much following the same line as he had proffered Denne twenty minutes earlier.

"What I'm really calling about is Treb Maple," Brad finally said, figuring he had concluded another exercise in hitting the high spots."

"The golfer? Thought you were in entertainment now."

"Golfer *and* entertainer, I understand. Mike told me you covered his brief senior tour career. His win, in particular."

"Missed his next tournament, abrupt as it might have been," Freeman added. "*That* was the interesting one. He walked off the course leading by four shots."

"So I read," Brad said, suddenly wondering that if there had been a Cracker Jack of a story in all this, Mike would have done it already. Freeman was Mr. AP Feature Writer in Texas, Louisiana, Oklahoma and New Mexico. And he'd published a couple of books on his subjects, on the side. One was about a famous Fort Worth murder he had covered that had been made into a TV movie. "Just trying to connect some dots via an idea my publisher had," Brad continued. "Probably won't amount to anything."

"Good ol' Tornado Thornton!" Mike mused. "The smartest son of a bitch who ever lived, when he married into a publishing fortune, then learned enough about the business to get by, hired the asshole of the universe to be his publisher while he sat on the sidelines in display advertising, had the resident professionals who lorded over upstairs for the two of them running scared, and when the time was right, moved into the big corner office downstairs. What's he worth now? Fifty million?"

Brad had forgot that Mike Freeman's start in journalism had been at the *American-Telegram.*

"More like a hundred."

"The old *American-Telegram*," Mike said with a whistle. "The vet staffers when I was there called it Peyton Place."

"So, what can you tell me about Treb Maple?" Brad asked, again.

"So, what will you tell me about your exit from sports?"

"Didn't I?" Brad grumbled.

"Not the nitty, pal. Give!"

Brad had never told anybody the whole nine yards. Not even Mandy. Now, for some reason, the prospect suddenly seemed interesting, perhaps therapeutic, and the timing proper, if it ever would be.

"OK," he said, resignedly. "Just don't tell Denne I told you. He pumped me real hard and I stonewalled. I still may have to work with you guys sometime. And Denne is your boss."

"Just in college football season, buddy boy. Now give!"

BRAD TOLD how six years earlier he had been brought to the paper from the Lubbock *Avalanche-Journal*, where he had worked up to being assistant sports editor after graduating from Texas Tech. He had met Betty there, and they had married right out of college.

Tom Richards, the managing editor at the *American-Telegram,* had his hands full with his sports staff. The paper considered high school athletics and, to a lesser degree, collegiate sports as its selling cards. The staff numbered seven, including desk man Chris Stemple.

"They all want to be sports editor, except Chris," Richards had explained to Brad when he had been interviewed by the managing editor in a Snyder restaurant, a strangely surreptitious meeting eighty miles from Lubbock.

"Not unusual, I'd say," Brad had answered.

"Well, not any of them is going to get that job. They're fair to good to excellent writers, if you proof their stuff well for grammar and spelling. But what's new about that for sports?" Richards had said with a nervous chuckle. "I don't want to lose any of them, actually. They all covet an APME sports writing award, and that's where you come in. You have one."

Two, actually, Brad had thought, if you count the UPI first place and the AP runner-up the next year, in the first two times any of his work had been entered.

In the two-hour interview, Brad had felt two red flags had been hoisted. First, the managing editor was afraid to clamp down on his staff, particularly Bart, who had become a popular if not controversial columnist. Second, Brad was being hired to ride herd on stampeding egos, not to develop his own turf.

But he took the job, which moved his family a hundred and sixty miles closer to his wife's beloved Daddy, nullifying her disdain at leaving Lubbock and the regular socializing she did with her sorority sisters, both young and graduated.

Actually, the move worked reasonably well in the beginning. The staff resented an outsider coming in and trying to set up schedules and call shots, after Brad's predecessor had pretty well let wide-ranging local and area sports coverage take care of itself. The former sports editor, a guy who actually smiled and told Richards "Thank you!" when he was fired, would put the names of beats in a hat and let the staff draw their assignments each season.

When Richards called Brad into his office soon after his arrival and said, "We've got a problem," Brad found himself at a crossroads.

"Uh, Bart came in the other day and said he wants to share duties," Richards explained.

"I came here with the understanding I was to be sports editor."

"And you are. But Bart suggested he get a title that won't seem like he was passed over."

"Which he was. Correct?"

"Right, Brad. He was. But Bart makes sense, actually, if we can keep McKnight from jumping ship. Bart said why not make him executive sports editor? You would be the sports editor and make the day-to-day decisions."

"In other words, Tom, I do all the dirty work and he gets the credit. Suddenly he's perceived as being the boss."

"But we'd know differently, right?"

Brad sat in the close confines of his managing editor's office, realizing his return to his old hometown had been a mistake. "Wouldn't McKnight object to your plan? Or, let's be honest…Bart's plan?"

"I'm sure he will. But if I lose one of them, I'd rather it be McKnight."

'Then what about Will?"

"Ah, he's an old-timer. As long as he gets to cover track and field each spring and do his Sunday area high school columns, he'll be OK with it. Everybody at Crescent University loves him, since he's one of their own, more or less. He's got contacts. He doesn't want to be sports editor like the other two." Richards paused a moment before continuing.

"Well, what about it?"

"No way," Brad had said, thinking that Bart would be as dangerous to his authority as the other two primary staffers. Maybe more so.

"I hate to hear that. I've got to do something."

"Tell him, 'No way,' Tom."

Richards had shaken his head and heaved a sigh, and Brad had realized that the ME already had promised Bart, without asking him. Brad had just moved his family here, and going back to Lubbock wasn't an option. Good newspaper jobs were drying up. But he was going to be miserable if this thing were strapped on his back.

"Tell Bart he can tack associate sports editor to his title," Brad said finally, putting as much resolve into his voice as he could muster.

"Associate? Hmmm. It might work," Richards said. "I'll run it by Bart."

"No, don't ask him, Tom. *Tell* him. You gave me this job and I'm already being compromised. That's as far as I feel I can bend over and take this...this screwing. Think about how this will look around town when what's going on gets out?" Brad rose. "Excuse me. We've got a staff meeting." Then he strode quickly from Richards' office.

Bart was not happy, but he accepted the compromise on his play for power. The rest of the staff was not too thrilled either, but they finally accepted Bart's promotion into a hitherto non-existent position over them, but just under Brad.

The first football season had gone reasonably well, except that Brad's love of the high school and small-time college game had taken a severe beating. But he was co-existing with his staff, ignoring their petty pot-shots at his authority and slowly organizing their efforts.

BRAD HAD become an insider at the Aggie spring football and golf outing while at the Lubbock paper. Tech and A&M were Big 12 Conference rivals, so a scribe from the *Avalanche-Journal* who got to invade the archenemy's camp and come back with a feature or a column on how the prospects looked was well-received. Brad got the outing because he carried a 9.5, lowest golf handicap on the staff. He could cover the game as straight news, even though spring training windups were less than competitive. What he liked most about Skip's outings was the availability for interviews of Aggie stars that would badmouth Tech and make for very readable columns in West Texas.

Prior to Brad's arrival, the *American-Telegram* had not been at the A&M spring fling in several years. For one reason, the three local universities' small college football programs had spring games, so there always was a good chance for a conflict with the A&M game, which would be difficult to justify covering on top of AP. For another reason, the three top figures in the six-man staff were fiercely jealous of one another getting individual perks. And yet another reason was, those three simply stank on a golf course. They'd be hard pressed as a threesome to break 90 if they played their best ball; individually they were above-100 shooters. So none was overly anxious to submit himself to the humiliation of being the worst hacker at College Station.

This made it easy for Richards to turn down annual A&M invitations extended by Skip. Until, that is, Brad showed up. He was a veteran of the junket, and he automatically signed on when Skip proffered a special RSVP invitation. It cut Richards out of the loop. And it caused a slow burn among the envious staff elite, in spite of their lack of golfing skills. Particularly Bart and McKnight.

"LAST SPRING, I returned from our little party in College Station pretty well worn out," Brad told Freeman. "You weren't there. But I'm sure you've heard about the 4 a.m. breakup of our Friday night bash, then our 8 a.m. tee time Saturday, followed by the 2:30 kickoff of the most boring of all boring A&M spring games I ever sat through."

"Yes, I heard," Freeman said. "I was jealous."

"Keep in mind, Mike-o, it was a co-ed junket, with wives invited. I was recently divorced, and I hadn't begun another relationship yet—"

"Yet? *Yet?* Give, Buddy-boy."

"Another story, another time," Brad replied in a patronizing tone, glancing at his watch and seeing that he had spent more than twenty minutes talking to the ace AP feature writer and occasional major sports coverage expert. "Anyway, I didn't write anything about the spring game. For one thing, the Crescent U. spring windup had been the same weekend. I figured I could stick in a column sometime later, when I was high and dry.

"For the golf tournament, which was a scramble, Skip had put me in Coach's foursome, obviously on orders since my coverage of the Tech-A&M game the previous fall, when I all but accused the Aggies of intentionally putting the Raiders' quarterback out for the remainder of his senior year. I remember buttonholing the kid who made the tackle in the victorious locker room and asked him how it felt. 'How great can it be? What a thrill that tackle was!' You remember, Rodney got put out for the year with a broken ankle. I watched the play closely. Maybe it was an optical illusion, but it sure looked as if the defender gave Rodney's leg a stiff twist at the end."

"Um-hum. I remember the incident. Not like you did though, seeing it through the eyes of others. And I read your coverage, plus the sidebar. Didn't you talk to Rodney on the sidelines near the end of the game, while he watched Tech get beat with a cast on his foot? And don't I recall your asking him if he thought breaking his ankle had been done on purpose? Hey, Brad. Were your veins pumping red *and* black that night? As in your old alma-mamma's school colors?"

"Right all the way around, I guess, though I had really sensed that A&M went after Tech's QB. And their stands! Boy, they stood and cheered during that crucial first quarter, when the stretcher crew came out and carted Rodney off. '*I...don't...know for...sure,*' I remember Rodney fairly hissing. I milked that *real* good, about asking him if he had been hurt seriously, perhaps on purpose. Not my shinning moment, I have to admit."

"Boy! Coach had to be pissed."

"That's why I figure Skip put me with him. Since the tournament was a scramble, high-fives with lots of bullshit in between birdies graced our foursome. Except, Coach managed not ever to touch me, or even speak a word. And get this. We shared a cart. Total freeze job.

"Anyway, I digress. About a month later, Skip writes me this letter asking why there had been no Aggie spring game story in our paper. He said I wasn't the only non-cooperative freeloader. He cried in his letter that Coach was thinking about junking the junket next spring.

"I remember Bart was at his desk, opposite mine. He must've seen the Aggie logo on the envelope, and seen me read the letter after I opened it. And then seen me stick it under my desk calendar. I sighed and told Stemple I would have a column next Sunday, after all, and to remind me to tell McKnight to hold his. I hammered out one on a short interview I had with that 300-pound, monosyllabic bowling ball of a fullback they were touting for the Heisman.

"'What'cha working on?' Bart asked me. 'Just doing a little repair work,' I replied. 'Gotta take care of the Aggie spring trip.'

"Well, when my column came out, the staff made a big point about bitching all the way to Richards, and then up to Scott Campbell. Bart swiped Skip's letter from under my calendar and showed it to them. As if on cue—which it was, I found out later—Rob Gerschwitz had done a nifty reporting job of what was going on behind our paper's closed doors to the staff at Crescent. Gerschwitz is Crescent's sports information director. Both Will and McKnight were tight with him, though I suspect Will set all this up.

"Here comes the head coach-AD at Crescent asking the editor for my head on a platter. Same thing at the other two universities here. All guys I had never done anything to, except do my job and let them bask in the spotlights that usually came with it. Now they were actually hating me. That really disillusioned me. My best friend from grade school was a basketball assistant at one of the universities. He was the only friend I had. He took up for me, though it put him square in the middle of the battle."

"So, the paper eased you out of sports?" Freeman surmised.

"Not yet. I had the feeling that as bad as all this crap smelled, Tornado had let it be known I was to stay put. However, pretty soon the screw got turned real tight."

"How's that?"

"Well, one of Bart's buddies on a local high school staff, a Hispanic, got passed over for the head football job. Bart wrote this tongue-in-cheek column about the sins of a school board that wouldn't give his pal of minority ethnicity a chance.

"At the last election, the board had become tilted in favor of one major church crowd over the other. Church of Christ versus runner-up Baptist. The column was pretty brutal, without naming names, in Bart's crafty, satirical way. Meanwhile, I was late to a date I had wrangled with this beautiful 25-year-old—"

"The now-girl, perhaps?" Freeman interrupted, gleefully.

"Beside the point. Anyway, I let Bart say that the same old bloc of school board members had banded together and would hire their man. In essence, this would reject the application of the Hispanic assistant Bart had been trumpeting.

"I left for the day, feeling a gnawing uneasiness in my gut. I had almost told Bart I couldn't approve the column, that he could take it to Richards if he wanted to, and maybe he would OK the piece. But with my low esteem at the paper as well as around collegiate coaching staffs in town, I thought I'd cut him a little slack. Let him take his little dig.

"Next morning, I opened up the sports section and saw the column head on Bart's piece. 'Tripping Over the Same Old Bloc.' No surprise. The head had came from the body. But I spewed my orange juice all over the counter when I got to that graph, where the culprit board members suddenly were identified as the *religious* bloc."

"Ouch!" Freeman interjected.

"I got to the paper as fast as I could. The switchboard was on fire with calls from irate Church of Christ readers—the bloc to which Bart obliquely referred. Nothing from Crescent, mind you. Just readers.

"No staffers were there. I told switchboard to tell all calls to us that sports wasn't in yet. Pretty soon, the deskman, Chris Stemple, wandered up. I was all over him, wanting to know what had happened to the proofed column."

"'That thing about religion? That was Will's idea,' Stemple told me. "We tried to call you at home. But you weren't there. So we went with it."

"'Without clearing it with Richards?' I screamed. He said Will explained that people wouldn't know what Bart was trying to say. I told him they sure would now, thanks to one of their own. Will's a member of the Church of Christ.

"About that time Bart ambles in, looking like a hound who had just dined on the raccoon he had killed the night before. I headed for him on a run, but the ME intercepted us both. 'In my office!' he roared.

35

"Richards shut the door and said, 'All right, I'm listening.' He stared straight at Bart, then me. 'Bart, bad idea. Did you get Brad's approval?' He nodded. 'Brad?' 'Tom, they changed the wording on me. Calling the four school board members a bloc is bad enough. I admit I OK'd that. But sticking in *religious?* That changes everything."

"'Will's idea,' Bart hedged. 'And it was just one word. You weren't around to discuss it.'"

"'Bart, I had already discussed the column with you," I sputtered. "Then you guys changed it.' Now, get this, Mike. Richards actually *agreed* with Bart. 'He's right,' he said. 'Everybody would know you're talking about Church of Christ people, either way. You guys go back to work. But I guarantee you, this thing is gonna get nasty! I want you to run every single letter you get.'"

"So they jerked you out of sports," Freeman said.

"Not yet. A funny thing happened on the way to the lynching. Church of Christ people, I understand, got the word out among themselves to ignore the paper and this flap. We hardly received a bad letter to the editor after that first day. But we were besieged by Baptists saying things like, 'I didn't know the *American-Telegram* had the guts to tell it like it is!' Bart became a hero to them. Tornado is a Baptist, you know. He loved it!"

"So, how *did* you get the ax?"

"A month or so later, after Campbell and Richards had really taken the heat in secret from Crescent's administration and sports people, and Bart and McKnight, along with Will, had told the editor and ME how bad it looked that I had breached the rules against conflict of interest with that stupid joke I told Bart about why I wrote the column about the Aggie fullback, they filled the A&E desk with me. Named Bart and McKnight co-sports editors, if you can believe that, and Will associate sports editor, Bart's old faux handle. I give this combine six more months, maximum."

"I'm surprised you got to stay, as bloodied up as you must've been."

"That's the funny thing about all this. They couldn't fire me, or Thornton and all the Baptists would be on them. And the Church of Christ people had settled on the high road, at least publicly. Also, in that month, I had met the most intriguing, beautiful young woman thirteen years younger than me, and I didn't want to leave town until I discovered how this budding relationship was going to play out. And the capper? I have grown to actually enjoy this artsy-fartsy beat."

MIKE SIGHED. "Some story. So I feel obligated to tell you what I know that you want to know about Trebor Maple."

"I'm curious," Brad replied, ignoring the red flag fluttering before his mind's eye as he spoke into the phone. "Why didn't you dig deeper into the mystery of Maple? And by the way. What were you doing covering a senior PGA tournament in Boise?"

"It was because the region's AP staffer was on vacation. I hadn't been to Idaho before. The weather was supposed to be fine in late August. It was too. I used to do this same thing for our guy in the Rio Grande Valley. That's how I got to know Maple way back yonder. He was a real party animal. Had the sweetest swing this side of golf heaven. But he couldn't putt worth squat. Every time he would play competitively, he'd choke. Then, with no flat stick to fall back on, his swing would come apart. He was an easy mark. The man could play poker though, as I remember from stories down there. And he was fun to be around. He was an assistant at Valley International Country Club.

"I lost track of Treb over the years. I heard he had a bad experience co-owning a small course in the Corpus Christi area. Or maybe it was Victoria. Then I heard he went back to the Valley, when they expanded to thirty-six holes. Spent his winters there and ran that little course in the mountains of New Mexico. What's the name…?"

"Ruidoso?" Brad asked.

"Nah. Close by. Oh yeah, Cloudcroft. You ever play there? Little nine-holer. Eight-thousand foot elevation. You can hit the ball a mile. Anyway, I heard his wife, Louise, got killed or hurt real badly in a car accident of some kind, ten or twelve years ago. Now, there was a looker! Beautiful brunette. Even in her fifties, I remember her as a knockout. Somebody just *made* for a guy's fantasies.

"So imagine my surprise when I got to Boise Tuesday of tournament week to find out my old Valley drinking buddy had been a Monday qualifier. My God! This guy was sixty-seven years old! He'd tried to qualify for the regular tour maybe 30 years earlier, at least two or three times. Never even made it past the first thirty-six holes."

"And he won the thing!" Brad said. "Yep. Played lights out. Couldn't hit the driver more than 250 yards, but his irons were flawless. And he sank *lots* of putts. Won by four or five shots, if memory serves me correctly. He was a different guy than the one I had known. A real Jesus freak too. Most of the press corps tore him a new one over that. 'God is My Caddy,' I recall one headline. 'Who Needs Yardage When You Have Christ on Your Bag?" said another. Although Treb had some old friends on the senior circuit, most of them abandoned him. His press conferences were a riot!"

"Actually, he won by four shots," Brad interjected. "So he wins, gets ridiculed by the press—not by you, though, from the archive stuff of yours I read. But he was the oldest pro ever to pull off winning a senior event. Or

Champions, as they call it nowadays. Then he picks up where he left off the following week at Napa Valley, leading by *six* shots through two rounds, only to walk off the course and, it seems, into oblivion."

"That's how it went," Mike Freeman agreed. "I was back in Fort Worth by then, so I missed out on the Napa fireworks. He got into it verbally with some of the pros. But still, he was whipping their butts. The PGA was not happy over his exit, believe me. I tried to get them to talk about it the next week, but I couldn't squeeze much from them except he had been fined, and until he paid that and made some explanation over his behavior, his short career as a touring senior golfer was over."

"So what about his Buddy Holly connection?" Brad asked.

"You know, I had always heard about that. But Treb wouldn't discuss it when I knew him in the Valley. It was late in the Boise tournament when someone finally called ESPN and said Treb used to be a backup singer for Holly when he started out with the Crickets. Treb reluctantly 'fessed up, but wouldn't expand on it. ESPN tracked down some credits and found he had doo-diddly-de-wahed on *Oh Boy!* and some of Buddy's early hits. It got pretty confusing in the press quarters, when Treb all but denied the connection that ultimately became undeniable."

Mike laughed, then continued. "I remember on Sunday, ESPN showed some early clips from Treb's round, and played *Oh Boy!* while he sank puts and drilled irons at pins. It was funny to see him hitting utility metal woods on par threes when some of the whipper-snappers only 50 or 52 hit seven and eight irons. But Treb was invincible that week. Who knows what might have been?"

"I hear he's in Las Vegas now," Brad offered.

"Me too. Giving golf lessons and playing poker downtown."

"Sort of strange for a born again Christian…"

"You'd think so. But why this interest? Treb walked away from a million-dollar career, maybe more, when most everybody else is drawing Social Security and milking sick 401-Ks. Hey, pal. You pumping me so you can do a feature on Maple?"

"I'm going to Vegas this week, and I got the idea to maybe look him up. Maybe I could sit in on some Hold-Em with him, you know?"

"I'd kibitz, Brad. Maybe Jesus is at his side at the table, just like on the golf course. I hear he can whip most anybody in poker. And he walked out of golf with a quarter-million-dollar stake."

"Just curious, that's all. I'm going to be there with my new girlfriend for a while. Did I mention she's twenty-five?"

"You cad! May she whip you into bedridden exhaustion!"

"Anyway, thought I'd take my clubs. You know. A newsman's curiosity."

"Sports guy's or entertainment hack?"

"Take your pick, Mike. And thanks."

NO SOONER had Brad hung up than his phone rang.

"Hey, mister, who've you been talking to?" the sweet voice of Amanda Scott cooed.

"Hi, hon. Just doing a little leg work on our man Maple."

"Leg work on the phone? I'm having a little trouble getting a picture of this in focus. Seriously, what did you find out?"

"Nothing we haven't known about. Except some people think ol' Treb cheated in the tournament he won."

"Really!?"

"Yeah. Had Jesus on his bag, clubbing him and giving him yardage."

There was a pause, then Mandy chided him. "You're pulling my leg."

"Ummm...now *there's* a mental picture I can relate to."

"Oh...you! Brad, you're awful."

"You getting packed yet?" Brad asked.

"Almost through," Mandy replied, excitedly. "What about you?"

"Won't take me long."

"Brad, what I really called about was, Grandmother wants to fix dinner for us this evening. You can pack, then come on over and we'll be ready to go early in the morning. Right?"

"We need to be in Midland by 8:30, if we're going to make that early check-in. It will actually give us an hour's extra time. We can sit there in the Southwest departure area, hold hands and talk about what we'll doing the next week or so."

"I am...*so*...excited!" Mandy bubbled, sounding a little out of place, as if she were a teenage actress in *Clueless*.

"See you tonight, hon. About seven?"

"Or earlier. Bye, Brad."

4. Welcome to Glitter Gulch

"This is exciting!" Mandy gushed, as the Southwest Airlines 737 neared the threshold of Runway 35 at Midland-Odessa International Airport.

"Seems as if I've heard *that* before, during preparations for this trip," Brad replied, smiling. The aircraft swung into position, hesitated for a few seconds, and began its takeoff run. "Our crew will have to accelerate to a pretty good clip, since we've got a full boat of red-necked high rollers."

"Ohhhhh!" Mandy responded as the 737 roared down the runway. They were sitting on the right side of the aisle, looking forward, with Mandy in the window seat. She reached across her lap with her right hand, groping for Brad's. He picked hers up with both hands, and held her gently.

"Now, that takes your breath away!" Mandy said, after the aircraft transitioned into flight, then rose quickly before settling into a shallow climb. "Whew!"

"Well, you've reached a milestone, hon," Brad whispered. "Congratulations. Scared?"

"Not anymore."

They sat close. "We're going to have some fun," he said. "Any questions?"

"Well, I was wondering about gambling. Do you think I really have to?"

"They're sort of expecting us both to engage in a little action. I'll do most of it. But I think, considering our accommodations, you ought to pull a *few* handles. Take a couple treys in dollars, pick out a machine that strikes your fancy, put your little card in the slot—don't forget the card, that's important, since that's how the casino people track your use of the facilities—and punch the 'play' button. Or pull the one-armed bandit's one arm, just to see how it feels."

Mandy didn't answer. She looked straight ahead, expressionless.

"Something wrong, hon?"

"Oh, I'm just being silly, I guess. I know gambling is supposed to be addictive. And it's sinful, if you take the Bible literally…"

"The way I interpret the morality issue, gambling is wrong if it hurts you or somebody else. I fail to see one hurtful situation in our arrangement. One, we use part of somebody else's money to make a teensy-weensy dent in the Fifth Jack's bulky bank account. They know we're coming, and they welcome the challenge. Two, they're not blind to what Tornado is asking, and that's to turn their heads just a little, for old time's sake. I reckon he has left plenty of that good ol' West Texas money in Vegas in years gone by. Three, we get great accommodations for a week, ten days or maybe two weeks, depending upon Buddy Holly's old sidekick, Trebor Maple. Four, if we get lucky, we'll let the Fifth Jack buy us tickets to some shows. I hear the MGM has enticed Fleetwood Mac back. You might like Shania. I'm a sucker for magic, or masters of illusion, if you will. I've seen Siegfried & Roy at the Mirage. They'll blow you away. And Penn and Teller are a hoot."

"So you're perfectly OK with it? All of it?" Mandy asked shyly, glancing sideways toward him.

"Sure. Trust me, hon. Anytime you get uncomfortable, we'll change things up a little. You don't *have* to gamble. I just think it might look a little better if you did. They're getting to hold twenty thousand dollars of Tornado Thornton's money for a while. They get to keep a tenth of that. Somebody who's somebody there knows the deal, and they're all right with it."

"Well...since you put it that way, it doesn't sound so...so dishonest," she said, then added, eyes focused on her lap, "Brad, you're not worried, uh, about being around all that what you call action, are you?"

"Me? Why should I? I know casinos. I know odds. The only way *I'll* play a sucker's game is to play it with another consenting adult's money."

"They don't play poker in a casino?"

Poole turned to his beautiful companion. "No, it's not a real casino game. They have poker tables they run for the players, supplying a dealer for a percentage or cut of the pots, is all. Why do you ask, hon?"

"Just wondering..."

"You know I used to play cards, don't you? But I don't remember telling you about it. Did I?"

"I don't think so. I...I heard it somewhere, I guess."

"Um-hum. I'm not surprised. People have big mouths. There was some poker in my past, and that's where it will stay. In my past. I can't afford it with my newspaper hack's salary."

"Brad Poole! You are *not* a hack writer! And forget I mentioned it. OK?"

"Sure, hon. *You* forget the tale out of school some good friend might have told you, and I'll forget you brought it up." He shifted in his seat, touched the shallow recline button, crossed his hands on his chest, lay his book open in his lap, and closed his eyes. "Think I'll try to nap the rest of the way."

"Good idea," she said, staring out the window and down at the semi-arid New Mexico landscape almost six miles below.

MANDY THOUGHT back to when her grandmother had suggested she ask around about Brad, after their first date appeared it might be the start of something. Now, she wished she hadn't.

41

Some friends at church had heard about the sports editor's reputation of being not only a card gambler, but—they said—a big loser at poker. One friend said she heard he got trapped in a game for—how did she put it?—for "huge stakes," and he got burned. His rich father-in-law bailed him out, and it cost Brad his marriage. The other friend said *she* had heard that Betty Poole was a spoiled rich kid who never grew up. That Brad had had his fill of her possessiveness and "I'm always right" attitude long before the fateful card game in Midland. The marriage was dead. The night of bad poker in the Permian Basin simply provided the burial.

Mandy's erstwhile friends also had plenty of gossip to dish on Brad's exit from the sports editor's desk and his exile to arts and entertainment. Several versions included Brad not able to control his staff, Brad being caught in conflict of interest, his run-in with coaching staffs from the local church universities, and Brad's general attitude problem—the latter augmented in no small measure, probably, by his divorce which occurred about the same time.

Around the fourth date—pretty much a record with the same guy for Amanda—Brad had asked if she had heard about the sports department war. She admitted she had. He asked her what she had heard, and she told him.

"Pretty much a little of all of the above," he had told her that evening, over enchiladas at Farolito's Restaurant. "Plus, I had two guys who wanted my job, and a third who wanted me out of his hair."

Mandy briefly got to know Bart Lindsey's wife, Karen, when Karen would bring their teenage daughter to Sunday night youth fellowship at the church. Karen had told Mandy that she had heard she was dating Brad Poole, and Mandy had acknowledged that they had been out a few times.

"Don't believe a lot of what you hear about Brad, when it comes to the newspaper," Karen Lindsey had said. "He's a good man who got stiffed by his own people, mostly because they wanted his job. I should know. My husband landed the first blow. Your poor guy never had a chance, the way they set him up with the college coaches."

Not long after, Karen divorced Bart for a different set of marital sins, according to the ladies at church.

So for Mandy, that chapter in Brad's past was closed. He had told her he was divorced shortly after asking her out. "Part my fault, part my ex-wife's," he had explained. "People shouldn't get married before they're twenty-five, at least. Maybe not until thirty." He had never offered to expand on the breakup, and Mandy had never asked him to. Plus, she quit listening to people who wanted to gossip about Brad. She had made it clear she didn't want that stuff brought up in her presence.

MANDY STOLE a glance at Brad in the next seat. His eyes were shut, but she didn't believe he was sleeping. She remembered their first date, how he had kept coming into the store and finally asked her out one Wednesday evening. Sure, she had told him. If he didn't mind taking her to the weekly supper and program at her church.

She smiled as she recalled Brad's pained expression he was barely able to dismiss after a second or two. "Actually, I'm really not a church-going sort of guy," he had told her. She had smiled and instead of run for cover, she had left the door open. "We Presbyterians don't twist arms," she had told him, smiling. "You might enjoy yourself."

"What's the program?" he had asked.

"You get to choose between *Today's Christian and The Internet* and some continuing studies, one on Old Testament heroes and the other a group discussion for pre-middle age adults who are suddenly single."

He had taken her, shaken hands with the minister, eaten a meal of fried chicken and English peas and salad and peach cobbler, made a valiant effort not to appear in discomfort at the exceedingly friendly, mostly older Presbyterians, learned considerably more than he cared to about the ancient Jewish heroine Esther, and escorted her home where he met her grandmother. Mandy and Brad had sat in the living room and talked for almost an hour, as if they were time-warped back to the fifties. She had laughed and given him a reassuring pat on the arm when he got up to leave and absent-mindedly reached out to touch her left hand that wasn't there. Mandy had watched Brad Poole walk to his car, feeling a twinge of excited restlessness deep inside her being.

Less than two weeks later, her suspicions had come true—Amanda Scott had fallen in love for the first time in her life. Two months later, she had unleashed carefully hidden passion and made love to Brad.

She smiled at the recollection of that weird, wild and ultimately wonderful evening. Mandy had not told Brad that she was a virgin.

BRAD LIKED to doze while traveling by jetliner. His was a half-sleep. He enjoyed drifting from catnap to idle thoughts, and back to soft snoozing.

He had brought aboard a copy of Ellis Amburn's *Buddy Holly a Biography* he had found amid the mountain of review hardbacks that publishers had sent to the paper. Heralded as the definitive Holly bio, it had been spot-read by Brad over the previous weekend. He had found only four brief mentions of The Picks, and none of Treb Maple, even though Amburn had written that the trio's contribution to the Crickets' now-classic album, *The Chirping Crickets*, "was a crucial element in the Buddy Holly sound (for which) unfortunately," the author noted, the Picks had received no credit.

Being a Texas Tech student for four and a half years, with a journalism diploma to show for it, as well as being well versed in the strange nature of Lubbock, Brad had got a kick out of former acquaintances of the rock legend remembering the night a teenaged Buddy Holly lost his virginity in the back seat of a car parked on a dirt road that paralleled an irrigation ditch in a South Plains cotton field.

After laying the book open in his lap and drifting into his half-sleep, Brad had squinted when he felt Mandy turn in her seat. Through half-closed eyes he had watched her look at him and smile. He felt the coming days in Las Vegas were the start of a special time for him and this lovely, intelligent and unique creature who had done a pretty good job of captivating his life.

After his divorce, Brad had figured on drifting among women of his own age, perhaps even a year or so older; women who like him had been disillusioned by marriage, and looked forward to reasonably uncomplicated, sexually fulfilling relationships.

No sooner had he embarked upon his carefully planned voyage on the sea of tranquility than he had taken note of Mandy swishing around her little shop. This much-younger woman, undaunted by a physical handicap that should've been shattering, was somebody one could not help but watch and admire.

Brad moved restlessly in his seat as he recalled his and Mandy's first encounter with intimacy. He had progressed slowly toward sex; in fact, he had a relationship of sexual convenience with a woman of forty-two going on the side during the first month or so of his infatuation with Mandy. Mandy had been ready and willing when he had ratcheted up the presence of growing passion for both of them.

He still winced when he remembered his confrontation with the fact that Mandy was giving her virginity to him. At the age of twenty-five! Who would've believed it? She had cried softly following that initial episode. It had been a first of sorts for him too—the first time *he* had made love to a virgin.

What does a guy do? Apologize? Run for his life? Take her in his arms and quietly reassure and comfort her? Fortunately, Brad thought, he had taken door number three. They had made love maybe five evenings since then—each time better than the first, but never with her sleeping over at his modest garage apartment. And each time, culminated by this beautiful child of God's soft sobs.

"I'm sorry to act this way, Brad," she had told him just a week earlier than their flight to Vegas. "I can't help but feel a little ashamed. But if I've been, uh, celibate, as I believe I ought to have, I think you're for whom I've been saving myself. I love you."

So what's a feller to do? Brad had thought, that fateful evening. "I…I think I've fallen in love with you too, Mandy," he had told her. It might not have been totally true then, but it was getting awfully close to the real thing now.

"BRAD! ARE you awake!?" Mandy asked excitedly, following a muffled radio message from the Southwest captain.

He looked up from his revere and smiled. "I am now."

"Oh, I'm sorry. But just look down there. Can you see it? The Grand Canyon!"

"Yep. We fly almost right over it. Lake Mead will be coming up pretty soon. And then we'll be there."

"Oooh, this is so exciting!" she said, reaching across her chest and grabbing his right arm with her hand. She snuggled close. "Thank you for bringing me!" she said.

"Thank you for coming." He watched other passengers prepare for landing, and nudged Mandy. "Get a load of that guy." He motioned to a man with a string tie and a turquoise-encased silver watchband. One row up and to their left, he was closing a paperback, *Winning Poker for the Serious Player—The Ultimate Money-Making Guide!* by Edwin Silberstang. "Actually, I've read it," Brad said. "It's one of the better books on the subject. If people could just learn it all and live by it, they could do OK. But few ever do that."

Soon they were on final approach to McCarren. She held tightly to his hand as they landed and the Southwest flight deck crew put the 737 in reverse thrust while braking. Soon they deplaned. Brad laughed when Mandy stopped just past their gate and remarked, "Well, would you look at that!" She had seen the rows of slot machines busily engaged.

They got their luggage, grabbed a taxi, buzzed past the gaudy new casino hotels at the north end of the Strip, some of which Brad hadn't seen since his last visit three years ago, and wound their way to downtown Las Vegas and the Fifth Jack.

He paid the cabbie and hefted their three pieces of luggage, then passed them to a bellman. They entered the lobby and he checked in while Mandy stood nearby, staring wide-eyed into the adjacent casino at the blinking slots and their incessant clanging.

"Those white lights on top—what are they doing?" she asked excitedly, as he guided her toward to elevators.

"Those, hon, have just hit a jackpot of some magnitude or another."

"Ooooh!"

AFTER SCOUTING their accommodations, Brad dutifully instructed the bellman to put Mandy's bag, hangups and makeup case in one bedroom of the suite, and his two pieces of luggage and laptop in the other. They took turns showering, put on fresh clothes and went downstairs to the Fifth Jack's grill for a light late lunch.

"Ummm, this is good!" Mandy cooed, over her chef's salad.

"Y'know, I'm not going to be too displeased if we have trouble tracking down good ol' Treb Maples," Brad said, putting his cheeseburger aside and dipping some fries in catsup. "Tornado done did us a big 'un whuff these here digs," he added, slipping into an exaggerated West Texas twang.

After lunch, they strolled through the semi-controlled mayhem of the main casino. Brad showed Mandy the crap tables, blackjack semicircles of green, and a roped-off area for baccarat. Skimpily clad young women were serving drinks to the players—"complimentary," Brad pointed out, chuckling when Mandy made a face—while other girls rushed back and forth, slips of paper in their hands. "They're keno runners," he explained, then added in response to her quizzical expression, "It's a numbers game that looks easy to win, but it's not. Other than picking numbers and marking them on his sheet, the player has absolutely no input, either physical or mental, in playing keno."

He led her to a gilded cashier's cage area where players were buying chips or slots coins. "Let's see how good our credit is, and log a little action before going out on the town."

He opened the letter Tornado Thornton had given him, and glanced once more at its brief contents:

> *This is to introduce Mr. Brad Poole, for whom the amount of $20,000 credit has been established, under certain conditions approved by Mr. Rick Conti. Please extend to him the courtesy you have in the past, to me.*
>
> *B.A. (Tornado) Thornton*

"You want to see?" Brad asked Mandy, who nodded and quickly scanned the instructions on the paper's letterhead. Brad then handed it through the teller's cage bars to a woman who punched some computer keys, then asked them to wait a moment. She reached for a phone and spoke a muffled message.

"Mr. Conti will be with you shortly," the attendant said. Soon enough, a nice-looking middle-aged man in a suit and tie approached, smiled, and waved Brad and Mandy to an adjacent window. His nametag, black embossed on what appeared to be silver, read "Rick Conti, Casino Manager." He reached under the bars, shook Brad's hand and said, "Welcome to the Fifth Jack. We're pleased to have you as our guests through your stay, up to two weeks. Do you understand the conditions Mr. Thornton has imposed with his letter of credit?"

"I think so, but I'd like you to spell them out, just in case," Brad replied.

"The letter authorizes us to extend to you two-thousand dollars in casino chips and coin, upon demand. Anything over that figure, up to twenty-thousand, during your stay is subject to my authorization, or one of my three shift managers in times I'm away from my post." He looked directly at Brad and smiled. "I'm sure Mr. Thornton, who is one of our time-honored, valued regulars, has gone over the terms. There shouldn't be any problem. We'd like you to do us the courtesy of showing us how you carry out your play. Just put these in the appropriate slots on our slot machines," he said, handing credit card-type plastics on little nylon cords, "and get your dealer or pit boss to sign these when you visit our gaming tables," giving Brad a stack of chits. "Let me know a day ahead of when you expect to return home and I'll have a receipt and cashier's check ready for you to take back to Mr. Thornton? Any questions?"

"I noticed you have baccarat, but I didn't see any poker or hold 'em tables in the casino area," Brad responded.

"Yes. Our main floor isn't as large as you'll find in other casinos. We can arrange a game of hold 'em in our second floor parlor. Those are by invitation. Normally, they start at minimum bets of $20," Conti said, fumbling with Thornton's authorization letter. "I notice—"

"Yes. Unless I was an idiot, I'd be buying in at 100 times the minimum bet, or two-thousand," Brad cut in, trying not to sound too irritated by his host trying not to sound too condescending. "In other words, our whole nest egg."

"That, plus the fact the poker room doesn't accommodate those," Conti said, tapping the stack of action chits. "At least, in our arrangement. Understood?"

"Not really," Brad said, sighing. "But it's your place, your rules and your games."

"Thank you. If you wish to play poker, perhaps you brought along some of your own cash? Or better still, maybe you or the young lady can get hot and you can win a stake on our money," Conti said, smiling.

"You never can tell," Brad replied, trying to imitate the casino manager's smirk.

"So, what can I get for you now?"

"Give us a couple trays of dollars for the slots, and I'll have a couple hundred in chips—fives and tens."

The pretty teller to whom Brad first spoke was standing nearby. She moved to Conti's side when she heard Brad's response.

"Excellent start," Conti said. "L'Quitia here will get you fixed up. I'm betting that this is your first time in a casino," he said, to Mandy, who nodded. "I can tell Mr. Poole is a player. Good luck, you two. Hope you take us to the cleaners."

"Right," Brad replied, as he took the tray of silver dollars and stuffed the chips in his pockets. "By the way, do you know Treb Maple?"

"The pro golfer? Sure. He's one of the semi-regular poker players around downtown. With us maybe once or twice a month."

"You know where he hangs out?"

"During the day? He teaches at one of the new courses outside of town. Ask at the desk. I'll bet they can help you. Maple has a web page."

Brad steered Mandy to the right and found the dollar machines. "See one you like?"

"Are there good ones and bad ones? How do you know?" she replied, looking up and down the row. More than half were not in use.

"They may not look it, but they're all pretty much the same."

"I read up in the room, while you were showering, that slot machines pay back 91 percent," she said, in true small businesswoman fashion. "I don't see how they can offer all this, with such a small margin of profit."

"Never feel sorry for the casinos," Brad replied. "I figure that 91 percent includes the very rare but regular super payoffs, resembling lottery pots. In the mean time, casinos here pull in a combined tens of millions every day, just on slots, and they don't pay back anywhere near 91 percent on a daily basis. These places divvy up billions every year."

"I...I think I like this one. Blue Diamond," she said stopping in front of a machine less grotesquely adorned than most others. "What do I do?"

"Put your trays down here, right in front of you. There are creeps who love to rip you off and dope heads off the street who get by security and stand on their heads to clean out a plastic bucket, if you're not careful. This is a two-play machine. In other words, to get the best of the payoffs here," he explained, pointing to a schedule that was headed "Two Coins," "you have to put two of these fake silver dollars in this slot here."

"Can I play just one?"

"Sure. Now, put your card in up here, and if you change machines, don't forget to retrieve it and take it with you. Then, you pull the handle. Or punch that "play" button there, if you get tired. Which will it be? OK. Pull it all the way down."

Brad watched Mandy eye the spinning computer-driven disks, suddenly feeling guilty. What if she gets hooked on these things? he thought.

"Oops. Nothing this time. You got two diamonds. But that icon there—"

"Icon?"

"Figure. What ever. It doesn't mesh with this machine's pay."

"Maybe I ought to play two dollars at a time," she mused, half to herself. "Maybe it's not impressed with just one."

"You might be right."

"I'll play two."

She pulled the lever with her right arm and watched the three spots fill, one at a time.

"Oh pooh! Nothing again," she said.

Brad let her keep going, noting that she was getting the hang of it, but coming up dry. Then, on her tenth try, the machine clanged.

"What's that!?" Mandy squealed.

"You're a winner, that's what. Look. You got fifty bucks! Congratulations."

"How do I get paid?"

"See the little window that says credits? You have fifty credit. You can 'bet the max' now, two dollars, by punching that button. And if you're arm is getting tired, just push that other button."

He watched as Mandy watched, pull after pull. Sure enough, in less than ten more tries, she came up with a hundred and twenty dollars.

"Woooo-ooo," she purred slowly. "I could get used to this!"

The payoffs continued—fifty, a hundred and twenty, twenty a couple of times—over the next ten minutes or so.

"I'm ahead. Right?"

"You're ahead, hon. By considerably more than the two hundred you brought over here. Somebody," Brad said slowly, turning his eyes to the ceiling, where cameras looked down on every corner of the gaming area, "somebody up there likes you."

"Silly! God doesn't give a whit about my playing slot machines!"

"I wasn't talking about God."

"Hum?"

"Forget it. I'm going to turn in your original two hundred. You can play on your winnings. We'll split it all up later. I think I'll spend a little of my two hundred on the crap tables or playing blackjack."

"You want me to stay here?"

"Unless you get tired, or busted. In that case, come over there," he pointed to the tables area, "and look me up. Be sure to use these buckets when you cash out—you push that button there, to do that—and keep an eye on your silver dollars. Be sure your purse stays in your lap. And don't forget to take your play card with you, whereever you go. We'll celebrate tonight at the main dining room. I'll make reservations."

After that, Brad spent half an hour going up against a pretty dealer at a five-dollar blackjack table. Since he gave up trying to count face cards and aces long ago, he was not surprised when he lost about fifty dollars.

He hung around the craps area for half an hour, playing "wrong"—or going against the "right" shooters and betting "Don't Pass" with the house. He took double odds, winning when the house did except against box cars (two sixes) which were a push, but not endearing himself to superstitious fellow players. Brad passed the dice most of the time, getting ribbed by the stickman, except once when he had watched three straight "right" players fail to pass, and put ten dollars on the pass line, with twenty behind, on odds. He threw an eleven, let his winnings ride, then rolled a five. Six throws later, he came up with a four-three, smiled as the dealer across him raked in his two piles of chips, and tossed a five-dollar piece to him, the stickman and the far dealer. It was nice when you tipped with other people's money, he mused.

He let the pit boss estimate his play and sign his chit, as he had with the black jack ensemble, then headed to find Mandy. He figured the nearly an hour of action had cost him just under a hundred. That ought to please the Fifth Jack's people, he thought. And it kept him about par for losing during the next fourteen days or less.

He watched from behind Mandy. She was just sitting there on her stool, not making a move to play.

"Uh-oh," Brad said as he patted her shoulder. "Has Blue Diamond turned on you?"

"Brad! Look!" She gushed, pointing at her machine's tote window. "I'm ahead…ahead—"

"You're up by fourteen hundred and twenty-six dollars, kid," he replied, doing a really poor take on Humphrey Bogart. "Get those plastic buckets. We're gonna cash out."

He pushed the button, and while Mandy stared as the stream of imitation silver dollars spat from the machine, he turned toward the ceiling cameras, and waved. Those smart-asses would love it, he thought.

THAT EVENING, they ate in the Fifth Jack's fancy cave-like main restaurant. Mandy celebrated their good fortune and the start of their dream trip with lobster tail. Brad had a surf 'n' turf special—fried and boiled shrimp and a New York strip steak. Both entrees had all the trimmings, climaxed by cherries jubilee.

Mandy, as usual, had bottled water with her meal. Brad sipped a glass of Napa Valley chardonnay. It was the first time he had drunk alcohol with Mandy. Not for any other reason than she was a non-drinker. She only smiled and nodded when he asked if his wine would be OK with her. He didn't mention the four freebie weak-sister gins and tonics he had, during his blackjack and craps sessions.

"Well, what'd you think of today, seeing as how we started out a hundred and fifty miles from the Midland airport about sixteen hours ago.

"It's been fun, overall," she replied, less animatedly than Brad had anticipated. "How'd we come out with our gambling?"

"You won. I lost. We're ahead by almost thirteen hundred bucks. I'll get us some show reservations and pay up front for them. Let's put the rest in the safe we've got in our room. I'll figure out a combination we both can remember. I suggest we use that money for entertainment. Each day, when we set aside time to gamble, let's check out money at the office. We've used four hundred of two thousand. I'll get two, three or four hundred each day, and we can stay with that equation until something else happens. After our shows and anything you'd like to buy while here, and after our sessions with Mr. Maple Esquire, we'll split our winnings. I'll bet you can't wait to get back to Blue Diamond tomorrow."

She turned her head and took her time answering.

"Brad, it was fun all right…I guess. But I…I just wasn't comfortable. At least, after I got through. I just don't feel right about it."

"Hey. Don't worry. Play five minutes a day, and cash in."

"Thanks. I can do that."

"Anyway, I've got a hunch your best action was this afternoon.

"Really? Why?"

"Oh, just a hunch. Slot winning goes in spurts. Hey! I bet you're tired. Want to get some shut-eye? I've already got a lead on our Mr. Maple. We can rent a car—Thornton gave me an el-cheapo company credit card for that purpose—and maybe hunt him down tomorrow."

"I'm with you, Brad."

They took in The Freemont Experience, the dazzling computerized light-and-music extravaganza outside the Fifth Jack on the sectioned-off four blocks of Freemont Street, then headed for their suite. They kissed long and hard before turning in tired out.

In their separate rooms.

5. Mandy Has "The Glow"

Brad rolled over and gazed bleary-eyed at the clock radio on his nightstand. He had been awakened by Mandy brushing her teeth in the adjacent bathroom. He heard her door close softly, so he followed her lead. Then he tapped on her door.

"You up?" he asked.

"Of course! Sorry if I woke you. I peeked in and you were sawing logs."

"Mind if I come in?"

"Silly. Come here."

Brad walked to her bed, sat down and kissed her. "Sleep well?" he asked.

"Oh, off and on. It was an exciting day for me. And, I had some things on my mind."

"Sounds ominous. Something wrong?"

"No," she said, smiling. "I had some*thing* on my mind, actually." She smiled seductively at Brad, who wondered if she was thinking what *he* was thinking—why he woke up alone in bed. But they had talked about it before the trip, of course; far be it from him to rock *that* little boat. Mandy smiled at him, put her right hand behind his neck, pulled his head to hers, and kissed him passionately. He pulled away, smiled, and quickly responded when she pulled him back and repeated the maneuver.

Without a word, he pulled back the covers and briefly let his eyes wander from the top of her light blue teddy, to her bare legs pulled tightly together, as if making more room for him to sit beside her. He gently stroked her breasts, pulled off the flimsy top and kissed first one, then the other. He stood. She reached up and pulled down the pajama bottom he had worn to bed. He slipped off her panties, and crawled in beside her.

She was extraordinarily beautiful and sensuous in her nakedness! She was slender, yet soft to the touch. Her handless arm defied him to take notice of it, so splendid were the exquisite figure and the warm, effervescent facial features.

When romance is good, it can be very good. And their half-hour of mutual responding and providing was an exercise in sex excellence. Ask most anybody exhilarating in the glow of such love-making for a comparison and he or she likely would reply that what had just transpired between these two was their best *ever!*

That is, until Brad rolled over on his back and closed his eyes. Mandy was crying. Again!

"Wow! You sure know how to shoot a guy down, Mandy."

She pulled up on her elbows and smiled through her tears. "Oh Brad! I'm so sorry. I'm mainly just happy. Completely happy."

He *almost* said something to the effect that he didn't want to keep feeling as if he were competing with God for the depth of her love. How glad he was that he had held his tongue!

"Brad, it's not you. And truly, I am just so...so happy to be with you. I *love* you! I haven't regretted making love to you. Not once! You know it was new for me, our first time. But so was true love. And when we...when we share moments such as just now, it is special. I...I guess I felt a little shallow, since I long ago had promised myself to save these special times for the right person. But really, I think I have."

Then she rolled over on her back and lay beside him. "But Brad, I don't want you to think I'm trying to trap you."

"Of course I don't," he replied, thinking he truly *did* feel she was snaring him, regardless of her intentions. He couldn't help it. But in all honesty, he was trapping himself. She couldn't be blamed for his realizing that she had become the single most important part of his life. His and Betty's love had digressed from pure passion to disappointment, with their relationship's only redeeming qualities the two daughters they had brought into the world. He honestly could tell himself, whether in the warmth of physical union or the cool light of day, that he had never known such special feelings as Mandy summoned in him.

She rolled sideways on her right elbow and looked into his eyes, smiling as the tears ceased. "I guess you think I'm silly. But I want something left over for later, if—and I am very content to say and really mean *if*—it all comes together for us. I can't stop making love to you. Not now. You're all I'll ever want. I...I just ask that we not actually *sleep* together, until..." She turned over again and lay beside him.

"'Nuff said, hon," he responded, up on his elbows and looking deeply into her eyes for a few seconds. "Now, let's get up and at 'em. We'll sample the Fifth Jack's best in breakfasts downstairs. I've got a lead on who can direct us to Sir Trebor Maple."

AFTER THEY had eaten, Brad plugged in his laptop to the modem that came with their suite, while Mandy sat in one of the easy chairs nearby and scanned the morning paper.

"Here it is, all right," Brad said, as a web page flickered to life. "Don't know what all the secrecy was back home, and with the AP guys. Maple isn't hiding out. Not if you know his www. Look here."

She came over, peered at the screen and read silently along with Brad:

> *While in Las Vegas, super senior golfers (65-older) with a 24 or less handicap are invited to spend an afternoon with Treb Maple, oldest winner of a PGA Seniors (now Champions) tournament...and in his first try!!!*
>
> *Treb will meet you at picturesque Desert King Golf Club. He'll show you how his game turned around virtually overnight not too long ago, from pedestrian club pro to the talk of the sport, world-wide. Let him teach you his method, designed to offset much of the damage age does to our swing. If it fits your game, you'll elevate your performance. If it doesn't, you should gain confidence by just trying Treb's way.*
>
> *The four-hour session includes Maple watching you swing, suggesting how you might work his winning method into your game, then going through the bag—woods, long irons (Treb doesn't really believe in them!), short irons, the wedge game, scrambling and putting—all on the club's driving range and practice green. You'll hit some, Treb will hit some, and aides will videotape the highlights so you can always refresh your efforts to improve your approach to golf.*
>
> *The package costs $1,000 and includes a cart and weekday green fee for 18 holes at this public-access club, located between downtown Las Vegas and Hoover Dam. There will be two 10-minute breaks. This exciting opportunity will close with a 15-minute Q&A session with Treb in the Desert King's 19th Hole bar and grill.*
>
> *Available reservations are scarce. A session with Treb is worth working around your trip to Las Vegas. Call now, 1-800-555-0141 and leave us your name, address and phone number. Give us three dates from which to choose, first choice through third. We'll send you a brochure, and upon receipt of your $250 non-refundable deposit, you will be on your way toward a new and exciting insight on improving your game.*

"I guess that's him swinging," Mandy observed, as Brad scrolled back to the beginning of the web site. "And him in the up-close picture. He doesn't look like he's almost seventy, but I guess you never can tell."

"No, you can't," Brad replied, a little snidely. "The mug shot could be twenty years old. But I recall some of the articles I researched last week showing him as not looking his age. Guess they checked his driver's license or took a saliva test when he won," he added with a snort. "You ready? I'll call and get us a car. The *American-Telegram* can afford a sub-compact, surely! We'll have it for a week, at least."

"I'm ready!" Amanda announced.

"OK. I'll call the club and see if they expect him around there this afternoon. Maybe we can catch him before he goes out for one of these high-dollar lessons. Or perhaps on a break. I'd like to set up a time for us to do some interviewing. Probably several hours' worth, if I'm lucky." He closed his computer notebook, then mumbled, "I have a hunch it'll work out. Guys with a gimmick love publicity, I don't care what anybody says. Figure it out. Three-hundred and sixty-five days a year, minus say a hundred and twenty to cover weekends and holidays, and good ol' Tricky Treb can pull down at least two-hundred grand, even after expenses."

"Oh, I'll bet he's a nice man!" Mandy countered. "You did say you were told he's very religious."

"And a poker player, don't forget." Brad stood and smiled at the apparent contradiction. "In Vegas for less than twenty-four hours, with hundreds of Blue Diamond's bucks locked away in our safe, and she's suddenly a betting lady. Well, let's go find out how you'd have done, had I called you."

"*Called* me?" Mandy asked, puzzled, as she followed him to the door."

"Never mind," Brad replied with a sigh, as he gave her a kiss on the cheek.

BRAD CONSULTED the map he had picked up at the desk. He had rented a Neon, helped Mandy in, and soon he had maneuvered the little Dodge onto Fremont Street. Then they got on 515, drove to Henderson, and tuned left on Nevada 142.

The drive out of the city and into the desert was pleasant. Mandy was truly thrilled with it all, and her enthusiasm gave Brad a lift. It took almost half an hour before they came to the rather faded billboard that proclaimed, "Desert King Golf Club, next right. Public welcome. Starting times advised."

Brad turned off the state highway and drove down a curbless, black-topped boulevard with mostly dead or dying palmettos aligned in the center.

"Certainly not Augusta National," he mumbled, squinting in the merciless sunshine to try and see what lay ahead.

He had called the pro shop from the Fifth Jack and had been told, "Yeah, Treb will be showing up. One of his two compadres is here, getting things set up. The lessons usually start around one."

"There!" Mandy squealed, pointing. "I can see it. Buildings. Green grass."

"Barely green," Brad groused. As they neared the shimmering, almost mirage-like setting, they discovered some of the architecture consisted of small, faux-adobe houses, built outside chain-link fences that cordoned off the golf course.

"Uh-oh. I see a double-wide back there. This ain't no high-class operation, my sweet!" he announced.

Two adobe-covered pilings served as the club's entrance. A small, well-kept sign to the right proclaimed, "Home course of Treb Maple." They proceeded around a circular drive past a passable main clubhouse and followed a sign that read, "Pro Shop."

"Well, at least the course looks better than the rest of this place," Brad said as they got out of the Neon.

Amanda followed him inside and walked to the expansive plate-glass windows that looked out on what she would be told were the first tee and ninth green. Brad strode to the counter and asked a young assistant pro if Maple was there.

"Not yet. He usually doesn't check in with us. That guy over there," he said, "works for Treb. His other sidekick usually shows up with the pro. Their client is out on the putting green and Treb's never late. You the guy who called earlier?"

Brad nodded. "Thanks," he said, and walked toward the older, hefty African-American the assistant had pointed out. No one else was in the pro shop.

"Hi," he said, extending his hand. "My name's Brad Poole. I understand you work with Treb Maple."

"Carl Struthers. You th' dude who called out here earlier this mornin'?" the large man replied, taking and shaking the extended hand.

"That's right," Brad said, noting a weathered paw, one that obviously had seen its share of hard work. He guessed Struthers was well into his sixties; perhaps older.

"You got business with Treb? He don't take on young guys like you. He figures th' only ones he can help are th' older farts." He chuckled. "Like him and me."

"No, I'm not here for a lesson. I'm from West Texas. Write for a newspaper. I'm out here with my, uh, friend over there," Brad said, feeling awkward when he actually thought about calling Mandy his fiancee. "I thought Treb might like to catch the people back home up on what he's been doing the past couple years."

"You mean since Idaho, I reckon," Struthers interjected.

"Well, that too I guess. But Mr. Maple is a Texas Tech grad—so am I, incidentally—and he spent a lot of time in Lubbock, Wichita Falls and Abilene. None of the three is in our circulation area, but they aren't too far off. We all like to keep up with each other out there. Not much else to do," Brad added with a nervous little giggle. He suddenly suspected, from

Struthers' cool demeanor, that his Treb Maple project might be in trouble before it began.

He was right.

"Newspaper guy, huh? Treb don't talk to scribes no more. Nosiree."

"Well, I think he might, to me. See, I've got this idea for a story that could land on the AP state wire, and easily increase Mr. Maple's clientele by dozens. Maybe a hundred or more. I don't mind telling you, your little business venture out here is pretty much a well-kept secret."

"Humph! Where we gonna put 'em, boy? We turnin' 'em away now. Treb felt so bad, he got to double-scheduling us. We call 'em the dawn patrol. They come out at eight a.m. at least twice a week. If it's a Monday through Friday, we turn around and get another'n goin' at one. Money's good, but it sure do make for long days. 'Specially when you might wanna do somethin' that night. No, I figure we don't need no publicity. Treb likes it that way, after Boise. And what Treb likes, Mike and I like."

"Mike?"

"Miguel Cardenas. He's Treb's 'n' me's partner. We split everthing we make out here three ways. Club don't charge us none. They like the idea o' havin' somebody like Treb around, much as he can be. Mike's known Treb since they went to high school together, back in the Rio Grande Valley."

"Brownsville?"

"Yeah, Brownsville. Down among the palms where th' sun *does* always shine. They played high school golf. Where ever Treb went, after he done used up all his chits at Tech—he never did graduate, like you, in almost five years—he always tried to get Mike aboard."

"And you?"

"Me? I was a fat-ass has-been caddy, done come down from th' main tour to hang around th' senior circuit. Older guys knew me from 'way back when. So if their regular boy didn't show, they'd throw ol' Struts a bone now and then. Since I could use a cart most of the time with the seniors, I was able to make a livin'. Send a few bucks back to Houston, to my daughter and m'grandson, Claude. She let me name him after Claude Harmon Junior. One of the greats from back in th' forties and early fifties. The daddy of all those Harmon swing gurus today."

"Um-hum. I've heard," Brad said absent-mindedly, worried about the proclamation that Maple is still a no-show with the press, but glad he had found perhaps a conduit through Struthers. He was ready to open his mind to mental note-taking, a technique he had mastered through the years. "They all call you Struts?"

"That's what I go by. You're welcome to use it."

"I'm curious. It's your business, but do I understand that Treb splits even-steven with you and—what's his name?—Mike?"

57

"You got it. The man's a prince, in more ways than one. I owe him my life. I mean, my *whole* life!"

Brad didn't pursue the esoteric tone of that pronouncement. He was more interested in the bird nest on the ground Maple had out here in the southern Nevada desert, less than ten miles and southwest of Lake Mead. A life he was sharing with a couple of very lucky buddies.

"A three-way split, with virtually no overhead—"

"Oh, we gotta buy VHS tapes. Our two video cameras are paid for, 'course. Five or so round trips a week out here in the middle o' nowhere adds up to four or five tanks of gas. We got two cars to feed, mine and Mike's. Treb leaves his Caddy at home, though it don't get used much. Louise—that's his wife—she's a wheelchair lady. Most days she's on her own, downtown. Got lots of slots pals."

"I understood his wife was dead."

"Nope. Shudda been killed there ten or so years ago, to hear Mike talk about th' wreck. Treb don't say nothin' about it. Happened in New Mexico. Louise is a nice lady. Treb takes good care of her. Their's is a funny kind of marriage. But," Struthers added quickly, "that's their business.

"Anyways, back to *our* business. We buy each guy a green fee—thirty-five bucks, including half a cart. Drinks add a little. I figure we keep nine hundred and thirty, maybe nine-thirty-five of each thousand. That's before Uncle Sam, o' course. Treb is th' whole show, naturally. Mike is in charge of our video setup. I'm sort of a go-fer, but I do some work on th' hand-held camera too. Mike and I take turns contacting prospective clients, me by phone and Cardenas with e-mails. We give our guys th' first-class treatment.

"I'm an ol' caddy, as ya know," he continued. "But I could break 75 on any course you could name, in my time. If," he added with the hint of a sneer, "I coulda got on it. Mike, he wuz a sweet-swinger who could've been somebody. With a break or two, he coulda beat Trevino to th' tour, as their token Mex. If I hadn't been so flabby and lazy, I mighta give Charlie Sifford an' later on, Lee Elder and Calvin Peete a run as th' black guy of the late sixties an' early seventies. But wasn't to be. Anyways, I'm real happy with th' way things've worked out."

"So. Mike's been with Mr. Maple off and on about all his life. When did you hook up with him?"

"Treb was a Monday qualifier, y'know. Well, there I was in Boise, without a bag. I see this old guy—old like me, not fifty-ish like th' rest o' those hundert 'er so hustlers gettin' ready to choke their guts out, tryin' for one o' four spots in the 54-holer over th' weekend. It was his first time.

"I didn't know him. We'd missed each other down through th' years. Treb was right out of the pro shops. Never really had tried to make it in th' big show, where I was workin' for lots o' the up-and-comers back there when the tour was peanuts. I toted for Doug Ford once at Colonial, when I wuz little more'n a kid. I've worked with Middlecoff, Paul Harney, Tommy Bolt, the puttin' man Jerry Barber, and even filled in on Sam Snead's bag one time. Those wuz great years.

"Well, like I say, I look over th' guys with no caddies, and my eyes keep comin' back to My Man. There was somethin' really special 'bout Treb. I asked him if I could tote for him, that I already had th' course stepped off and charted for yardage. He smiled and nodded. An' he's been My Man ever since."

"See, Struts? *That's* the kind of guy I want to write about!" Brad effused. "Think you can help me get on the ins with him? To do a couple interviews away from the course?"

Struthers smiled. "Like I done tol' you, ace. Ferget it. Whoa! There he come now," Struthers said, getting up laboriously and walking slowly toward the door. "He an' Mike are right on time. Won't be comin' in." Sttuthers stopped and turned. "Nice talkin' to you." Then he turned and stared at Mandy. "What a beautiful young lady you got there, Ace." He smiled. "Seems a mite young fer you but that's your business. Yours and hers."

"Hey Mandy, come over and meet Mr. Struthers, Mr. Maple's partner," Brad called out.

'Hi, Mr. Struthers," Amanda said, strolling to the two, smiling and extending her hand. "Mandy Scott."

"Struts, Mandy. Call me Struts." He smiled, and stared intently into her eyes for a couple of seconds. "Hopes to see *you* again."

Brad was curious to see if Struthers had noticed that her left arm was missing. He seemed to have not.

"Think I can walk with you and meet Mr. Maple?" Brad asked the big man.

"Sure."

They stepped out of the pro shop and into the baked sunlight. "That Amanda. She's a keeper, I suspect."

"I figure you might be right," Brad replied.

"She got a glow. Know what I mean?"

"I guess so. She smiles a lot. That it?"

"No, not really." Struthers stopped and in a slow, almost hushed tone, asked, "She got th' Lord, ain't she?"

"Excuse me?"

"She a believer?"

"In God? Jesus?" Brad laughed. "You got *that* right."

"I can spot th' *real* ones real good. Not like Treb can. But close. An' your lady done got th' glow. Hey Treb, Mike," he called out to the two men who were approaching. "Meet this newspaper guy. What is it now, Ace?"

"Brad Poole. Sure glad to know you, Mr. Maple."

"Treb," Maple said softly with a smile, shaking Brad's extended hand. "This is my other partner, Mike Cardenas."

"How you doing?" Cardenas greeted.

"That our man from Atlanta over there?" Maple said, turning to Struthers.

"That be him. I'll go tell Mr. Biggerstaff we're ready. *He* is, that's fo' sure. Been chompin' at th' bit for half hour."

"Say, Mr. Maple—Treb. I was wondering. If I stayed around, could I maybe watch you give your lesson?"

"Nope. Mr.—what's his name again, Struts?"

"William Biggerstaff."

"Oh yeah," Treb drawled. "The Coca Cola guy. Brad, Mr. Biggerstaff has paid for this afternoon. I don't figure he wants to be kibitzed. Even if he didn't mind, I would."

"Gee, Treb. This is kind of important to me. I had in mind doing a piece for my paper back in West Texas. Interview piece, hopefully. If I got out there and hit a few balls say, fifty or so feet away, and took a few pictures, would that be OK?"

"I'm not too keen on the photos. But I don't own this range. Let's make it a hundred feet. The club *does* allow me to have the south end of the practice tee pretty well to myself, if there isn't a rush on. Usually there's not. Struts can be pretty forceful-sounding, shooing a guy off if he brings his bucket right next to us, when there's an open range up and down the tee. And you say this is important to you? Not just a casual meeting, then, I take it. Tell you what. If you want to wait the whole afternoon, fine. After we have drinks with Mr. Biggerstaff, I'll buy you one. And then I'll give you ten minutes, strictly—and I do mean strictly—off the record and explain to you why I won't be giving you an interview. You or anybody else."

"I'll look forward to it," Brad replied. "Just give me two of those minutes to listen to why I think you ought to reconsider."

"OK. See you then. And remember," Maple said, hoisting his black tour bag on which his name, but no sponsor, was emblazoned in bold white letters, then slipping the strap over his right shoulder and heading for the practice tee. "One-hundred feet. No closer."

"SON OF a bitch!" Brad mumbled, unaware that Mandy had just walked up behind him. He had returned to the pro shop and stationed himself near a plate glass window from which he could look out to the practice tee in the distance.

"Brad!"

"I'm sorry, hon. Didn't know you had come up. I shouldn't have said that," he apologized, sheepishly.

"No, you shouldn't have. Are you talking about Treb Maple?

"Forget it. OK?"

"Brad, I've never heard you say things like that before. What's wrong?"

He sighed. "It's just that the guy is stiffing me, on the interview. I can't figure out why. The whole thing depends on him cooperating. It sure won't look too good to Tornado Thornton if I come up dry."

"Well, it *is* his right, isn't it?"

Brad turned back to the window. "Public figures, even flashes in the pan, don't have rights. Not like the rest of us."

"What do you mean?"

"I mean, I can get the story *I* want, one way or another. If the...the star-spangled snot thinks he can stiff *me,* he's got another think coming!"

"Brad, this isn't you," Mandy said softly.

"I think I can get Struthers to open up," Brad said, ignoring Mandy and turning back to the window, as if talking to himself. "Don't know about this Cardenas guy, but it's been my experience that people who never made it usually like to get pumped about what was, and what might have been. And I've got the name of their so-called client out there. I will bet he'll do some talking about the fleece job they're applying to him right now. Only I also bet he'll *love* what they do to him. He can afford getting the star treatment." Brad turned to Mandy. "Say, did you see me put my Nikkon in the car?"

She nodded. "It's in the trunk, along with the small tape recorder."

"Good. Do you mind coming out to the practice tee with me? While I hit a few shots and take a roll of film with the distance lenses? I'll buy us a couple of hats and some sunscreen. The son of...the senior sensation won't let me get closer than a hundred feet to him and his precious practice session."

"I'll do whatever you ask, if you'll just calm down, and *not* talk that way again," Mandy agreed.

"Hon, this is business. And my business does have what I guess could be described as an ugly side now and then."

"Brad, promise me."

"All right, all right." He moved briskly to the pro shop counter and addressed the assistant.

"I'd like a bucket of balls, please."

"Large or small?"

"Large. And can you loan me a couple of used clubs off the rack? A driver, maybe a three-iron and seven-iron?"

"You got shoes?"

Brad smiled. "Nope. But these sneakers will be OK, if I swing easy." He looked back toward the range. "With those old guys out there, I'll just gear down and take it back like they do. Like I might break my neck or something."

"I'd appreciate it if you don't get too close to Maple and his bunch," the assistant pro said.

"I've already been given my working orders. I guess we better get a couple of Desert King logo hats too. And some sunscreen. Thirty-five or so."

"No problem."

"By the way, what's your name tag say?"

"Jack. Jack Hill."

"Say, Jack. Do you know Treb very well?"

"Just from out here. I've been watching him give lessons for about a year or so."

"Watching? And listening?"

"I guess."

"Y'know, I might like to talk to you later on. I'm doing a feature on Maple for some Texas newspapers.

"Like the *Dallas Morning News?* "

"Could be, if I get some great interviews and AP picks it up.

"Sure. My mom and dad live in Cedar Hill, just south of Dallas."

"Then let's make a date, after I hit some balls and take some photos. Treb said I could do that."

"I'll look forward to it, Mr..."

"Poole. Just call me Brad," he said with a phony grin that made Mandy, who was standing to the side, shake her head.

For one of the few times during any of her waking hours, she wasn't smiling.

"OK, LET'S go over this last hour, Bill," Maple said to the Coca-Cola executive from Atlanta. "One, we accept the fact that we've lost a whole lot of swing speed the past couple or three years, after—as Lee Trevino said—'hitting that brick wall' of diminished strength ten or so years ago."

Bill nodded, sweat dripping from his forehead.

"So we're going to counteract our body's decline with some alterations, and maybe a gimmick or two," Maple continued. "You're going to keep in mind that this afternoon is not so much a *lesson,* but a show-and-tell. I waited more than half a century to do something in golf. Or, more accurately, have something good done for me. I'm going to show you the basics of what I changed in the physical side of my game to get to Boise and into the senior tour spotlight—however briefly that turned out to be."

He stepped to the place where Bill had been hitting balls, motioning him to stand at right angles to the line of flight they had been practicing.

"Tell me. What's first that we discussed last hour?"

"Uh, your stance is—"

"No, *first.*"

"Oh sure. The grip. Vardon is gone. Ten-finger is in."

"Ten-finger, baseball grip. I prefer to call it baseball-bat style. Now what?"

"The stance? Yeah. It's square to my line."

"Right." With his feet positioned about 26 inches apart, unusually wide for someone barely five-nine, Maple lay a club next to his toes.

"You watch pro golf, of course. Every guy out there on the regular circuit is on camera more than number 130 on the money list for at least one reason. Might be putting. For sure, that's half the game. Could be irons. Mid-iron excellence, if he's a short-knock. Might be booming drives, most of the time in the short grass. Trouble-shooting out of sand and greenside fringe is crucial. All the pros have special strengths. You can learn a lot from watching many of them.

"When I was a kid, Hogan was my hero. Still ranks way up there. I saw him twice at Colonial. He was pure pleasure to watch, his swing was such perfection. But it was too complex to be a pattern for anybody else's game. Snead was too beautifully fluid. Like Bobby Jones had been. Not many of us can be that way. But theirs sure was fun to watch.

"Today, of course, Tiger is great to gallery, if you can stand the unruly crowds. But the young man's dedication, athletic prowess, conditioning and virtually unreachable level of competitive instincts make him difficult to try to emulate. Pretty swings include Mickelson and Fred Couples in quirky kinds of ways. The retiring—at least from the regular grind—Tom Purtzer has a picture swing. So does Jeff Maggert, with that superb left elbow action at the top.

"But the one who helped me find something to which I could apply my own variations was Bob Estes. When he's on his game, he can't be beat by *anybody,* tee to green. And he's on more often than not, because his swing is more functional," Treb explained, using his client's five-iron as a pointer. "His body is upright rather than slouched. He has a slow take-away, but his square setup helps him swing through the hitting area with extra strength. You and I couldn't *begin* to think in *those* clubhead speed terms, but Bob's turn through the ball and his strong, high finish are excellent elements to copy. I got my baseball grip from him."

Cardenas with his stationary video camera set-up on a tripod behind Treb, and Struthers moving about with his hand-held, taped both men during the discussion and exhibition.

"The ball goes where? More toward the center of my stance. OK. The address. If you buy into my older-senior swing, you're going to dedicate lots of hours on the range hitting balls, when you get back to Atlanta. *Right?* OK, now lean your weight back, as if most of it is centered more toward your heels than insteps. Certainly not the toes. Feel as if you are slightly, just slightly, weighted to the left foot. Remember. *Use the hosel* to address the ball, *not* the meat of the clubface. Picture your shaft lining up with the center of the ball. That's my main variation in copying Estes."

He paused a moment and smiled, then continued. "I know, I know. You'll be thinking that dreaded word—*shank.* That's when practice will come in. You'll develop a slight loop, and bring the meat of the clubhead in, like this."

Maple hit the five-iron with an effortless swing and his student marveled at the ball's flight, ending less than five feet short and dead into the 170-yard sign.

"I used to take away with my hands and lower arms. Now, with my hands hanging down to maybe five inches off my midsection and my arms forming this 'V'"—Maple put his right index finger first on one elbow, then the other—"I try to concentrate on feeling that I'm swinging with my shoulders more than anything else. Try to remain stationary around the hips. You won't. You'd *break* something if you were able to do that. And grip the club *lightly!* I remember when Bob Toski, one of the game's great teachers, came to Rancho Viejo near Brownsville when we opened our first course there. He preached the easy-feel doctrine to extreme, but it sure caught your eye.

"Toski told the old Sam Snead tale about holding your club as if you were wrapping your fingers around a little bird or a butterfly. Then Toski teed one up, took his driver and made a full swing. He had such a light grip, the club flew a good twenty yards down the center of the driving range. But the ball led the way, on the same line, and wound up more than two-fifty. Not bad.

"Anyway, until I made these changes, I never knew what I would be doing from one day to the next. Now—and remember this, it's essential—after thousands of practice balls, I *know.* OK. Let's look in the rest of your bag. Um-hum. About what I figured."

Bill Biggerstaff had a set of Callaway Big Bertha irons, two through pitching wedge. Cleveland sand wedge, 55 degrees. A Titleist floppy wedge that looked to be 60 degrees. Great Big Bertha one, three and five woods by Callaway. And an Odyssey "two-ball" mallet putter.

"Look in my bag," Treb offered. "I don't have anything under a five-iron. Not that I *can't* hit longer irons. I just can't get them up like I used to. Among other things," he added, as Struts guffawed and Cardenas giggled while their student smiled. "But I can loft my longer approach shots, hitting a five, seven or nine wood. These babies are my favorites. Also, you might want to add another utility club instead of that floppy. Those things are great for Mickelson and Tiger, because they learned early and work hours a week with L-wedges. But you'll miss 'em more than you hit 'em, I guarantee. And around the green, you can embarrass yourself big time with a bladed or chili-dipped flop shot. Here," he said, taking the Cleveland sand wedge from the man's bag and hastily scraping a ball into position. "You want to flop? Use this club, and lay the face *way* open, while coming out of our regular square stance and opening to your left. See that bucket over there?"

Maple pointed with the club, at the object maybe twenty yards away. Then he took almost a full swing, clipped under the ball which he had addressed well back in his stance, and sent it at least twenty-feet straight up. It plopped down four feet short of the bucket and stopped almost dead.

"Wow!" the elder student effused, with a whistle.

"I like your choice of a putter, incidentally. Now, what ball do you hit?" Treb asked.

Bill dutifully unzipped his bright red and white Coke bag and produced a Titleist Pro-V-2.

"You think you can do justice to this souped-up pro product? Or do you just jack it up for looks?" Treb asked.

"I use it because the pros do, and because it gives me confidence."

"There! You said the magic word! Confidence! Golf is all about confidence. But in reality, with a swing speed of between eighty and eighty-five miles per hour—and I'll bet money yours falls in that range—you can hit whatever you want, so long as it's low-compression. Me, I won at Boise with a Top Flight XL 2000, and not an XL 3000 mind you. And not 'extra distance' or 'extra spin,' either. I hit an XL 2000 *woman's* ball. You can imagine the looks I got on the first tee, where they chart who uses what ball. Lots of smiles. Even a laugh from one of my fellow competitors I was playing with that day, bless ol' Paul Sheffield's heart. But mine's a *soft* ball, and I'm not going to vibrate my skeleton from my toes to my neck when I hit it. And I promise you, I'll not give up any yardage either, thanks sadly to my slow swing speed."

"I should be taking notes," Bill said, frowning.

"Plenty of time for that at home back there in your den on Peachtree Battle Avenue Northwest," Treb said, remembering the street address from reading the man's file that morning. "It'll all be on the tapes you'll take home."

"Hit another for me?" the student asked.

Maple moved a range ball to a grassless bit of hardpan, set up more open as he had instructed, and hit a high sand wedge to within three feet of his previous effort.

"Uh, pulled it a little, boss," Struthers remarked.

"You don't ever want to swing outside yourself," Treb remarked, exchanging the wedge for a five-iron and ignoring what came off as Struthers' well-rehearsed bit of practice tee dialogue. "Always have a little left. Now, step behind me—be sure to stay out of Mike's way with his camera. See where I address the ball? I can look right down the shaft to the hosel, which is centered on the ball. Now, I move the club back about four inches behind the ball, and..."

Maple swung, sending the ball right of the one-seventy sign, on a high arc that slowly began a slight draw to the left at the top. It came down maybe two yards directly behind the sign.

"I purposely swung full on that," he said as Bill gasped. "Looks good, but swinging outside of yourself won't hold up. Develop your rhythm and your distance, and stick to it.

"God...DAMN!" the Atlanta man gushed. "I hate my fuckin' slice so bad. I'd give up my seat on the express jet to heaven if I could hit a draw just *half* the time I take a swing!"

Maple looked at his student for maybe eight seconds. "It's been my experience that people with that kind of language don't have a place waiting in heaven to give up," he said, unsmiling. "And that breaks my heart. Really!"

"What?"

"*Surely* you're not proud to have that garbage talk on your tape. Just an observation. Don't mean to intrude on your personal business. I guess it is *your* business, even if as noise pollution it might offend somebody with you. And I sure don't know what good it does you, personally."

"Well, I've never—"

"OK, forget it. Maybe I'm out of line, since this is your dollar," Maple said, smiling slightly and touching the man on his shoulder. "Just my way. Can't help myself...like I reckon you can't help yourself either. But I'll tell you something. I talked pretty much that way back in my frustrated years. Then I got help, and I do mean help," he said, glancing skyward. "But I'm not a preacher. Just a mild-mannered soul who has to speak his mind now and then."

"OK. I'll watch myself the rest of the afternoon...I guess," Bill mumbled.

"Good enough. Let's take a break, then I want you to hit some more with me. It'll feel like you're falling off the edge of the planet, especially with that hosel address and the clubhead four or so inches behind the ball. But it's worked for me. Then, we'll pitch and chip some, and finally spend an hour on the putting green with that Odyssey of yours. Now, follow Mike over there to the Igloo, and grab yourself a Gatorade."

Struts placed his camcorder on a worktable they had stationed on the practice tee, and silently busied himself with it.

"I know. I know. I was out of line," Maple said with a sigh.

"You has to do what you has to do, I guess," Struthers sighed. "You knows I hate that stuff too. Now. But we done all agreed, back there in Boise and later in Napa, that we ain't gonna change folks by preachin'. Only by doin'."

"How right you are," Treb said, slowly. "I make about ten mistakes a day, worthy of attention during my evening prayer. I figure that's about number seven for today."

"Fair enough. Say, you been lookin' at our friend over there, hittin' balls?" Struthers said, nodding toward Brad Poole. Mandy was standing nearby, watching him hit range balls with the borrowed clubs.

"Every now and then. Not a bad swing. If he can putt worth a hoot, he can break 80 a majority of the time, from most middle tees."

"Been takin' pictures of you," Struthers said.

"I know," Maple replied with a sigh. "I sort of told him OK. I just hated to keep telling him no, no, *no*."

"About th' interview. Don't you think it's pretty near time to change yer mind on that?"

"Nope. Closed subject. That young lady with him. It's pretty far off, but she looks familiar. Except for the one arm missing."

"Arm missin'? Well, I be! I hadn't even noticed, an' I wuz with her, up real close. Treb, she got th' glow about her."

"Really? You sure?"

"Positive. It's real. If that ain't a angel over there, it's one fine, Jesus-saved person."

"Maybe she's both, eh pard?" Treb said, laughing and slapping the large black man on his shoulder.

"Could be. Could be."

6. Weaving a Wicked Web

Brad's watch showed 5:35 when he glanced at it after seeing through the pro shop picture windows Maple, Struthers, Cardenas and their client from Atlanta leave the putting green and head to the parking lot. Then they were loading their gear in two cars while helping the Atlanta man put his bag in a Lincoln Continental with Nevada plates, obviously a rental.

"I'm going to the ladies' room," Amanda said, rising from the table that Brad had selected. Actually, there were only six in the bar and dining area of the shop. Brad had taken one at the far side of that part of the room. "Don't want to cramp the pro's style while he chats with Mr. Moneybags and we wait our turn for an audience," he had told Mandy. Brad had brought in his brief case when he had returned his camera to the Neon's trunk.

"Hi, again," he addressed the combination barmaid, waitress and short-order cook. "Sally, is it?"

"Hi again yourself," she replied. "And yep, it's Sally. You and th' lady need somethin' else?"

"I think I'd like a gin and tonic this time," he replied. "My girlfriend could stand another Minute Maid lemonaide, I'd wager."

"Comin' up," Sally said, turning and then stopping when Brad continued.

"Say, I've got a date to talk over some stuff with Mr. Maple when he finishes with his visitor, but I don't want to be a problem until then. Will we be out of the way over here?"

"Sure. Treb always sits at th' table nearest th' counter." She turned again and headed to the kitchen. Quickly Brad opened his brief case and removed a small Radio Shack tape recorder. Checking to see that Jack Hill, the assistant pro, was busy with a range ball customer at the cash register, Brad then walked to a large ivy plant next to a door six or eight feet from the table to which Sally had pointed. He pressed the "play" and "record" buttons, and slipped the recorder in among the ivy. He was back at his table when the four men entered the shop. Maple looked at Brad, smiled and nodded while pointing at his watch and flashing five fingers three times.

The entourage took their table as Mandy returned to hers and Brad's. As she sat, Brad noticed that Trebor Maple took an immediate, almost intense visual interest in the twenty-five-year-old beauty.

Mandy also noticed his sudden preoccupation with her presence, since she and Brad were sitting where both could see the men by turning their heads forty-five degrees. She smiled at the older man, who smiled in return before resuming conversation with the men at his table. There was occasional laughter, non-stop conversation and continued glances by Maple toward Mandy.

"Looks like they're having a good time," she said to Brad. "Bet you wish you could be in on that!"

"Hum? Oh yeah. Well, he'll either join us or wave us on over when they get finished. Y'know, hon, I'm getting a little tired of the old coot eyeballing my girl. He is, you know."

"Pooh! He's just being nice. That's the way I see it."

"The way *I* see it, he's ogling."

"Ogling!? Why, Brad Poole! You sound downright jealous, as well as really, really out-dated. Ogling indeed! Anyway, he's old enough to be my grandfather, you know."

"Look, there's something to that stare of his. Either he simply can't take his eyes off you, for whatever reason, or he's making a pass. I know guys. And even the old ones used to be on the make, before their equipment gave out."

"Please, Brad," Mandy said, losing her light banter.

"OK. Sorry."

LESS THAN half an hour later, Trebor and his associates bade farewell to their customer from Atlanta, walked him to the door, shook hands and waited while he left. Then they came to where Mandy and Brad were sitting.

"Mind if we join you two?" Maple asked.

"We've been looking forward to it," Brad replied. "Fellows, this is Amanda Scott. Mandy, you know Carl Struthers. This is Mike Cardenas, and finally, the man we came all the way from Texas to see, Mr. Trebor Maple."

"*Buenas tardes,*" Cardenas said, smiling. Mandy quickly decided that he, like Struthers, was well up in his sixties. Maybe more.

"A pleasure," Maple said, enveloping her only hand with both of his palms. Brad stared at the gesture for a couple seconds too long, Mandy thought.

They pulled over a fifth chair, and Maple wasted no time fessing up to his earlier visual interest in her.

"My dear, I'm sorry if you caught me staring at you a while ago," he said, looking into her eyes. "It's just that you remind me of someone I knew a long time ago, someone who was very special to me. Not only do you remind me of her. You look exactly as she did, the last time I saw her."

"So we can rule out your wife," Brad said with a nervous laugh. "Relative? Old girl friend? Or none of our business?"

"I'd be rude taking number three, since I brought it up. And she wasn't a relative. Regardless, it was a long time ago. But the physical resemblance is startling. I apologize if my discovery was unsettling. You'd understand if you had known her. Right, Mike?"

"You mean Clarice? *Compadre,* that's been a long time ago. But now that you have it out in the open, yes. I can see the strong resemblance. Same slender figure, if you'll pardon me for saying so. Same dark, flashing eyes. Clarice's smile too. Miss Scott, you can take my word for it. You are being compared to a very beautiful young lady, albeit one in her early twenties the last time Treb saw her, nearly fifty years ago Me either."

Mandy blushed. "No harm done. I take the attention as a compliment."

"So, Treb, I really...*really* am interested in telling the folks back home about what you're doing these days," Brad said.

"Fine. You've seen our operation, and I take it your being a reporter, you can put together how it works. Be my guest."

"Well, sure. But I was hoping to talk to you and wind up with a pretty extensive story about Treb Maple. You know. The man of mystery, since your great victory at Boise two years ago. Also, I'd like to explore your connection with Buddy Holly—"

"Holly?" Maple laughed. "Now there *is* some old business. That goes back to 1957."

"Dum-de-dum-dum...Oh Boy!" Cardenas vocalized.

"I dug through your morgue file back at the paper, and there wasn't anything of major consequence about your brush with rock 'n' roll fame," Brad said. "I tapped into AP's library and didn't do much better. My idea is to sort of dove-tail your success on the senior tour—"

"Now history too," Maple cut in.

"Regardless, I envision bringing Trebor Maple back to the public's attention. Sure couldn't hurt your enterprise here any. I think AP might pick up the piece, which then would be available to all the subscriber papers in Oklahoma, Arkansas and Louisiana, as well as Texas. And if I do my job right, assuming you let your hair down and talk about yourself, back then and now, AP might pass it along to the rest of the U.S. How does that sound?"

"Would you be able to stick our website in there somewhere?" Cardenas asked, to which Maple smiled and nodded.

"I could. I would. Whether it stayed in would be up to the editors, back at my *American Telegram* and at AP. But you help me with this, and I can pretty well guarantee my paper will leave it in. Also, I know the right people at AP who might be able to play it as it lies, too."

"What's everybody havin'?" Sally asked, as she walked to the table.

"Order up, folks," Treb offered. "I'm buying. Sal, give me about half a tea glass more of sangria and Fresca."

"Same for me *senoria*," Cardenas replied. "Treb finally got me hooked on his half-and-half cooler concoction."

"I'm fine, thanks," Mandy said, followed by Struthers adding, "me too."

"Oh, I'll take another gin and tonic," Brad said, unmindful that he was showing Mandy yet another side of his demeanor she hadn't seen before.

"OK Brad, let me get right to it," Treb said "And from now on, this afternoon, we're off the record." When Brad nodded, he continued. "Somewhere in those stories from Boise and Napa, you're bound to have come across some pretty damaging press, at least from my viewpoint."

"Probably not as noticeable to others as to you, since I'm sure they were your first exposure to being quoted in the big-time press," Brad replied. "But yes, I can see where you'd be a little rankled by some of it. That's the beauty of this story of mine. You'd get to set the record straight."

"You're saying you'd let me see your article when you've finished, and have veto authority over any part or all of it?" Maple asked, smiling.

"Uh, well, I couldn't do that, no—"

"I didn't think so. Son, I take it you know I am a religious man. At least now." He glanced into Mandy's eyes, which were focused keenly on his. "I wasn't, up until fourteen or so years ago. So when I decided to try competitive pro golf one more time, my life had taken on a new and improved meaning. Pressed suddenly into the spotlight as I was, when I won at Boise, I must've looked like fresh meat hanging in a market window to some of those writer guys. Especially when they found I would answer most any question, up front, without any spin. That made most of the regular guys on the senior tour pretty angry. Incidentally, I'm sure you know it's called the Champions Tour now. Anyway, I didn't mind that. I was made to look like a fool at times. I didn't really care that much about either contingency."

Maple paused. He took a sip of his wine cooler Sally had just set before him, then continued, staring at his hands he had folded and put on the table. "Then, when my relationship to God, through Jesus, was butchered by several of those writers and a local TV guy, it hurt. Even though I made it plain that I didn't think God cared one way or another if Treb Maple sank a birdie putt or shanked a nine iron out of bounds, much less took home what to him was a bunch of money. I still don't.

"After being a loser in tournament golf all my life, I suddenly found myself playing fifty-four holes in a circuit whistlestop with the lowest combined score of seventy or so guys. At least half a dozen of them were household names. So here came the stories of how I must've prayed my way to a win. 'Was that Jesus on the bag for Treb?' one real fine fellow wrote. 'God's no match for the field at Boise,' a headline read.

"In other words," Maple continued, leaning back with both elbows on the table while he looked straight into Poole's eyes, "they used me to make fun of a person with religion. Which," he added with emphasis, "was misleading, since a great number of players on all three men's tours, and the women's as well, I'm sure, are very God-oriented. It's just that they have enough sense to be wary of the sensational ends of the media. You know, don't you, that my relationship with God and golf made a couple of the supermarket tabloids. You didn't? I'm sure you can imagine what fun *those* rags had. Remember the old World War II movie, *God is My Co-Pilot*? Course not. You're too young. Anyway, one of the tabloids had a head that read, *Christ is My Caddie*. I can only imagine what it was like."

"You mean, you never read it?" Brad asked.

"Nope. Mike did, though. Mike?"

The aged but still-handsome Mexican American smiled. "I told Treb he was wise not to have read it."

"Just one more reason, I think, to get all this out in the open," Brad said. "Maybe you're right. But knowing my inborn naivete, I would answer a question frankly and honestly, just as I had done eighteen months ago. And I would be at your mercy. Believers wouldn't believe any stronger, probably, whatever you might write. Some whom I don't particularly care for might use me for their own agendas. Not that Jesus through God can't take care of himself. But just the fact that a person out there who might be on the *verge* of a Christian rebirth would take a look at me and see something over- or under-emphasized in print that would set him or her back, now that just chills my blood."

"Why in the world do you think I'd do that to you?" Brad asked, his voice shaking.

"I don't. You probably wouldn't. But I made my mind up back then that I'd never let myself get in that position again."

"Mr. Maple, excuse me for butting in," Mandy interjected, quietly though firmly, "but I *know* Brad wouldn't let you down. And the Buddy Holly connection would be interesting to a lot of people. One's my grandmother. She said she liked him almost as much as Elvis, when she was young. She's told me that of all the old fifties' rock 'n' roll stars, most experts rank Presley and Buddy one-two."

"She's right. And in fact, I'd bet you could reverse the order if you were talking about England," Maple replied. "At least today. Had it not been for John Beecher and some folks over there, Buddy's legacy probably *everywhere* would've died with him, in that Iowa cornfield just after midnight on February 3, 1959.

"There *are* some good stories that *could* be told about the Picks, though certainly not because of me. After *That'll Be the Day* our trio on the sly

72

comprised the voices of the Crickets, who besides Buddy and with one exception, a guy named Niki Sullivan, actually either couldn't or wouldn't sing a lick. But there're only two of us Picks left now. The other one, John Pickering, can tell you what you need to know."

"But he's not a celebrity like you, is he?"

Treb laughed. "In *his* eyes, I imagine he is. Regardless. I want you to understand that I'm serious about this. No story about me, at least not from my lips, about my golf tournament, about God or about Buddy Holly. OK?"

Brad stared at the drink Sally had just left for him. Then he looked at the other two men at the table. They had remained silent.

"You don't think this is a good story idea, Mike? Struts?"

"Hey, I think it's great. Gotta admit it wouldn't hurt our business. Right, Struts?" Cardenas said.

"You got it, com-*padre*," the big African-American replied. "I don't think you an' me's anywhere near in a position to retire. But it's my man's call. Not ours. Even if he could live right nicely playin' hold-em downtown from now till th' sun sets on all o' us."

"Struts, don't give our friend here another excuse to shop any more story ideas," Maple cautioned with a smile. Then he turned to Mandy. "Where you guys staying?"

"The Fifth Jack," she answered, when Poole sat mute.

"Yeah? I'll be downtown tomorrow night for cards, right across the street. Let me buy you two dinner at the Golden Horseshoe. I feel badly about all this, but I gotta stick by my instincts. I would not like to go through nights without sleep again."

"I think dinner would be nice, Mr. Maple," she replied.

"Good," Treb said, standing. "I'll call you and leave a message if you're out, some time tomorrow around noon. I'll even bring these two outlaws with me. We got two jobs tomorrow, don't we?"

Cardenas nodded.

"Again, forgive me for staring a while ago, Amanda. You were a major blast from the past, as they say. And," he added, looking again into her eyes, "I think *you* probably understand where I'm coming from, concerning the story. Right?"

It was as if he had taken a peek deep into her soul. All Mandy could do was nod, as usual while smiling.

"I'll look forward to seeing you two tomorrow evening, then. And if you like, bring along a tape recorder. If we can steer clear of talking about Boise or Napa, and if you want to write something about our little operation here, to satisfy these two mercenaries, that's OK. Just nothing about what you *really* want, I guess, and for that I apologize."

"Just a *little* about Buddy Holly? Pleeese!" Mandy pleaded, as the three men moved away.

"Oh...we'll see," Treb said with a laugh. "Now you're taking advantage of my blast from the past. Hey guys. Let's all three go back in one car. We got a job in the morning as well as the afternoon. The early bird will be all right if he gets here before eight. We can lock everything up in Strut's Wagoneer, and take Mike's Explorer back home. You guys plan to come on ahead tomorrow morning about seven. I'll bring my car since I'll meet our Texas visitors for dinner. You two can join us if you want."

"You buyin'?" Struts asked, the last to stand up and then with no small amount of difficulty.

Brad was still staring silently at his drink as they walked away.

"WELL, *SOMEBODY* say somethin'," Struthers growled, as Cardenas pulled his Ford onto the main highway and headed for Vegas.

"Like what?" Maple asked.

"Like, can we maybe discuss th' pros and cons about this young writer and his idea?"

"What about it, Treb?" Cardenas seconded, as he pulled down the viser to partially block out the setting desert sun. "We haven't talked about it much, but we *know* our enterprise is gradually slowing down. We don't advertise in any golf magazine. We've—and by *we* I mean you, boss— we've turned down half a dozen of their requests for interviews and features since Boise that would've been the greatest free plugs we could ever hope for. Now you're old news. My take on the stats is, this deal of ours will dry up one of these days unless we—you, Treb—do something."

Maple sighed. "You know how I feel about it, Mike. You, even more so than him, should too, Struts. You remember the screwing we took at Napa?"

"How well I do," Struthers said, leaning forward in the Explorer's back seat and resting his elbows between the other two men. "Good Lord, Treb. Y'know how much I appreciate what you've been doin' for me, with these super senior lessons. I know Mike does too. We love ya', man. It's your call 'cause it's your life we've hitched our wagons to. We all know more or less everthin' about each other, and my guess is that you're pretty well set, financially, but not *quite* where you'd like to be. 'Specially with, uh, Louise."

Treb turned in the right front seat and looked back at his friend.

"I mean, it's good money." Struthers continued. "I know I've sent a wee bit too much of mine back to Houston, but I could get by jus' fine without our deal, if it ended tomorrow."

"Me too," Mike added. "But we all sort of enjoy working with these guys, and if we're honest, we like the comfortable life. I'm *proud* of what we do too. I will bet there's *nobody* who gives struggling 65-and-over amateurs more for their money than we do. It's worked out well. The club loves it, and our virtual zero overhead couldn't be beat anywhere else. But it's peaked. Unless we market ourselves some way—and what could be better than free publicity?—then let's get ready to close up shop one of these days. Sooner than we might expect."

"Th' man speaks with unbridled wisdom," Struthers said.

"*Unbridled* wisdom?" Maple said with a laugh. "Struts, you've been reading again." He turned forward once more and stared down the highway as the Las Vegas lights began to battle encroaching twilight. "The thing is, I figure God's been taking good care of three twice-over has-beens. I also figure he'll keep doing it, one way or another. But you guys know how I am with answering a question. I *answer* it. Jesus doesn't need me to take care of him. But why would I want to put myself in the position of *feeling* I let my Lord down—ever again?"

They drove without speaking for a few minutes. Soon Cardenas hit the freeway and maneuvered between the three lanes of traffic. It was he who broke the silence.

"Been thinking, Treb. What if Struts and I met with the writer feller? You and I go back to the first grade. We've been around each other just about every year since, except when we were in the Army. You and Struts couldn't be any closer than you are, after what you all went through those two weeks when you met. We *know* you, Treb. Like a book. Any questions, just about, that he might ask, one or both of us could answer. Sweet Jesus *knows* you can trust us!"

"Trusting you isn't my worry. You know that. It's putting my life—especially my walk with the Savior the past fourteen years—into the hands of a man whose livelihood depends on grinding out stuff on deadline, stuff that some people *might* want to read if it's sensationalized."

"Not every writer guy is a Duke Pleasance, Treb," Struthers interjected.

"And did you catch the pure sincerity surrounding that little girl he's with?" Cardenas argued. "The one you think is a spitting image of Clarice? I figure he's stuck on that sweet thing, and I also figure she wouldn't *ever* let him do a job on you. And I think if we, Struts and I, present it to both of them just why you're gun shy, well this just might be exactly what all of us need."

"Hey Treb," Struthers added. "Ever cross your mind during this drive home that maybe, just maybe, the guy and his story ideas might be God's doin'? Th' *real* Treb Maple story finally told? Why, I bet you could sit down with sweet Mandy one evenin' and tell her all about Buddy Holly and you and…and…"

"The Pickering brothers," Maple assisted.

"Right. Them Picks. What little I done gathered along th' way, it *could* be a neat story within a story."

"I…I just don't trust the guy," Maple said. "I really, *really* don't. There's something about him…"

"OK. Think about this then," Cardenas said. "You *know* he's bound to have brought a tape recorder from Texas. We got a tape recorder. Two of 'em in fact. What if, as a condition, we tell him that we want to record the interviews he does with Struts and me. And that *if* everything seems to be going all right, you'll plan meet with him after we're all through, to tie up any loose ends. Struts and I could be there too. We'd break in and holler 'calf-rope' if things got sticky, and you started running off at the mouth. Again."

They all laughed, then Treb sighed, and took a cell phone from the glove compartment.

"Let me sleep on it. OK? I'm going to call Louise and see if she's still feeding slots and wants a ride home, or if she's already there."

"Boss, I really believe it's the right thing to do," Cardenas said.

"Me too," Struthers added, animatedly.

"Don't call me boss," Maples grumbled as he dialed. "Both of you know that."

"You got it…boss," Cardenas mumbled, grinning.

"BRAD, WHAT'S wrong? He said he'd talk to us tomorrow night," Mandy asked.

"Sure!" Poole hissed.

"C'mon, Brad. We've got time. Let's be patient and see what happens. He seemed *really* nice to me."

"Why wouldn't he? Treb Maple is just like most other born-agains. He wears Jesus Christ like a miner's hat with the flashlight on."

Mandy stared at him. Her eyes grew moist. "Is that what I do, Brad?" she asked quietly.

He looked up, then reached for her hand. "Hon, I'm a jerk. I had no call to talk that way. It's just that I'm disappointed."

"You two want anything else? I'm closing now," Sally said, picking up the glasses and scooping Maple's twenty and ten into her apron pocket.

"I'm through," he replied, taking a quick glance toward the ivy plant. "Mandy? Nope, thanks anyway, Sally. I hope we see you again."

"Likewise, then. You guys have a safe ride back to Sin City."

Brad stood, and helped Mandy with her chair. "I really do apologize, hon," he said, pouring as much sincerity into his voice as he could. "Let's get on back and have a nice dinner. On Tornado Thornton. Or the Fifth Jack. Or whoever."

They walked to the door just as an older man who looked every bit as if he belonged in a golf pro shop entered. He smiled and nodded as they walked by and held the door for Mandy. Brad waited just outside, being sure the visitor was engaging Jack Hill in conversation.

"I think I'll take a rest stop before starting back," Brad said, handing her his briefcase. "You go on ahead, Mandy." He re-entered the shop and heard the visitor address the young assistant pro.

"Hi, there," the man said. "Name's Baxter Randall. You th' pro?"

"Assistant. Jack Hill. Our head pro, Charlie Crow, is off today. I'll be closing up soon. Only a couple twosomes still out on the course."

That's OK. I'm just lookin' around. I take it from your sign out by the gate that your little facility here is where the great Treb Maple calls home."

Brad slowed, looked around the corner and saw that Sally was not out front, then walked quickly to the ivy plant. He glanced back at the golf end of the large room and, seeing the men talking, reached in and quickly grabbed his tape recorder, which was small enough to slip into his pants pocket. Then he walked back toward the entrance, only to slow at the counter and pretend to look over the different boxes and sleeves of golf balls on display under the glass. A large basket on the counter had a sign that read, "Slightly used. Your pick, seventy-five cents. Or three for two dollars." He turned over first one and then another of the balls, most of which had been rescued, or perhaps just barely revived, from a watery grave. He was back in earshot of the assistant pro and his visitor.

"Your name was…?"

"Baxter Randall. Bax. Ring a bell?

"Kind of…" Hill said slowly.

"I used to play the tour. Both actually."

"Oh sure," the young assistant pro replied, though still with a puzzled look on his face.

"Not a household name, of course. Certainly not like ol' Treb, my buddy from the senior circuit, however briefly. Does he play here?"

"Not often. But he stays real busy giving lessons on a regular basis…"

"Does he now! That's what I had heard. My-my. Two weeks out of a lifetime and our guy's a friggin' genius. I was hopin' to bump into him."

"He's here most afternoons, around one. Sometimes in the morning. I'll tell Treb you were asking about him."

"Do that. It'll make his day," Randall said with a grin.

"Need some balls?" Hill said, eyeing Brad as he tossed a used one back on the pile.

"Nope. Just looking. Say there, Mr. Randall, could I shake your hand? I sure remember you from the old days," Brad said, thinking he recalled something from an article about the Boise tournament, but not really sure. "Brad Poole. Used to write sports."

"Do tell?" Randall replied, smiling as he took Brad's outstretched hand. "Glad to know you."

"In town for a while?" Brad asked.

"Yep. Staying at the Excalibur."

"I'm doing a story on Treb. Maybe you'd like to meet with me sometime, and tell me about life on the tour."

"You're doin' a bit about Treb?" Randall laughed. "My my. Love to, son. Give me a call around ten some morning before next Sunday. Might help me wake up. And call me Bax."

"I'm at the Fifth Jack, downtown," Brad said, opening the door and waiting for Randall to exit, after the old pro had waved goodbye to Hill.

Brad looked toward the rental to see if Mandy had gotten in, then remembered that he had locked the car and had the only set of keys. He looked around quickly, then saw that she had walked alongside the shop windows, out toward the paved cart path that led from the ninth green. She was looking through the wall of glass. It immediately dawned on Brad that Mandy could have seen him slip over to the ivy plant, look around to make sure he was alone, and retrieve his tape recorder.

"Hon, you ready to his the road?" he asked lightly.

The unusually unsmiling young woman turned to him and walked silently toward the Neon. He caught up with her, unlocked the door, helped her in and pushed the switch to unlock his driver's side. He walked around the car, got in, started the engine without speaking, and drove out the front entrance, waving to Baxter Randall when the old golfer exited the pro shop and headed for his Cadillac. Brad idly guessed that the Sedan de Ville was getting long in tooth. Probably around a ninety-four.

"That guy?" Brad said, groping for idle conversation. "He knows Treb. In fact, he was looking for him. The way he talked, I couldn't tell if he was an old friend who likes to kid around with Maple, or what."

"Did you go to the restroom?" Mandy asked, coolly.

"Excuse me?"

"The restroom. That's what you went back for, wasn't it?"

She had seen. That was certain now. This was not like Mandy, to play cat-and-mouse. He didn't like it, nor did he care for the defensive posture into which he was being forced.

"Y'know, I completely forgot it. I was headed that way when I remembered I'd left my tape recorder in the snack bar. Then I saw this old pro over there talking to that young Hill guy and got interested when I heard Maple's name. But I'll be all right. I can hold it till we get back to town."

"I don't remember your taking the recorder in with you," Mandy said, as Brad shot a quick glance her way. He didn't like to see her without her perpetual smile.

"No? I don't remember. Maybe you were out. It's the small one. I was going to trot it out when Maple and his guys met with us, but—"

"But you didn't."

"Um-hum. Anything the matter?"

"Brad, what was in doing in a flower pot?"

"Hell, Mandy, I don't know! I guess I just laid it down. Now, forget it! All right?"

She stared straight ahead into the gathering gloom.

7. **Bread is Spread on the Poker Waters**

Brad and Amanda returned to the Fifth Jack about the time the crowd awaiting the Fremont Experience was gathering along the famous old Las Vegas street. About four blooks' worth of overhead light shows scripted to high-technology sounds of easily identifiable music would be presented three or more times a night, each a different format. One might be a cartoon-character western theme featuring Willie Nelson and Waylon Jennings warbling *Momma Don't Let Your Babies Grow Up to be Cowboys,* and ending with Roy Rogers and Dale Evans wishing *Happy Trails to You.* Another starred U.S. Air Force aircraft in eardrum-splitting flights, from one end of the four-block overhead stretch of hundreds of thousands of multi-colored lights, to the other. Amanda had enjoyed seeing one of the shows their first night, and had seemed anxious to follow up with subsequent visits.

Clearly, though, she had lost her appetite for entertainment as well as food during the afternoon. She had hardly spoken to Brad during the hour-long drive from Desert King Golf Course and through the city, the trickiest part of which was getting to the Fifth Jack's parking garage.

"You want to freshen up before dinner?" Brad asked as he stopped the Neon.

"No. I'm not hungry. I may get a sandwich later."

"Well, I'm famished!" Brad said, silently promising himself not to let Mandy put him on some guilt trip, or whatever she might be cooking up. Hell, he had gone through a lousy marriage with this kind of crap going on. Maybe it was good that he was now learning about *this* side of his young companion. "We need to provide the casino a little action. You think you'll feel up to that later on in the evening? Vegas never sleeps, you know. And we can stay in bed till noon if we so choose."

She sighed. "Brad, I guess the slot machines were a novelty last night, particularly when I won and didn't have your or my money in it. I feel real bad about this, but I just don't want to do it anymore. Unless you say I just *have* to. But I will be very uncomfortable doing any more of *that.*"

He surprised her by telling her, "No problem. I can gamble for the both of us. My God, with that ass Maple—"

She sucked in her breath, but didn't say anything. Poole decided now was not the time for a confrontation.

"Sorry. With Treb seemingly intent on being uncooperative, I'm gonna have a good bit more time on my hands here, until I call Thornton and report that our guy is in hibernation."

They walked to a door leading from the garage, and headed for the elevator.

"Don't you think *something* might work out?" Mandy said as they walked down the hall.

"Doubt it. I don't care for his alternatives. But we can give it a day or two. Maybe if he hangs out with *you* a while, he might soften up. I can tell he doesn't care for *me.*

He punched in the upper floor designation where their suite and five others for high-rollers were located. "I just want you to have a good time," he said, as the elevator door closed. "I know this afternoon was a bust—for both of us."

"I'll be OK," Mandy replied, attempting a smile.

The elevator stopped. They exited, and walked to their hallway door. "I'm going to take a shower, change clothes and drift down to see if I can shoot a crap or two," he said, smiling broadly at making a joke, though it sailed right past her. "I'll have a sandwich or something later on, and check on you. I may be gone for most of the evening. If you don't want to get out, call room service and order what you want." He opened the closet in the main room and punched in the combination to their safe. "I'm going to take a few hundred from our winnings, in case I decide to go across the street and play a little poker."

"That's fine," Mandy mumbled half-heartedly as she sat in an easy chair. "Staying out, I mean. I'll be OK. Is it all right if I call Grandmother? I'd like to check on her."

"No problem. You remember the combination to this thing, don't you? Half this money is yours. Help yourself anytime you want to buy something outside the Fifth Jack. OK?"

"Sure."

AFTER HE he had cleaned up, dressed and bid a rather strained "good night" to Amanda, Brad ventured downstairs. Suddenly he was hungry, and wished he had thought to make reservations for the cave-like formal dining area called the Silver Lode. But a plateful of fried shrimp and french fries in the Jack's café worked out just fine.

After eating, he ventured to the main business area. He didn't see the casino manager in the guy's office. Instead, an officious-looking middle-aged woman was sitting at his large desk.

"Can I help you?" an attendant asked through the cage bars.

"Is, uh, Mr. Conti—Rick Conti—not on duty tonight? I was supposed to check in with him."

"Mr. Conti was called to Atlantic City, rather suddenly. I don't think he'll be back for a couple days or so. What can I do for you?"

"I've got an account," Brad replied. "I'd like to draw on it. Name's Brad Poole. Room 1212."

"Poole...Poole. We have you on the guest list, but I don't find an account. Let me call Mrs. Huckabay. She's assistant manager and in charge while Mr. Conti's on the East Coast."

Brad gazed around the casino, noticing only moderate action. Just three crap tables were up and running, and probably only half of the semicircles accommodating blackjack and its variations.

"Yes? I'm Sondra Huckabay," the attractive African-American assistant manager greeted, with a smile.

"Seems you've misplaced my account," Brad said, smiling.

She got on the computer. "Pool or Poole?" she spelled.

"With an 'e'."

"Well, it's all here, it seems. Just not the account. How much were you cleared for?" She kept attacking keys when Brad suddenly remembered that Conti had reminded him to ask for "Thornton-Poole" in case Conti was not at the casino. He was about to relay this to Mrs. Huckabay when she spoke up. "Ah! Here it is. I had to try a couple of other avenues. Now, I just need your PIN."

"Let's see. It's our room—twelve-twelve plus...oh yeah. Plus six-eight," he replied, vaguely recalling the last two digits on a paper Conti required him to sign.

"There it is! Chips, I take it? No coin?"

"Yes."

"How much of the balance would you care to check out?"

This caught Brad by surprise. "What's the total now?" He asked.

"You have nineteen thousand, six-hundred."

Hummmm, he thought. What gives? He laughed. "How about five thousand?"

"No problem. Most in hundreds?"

"Uh, yes." His mind suddenly shifted gears into high. If he continued with this strictly forbidden move, what were the consequences?

"Say, I, uh, have a problem keeping up with what I have left. If I don't blow the whole five grand tonight, can I re-deposit it to my account? We're going to be here a while, and though I appreciate the hospitality, I don't want to wake up busted with several days left."

"Of course. You may return either cash or chips, and give whoever waits on you this slip. They'll put your stake money that's left back into your account."

"Just like I never took it, I guess," he said, laughing.

"Naturally, there'll be records of withdrawals as well as deposits, just like at the bank."

"Naturally," Brad acknowledged, unable to keep from grabbing the little satchel of chips that was pushed under the bars. "But I reckon the bottom line is what will count most. At least with me."

"Good luck, Mr. Poole with an e," she said, smiling.

He left the cage, beginning to think ahead to his sudden good fortune. How would he play this? It stood to reason that, since their little deal affording them up to two weeks in a swanky suite was on the sly, a salute to Tornado Thornton's past patronage, it would necessitate two *separate* accounts. One would be the Thornton-Poole listing, to which Conti would monitor upwards of three thousand dollars in total, two-week casino action, over and above winnings. The limit would be to satisfy Thornton's watchdog request. The face value would be so Conti could justify giving Brad and Mandy the best in accommodations and food.

The other entry, requiring the PIN, would be the official yet phony account. It showed no limit on Brad drawing from the total twenty-thousand. That would be to satisfy Fifth Jack's checks and balances, were they to do an audit. When Brad had whipped out the PIN Conti never expected him to use, and Brad couldn't remember just how he came to get it, the PIN triggered this phony account. So far as anyone but Conti knew, Brad could draw on the full twenty grand for Fifth Jack chips and coin.

Conti had failed to clue in his most trusted staff member. So long as Conti was gone, Brad could use the money to stake himself to some poker action, if he could figure a way to accomplish that. He figured Conti wouldn't care that he had slipped into the fake account, so long as Thornton's seed money—less three thousand—was available to send back to West Texas. If he squealed to Tornado, Brad could lie his way out of a firing. Especially if he had a story for the paper, which he'd come up with, one way or another.

What if he lost? Despite Brad's sudden enthusiasm, he had to factor in that prospect. He was in a city full of sharps and sharks. But most would be at bigger games than a ten-twenty-dollar table of hold-em. If it's casino-run, you'd have a dealer, greatly reducing any worry about a card mechanic. The house took a nice chunk out of every pot for providing a place to play what would be all but guaranteed to remain a safe game.

He sat at a blackjack table run by a good-looking dealer. Her nametag read "Sheila." He played her one-on-one, two hands at a time, twenty a pop after she exchanged a few of his hundreds. Idly he ran the prospects for bigger games through his mind, since he could play twenty-one almost in his sleep.

Suddenly he knew he had it figured out. He couldn't help but smile.

"Double-down this one, Sheila," he said, of its two-card deal of five-four, with the dealer's up-card a six. He was dealt a four for a locked-in total of thirteen.

His second hand, a pair of eights down, prompted him to add, "split these, please."

The dealer provided one card for each of the two eights. He waved his right hand over the ace that now joined the first eight, signifying he was staying with that nine or nineteen, automatically converting it to the latter. A tap of his index finger on the second set of cards—a three had joined the eight—signified a "hit." Sheila did, producing a four. Brad waved his hand over this usually-bad fifteen and waited for Sheila to flip her hole card. He expected a face card and got a jack. She was forced to hit her sixteen, and a queen busted the dealer.

"I thought you were asleep there for a while," she said, pushing eighty dollars in chips to Brad. Now he was pumped. He discovered Sheila was from New Hampshire, through chatting with her between shuffling. After half an hour, he tipped her two twenty-dollar chips, gave her his "action slip" to sign and bade her farewell. He hadn't done badly. He had clipped her for about six hundred dollars.

"HI," MANDY said into the telephone in the main room of the suite, dredging up all the phony cheerfulness she could from her downtrodden state.

"Well, do tell!" Thelma Walker responded. "If it isn't my long-lost granddaughter, caught up in the lights of glitter gulch, but still sweet enough to remember those who love her back home."

"Pooh! How're you doing, Grandmother?"

"I'm fine. The shop's fine. I *am* wondering how you're doing?"

"Oh...great!"

"Try again, my sweet."

Mandy sighed. "It's just the long trip, I guess."

"You've had words. Is that all?"

"Yes. More or less."

Thelma laughed. "You've never been this close to another human for such a time, other than me, in your whole life. By more or less, you don't mean you've had a screaming fight, or maybe he has done something physical."

"No, nothing like that. I guess I see him a little differently. I'm sure he feels the same way about me."

"Then he's a fool. Mandy, when your grandfather and I used to take one of our infrequent trips to someplace exciting—Possum Kingdom Lake comes to mind—we'd be anticipating *so* much and be so into the thrill of something new. We'd expect the excitement to keep building. But none of us lives in a world where the ups always whip the downs to pieces. You gotta expect a balance. Plus or minus. Day after day. Hang in there with Brad, dear. I'll bet you wind up the two weeks with a plus. And that's as good as you can ever expect to get."

Mandy laughed. "Gee, am I glad I called you."

"Promise me another call in a couple of days. Make up with Brad. Spread your wings a little and have fun. And always remember, Amanda. You're *special*. God knows you're special! By the way, I have some news from another front."

"Oh?"

"Your momma was in town last night. She and that slick Caribbean husband of hers—"

"Cuban, Grandmother. Cuban-American."

"Whatever. Don't get me started. Anyway, they popped in and Mary Katherine was disappointed her daughter wasn't here. But she was delighted when I told her where you were. She and Desi—"

"Oscar, Grandmother. Oscar Arnaz."

"Whatever. She and Oscar are driving from Miami to Las Vegas. On business, he said. Expect a call sometime tomorrow. I told her where you're staying, before I could think of something else to say."

"That's fine, Grandmother. I'll look forward to seeing her," Mandy uncharacteristically lied.

"Remember, dear. One, cut Brad some slack. Two, call me in a couple of days. Three, good luck with your momma."

"Bye, Grandmother."

Amanda stared at the phone and sighed. So this is what they call life. She realized she had been way too shielded for most of her twenty-five years.

BRAD HAD figured that he knew the place where Maple played cards. It was two blocks away. It should be a safe game, one peopled mostly by out-of-towners hoping to turn mediocre attempts at the fast-paced poker game into something they could brag about back home. He'd look for a ten/twenty-dollar table.

Common sense dictated that he buy in for one-hundred times the maximum bet's amount. His night's winnings, plus what he and Mandy had in their room safe, would not let them be wiped out via the three thousand-max account, were Brad to lose his two thousand tonight. The trick would be to convert two thousand in Fifth Jack chips into cash.

This he had been able to do by visiting a cage away from Sondra Huckabay's office. It worked like a charm. The teller gave him twenty hundred-dollar bills for two-thousand in chips.

Then Brad had ambled through the Fifth Jack Casino's main room, drifted back to where a sucker's progressive slot area was drawing attention from the unenlightened patrons, then slipped out the door and onto Fremont Street.

Fifteen minutes later, after asking a few questions, he located the older, smaller Adobe Casino where Treb Maple spent one night a week at his hobby of plucking would-be hold-em heroes. Nice avocation for one of God's chosen, Brad thought.

He stood around the nine-man, ten dollar-twenty dollar game. Being the Las Vegas variation of Texas Hold-Em, he watched as a large white plastic disk was passed from one player to the next, clockwise against the table. This signified which player would act as dealer, even though the actual dealing was done by a casino employee. The player directly to the left of the disk, or button as it was called, was the first blind. He automatically "bet" five dollars prior to each deal, with the player to *his* left, recognized by Brad as the second, or big, blind, adding ten dollars, as always. If no other raises among the callers progressing left around the table were made, then the small blind could either fold and "donate" his original five bucks to the game, or call the ten dollar raise. Or, in rare occasions and almost always by shrewd gamblers who knew what they were doing, the small blind could call the ten raise and bump it—or raise it—five or ten more.

Brad was comfortable watching the action progress. The actual dealer gave each player first one down card, then another. These Brad and his West Texas cronies, plus those two assholes in Midland who had changed his life that fateful night, had called pocket cards. Brad was happy they were so designated in Vegas.

Betting on the first two of seven cards, the best five of which ultimately would constitute hands, came next. It would be the first of betting, calling, raising and folding.

All set at this point of a game, the table might have lost perhaps four of its original nine, since there might have been two raises within the action following the pocket deal. Brad knew that the best cards to keep one in the game are ace-ace, king-king and so on, through the jacks, plus an ace-king suited—both cards being diamonds, clubs, hearts or spades.

Then comes the flop. The dealer burns a card (takes the top card and pushes it to the side, out of play), then deals three cards up, in the center of the table. These cards belong to *all* players, if they wish to use them. One can readily see where a player who is blessed with having, say, two aces hidden in the pocket, might watch an ace surface in the flop. He will be looking to win the hand, especially if he is able to chase potential draw-out straight and flush hands with aggressive betting. Better still would be two garbage cards coming up in the flop that are not suited or in progression with the ace, but still hanging around the edges of a medium-high straight. Like an eight and a ten. Or perhaps two low cards suited, like the seven and deuce of hearts. This flop would be cause for hope for either a straight or a flush, depending upon that opponent's pocket draw.

Understandably, the player with the two aces hiding in his pocket will be in great position as the first round of betting commences. He can bet (ten dollar limit at this time) if he's on the front end of the blinds, or hide and watch one or two raises, then raise at the tail end.

Another card is dealt up and placed in the middle of the table, and this, Brad noted with familiarity, is called the fourth street. More ten-dollar betting and raising. Another fold or two.

Those contenders still left are now poised for the fifth street, or as he found it called in Vegas, the River. That's the final card dealt up, following the actual dealer burning another card. Maximum bets now double to twenty dollars. There will have been five "community" cards up and, together with the two originally down to everyone, each individual left in the game has seven possible cards to use toward making a five-card poker hand. Much as in seven-card stud, but considerably wilder due to the betting.

"I'm through," a player who was to be the first blind on the next hand said with a sigh, while picking up only about fifty dollars in chips. Brad quickly lay claim to his seat and gave the dealer two thousand in cash. He spent the first half-hour playing "tight," or cautiously, trying to stamp himself as ultra-conservative. Or at least, not inclined to be "loose." That's one who plays wildly, bluffs frequently, and stays to nurse inside or ignorant-end straights. He might make a moderate score now and then, but more often than not he exits the game sooner than later, all tapped out.

After two hours, Brad had read the perennial losers properly and was comfortably ahead for the night. Probably a thousand up, though he wouldn't dare even hint at counting his chips.

Then, after figuring he had spread enough bread on these waters, he got the hand he had been waiting for. His pocket cards were the ace-jack of clubs. The flop was promising, though not for trips, or three of a kind. A pair would have signaled the start of a full house for someone else—perhaps two, both with one of the remaining card denominations in the pocket while they worked with doubling another flop or street card.

The king of clubs, the queen hearts and the nine of clubs came up next, tempting those trying to make a big straight stay in the game. Plus, with ample paint, or face cards, around when the three of clubs at the fourth street gave Brad the nuts (already an unbeatable and well-hidden hand), lots of players had invested considerable money in the game. There might be another club flush, but it couldn't top Brad's ace (pocket)-king (flop). Straights looked promising, but a flush would sink them.

Brad was in the first blind. Knowing he couldn't be beat, he checked! This kept two or more loose players in the game. The next player, a loud-talking guy from Oklahoma, then bet. An obvious high straight raised him, and when it came Brad's turn, he raised again! The check-raise was either a blow or a frightening puzzlement to those who had pegged the stranger as a conservative. This left the River, or last card, in which Brad came out betting and jumped all over the foolish soul who had telegraphed his own club flush that was no match for Brad's hidden ace-high. Brad pulled in the stack of chips. The one hand alone was worth more than a thousand.

Later, when his new ride-with-a-winner reputation had been assumed, he literally stole a nice pot with a pair of sevens. A raise and re-raise at fourth street had chased three potential winners who were drawing for makeable winning hands. They had seen his action before and pegged him for another nuts hand. Since the game's two loose players had uncharacteristically folded early, Brad was in the position of making a traumatic bluff.

It worked, and earned him almost a thousand more.

Brad left the table at 2 a.m., sheepishly linking to his fellow players his cache of three thousand, six-hundred dollars and change to "pure luck." He tipped the grinning dealer a hundred in Adobe Casino's chips, converted the rest into cash at an Adobe window, then walked out. He strode gingerly a half-block, crossed Fremont Street and slipped into the Fifth Jack.

He made his way slowly through the casino, mindful of the overhead mirrors hiding cameras linked to a control room. Brad stopped by a craps table, took a hundred in twenty-dollar chips won earlier at Sheila's blackjack table from his sack that had been tied to his leg at the Adobe, and lost the hundred in less than fifteen minutes. He had the pit boss sign his action marker, then made his way to the main business area.

No one was in Conti's office, but Ms. Huckabay, seemingly ready to call it a night, was talking to an employee near a teller's window.

"Hi," Brad greeted, walking up to the window.

"Hi yourself," she responded with a smile. "How'd you do?"

"Oh, a couple or so hundred. Can I return my stake to my account?"

"Sure. Help the man, Doreen."

Brad gave the attendant five thousand of Jacks' chips, which he had fleshed out by buying two-thousand at the craps table. He handed over his original receipt, then gave Doreen the remainder of his earlier blackjack winnings. "I'd like to cash these," he said.

BRAD TOOK the elevator to the twelfth floor, and slipped quietly into his and Mandy's suite. He looked in on her, saw she was sleeping, then dialed their safe's combination and added more than four-thousand dollars in cash to the small amount they had left from Mandy's first-night winnings.

He doubted Mandy would be going to the safe again, since she was no longer interested in slots. He would keep this cache handy, as he made plans to turn a lackluster working trip to Las Vegas into maybe tens of thousands of dollars' profit.

Brad then got his small tape recorder and a reporter's notebook from his briefcase and sat in an easy chair, illuminated by an overhead lamp. Using earphones, he made notes while listening to the four-way conversation during Maple's pro shop grill session the previous afternoon. The one to which he had not been invited.

Brad smiled often, writing in his own version of shorthand remarks that might come in handy, even if they could easily be taken out of context, were Brad forced to play hardball with Trebor Maple on a story.

"You mind me asking, Treb...was Boise a religious experience?" a strange voice spoke into Brad's ear, one obviously belonging to the Coke guy from Atlanta.

"Not really. I already had that."

"Forgive me, but I'm curious," the inquisitor insisted.

"Well...I'm a born-again Christian. And don't confuse me with one of those TV ministers, prophets or healers," Maple replied. "About half of them are phonies. At least, in my opinion.

"The truth is, I didn't take God with me just to the Boise tournament. He goes *everywhere* with me. Has, since that day in 1988 when my life seemed just about over, just about hopeless, and I lay on my bed trying to figure how the end would play out—"

"Hey, Boss. Tell him about the five-iron from the trap on fourteen during the second round that turned it around for you." Brad recognized Mike Cardenas' voice.

"No wait," Atlanta insisted. "If you don't mind, I am curious. Is this what you call rebirth? I sure would like to know how it happens."

"You sound like a man looking for his. I hope so."

"Man, I think I've had an experience sort of like this. Do every December, right after Christmas, when I make out a twenty thousand-dollar check to the First Peachtree Valley Baptist Church. It's happened like clockwork, for five years now. And I *do* feel good when I hand over that check to our church treasurer."

"I see. How often to you go to church?"

"Try to, on Easter Sunday. Except sometimes the Masters' fourth round falls on Easter. The kids come Mother's Day and want their mom and me to go to church. Once or twice more a year, though Sunday is a big day at my golf club. But let's get back to your feel-good stuff."

"Mine," Treb resumed, slowly, "came on simply. I remember saying something like, 'God, I've had it. I wish I were ten again, just for a minute, and could feel the presence of Christ's great promise, the Holy Spirit, like I did back there one evening at Brownsville's First Presbyterian Church.' Nothing happened for maybe a minute. Could've been more. Could've been less. But all of a sudden, my left heel started tingling. I felt a chill creep slowly up that leg, then down the other. Then my body shook all over. I sat up with the most *unbelievably* peaceful feeling just *flooding* over me. Like water. I *knew* it had happened to me. The Holy Spirit had taken hold."

"Uh, Treb...bet our friend here wants some more on golf. Maybe th' way th' last round went in Idaho," Carl Struthers' unmistakable urban inner-city Texas drawl broke in.

"No please, Treb. Go on with this," William Biggerstaff from Atlanta all but begged.

"Well, later 15 or so years ago, when I began reading the Bible regularly, I discovered what would become the greatest revelation of my life," Maple continued softly. "That was, the Holy Spirit would never leave me. I was saved for eternity. A thousand cases, more or less, of Pearl and Lone Star Beer before, capped by a thousand bottles, more or less, of Oso Negro gin and vodka, and Jack Daniel Green Label, some Black Label, and a truckload of Sauza tequila liters that had made me do crazy things and say hateful stuff to people whom I loved, all of that was wiped clean.

"Now, I can have one vodka martini, or one shot of tequila, and enjoy the warmth. But I wouldn't crave more. I sure wouldn't *need* more, to hide my insecurities and uncertainties, which all but went the way of booze. Wine became my social drink of choice. A cooler," Brad could almost visualize Maple holding up his sangria and Fresca, "like this."

"I had a guy at a dinner party tell me one time that he was a born-again Christian," Atlanta said. "'What'd you do?' my wife shot back at him, right there at the dinner table in front of maybe six other people. 'Go back into your mother's womb?' I felt real bad for the guy. My wife had downed a few scotches, and she dearly hated the term 'born again.' She always told me it reminded her of some ignorant soul at a backwoods tent revival, swept up in the moment of hell fire and damnation being preached by a faith healer who would be in the congregation's pockets real soon."

"You shouldn't have. Felt sorry for your friend, I mean," Maple said, as Brad kept stopping and re-starting the tape recorder, letting his simplified shorthand catch up.

90

THE SUBJECT got back to golf again, with Struts telling about another pro's caddy and his bets that his man would do this and do that and how it all would demoralize Maple, during the second round at Boise.

"Treb an' I was just getting' good acquainted," Struthers said. "I must'a took that boy fer a hundred, five an' ten at a time. He doubled up fer fifty on eighteen, when Treb had this ten-footer downhill, breakin' to th' bad side—ya know, to th' right—while his guy had eight feet straight and blow th' cup. Treb slipped his in th' center cut—"

"You know how I *hate* that silly TV guru expression, Struts," Maple sighed. "Wish I knew what talking head on TV came up with it first. Probably one of CBS's.".

"Never th' less, Treb sank an' Corky never got his putt to th' hole. Thought Treb was gonna make me give my winnin's back, when I tole him 'bout it later. But then he jus' laughed."

Atlanta wanted to know once more the secret of Treb's chipping. "I move the address for my full shots from the hosel to the toe, play off the back foot, take ten or fifteen inches back and then the same ten or fifteen inches forward, parallel to the terrain from which I'm hitting."

He asked Maple about inconsistency from greenside bunkers—"Usually too much body movement. Lock those dug-in feet in the sand, take a slow backswing and above all, *finish."*

And so on, with several more jokes and easy banter, but no more on religion.

Treb's able assistants, Brad surmised, had craftily guided the conversation over drinks away from their man's transparent eagerness to talk about God.

After an hour or so of sometimes frenzied note-taking, Brad shut off the machine, put it back in his briefcase with the notepad, and headed for the bathroom. In no time, he was in his bed, in the room adjoining Mandy's. He slept like a baby, even when Mandy slipped out at 8 a.m. to eat breakfast alone.

He had never sensed that she had watched from her darkened bedroom through a cracked door as he had listened to the tape and taken notes on his electronic eavesdropping.

She had returned to her own bed before Brad had finished. But *she* had not slept like a baby.

8. Mandy's Momma Has Great Timing

Mandy awoke before 6 a.m., sighed when she realized she couldn't sleep anymore, got up and dressed, and slipped from the suite without looking in on Brad. She knew how late he'd been up, and she figured he'd stay in bed for hours. She also was in no mood for a confrontation after the events at the golf course. Not yet, anyway.

Mandy rode down to the small main lobby and was about to turn to the left to head for the mezzanine grill when she saw Treb standing at the desk. She walked up behind him and greeted, "Hi, Mr. Maple."

He spun around and smiled largely. "Why if it isn't Amanda from West Texas! I was just leaving you and your, your boyfriend—?"

"Yes. Boyfriend."

"I was just leaving you all a note. About tonight. I figure we'll meet you at the Golden Horseshoe around 8:30. Sound OK? My guys might or might not be with us. They make up their minds at the last minute. Sort of tends to depend on how a pretty-full day goes."

"Fine," she replied, smiling. "Why don't you go ahead and leave the note anyway? Brad is sleeping in this morning. I may not see him until later."

"You headed for breakfast?" he asked.

"Yes. I'd love for you to join me. If you have time."

"Time enough for a cup of coffee, at least. I meet the guys in about forty-five minutes, including maybe ten from here. Louise—that's my wife, c'mon over here and meet her—she lost her mid-morning ride when her sister had an interview at 8:30. She's right over there," he said, pointing in the direction of the first slots one sees from the lobby. "Coincidentally, the Jack is one of her favorite places to play slots; at least downtown."

"Sort of early, isn't it?" Mandy wondered.

"Louise is a daily slots player. She's handicapped, and it's her main pleasure in life. That, and bingo. The Fifth Jack has *that* losers' game too, midmorning each week on Wednesdays."

Mandy followed Maple to a gallery of quarter slot machines. Even before 7 a.m., this section of the casino *clanged!* and *dinged!* with the unmistakable sounds of activity, though only about a third of the machines were being used.

"Louise, meet the new friend I was telling you about. Amanda…"

"Scott," Mandy assisted.

"Amanda Scott, this is Louise."

Mandy looked down on a face that had to be seventy years old, but one that framed what twenty to fifty years before had been strikingly beautiful. She could tell. And plenty of mature beauty still remained.

"Hello Amanda Scott," Louise greeted from her mechanized and motorized wheelchair, quickly glancing away from Mandy's handless left arm, from which the young woman's ever-present shawl had briefly fallen. "My husband was quite smitten by you. I surely see why."

"Guilty as charged," Maple said with a laugh. "Only not for the reason someone might imagine."

"Yes," Louise said, smiling while holding her bucket of quarters. "She does look amazingly like your old sweetheart. At least so far as I can tell, in the face and with the curly black hair. Oh, don't look so surprised, Treb! I've gone through your dusty old Brownsville High annuals enough times and read ad-nauseate the two years of drippy odes to love Clarice penned to you."

"No secrets kept from this lady," Treb said, shrugging. "We're about to have coffee and, for Mandy, some breakfast. Want to join us?"

Louise turned back to her machine, curiously enough a Blue Diamond quarter version of the dollar slot Mandy had picked the first night they had been at the Fifth Jack. "No, go ahead. I've had all I need. And with this infernal contraption, the fewer potty stops I have to make, the better."

"I'm taking her and her fella out for dinner tonight. Want to join us?"

"No," Louise said, stretching. "I'll be done in, as usual. Sis is going to pick me up just before noon and take me to the Strip. Probably Caesar's. Maybe on up around the MGM Grand or one of the new places. I imagine I'll be home well before you all start back from the course. I figure it's TV tonight, with Melba maybe coming over."

Treb bent down and bussed his wife on her cheek, which was neither offered nor hidden. "See ya. Have fun. Let's go to the grill, Amanda."

"Good bye, Mrs. Maple. Sure was nice to meet you. Hope we'll get together again."

Louise gave a half-wave with a hand, her face firmly locked on the three tiers of illuminated icons while she pressed the "max play" button.

"IF YOU don't mind my asking, how…uh…" Treb asked, haltingly, as they sat in a booth that overlooked the craps and blackjack portion of the casino.

"How did I lose my hand? Car accident, when I was a little girl," Mandy replied matter-of-factly, after she had ordered orange juice, a poached egg, hash browns, and an English muffin with honey. Both she and Treb were served their coffee. "Your wife's misfortune came about the same way, Brad tells me."

Maple nodded. "Mountain forest highway in New Mexico, fourteen years ago. Another question, Amanda. Do you prefer Mandy? Or is Amanda OK? Personally, you strike me as an Amanda."

"That's just fine," she replied, unconsciously yet automatically adding a special sparkle to her ever-present smile.

"Amanda, you're a believer. I mean, a *strong* believer."

"In God? Yes I am. Always have been."

He grinned. "Struts thinks you may be an angel," to which Mandy put her napkin to her mouth and shook with laughter.

"Oh that it were only true," she responded. "I must thank Mr. Struthers the next time I see him."

"But he *is* right in one sense. You *do* have what he and I got to calling 'the glow,' back on the fairways at Caldwell Golf and Racquet Club just outside Boise. A believer all your life, eh. Church-goer?"

"Yes. Presbyterian."

"I grew up in that denomination," Maple said. "God and I are mighty close these days, finally; after he and I both endured my horribly misspent life during most of my years. Now, since a spectacular yet private rebirth, the Holy Spirit that Jesus promised each of us *could* have just for the asking sometimes floods my inner being with something akin to beautiful music, sung by a choir that is accompanied by the New York Philharmonic. At others, he whispers comfort to my soul when it's troubled, guidance when it's tempted, and counsel when it's confused. I know I should be more active in church life—the Apostle Paul instructs it in no uncertain terms—but my spiritual comfort zone is more on the solitary side. Then again, Christ told us that "when two or more gather in my name," so Struts and I should fit *that* bill. Also, I do have three or four Protestant or non-denominational congregations I visit now and again. Struts usually goes with me. Mike sometimes. Louise maybe once a year. But I don't get involved in the regular activities very often. To my discredit, I'm sure."

"Oh, I couldn't get along without Sunday School about every week—unless I'm someplace like Las Vegas, which is a first for me," Mandy said, her glow transferred to her voice. "Next for me each Sunday is the regular service, then Wednesday night suppers and classes, and most everything else that comes along at Central Presbyterian, back home," Mandy paused, then continued. "Would I be correct in assuming you helped lead your friends to relationships with Christ?"

"They *both* know that road. Struts and I went through so much intensity in Boise and, the following week, at Napa, when I played senior golf for the only times, that he just sort of picked up where he'd been forty years before.

He's a sprinter down that road I was talking about. Mike, he's more of a plodder. Grew up Catholic. Hasn't been what you could call a good one of those for a long time now. But he's a good *man.* A very, *very* good man. We go back to our grade school days."

Treb chuckled. "Mike lives in deathly fear that I'm going to proselytize with our customers. That would make him most uncomfortable. Would me too, if I thought I did. I believe in the individual finding his own way, which if truth be known, the *way* had *already* found *him.* Or her. Only he or she didn't know it at the time. But there's room for all kinds of approaches and roads, and most everybody needs a little help or push in the right direction. In the end, however, read the core teachings of Jesus, and it's pretty simple."

"You're an interesting man, Trebor Maple. Trebor. Where did you get that name?"

He smiled and toyed with his spoon and coffee cup. "My mother was a lover of all things limey. She coveted the ways of the English, though she never got near the British Isles. My dad—pretty much a no-show all my life, till he disappeared for good when I was nineteen—no-showed big time the early February 1935 night in Mercy Hospital; the night when I was born. To hear her tell it, somebody asked her questions about her newborn while she was still pretty well grogged out. When asked what the baby's name would be, she mumbled 'Trevor.' 'Come again?' the hospital lady asked. 'Trevor.' 'Spell it,' she urged Mother. 'T-r-e-v-o-r. Trevor…Timothy…Maple.' Well, she was slurring that 'v,' even when she spelled the name for the hospital lady, who kept hearing 'b'. She finally shook her head and said, 'Well, that's a new one.' When the birth certificate came several days later and the error jumped out at her, Mother was too superstitious to change it. Bad luck, she believed, would befall her beloved son, if she tampered with it. So she let the substitute first name stand."

"Now *that's* rich!" Mandy said, laughing. "I can't *wait* to tell Brad. Unless," she added quickly, "you'd rather I not—"

"Nah! That's OK. Actually, I might have been too hasty with your boyfriend. See? I can talk easily with you. But I still feel the hair on the back of my neck bristle when I get around newspaper guys. I don't want to ever read *again* somewhere how I use God to embellish my credentials as a golfer or a man. How maybe I let Jesus line up my putts at Caldwell, near Boise. How the Archangel Michael, perhaps in the form of Struts Struthers, toted my bag. Or how the Holy Spirit checked yardage and clubbed me; maybe even spirited himself to the par three seventeenth that last fateful day at Caldwell, when my tee shot hooked toward the water after barely clearing a trap that would've left a near-impossible up and down. My Top Flight hit something and actually bounced *uphill* toward the green, leaving me a pretty simple lob shot that set up a par. Did the Holy Spirit intervene, maybe slip to

95

the bunker and blow the ball over, then reach down and make it skip away from the *agua?* I think not. It demeans true spirituality, for the sake of selling cheap newsprint. Especially demeaning for those groping to get there."

"I can see you're very protective of your station in Christianity," Mandy countered. "Still, it's just so *refreshing* to hear you witness. Would I be out of line to ask you to have a little faith? In Brad?"

"You *and* Struts. *And* Mike," Treb sighed. "Especially Mike, who handles our books and bookings, which a couple months ago may have peaked. We talked about it last night. I'll have a proposal to make to Poole this evening. Sort of a compromise."

Then Mandy remembered, and quickly decided to tell Maple about catching Brad secretly taping him and his client and two aides at the pro shop grill yesterday. Hiding his recorder in a potted plant.

Treb laughed. "Well now, *that's* ingenious, in a conniving sort of way. I don't really mind tapes. I just want what's on them to be quoted correctly, and more or less in context." He stood, and took a twenty from his money clip. "I've gotta run, Amanda, to catch up with my henchmen."

"No, coffee's on me," Mandy said, placing her hand on his bill and pushing it back. "All of our in-house food is paid for, along with our room."

"Comped, eh? Is Brad a player?"

"Yes. But *this* trip is because his boss is a bigger one. Or was."

"Tonight, then," Maple said, extending his hand and smiling. "Do me a favor. It really would be good for Louise to get out. Drop by and tell her I said if the time angle works out, I might take you all over to the Mirage and meet up with my pal and work in progress, Josh Leventhal, and his wife Missy. You want to meet a character, he's the ultimate. A highly unorthodox Jewish reprobate. We have classic arguments. Louise doesn't join in, but she fairly shakes sometimes. You get the idea she'd like to wheelchair-joust with him, and the winner lives. Or perhaps dies. I never know with those two. He's pretty close to his last legs, due mainly to emphysema."

"Josh. At the Mirage. OK."

"Miss Scott, Struts *is* right." Maple said with emphasis, as he started to walk away. "You *do* have the glow. Maybe you *are* an angel, after all."

"You too, Mr. Maple," she replied as their waitress placed her breakfast before her, Mandy's smile as warm as Treb could imagine one ever being. "Maybe you too."

BRAD SLEPT until 1 p.m. After a late breakfast, he answered the page to their suite and picked up the message from Maple. Then he withdrew four-hundred dollars in chips from the restricted account, played more blackjack and shot craps, and almost four hours of boring play later, returned just over three hundred to the account after getting his dealer's and pit boss' chits signed, signifying the tenor of his play and the minor losses.

He met Mandy in the living room of the suite, seeing her for the first time in about twenty hours. She offered her cheek when he attempted to kiss her more warmly.

"So it's all set for tonight?" Brad asked.

"Far as I know—"

The telephone interrupted their strained attempts at conversation. Mandy was closest, so she rushed to answer. She figured she knew who it was.

"Hello? Oh hi, M.K. Yes, I talked to Grandmother last night and she told me you had left there, on your way here, the evening before last. You and Oscar must've driven almost straight through."

She looked up and gazed absently at Brad's wide-eyed, quizzical look, his palms extended outward in a *"What gives?"* expression.

"So where are you staying?" Mandy asked. "New York New York? That's a new place on what they call the Strip, isn't it. No, I haven't been there yet. Um-hum…um-hum…Uh, no. We'll take a rain check on that. We've been invited out to dinner by this nice man on whom Brad's doing a feature story. Where?" she looked at Brad, who shook his head. "It's at the Golden Horseshoe, but it's a business type thing. So we'd be pretty well tied up." Mandy listened for half a minute, then rolled her eyes toward the ceiling as she turned to Brad. "Well, I guess it would be OK to stop by the table and say hi. But please remember. It's a pretty important meeting for Brad. Promise you won't stay. It might detract from what he wants to accomplish…Oh, I *know* you wouldn't! And I'd like to see you too…and Oscar…Sure! We'll be glad to say hi, introduce you around, and then set a time day after tomorrow when we can see you longer. Maybe lunch…Um-hum…um-hum. 'Bye."

"Well?" Brad half-asked, half-commanded.

"I didn't tell you they were coming in, 'cause I hadn't really seen you, uh, to speak of since I talked to Grandmother. I have no idea why they're here. They were on their way and stopped by to see Grandmother. She said to tell you that Oscar has taken up golf, and he knows who Treb Maple is. And to tell you that he's impressed. Grandmother had filled them in about our trip. Oscar comes here every so often. I think I told you that. It must be business too, but I don't know anything else about it."

"Great. Just *great!* Mandy, I hope they don't waltz up there and crowd themselves in to sit down with us. Or agree to, if Treb gives a perfunctory invitation."

97

"Brad, please don't be angry. Not when we're about to go out. She said they wouldn't. They just want to say hello. Then get with us in a couple of days. Or maybe just me, if you'd like to skip out on that."

"Just damn great!" Brad mumbled, noting out of the corner of his eye that Mandy displayed neither shock nor discomfort.

Could be getting used to it, finally, he thought. Then he turned inwardly pensive. *Or maybe she just doesn't care anymore.*

"THIS PLACE is great for steaks," Treb Maple suggested, as the table for four was rearranged slightly so he could wheel Louise in between Brad and him.

"I remember, though most of my past visits have been on the Strip, as opposed to downtown," Brad said. "Sorry Struts and Mike couldn't make it, but I'm happy to meet you, Mrs. Maple. Glad you could join us."

She smiled slightly, almost as if she were masking a sneer. "Please. It's Louise. Mrs. Maple was Treb's domineering mother, rest her never-pleased, never-wrong soul. When your young lady told me late this morning that we might be having drinks with his highness, the right Reverend Rabbi Sheikh Joshua Leventhal, I couldn't *miss* coming. You never know what that idiot is going to spout off about. He's a piece of work."

"Now, Louise, Josh is dying," Treb said softly. "Let these kids make up their *own* minds. But," he added, addressing Brad and Mandy, "he *is* a character all right. Used to have a well-read entertainment column on Vegas nightlife. Fantastic insight, for an avowed atheist, though he does tend to run off at the mouth. 'Opinionated' isn't close to defining his acerbic outlook on life."

"Wish I had brought my tape recorder," Poole said.

"Probably best that you didn't. Not worth taking a chance on inhibiting the old profligate. He loves to wallow in his own dissoluteness.

"Is he your age?" Mandy wondered, as the waiter began readying their table-setting.

"Almost. A year younger. We've only known each other for eighteen months or so, but we had mutual connections. Like Don Cherry, the singer and my partner in money matches here now and then, as well as back in Brownsville, about 30 years ago. He and Josh have been big buddies for decades. I've known Cherry well since the late sixties, when he began coming to Valley International Country Club's member-guest where I was assistant pro to Ranch Guerrero. Bill Bass, one of the nicest guys to work for and a heck of a real estate entrepreneur, bought the old Brownsville C.C. He redesigned the layout, bought adjoining real estate, sold home sites and put in condos and small rental units. He gave Cherry one of the houses on course in return for sharing tournament function entertainment duties with Rusty Draper. Cherry got Jimmy Demaret—he's a famous and colorful pro golfer of the 1930s and forties, Amanda, now deceased—he got Demaret to come to Brownsville. That opened up lots of other guest celebrities, such as astronauts like Gene Cernan and Charlie Dukes. Also lots of Dallas Cowboys."

"Names from out of the past, all right," Louise mumbled. "And you're rambling, Treb."

"Who was Mr. Draper?" Mandy wanted to know.

"Most famous for *The Ballad of Davy Crockett* in the early 1950s, then became a dinner club entertainer, though never past the minor leagues. Draper's show-stopper was a movie title song he borrowed. *Jean, Jean* became his Brownsville signature. Two married ladies, one named Jeanette and the other Genie, had to be separated from a potential catfight one day over a women's brunch when they *each* claimed Draper was singing directly to *her.*

"Cherry, he was a crooner, could've been one of the best if his career timing hadn't been so unlucky. Pro golfer too. When I was a kid, I used to visit my grandmother during summers in Abilene. They had a July Fourth amateur tournament there that dated back to the thirties. I was a twelve-year-old caddy the first time I saw Cherry play, and he was something to watch. At nineteen, he had everything. Sad to say, that included a temper to match his rapidly disappearing buff-red hair. He could blow like Old Faithful when the putts wouldn't drop, and when he'd blow, he was done. But man, could that guy play!

"Don was Dean Martin's buddy. Cherry hit it big in the early fifties with the pop song *Band of Gold*. Columbia Records. He sounded a lot like Guy Mitchell, or vice versa. Never would talk much about being in Mitch Miller's stable. I always wondered if that storied A&R genius decided they were too much alike for one label and cut Cherry. Then again, Elvis soon took care of changing careers for most *all* crooners. Neither Don nor Mitchell made it big on records after that. However, Cherry earned a respectable living in Vegas, and still does to this day, mostly in lounges. Appeared on Martin's TV show a lot in the late sixties and early seventies—even partnered him in the Crosby Clambake at Pebble Beach. A few years ago, he opened for Vic Damone, who's now all but retired. And though in his seventies, Cherry recorded a CD album of Old West and Texas songs with Willie Nelson, titled *The Eyes of Texas—A Tribute to Lady Bird Johnson.* That was just a couple years ago. He sounded fantastic. So'd Willie."

Louise reached for a cigarette, which Treb lighted. "Ramble…ramble," she sighed.

"Sorry. I've tried to explain to Brad why newspaper guys make me nervous, that I tend to run at the mouth. You all ready?" he asked, as menus were placed before them.

"By the way, Treb," Brad asked, "You know a golfer named Baxter Randall?"

Maple stared at him over his menu. "Why?"

"Well, out at the golf course yesterday afternoon, after you all had driven off, he showed up at the pro shop. Asked the assistant a lot of questions about you."

Treb shook his head and smiled. "Good ol' Bax. Great timing as usual, just when a scribe is scratching around my back yard."

"Not one of your close buddies, I take it," Brad said, unable to resist a grin.

"Changing the subject, Brad, I've been thinking," Treb said. "Not to mention that this lovely young woman here," he patted Mandy's left arm, just above where her hand had been, eighteen or so years earlier. "She's pretty persuasive. Anyway, I talked to the guys, who want to tell you about golf and me. Which is fine. They're their own people, and I *sorta* trust them. Amanda and I hit it off this morning, when we had a quick chat. Why don't you whack out a list of questions, and she and I sit down for an hour or so and I'll promise to spout off in your tape recorder. I'll tell her what you want to know about me, personally. I take it you are interested in religion and me, so thoroughly trashed by the press during my very, *very* brief fling with fame."

"Well, that's fine, Treb. But it kind of makes me out to be a non-participant in my own enterprise. Like I'm not capable of conducting—"

"Brad, forgive me, but I'm not interested in your ego. Only in protecting my interests. Let's give you some room though. How about if I get with you and tell you all I know about Buddy Holly—which might not be nearly as much as you'd like, even if I did sing on some 34 million copies of the nine songs on which we backed him. But I'll be all yours for an hour, two, four or whatever it takes. Deal?"

"Well..."

"Why, that sounds *very* nice of Mr. Maple, Brad," Mandy gushed, causing Poole to briefly flash her an exasperated stare.

"OK, you win," Brad finally agreed. "But cut me just a little more slack. You said Thursdays are your poker nights? At the Adobe?"

"Somebody's been snooping," Treb said, smiling, nodding to the waitress who was set to take dinner orders.

"Can you get me in your game tomorrow night? Sort of let me watch you in action? Or maybe you're ultra-protective of that, too. A *Christian* who plays casino *poker* in Vegas."

"Not at all," Treb replied, narrowing his gaze. "Actually, I was going to play tonight instead of tomorrow, but I wanted to go out with you two, plus do some catching up with Josh and Missy. Sure. Think I can get you a seat. I'll call in a little while. It's an honest game, and I like competition. Only," he added, his smile returning, "it might be a little pricey just for researching an article. Maybe if you stood outside the ropes and kibitzed…"

"No, I'd rather play. Get the feel of the game."

"OK, but you'd better bring along about three thousand bucks, just to get started."

"No problem. I've got expense money for that, plus the fact Mandy and I have had a little luck the past day or two."

Mandy blushed, Maple noted. "*Beginner's* luck. And I'm *through*. Remember, Brad?" she inserted.

"Hummm. So you've come to town and already plucked the casino some?" Treb said, looking at Brad. "I'm impressed. But if we get head-to-head, expect no mercy."

"None expected, or sought," Brad replied, grinning like a confidence man on the prowl, "and none extended, either."

"Fair enough," Treb said, as salads were set before the diners. "Let's eat, then drop by to see ol' Josh…Uh, hello?" he added, when an attractive woman, forty-fiveish, came up behind Mandy and squeezed her shoulder.

"Hi, sweetie," the woman greeted.

Mandy rose, and gave her mother a light hug. She went around the table with introductions. "This is my mother," Mandy said, her hopes dashed that the family reunion would not take place at the table. She couldn't resist the chance to show her displeasure by telling them, "meet Mary Katherine Walker Collins Gerard Arnaz. And this is M.K.'s husband, Oscar Arnaz."

Oscar stepped forward, kissed his step-daughter lightly on her cheek, gave a smart little bow that flipped his six-inch-long ponytail to one side, and responded with, "Pleased."

"Hey, we're just starting. Maybe I can get the people here to set you up at the next table," Treb suggested with feigned courteousness.

"No, we're going out for the evening. Thanks anyway. I just wanted to come by and say hello to my little girl, and," M.K. added, walking over and placing her cheek on Brad's, "to meet her *fella*. Mandy, call me tomorrow. OK?"

"Here for vacation?" Treb asked.

"A little business, a little pleasure," Oscar replied, flashing a warm, toothy smile that went well with his darkishly handsome Latin looks. "We try to get over here three, four or five times a year."

"Any kin to Desi?" Treb asked lightly.

"As a matter of fact, a distant cousin."

"Ever meet him or Lucy?"

"Sorry, no. We'll be leaving you nice people to your dinner now. Glad to meet all of you. And I'd sure like to play a round of golf with you, Treb, if that's possible."

"My days are hardly my own. I tee it up on Sunday afternoons, but it's a regular game, hundred-dollar robins and individuals, and ten-dollar skins, with carry-overs. Maybe next time you're out this way."

"It would be my pleasure," Oscar replied.

"What's his business?" Treb asked Mandy, after her mother and step-father had exited.

"I really have no idea," Mandy replied sheepishly. "And I do apologize for the interruption."

"No problem," Treb responded jovially. "*Now* let's eat."

"MANDY LOOKED lovely, didn't she?" Mary Katherine said as she and Oscar sat in their black Lincoln Navigator, in the almost-dark parking garage."

"Yes. As always," Oscar Arnaz agreed, reaching into his coat vest pocket and extracting a cell phone.

"I'm all done in, honey," she said, stretching her arms above her shoulders. "Let's turn in early."

"Have to do a little business first," Oscar replied. He flipped open the phone, eyed a scrap of paper by the still-glowing dome light, and punched in a phone number.

"Oh Oscar. Really? So *soon?* Do I have to tag along? You know how I hate these, these deals. I'm frightened to death! What if someone tries to kill us? You know what happened to Catarina—"

"Jaime got sloppy! I don't get sloppy, MK. Quiet now."

"Please take me back to the hotel first. *Pleaseeee?*"

"OK! *OK! Quiet!!!*...Hello, to whom am I speaking? Yes, this is the Cuban. Is Mr. Gabe White there? He's expecting me to call. Oh? That's strange. We were going to meet face to face, I understood. Um hum. I see. Well, you will understand if I *am* a bit apprehensive. Good. Just so we understand each other. Hold on a minute..."

He snapped his finger at M.K. who gave him a quizzical look, her hands open. Oscar put his index finger on the opposing palm and made like a pen or pencil writing, prompting her to quickly fish a ballpoint out of her purse and hand it to him.

"Um hum...Trucker's Haven? Don't expect any exchange there, OK? You gonna be alone, *mi compadre?* Fine. I think it will be best to do our, uh, business someplace remote and secure. Five miles toward LA? On the right side. Got you. See you there. How long from downtown to Trucker's Haven? Yeah, where we're staying." He put his finger to his lips when M.K. appeared ready to correct her husband. "Give me twenty minutes more, so I can run up to the room. You driving a white DeVille with a blue fabric top…got it. I'll be in a black Navigator. And say, remember. No surprises. *Bueno?"* He smiled as he closed the phone and stuck it back in his coat, then started the SUV and backed out of the parking space.

"So, you're taking me home," M.K. said.

"Of course."

"This doesn't sound very good, from what I just heard," she said. "I won't be able to sleep a *wink* till you get back."

"Then come with me."

"Uh-*uh*. Catarina and Jaime…"

"Shut up, M.K.!"

9. Bad Night at Black Rock

To Mandy, entering the MGM Mirage was not unlike what she imagined one would experience if one somehow were to suddenly find oneself in an indoor rain forest.

Maple led the way to the main cocktail lounge and slowly panned around the dimly lit room. "There they are," he soon said, pointing to an elderly woman standing next to a gray-haired, goateed man in a wheelchair.

"C'mon, make my day!" Treb teased, pointing a gun-finger at his friend.

"Make mine, Maple, and don't mention your biblical pals *once* during the next hour or so," Josh Leventhal groused.

"Won't have to. I figure you will, for me. Already have, haven't you? Thrown down the gauntlet, I mean."

"Now, let's be nice tonight, boys," the matronly Missy Leventhal said. While her husband had a decidedly wrinkled look and wore a string tie, Missy was fashionable in a navy pantsuit, white shirt and a printed scarf around her neck. "It's so good to see you, Louise. And we have *guests.*"

Treb made the introductions, and drinks were ordered. Mandy had a Vanilla Coke, Brad a gin and tonic, Louise a vodka martini and Treb his usual Fresca and sangria cooler. The Leventhals were filling their glasses for a second round from their carafe of house chablis.

"Where're the boys?" Josh asked, hoarsely. He occasionally took a drag from the bottle of oxygen strapped to his motorized wheelchair.

"In bed. We've got a full day tomorrow."

"Still jacking it up...and letting it fly...so the rich suckers can see how a pro can whack a golf ball, even...an old fart pro," Josh wheezed. "Do you still promise them...you'll teach 'em how...you do it?"

Treb smiled. "You've seen my web site, you old grouch, so you know what promises we *don't* make, and what we tell them we *will* do."

"Amanda...you are a...lovely young woman," Josh said. "And—"

"And he *knows* lovely young women," Treb said. "Right, you letch?"

"Well, since you so rudely...cut in on my...conversation with this...sweet girl...yes. Yes I do. I...married one, didn't I?"

"That you did," Treb said.

"And I thank you," Mandy said.

"Young man, what...was your name now?"

"Brad. Brad Poole."

"And you do..."

"I'm a newspaper writer back in West Texas."

"And what...do you write?"

"Entertainment, after a few years in sports, sir."

"Treb! You matched...us up! How...*quaint!* I wrote entertainment before...my lungs retired me, young man."

"You wrote gossip," Treb said, playing at relishing a corrective tone.

"The only gossip...I recall writing...was when I announced...that the rock'n'roll...*doo-wah* sensation...of the fifties, turned...golf pro was now making his home...in Las Vegas, and he could...be had at the poker table."

"All right, you guys, can it!" Missy cut in. "These young people will think not too kindly of us. Louise, you're looking great, as usual. And you're feeling...?"

"Like shit," Louise replied. "But that's par for *my* little course of life."

"I see," Missy replied, smiling.

"So, what's on your agenda for this evening?" Treb asked, leaning toward Leventhal. "I promised our visitors here you were the answer man."

"Politics is...the bowel movement of...our society," Leventhal shot back, using his oxygen mask to garner up emphasis.

"Hear hear!" Louise shouted, over the usual lounge din, while Mandy and Brad slowly placed their drinks on the table, and Mandy put her only hand over her open mouth.

"That right?" Treb asked.

"As with individuals, a repulsive...stinking, often vulgar and...downright crappy undertaking...but one vitally...necessary to the survival...of our not surprisingly crappy...society," Josh explained, the verbiage seemingly exhausting him for a moment or two.

"Tell me, Brad...how do you handle *the*...in your writing?" Leventhal asked, as soon as he had collected sufficient breath to carry on.

"Excuse me?" Brad asked.

"Another sign of...the times, for us word merchants," Josh sighed. "Happened somewhere...in the 1970s, I think...a generation decided it could...craft individuality, instead of...earning it. 'I beg your pardon' not only...was sufficient for the better part...of the twentieth century, but preferred due to taste and, at...times, the opportunity for an...icy retort. Usually by some snotty female...wishing to shoot down...a poor slob's attempt...to get to know her better. But I digress. The article...*the* is used by writers mostly...on the short side of, say, forty five, to impress...their peers and to talk down to those...readers whom they consider less sophisticated...usually the older ones...if they have any."

"You've lost me, sir," Brad said.

"An example: 'The guest speaker...was poet John Doe, who read from his works'...My guess is, you'd write that...'The guest speaker was *the* poet John Doe'...Am I right?"

"Now that you mention it, I guess so," Brad replied, failing to keep from sounding apologetic.

"Totally redundant…Unless Doe is *the* only…poet, which I doubt…in today's sadly…overpopulated world. Some prissy…college prof somewhere…started it, and some high profile penman…took it up; then it snowballed…The 1970s…was a dumbass, lackluster decade."

"There's another of many examples, though I often fail to grasp Josh's take on significance, that further separates the generations' literary concepts, not to mention their basic speech," Treb said. "And I know exactly when. Today, especially the young people but again, forty five or so and under and especially females, can't speak more than a few sentences without exclaiming, 'My God!' or 'Oh…my…GOD!' or just plain 'God.!' To them, it's acceptable speech. And I must confess, the lord's name came in vain with me, more often than I care to remember, before my…before things *changed* for me.

"Now days, these people don't *consider* it to be blasphemy, which would be their saving grace, if they cared one bit about salvation in the first place. But us older codgers do, and I for one shudder every time I hear it. Particularly in TV sitcoms. Just isolate the objectionable phrases in your mind for a moment, and try to recall an episode of *Friends* when all three aren't overworked."

"Treb, I have to correct you," Mandy sheepishly interjected. "Many of us in and around my age bracket *do* consider such idle talk blasphemous. And we don't want to be lumped in with our contemporaries. At least not on *this* issue. But you said you know exactly when the practice began."

"I stand corrected, my dear," Treb replied. "And yes. I know *exactly*. Archie Bunker's favorite exasperated exclamation was, 'Oh…my…GAWD!' Curiously enough, that seemed to fit most *All In the Family* situations, at least early in Norman Lear's experiment with pushing the envelope. It pretty well completed the picture of Archie. We all could laugh at that buffoon, it seemed. Now, though, throwing 'God' around usually comes off as an overworked cover-up for nothing substantial to say. Either on a TV show or in real-life America."

"Love it…or leave it…Treb old boy," mused Leventhal.

"Meaning you have a better place to live out your days?" Maple asked.

"Minutes, probably…I have this…horror of having my…obituary report that…I expired while dining with…Trebor Maple…though perhaps our…other guests listed…would…compensate in taste," Leventhal replied, his last few words dwindling to a barely-audible whisper.

"So, tell these people where you'd rather be living than the good ol' U.S. of A." Maple challenged.

"Oh, Costa Rica maybe…except I don't…trust *their* crappy politics to last…I'd love to waste away…in Cancun…but that idyllic isle is getting overrun…not to mention the…sky-high cost of living."

"Uh, Josh, I don't think Cancun is an island," Treb interjected.

"Not talking…about Old Cancun…I'm talking about the tourist trap…which for your…information *does* qualify as…an island…Ah, that beach! Worth all…the Ugly American saturation it has to endure."

"What about you, Missy? Where would you want to live?" Mandy asked, hoping to steer the conversation from confrontation.

"Me? Paris!"

"Th' French…*hate* us! Openly!" Leventhal sneered. "Most Mexicans probably do too…but most of *those* have…learned to hide it with humor and tact." He paused, took a sip of wine, then pondered, "Ever wonder where…the anatomy of one…country or society's hatred for another…begins?"

"I'd say with politics, like the Germans, for us," Brad opined. "A guy running for chancellor, say one with charismatic speech, samples a poll, finds sixty percent of his countrymen have finally had it with us, sees where twenty-five percent more are undecided, and mounts a slick campaign aimed at swaying *them,* all the while keeping in step—goose-step if you will—with his core audience. He gets his office, but the slogan that got him there doesn't die so easily. In fact, it just seems to grow, feeding off suspicion, distrust and probably no small measure of jealousy."

Despite Treb's scowl and his nod toward the wheezing Josh Leventhal, Louise lit a cigarette. She blew smoke toward Brad. "So, young man, every German who doesn't approve of America suddenly must be classified as a Neo-Nazi?"

"Hey, I thought we were picking the French apart, for Missy's sake. Not the Germans," Treb wondered.

Leventhal took the bait, and swam with it. "If truth were known…probably some hot-shot…frog editorial writer maybe fifty years ago…slipped in a reminder…to still-struggling Parisians…how the stupid, rich Americans…come to their fair city…suddenly emerge as impressionist experts after…one visit to the Musee' de Orsay…or culinary critics following…a couple nights trolling…their—excuse, me, while…I catch…my breath—their beloved…restaurants. Like Brad said…the seed is sown by some seemingly credible opinion-*meister*…and the seed feeds on itself…till it's an uncontrollable monolith…too powerfully, politically correct to be challenged."

"OK! OK! So I don't want to live in Paris!" Missy exclaimed with a sigh. Mandy only stared, apprehension clouding her countenance.

"Like the Muslims, I guess," Brad wondered, suddenly transparent as Leventhal's willing straight man.

"Different ballgame," Josh replied, shifting uncomfortably in his wheelchair. "Religion!" he fairly spat out the word. "Clerics generally...control the minds...of the masses. Once we...lifted a finger to...help Israel...we had no hope. Now, it's a done deal...Coexistence is impossible..."

"Nothing is impossible, with *my* God," Treb said. "*The* God."

"Interesting," Josh replied, a rare smile creeping across his face "Were I to...renounce my atheism...it probably would be because...of the book of Revelation. Symbolic prophesy. Apocalypse. Armageddon. You can't...overlook the parallels toward which...mankind seems to be marching." He laughed. "Three dominant yet distinctly...differing religions...all continuing to trace their...modern concepts back to one man and one of two women...Abraham. And barren Sarah, who first insisted...her husband seek out and...bed down Hagar, her handmaiden...so he could have the promised offspring...he so desperately needed...to fulfill his promised mission. Enter Ishmael."

"Oh lord!" Missy exclaimed. "A Bible lesson by Josh Leventhal!"

Josh took a breath, while most at the table shifted uncomfortably in their chairs. "Then Abraham...a pretty spry hundred-year-old...more or less...gets this...bolt from the blue...Old, wrinkled-up Sarah, at ninety well beyond...child-bearing years, conceives! Hallelujah! Now enters Isaac...Suddenly, two fathers...of future generations! What to do...wait till they...come of age, and fight...to the death...to please their malevolent...creator? Or kick one...out of camp, with his mama...and into the desert...to seemingly certain death. Bye-bye, Ishmael.

"Or is it Isaac? When that same malicious...creator tests old man Abe way up on the...mountain, ordering the killing...of his own son...then at the last second...calling off the joke...it's *Ishmael* who's under the knife. So said Mohammed! But no...the older half-brother has been sent packing...say the Israelites' history books.

"Apollo in all...his wild and crazy...party pranks...never jerked the chains...of human puppets...so profoundly."

"What seems to be one thing can appear decidedly different in the eyes of the Creator, whose motives and in whose ultimately perfect mind, or thinking process, or eternally preordained concept we cannot begin to comprehend," Treb offered, surprising even himself with his attempt at uncompromising theology.

After a pause, Josh took off on another tack. "You people know that Treb...here, the born-again, par-busting, poker-playing phenom...believes in evolution?"

"That I do," Treb replied, not at all defensively. "Just as I'm basically too simple to comprehend how any agnostic—or even an atheist such as my good friend here *professes* to be—could look up at the heavens on a summer night and not feel the presence of a superior being, a creator. I have to dismiss those with the notion that God's word, having been filtered through several languages—some *really* alien to others—has to be locked into a time frame that God himself dismisses with his concept of eternity. If a thousand years is only the blink of the creator's eye, why can't a hundred and twenty-five million years thus be translated into, say, a day? Locking God into *any* natural restraint is to subject the ultimate creator to constraints."

Another pause. Brad looked across at Mandy. Even in the dark of the lounge, he could see crimson creeping across her cheeks and furrowed brow, with no smile on her face. Too bad, he thought. I'm enjoying this. No more booze for me. No tape recorder, damn it! Gotta concentrate on remembering *all* of this rich stuff, word for word as closely as I can get it. And I predict that it's gonna get better!

"I mean," Leventhal wheezed, "almost forty-two hundred...years ago...out there is the miserable Mideast...three seeds of religion will...be sown amid the scorpions and scorching sun...Even the Jewish texts...concede that no harm will...befall Hagar and her son Ishmael when they are sent packing...by Abraham, well into his twelfth decade!...The Jews, as luck of the genetic draw...would have it, my tribe...became the chosen people...Jesus, said to be...their long-expected Messiah...is executed as...an imposter...But his teaching...spawns a *new* religion named for him...Now enter a connection...to Ishmael's wandering tribe. Seven-hundred years after his time on earth...Jesus becomes a major Muslim...prophet, alongside the likes of Noah, Moses, Ishmael, Jewish heroes Isaac...Jacob and Joseph...even sorry old supreme dumbass Adam. Today's Christians would seem to at least be tempted...to give a nod more to...Moslems than my guys...since after Jesus' controversial death and maybe-yes, maybe-no resurrection, until Mohammed's wild dream ride...there was no other Muslim-recognized prophet. Also...it might be noted, Mohammed...had been raised...by a Christian uncle! And received via his vision, that fateful night, the confirmation that...yes, Jesus' birth was of...what would become the Immaculate Conception! The only one...of its kind...ever, even though the term originated far from the...package called Islam that was...crafted by Mohammad's followers after his death.

"Ah, but does...this make Jesus the Son of God? 'No!' Mohammed insists that he was told...God can do anything...all he has to do is say, *be,* and it is done'...But he cannot stoop to have...a *human* son...nor can he become human himself...sort of shooting down that...glorious concept of 'He just says *be'.* Mohammad said he learned that...Allah is incapable of lowering himself to human standards…other than watching…the little twits mess up his stuff…He could…*never* share power with his lowly creations…And forget about that wild concept, the *Trinity.* Also, jettison the…myth that Jesus…was crucified! Since he…was taken straight…into heaven, surpassing…human death, he didn't…die. Thus, he never was…ergo couldn't have been…raised from the dead."

Josh gathered himself for a few moments before continuing, a self-satisfied look taking over his beleaguered face. "Jesus is the most…interesting concept…in Islam, one would find…That is, if the clerics could be kept away from…a thought-provoked student's poking around…the edges of the Koran."

It was as if suddenly-inspired Josh Leventhal's lungs found new repositories of breath. His excited words generally came forth in quick, unbroken phrases.

"Meanwhile, the Jews continue to await their Messiah…but welcome Christian intervention in their really tough struggles to survive. The Moslem tribes take more than fourteen centuries to leap-frog from largely backward, nomadic existence into modernity, far removed from their historical roots in which they had contented themselves, while mired mostly in what would seem to be the world's most unappealing real estate, short of the two poles. But when you're sitting on top of most of the world's oil reserves, themselves important only in the last seven decades, you've got the infidels…by the ying-yang. Christians like ol' Treb here…follow the marching orders of their leader, whom they expect to return any day now, and preach love while pursuing peace. Their credo? *Come aboard, damn you, or we'll blow you to bits!"*

The few seconds of silence around the table in the Mirage's lounge, punctuated only by Josh gasping for air, were broken by the waitress.

"Everybody all right here? Anyone need a refill?" she asked, shaking the Leventhals' empty carafe and looking around the table. Brad and Louise raised their hands. Amanda and Treb shook their heads. Josh nodded as Missy said "No!" thus prompting her husband to ask for "maybe one more…glass here."

"I think it's time for a trip to the ladies' room," Missy announced. "Louise, I'd love to help you, if I can."

"I'll manage fine, as long as they have a handicap stall, and I seem to remember, they do," Treb's wife answered, matter-of-factly while backing her wheelchair, shifting gears and following Missy Leventhal. "You develop these upper-body muscles when you're in my state of semi-paralysis. That's in order to salvage some small degree of dignity."

Mandy got up and followed the older women toward the restrooms.

"Sounds like a good time for me to see a man about a dog too," Brad said, smiling. "Be right back. Don't continue Philosophy 101 without me, now."

"WHAT'S WITH this…young guy?" Josh asked, after Brad departed.

"He wants to do some sort of feature article on me."

"Entertainment?"

"He has a background in sports. I guess he wants to link my brief pro golf career some way with Buddy Holly."

"Interesting," Josh mused. "Glad you…decided to link up…with us. I miss seeing you, and Louise too…She's not doing…any better, emotionally, I see."

"Same old stuff," Treb responded, with a sigh. "She doesn't have it very easy, and you should know that."

"You think your young scribe is getting the…wrong idea about you…and me?"

"You mean because of your rosy outlook?" Maple asked, with a laugh. "I warned him about you. Which brings me to wonder just how badly *you* feel, physically. Is it just tonight? Or are you slipping?"

"Who knows, except for…*your* God maybe. Actually, I am…feeling worse. The doc says…it's irreversible, something we've all…known for two years. I don't talk to…Missy about it much. But…she knows what…I know. And that's that…I won't be stepping…out like this much longer. *Damn!* I hate the…thought of wasting away…at home."

Treb reached over and patted Leventhal's arm. "I'm sorry, old friend. I should've made sure I got with you more often, over the past few months. My fault. I will make amends. Is there anything else I can do for you? Other than," he said with a chuckle, "pray for you, which I have continually done, and don't go off on a tirade now."

Leventhal was silent for a moment, then surprised Maple with a soft response. "I know you do. I know how much…you want to save my soul. Maybe…maybe it's close to time…that I spend an afternoon…or evening just talking to you…without the bullshit." Reaching for his oxygen, he wheezed, unable to stifle a cough-inducing laugh. "If nothing else…I can go where *ever* with…the knowledge that I…gave you cause for hoping…my soul would escape fiery eternity. If anyone could save me…it would be you."

"Has nothing to do with me, pal. It's all you. I'm here to hold an old friend's hand. You talk a mean streak about not believing in God, through Jesus, but I've always figured that was a gruff front you enjoyed showing, for shock value if nothing else. Now, I sense that the louder you talk down salvation, the more you hunger for it. Uh-uh! Don't interrupt with more of your pseudo philosophizing. That's a smoke screen which is becoming transparent. You old codger, you don't fool me. You want salvation. You're just too ornery to admit it. So far, that is."

"You're wanting me to...say, 'Gee Treb, I think you're...right as rain!'...But I'm not gonna," Josh countered, as Brad returned to the table.

"You will, old friend. You will," Treb replied with a smile.

MANDY SAT before the wall-length makeup mirror in the Mirage's ladies room and watched as the image of Louise Maple came clanging and banging out of the handicap stall, complaining and swearing to herself. Mandy glanced to her left and made eye contact with Missy Leventhal, who also was watching the same struggle. Mandy wanted to help, and her eyes must have indicated as much to Missy, who gave an abbreviated shake of her head in the mirror.

"Need some help, Louise?" Missy asked.

"Hell no!" Louise shot back, as she guided her wheelchair to the spot to Mandy's left. "I do this for myself all day, every day, and you know that!"

Mandy attempted a quick subject-change maneuver. "I'm so sorry for your husband's discomfort, Mrs. Leventhal—"

"Missy."

"—Missy," Mandy said. "It is so unfortunate. And I *do* wish there was something I could do to help you a little, Louise."

"I'm sure you do, Mandy," "Louise sighed, then laughed a little. "My, we would be a pair, wouldn't we? You pushing my wheelchair through the casino and lounge...I'm sorry. I'm not intentionally making light of your, your—"

"Left hand, that isn't there? Don't worry. It's been that way since I was a little girl. You have this around for all your life, you get used to it."

"Still, I guess I feel a little ashamed, griping about my own woes when a beautiful young woman such as you has to...well, I hope you know what I mean. I'm sorry."

It was the first time Mandy had been around a mellow Louise Maple. "No apology necessary."

"Something else, my sweety," Missy Leventhal said, closing the latch to her purse. "Please don't think ill of my husband, for the way he talks to Treb. He simply adores the man. Josh was a big Buddy Holly fan when he started out in college, after growing up in Des Plains, just outside Chicago. He attended Northwestern, and bought *The Chirping Crickets* album. Still has it, by the way. He already knew he wanted to write entertainment. This must've been 1958 or '59.

"He told me later how he wondered about the sound the Crickets had, and how much it differed from their first hit, *That'll Be the Day,* to their second, *Oh Boy!* And then the third—oh, what was the title?"

"*Maybe Baby,*" Louise offered. "Then *Tell Me How,* off the same album. Brunswick label. I know 'em all. I used to have to hold Treb's hand back in the early sixties, when we'd come home from a party or somewhere, and the Buddy Holly stuff would emerge. How he'd try not to say anything about being on the records, but would finally crack. Then people who didn't know him well figured this dumb club golf pro was crazy, drunk—a state which we *both* frequented back then, by the way—or a little of both."

"Why?" Mandy asked, putting her small black purse in her lap and shifting in her chair to where she faced Treb's wife.

"Because, Treb told me, it was a sham," Louise explained, seeming to relish a relaxed setting in which she could contribute. "Let's see if I can remember. Yes. Norman Petty, the guy who produced and managed the Crickets, and later Buddy as a solo, briefly at least, before Buddy got ready to sue him, only he got killed. Petty got the Picks to furnish voices for the rest of Buddy's band. The guys couldn't sing well enough to pass, except for one, I think Treb told me. This husband and wife combo, Gary and Ramona Tollett, had put something together as background for *That'll Be the Day.* When that record took off, Petty looked elsewhere for backup. He liked the Picks. Buddy did too, apparently. At least at first. But Holly never was in the loop for making a decision on the Picks, Treb told me.

"Anyway, there was a decidedly different sound from the Crickets' debut and their follow-up, including *Oh Boy!* and the album. And keep in mind, at this time it wasn't Buddy Holly and the Crickets. It was just the Crickets. Treb said Petty masterminded a bit of voo-doo that got Buddy Holly coming out as a solo act at the same time, singing *without* vocal background even though the Crickets—the musicians—were backing him instrumentally. So the same summer that *That'll Be the Day* charted, here comes *Peggy Sue*—as a Buddy Holly solo hit. Couple that with *Everyday,* the favorite Holly song of all time for a lot of his fans. Right on its heels, in synch with the release of the album, came *Oh Boy!* by the Crickets."

"Wow! And the Picks didn't get *any* credit?" Mandy asked.

"Not only that, they didn't get paid. Petty promised he'd get them on record as themselves, if they'd just go along with him on the Crickets thing. *That* might be an early take on the late 1980s' scam known as the Milli Vanilli fiasco. Where those guys were caught lip-synching their stuff in live concerts. Treb figures the first time Buddy and the Crickets went to England, was where it hit the fan. *Oh Boy!* was a particular favorite over there, and when Buddy tried to get by without the Picks' decidedly featured vocal background, he got into a bit of trouble. Norman Petty finally came clean with the Brits, after his feet were held to the fire, mainly by a guy named John Beecher, we've been told. On subsequent issues of the *Chirping Crickets* album, Treb and John and Bill Pickering were given credit.

"Perhaps the supreme insult in all this came early in 1958, when the original recording industry annual awards show named the Crickets 1957's best *vocal group*, when only Buddy Holly—*still* not listed as the lead singer for the four—and the Picks sang on nine of the twelve songs."

"My, Louise, you sure have a good memory when it comes to Treb's rock 'n' roll roots," Missy exuded, happy to see Louise Maple so animated, for a change.

"I had to live through enough replays, beginning shortly after we were married," Louise replied. "John Pickering would call Treb or vice versa at Christmas each year, and they would relive all that Clovis, New Mexico crap every time. I felt sorry for them. They *did* seem to have had a chance. But in that business, if you're lucky enough to get one grab at the brass ring, you'd better make it pay. Seldom do you get another opportunity. They got theirs, and it took a real mess-up within their own ranks to sink the Picks' ship.

"But," Louise concluded, backing away from the dressing table, "that's another story. I'll let Treb do the telling. You ladies ready to rejoin the philosophical fracas out there?"

"Do I *have* to?" Missy moaned.

"Well, I for one don't feel as uncomfortable about them *now*," Mandy said, standing and giving one last brush of her hair, curiously with her missing hand, Missy noted. "Thanks to you both, for explaining things."

OSCAR ARNAZ maneuvered the Lincoln into the brightly lit, expansive parking lot of Trucker's Haven. Several eighteen-wheelers were parked around the restaurant, which had a band of glass windows stretching around three sides. They looked out onto the vehicles. He glanced at his watch and drove slowly around the autos parked outside the entrance. He saw an empty space next to a white Cadillac four-door with a blue fabric top, and pulled in.

Oscar sat behind the wheel for almost half a minute. A guy didn't stay in the independent drug trafficking game very long if he didn't have good instincts. Oscar fit that bill, with a cool, deliberate attitude thrown in. Those instincts told him something didn't seem right about this deal. He would stay on his toes. Then he got out, locked his Navigator, walked up three steps constructed out of four-by-fours painted gray, as were the handrails, and entered the eatery.

He stood a moment, scanning the dining room. He quickly picked out the man he figured was his contact, but took his time while eyeing the rest of the diners. No one at other tables seemed out of place. He smiled as the guy stood, and motioned for him to come over.

"Saw your SUV pull in," he said, extending his hand. "Have a seat. Wanna order something?"

"Just coffee," Oscar replied.

"One more, darlin'," the stocky, red-headed, freckle-faced man who had said his name was Smith called out to the waitress as she walked by. "Now, how do we do this, *muchacho*?"

Oscar eyed the man a moment, then smiled broadly. "Well, *cowboy,* it's your turf. You tell me."

"About ten miles on down I-15 is a gravel mountain road, off to the right. An old rickety sign reads Black Rock Ranch. You follow me. We'll exit, go a couple miles from the interstate access road to a double-wide that serves as a ranch house on a real small spread nobody works anymore. There's a barn in back. Let's pull in there. There'll be lights. You give me the coke, and I'll give it th' ol' sniff 'n' dip test—ah, I can hardly wait!— while you count out ninety stacks of hundreds, a hundred to a stack. Then we shake hands, tell each other 'bye, and go our separate ways. What do they call you, *muchacho*?"

"Your employer didn't tell you?" Oscar asked, nodding at the waitress as she placed a cup of coffee in front of him. He put in two Sweet'n Lows and reached for a creamer.

"Gabe? Nah. Just told me to hang around his cell phone tonight, till you called."

"I've dealt with Gabe four times before. Never was anyone else involved."

"Now there is. Fergit Smith. Me. I go by Billy C. And I work alone. You notice I ain't a-feared to give you *my* handle."

"Good for you." Oscar flipped out his cell phone and punched in a number.

"Who you callin', *muchacho*?"

Oscar held up his hand, just as the cell in Billy C.s pocket rang. "Oh I git it! You a-callin' me! How spiffy of you! Now ya satisfied? *Now* can we get on with our stuff?" His smile was broad and displayed with a sinister touch—a missing front tooth.

Oscar smiled, punching off his phone and silencing the ring of Billy's.

"Friend, I got a question fer *you,*" Billy said. "You comin' here from Miami, right?"

"Thereabouts."

"Notice your Navigator's got Louisiana tags."

115

"You notice correctly. In Louisiana, it had Texas plates."

"So you just tool on down the interstates, with all them Drug Task Force Dodges sittin' along the roadsides, watchin' fer a suspicious character—say, a Cuban with a pony tail, drivin' a sixty- or seventy-grand luxury SUV. You don't git stopped?"

"Now and then," Oscar replied, sighing. "We've got a triple-sealed carrying apparatus under the seats just behind mine—

"We?"

"My wife travels with me. But she's back at our hotel right now. Anyway," Oscar continued, trying to guard against suddenly giving a lot of information without being prodded, "our vault is made of titanium. It's got coatings to guard against x-rays and is triple sealed. The seat has been carefully redesigned to configure with the vault. A relatively new model like the Navigator isn't a common search for the drug guys. We wrap our cocaine carefully, as if we were in a hospital operating room. Dogs can't sniff it out. If we *are* stopped, we're soon or our way again. We run a low-key, low-profile operation.

"I have a trigger under the car that I have to disengage before we can slide off the seat and expose the vault. My partners and I have other makes of cars that are likewise outfitted, in case," he smiled, "some wise guy decides to sell us out. We all make deliveries, solo. But we keep up with each other. If anything ever happens to one of us on the exchange end, we are experienced in tracking down the problem, and fixing it. Permanently."

"You *are* unarmed, ain't you, *muchacho?*" Billy C. asked as he scooted across the booth's slick plastic covering.

"Of course. Like you I'm sure. But let's pat each other down at the ranch, anyway," he said, pushing Billy C.'s five across to him and leaving his own on the table.

"Sounds like a winner. You follow me."

"Lead the way, Cowboy."

WHEN THE three women returned to their table in the Mirage lounge, Mandy asked Treb to expand on the story of Buddy Holly and the Crickets and the Milli-Vanilli role the Picks played.

"Nah! Why spoil the evening?" he replied.

"C'mon, Treb, honor the…little lady," Leventhal wheezed, as Brad Poole edged forward on his chair.

"You sure you want to hear this stuff? I promised Brad I'd tell it and the rest of *my* Buddy Holly story to him. The rest of you will just be bored. Missy has heard it—"

"And I'd like to hear it again," Josh's wife broke in.

"I opened the can of worms, Treb," Louise sighed. "I guess as punishment I should sit through your version for the ump-teenth time."

He told the story much the way his wife had described, but adding color and fleshing out the edges now and then.

"The interesting thing was, Norman Petty through confusion in the home office at Decca had Buddy double-dipping at the money trough. Coral was a subsidiary of Decca Records, which originally had Buddy under contract for a horribly produced country album recorded in Nashville a year or so earlier. Decca gave approval to let Buddy try rock 'n' roll stuff with Coral, and good riddance, it seemed was their attitude in the Nashville country music end of the label. But not *That'll be the Day,* which had been on the Nashville album. Buddy and Jerry Allison, the Crickets' drummer, had co-written the song that had been inspired by a line John Wayne used frequently in *The Searchers*, one of his westerns.

"Anyway, as I understood the situation from studio gossip in Clovis, Coral was starting to spread its independent wings. It had latched onto an old abandoned label from the 1920s and '30s. Brunswick Records was picking up offbeat releases, usually destined to die quickly. Somebody in Coral's office, upon Norman Petty's prompting, I understand, decided to cover Decca's *That'll Be the Day* by Buddy Holly on Brunswick, with the newly formed Crickets as the artists. Might enhance *Peggy Sue* by Holly on Coral, when Decca and the record-buying public got around to figuring out the end play.

"The result was the birth of a rock 'n' roll legend with *That'll Be the Day*, prompting Brunswick to hastily make plans to put out the *Chirping Crickets* album, all while Buddy Holly's separate rock 'n' roll solo career was taking off on Coral with *Peggy Sue* and *Everyday.*

"Tell them about…the songwriting credits," Josh prodded.

"When Norman re-recorded *That'll Be the Day* in his Nor Va Jak Studio in Clovis, he lowered the key from the sissy-sounding reach for Buddy that Decca had produced. For that little production suggestion, Norman cut himself in on songwriting credit, sharing three ways with Allison and Buddy, where they had co-written the song that Decca recorded. It must've been a nightmare to sort out, money-wise, but in later years royalties from that one song alone, a classic that would be covered by dozens of artists through the decades—notably Linda Rondstadt—provided hundreds of thousands of dollars for the shareholders.

"Norman's soon-dominant cutting himself in for credit as songwriter was born with *That'll Be the Day,* I believe. But it sure didn't end there. Also, he had already formed his own publishing stable, working through Southern Music Publishing in Nashville. So if you came to Clovis to peddle a song, chances are Petty would agree, *if* he could publish it and record it through Nor Va Jak. And if he could get it recorded, well it seemed only fair to him that he be cut in for songwriting credit."

"That's...where the *real* money...in music recording came," Josh explained. "Royalties for air play...made a lot of non-performing...songwriters very rich. This started in the Big Band era, but...the practice *really* got sophisticated when rock 'n' roll...became a producer's...and publisher's paradise."

While Brad had taken out a small reporter's notebook and was hastily taking shorthand-like notes, Mandy was shaking her head.

"It's all way over my head," she said.

"Yes, but this...is really great stuff," Josh said. "Rock 'n' roll memorabilia from the only *valid* period of R&R—the fifties!"

"So what happened next?" Brad asked.

"What happened next is history," Treb answered, "and you and I will go into it more another time, like I promised. It's getting pretty late, and I am an old man still working long hours, a full day of which I have scheduled for tomorrow. I think we'd all best head home." He waved for the check, then added, "Brad, you said you wanted to play a little poker. If you're still interested, I've got you tentatively set for our hold 'em table tomorrow night, nine, at the Adobe. Interested?"

"I'll be there!"

"Bring cash. And don't expect there to be many patsies around *that* table."

THE NAVIGATOR kept a couple or three hundred feet behind Billy C.'s caddy. Oscar watched its headlights knife through the desert darkness up ahead. He smiled at the Black Rock Ranch sign, thinking about the old Spencer Tracy adventure thriller he'd seen on TV. The title was Bad Day at Black Rock, and Oscar wondered, could that be a portent of doom?

He and his partners had a pretty neat deal, working on their own and handling their drug-running operation from Colombia themselves, via several safe stops and transfers in Central America, and on to an innocuous entry into the U.S., usually through Gulfport, Mississippi.

They kept a tight ship, working out of Coral Gables, and didn't go the greed route. All three men were either Cuban exiles or sons of such. The only trouble they ever experienced had ended tragically, with the death of Jaime, their fourth original partner, and his Cuban-American girlfriend. But since their operation, one that lived comfortably outside gang or mob ties, had been percolating for almost ten years, a twenty-five percent mortality rate against no busts seemed a reasonable enough success story.

The shooting of their partner had come during a doublecross. Jaime was working a solo deal, but had taken his wife with him, much the same way Oscar did when he traveled to Las Vegas to sprinkle a little goofball dust. Their deaths had taught the small cartel to take steps that such wouldn't happen again.

Their contacts usually would become regulars. They built up a fleet of delivery autos, with Oscar's Lincoln SUV the latest addition. Along with state-of-the-art methods for transporting their cocaine, each installed and monitored periodically by a paid associate who was a DEA agent on the take. He had access to dogs and the latest in surveillance. The trio fitted each of their six vehicles underneath with a small waterproof pouch that contained a handgun, fully loaded. Arms were not permitted during exchanges, so the partners had always tried to explain beforehand that they must slip under the auto to trip a lever for access to the drugs cache. The partners always wore dark sport coats when making deliveries, and had devised slick moves permitting them to slip the guns into one of their side pockets. Just in case.

Oscar had never used his Kahr K9 in anger, or any other weapon for that matter. But he had become proficient in its use on indoor ranges. He considered the tiny locked-breech 9mm to be his ultimate insurance policy.

Arnaz was always careful, and could read people well. Tonight, he had not liked what he had read into Billy C.'s psyche. No Gabe, a new place to exchange and a new client with whom to deal made him uncomfortable.

Still, the ranch house and barn appeared pretty much the way the red-headed redneck had described. The place looked deserted. While Billy stopped and unlocked the barn, Oscar wheeled around the structure and back of the doublewide, and took a quick look. Then he pulled into the barn behind Billy, who closed the door after the Lincoln was inside. Billy turned on overhead lights that brightly illuminated the place.

"I got th' cash in my trunk," Billy said, after they had patted each other down.

"Good. Why don't you take it out, put it on that table over there? I'll watch real close, if you don't mind. Then I'll slip under my car and engage the electronic release on my compartment inside."

"OK, *muchacho.* Let's go slow 'n easy." Billy extracted a large suitcase, carried it to the table and let it fall open. Stacks of bound bills shown green and white in the fluorescent lighting. Oscar watched him carefully. "Don't trust me, huh?" Billy laughed heartily.

"OK, I'm going under for just a minute, pop the vault that's below the rear seat, and we'll be out of here in a flash," Oscar said. "Come on around and watch."

Billy C. stood a few feet away as Oscar spread a thin blanket that had been on the rear seat, and scooted under the Navigator. He had a grip on the K9 and had disengaged the safety in less than 10 seconds. Quick hand movements as he grunted a couple times hid the motion that put the weapon in his right side pocket.

"There!" he said, half a minute later, about the time he felt a draft and thought he heard the sound of a door opening. He looked past Billy's garish pink ostrich boots and saw a set of fancy Italian loafers tiptoeing in the direction of the Lincoln. "OK. Coming out now," Oscar said, his hands suddenly shaking and the taste of bile bubbling up in his throat.

"Nice 'n easy there, *muchacho*," Billy said slowly, his command punctuated with a vicious little laugh.

In an instant, Oscar's survival instincts took over. He had replayed such a scenario many times in his mind. Instead of backing out from under the Lincoln, he shifted to where he was parallel with the auto body under which he still lay. He could see that the intruder had a large revolver. It was held along his side, the muzzle pointing to the floor.

You just died, compadre, Oscar whispered, as if to the intruder but actually to himself. He sat on his butt, looked up, extended his left hand for Billy C. to grab, and as he stood, he reached in and brought the K9 up, firing twice almost instantly. The intruder never got his weapon up. His knees buckled and he fell to the floor.

"God damn you!" Billy screamed, trying to turn loose Oscar's hand and lunge for the gun that lay beside the dead man.

"You next, Billy? Or do you want to live?" Oscar hissed, releasing his grip and pointing his K9 at the fuming man's head. "You got three seconds after I quit talking, or I'm gonna shoot you through your jawbone. With this ammo I use, the slug will come out the back and take half of your head with it."

"OK! *OK!* I want to live, damn your Mexican eyes!" Billy hissed.

"Cuban, *muchacho,* Cuban," Oscar corrected, suddenly feeling confident. "And it might've helped your cause if you'd known that *that* was what Gabe knew me by. Now, you want to tell me what was going down here? Keep in mind, I had you pegged. If I hear *one* word that doesn't sound right, *bang! Adios,* shit-for-brains."

"Hey, we got a little greedy. OK? Now, let's you and me do a little business."

"Doesn't compute, *muchacho!* Who else is in on this?"

"Just us. I swear!"

"What about Gabe?"

"He…he don't know what's happenin'. Me an' pore ol' Earl here got wind of the deal and decided we'd see if we could wind up with Gabe's cash *and* th' sfuff to boot. Hey, man, I apologize! Please cut me a little slack on this. I know where Gabe keeps his money at his house out there near where Wayne Newton used to live. I can show you. I bet he's got five *million* in that closet safe. I know where the combination is too!"

Oscar knew he was lying now. "OK. Does Earl here have a car outside?"

"Nah. I brung him out earlier. He's been hidin' up in th' rocks."

"Is there a place where we can dump the body?" Oscar said, slipping over and picking up the dead man's handgun and wondering how to clean up the blood the guy had spilled.

"Yeah...yeah...sure."

"OK. Forgive me if I don't trust you...yet," Oscar said slowly. "But while I got the upper hand here, I figure it might be all right to go along with you, and become partners for the rest of the night. First, put the cash in the back of my Navigator. Then drag Earl over to your car and see if you can stuff him in the trunk of your Cadillac. Careful now...let's don't get this blood all over *everything.*"

"It's my step-daddy's old place. Nobody's...been out here...fer weeks," Billy C. said, laboring under Earl's lifeless load.

"Who is—was—Earl?"

"A nobody. We done got together last week, over a pool table. Had a few drinks. Decided...umph!...to go pards an' see what we could cook up. I'd done some legwork for Gabe, and got wind of your deal. That's all."

"So, where we gonna plant old Earl?"

"There's th' foundation of what used to be an old shack 'bout a mile from here, on up in the mountain. Had a pretty deep cistern nearby that's been dry an' boarded up fer as long as I can remember. And I knowed my late step-daddy fer at least twenty-five years. Nobody'll ever find him in there."

"OK. Let's go in your car. You can drop me back here to get mine after we dump Earl, then I'll follow you to Gabe's and split up *that* take. I keep my money *and* the coke." He could almost hear the wheels turning in the redneck's head as Billy tried to figure how he was going to get out of this fix. "Oh yes. *Not* that I *don't* trust you or anything like that, but let me hold your—or Gabe's, I figure—cell phone for a while."

IT HADN'T taken long to get the barn's dirt floor cleaned up. Oscar had overseen Billy C. shoveling up enough bloody substance, then putting it in a five-gallon can which the man had put in the trunk with the body. Billy had remained quiet on the drive up the gravel road, still figuring, Oscar was sure, that as long as he could stay alive, Billy felt he had a chance.

Soon the headlights picked up the old foundation, then the cistern. At the surface it was a concrete cone, with a three-foot opening on top that was covered by an aged thick piece of plywood. It was painted black and cut the exact size of the mouth of the cistern.

"You...not gonna help me?" Billy huffed as he dragged Earl's body to the cistern, then pried open the covering.

"You're doing just fine," Oscar said. He was standing close by when the cover came off. Oscar caught a hint of recent death that wafted up, and turned in the headlights to eye Billy C.

"It's been used before, I take it," Oscar said slowly, "and not too long ago. That where I was headed tonight, *muchacho?*"

"No no, I swear!. We were just gonna scare you a little, tell you where we'd leave your keys along th' road out, an' take on off. I promise."

"OK, partner, I believe you," Oscar lied, as Billy lifted Earl's feet over the edge and briefly looked into the blackness while the body headed to the bottom, which Oscar figured had to be a good thirty feet from the surface.

"Goodbye, pal. It was nice knowin' ya," Billy mumbled. Then he turned around and gasped as Oscar pointed the K9 between his eyes.

"Your turn now, *muchacho,*" Oscar purred.

"No please no dear God! Jesus I love you I promise. Don't do this, guy! We got a deal. Remember? God no!"

"There is no money in a closet safe, you stupid son of a bitch! And I'm gonna bet there is no Gabe. Not living at least. Right? Come clean and maybe you'll live for another few seconds."

"Here's th' truth...We done this fer Gabe. He's th' one who decided to make this deal his last with you, an' take a double-dip while he was at it. That's his cell phone you got."

"I already figured *that* out. Remember?"

"OK. Yeah. I'm supposed to use it to call him when we're finished. He'll be expectin' a call."

"What number?"

"I...I don't..."

"What NUMBER?" Oscar hissed, pushing the K9's muzzle into Billy's head. The frightened man spat out another cell number. "Call it," Oscar ordered.

"What!"

"CALL IT! Tell Gabe the mission's accomplished, or whatever you were supposed to tell him, then hand me the phone. *Slowly!"*

Billy began to sob as he punched in the number. He waited a moment, staring back at the muzzle of the Kahr, then blurted out, "Gabe! Hey. Billy C. here. It's...it's a done deal."

Oscar took the phone with his left hand, then fired. Billy's eyes and mouth were wide open as Oscar pushed the man backwards, and over the edge of the cistern. Billy C.'s body tumbled into the darkness to join Earl's. Then Oscar put the phone to his ear and heard a voice he recognized as Gabe's.

"Billy? Billy? What was that?"

"Hello Gabe," Oscar said softly, unabashedly impressed by his own suddenly cold and calculating voice, given the fact that he had just killed for the first time—twice.

"Who...who's this? *Cuban!?* "

"You just listened to your dumbass errand boy die," Oscar hissed. "His pal got it first. Now, I wonder who's gonna be next?"

"Huh? What *is* this?"

"You just screwed up, big time, Gabe."

"I—I don't know what you're talking about! Billy was calling me to tell me you and he made the exchange. At least, that's what I thought. Now, what's going on—"

"You're lying, Gabe. I got your money and I still have my coke. Now, you want to put things right, you take some time to make sure you don't screw up again. Figure it out. Call me on your cell phone, which I'm keeping with me. And you *might* get out of this alive. With the coke you ordered too. Only, the price just doubled, pal," he added, listening as Gabe quickly disconnected.

Oscar tossed the five-gallon can of blood and sand in the cistern, replaced the wood covering, drove Billy C.'s caddy to the barn, pulled it in and backed out the Navigator. He shut the barn door, figuring Billy hadn't been lying when he claimed the abandoned ranch was not visited often.

He had some thinking to do. And some gambling on just how involved his former trusted client was with the half-idiot Gabe seemed to have sent to whack him.

He drove back to the Strip and to the hotel, ideas turning over in his head.

10. The Wars of the Maples

"Well, it's obvious he's not going to show," Treb sighed, putting his last potato chip into his mouth and pushing the empty hamburger plate aside.

"At least we got his deposit in the bank," Mike Cardenas said. "And we *did* have a good session this morning. The guy from Ohio said he'd recommend you to some of his buddies back in Shaker Heights. But it's like we talked about the other day, boss. We're slowly slipping off the radar screen. We *could* use a little publicity, and the freer the better. Struts and I can hang around here for a while, just in case the guy calls and wants to reschedule, but I don't expect that to happen. You might as well go home and take a nap, since you'll be shuffling the cards tonight."

Maple stared out the pro shop grill's window. A senior golfer and his wife were holing out on the ninth green.

"I guess you're right. Here's an idea. We've got the whole afternoon off. I think I'll call our reporter friend. He can come out here and you guys can give him what he wants on my largely un-illustrious golfing background. I'll go to the Fifth Jack and offer Amanda the lowdown on me. Then I'll get together with Brad in a day or two and discuss Buddy Holly and the Picks. What about it?"

"OK with me, Treb," Struts Struthers replied.

"Sure. No problem," Mike added.

"Hill, would you look up the Fifth Jack's number?" Treb called out. The assistant pro hefted the large Vegas business pages phone book and called out the number, which Maple punched into his cell phone. He asked for Brad's room, hoping both weren't out.

"Mandy. Good. Glad you're in. This is Treb. Brad there? Um-hum. Downstairs. OK. Here's the deal. We've suddenly got the afternoon free. I suggest you tell Brad to come out here and grill my *compadres,* and I'll come in to town and tell you all about the *real* me. Real, as in real boring. Great. Brad has two tape recorders, huh? Make sure he's available. He might be on a cards or craps run that he doesn't want to leave. Either way, have him give me a call pronto and confirm, or back off. Remind him to give you some questions he wants to know about me. OK? Here's my cellular phone number."

Treb then disconnected, and stood. "I may as well head on back. Brad should be out here in an hour. If I hear otherwise from him, I'll call you through Jack over there."

"DON'T USE that one," Oscar Arnaz told his wife, taking a cell phone from their New York New York room and exchanging it for Gabe's.

"I'm just going to call Mandy," M.K. grumbled. "Guess I should've used our room phone. Things didn't go well last night, I take it."

"You take it right, babe. It did *not* go well."

"I could tell you were worried about something. Did...did it get ugly?"

Oscar turned his back to her and ran his fingers through his black hair. His confident air from the previous night had been replaced by a foreboding. Maybe he had got the wrong take. Billy C. surely had given him enough different stories. Pissing on Gabe while he killed the redneck might've been too hasty. It had been strictly business between them for almost five years. He knew nothing of the client, not his real name and not where he lived. Gabe knew nothing about Oscar, either, except the e-mail chat room used to signal a desire for contact when the Las Vegas man wished to order cocaine, the only controlled substance Oscar and his partners handled.

What if Gabe was *not* a mild-mannered, rich Las Vegas contact who could be frightened into a wrong move? What if Gabe was better connected, perhaps with people who knew mob types, who in turn could track down a Cuban American with a pony tail? Oscar was on the verge of pulling the plug and heading back to Florida.

"I don't want you to be worrying about it, M.K. I'm handling things. We're on the offensive right now," he said, trying to convince himself as much as ease Mary Katherine's mind.

"Then you didn't make the exchange."

"Not altogether. I've got the money. And I still have our dope."

"Oscar! What happened?"

Gabe's phone rang. He picked it up quickly. "Yeah?"

"Cuban, we gotta talk," Gabe said. "Where are you?"

"Downtown," Oscar lied. "And you?"

"I'm at home. Can I come get you?"

"I don't think so. What's on your mind?" Oscar walked to the bathroom and pulled the door shut.

"Look, I don't know what happened last night, but you ought to know me by now, after five years of straight deals," Gabe said. "I tried to raise that stupid go-fer Billy Carson this morning. No luck. Did you *really* ice the guy last night?"

"You heard it, fella," Oscar replied, reaching inside to try and find some of the machismo he had discovered last night, out at the Black Rock Ranch.

"Why, for God's sake?"

"He and some clown he called Earl tried to cross me. Billy finally told me the truth, under the gun. That you ordered the hit on me, to end our little arrangement and let you wind up with almost a million in the very best

Colombian you could find, free of charge. I couldn't believe it. But a man doesn't figure to lie when he's looking down the barrel at eternity, which I imagine you know from experience. Not even a dumbass like Billy. He said you wanted me whacked. I believed him."

"Cuban…Cuban," Gabe murmured. "You got it *all* wrong. That stupid son of a bitch tried to pull a fast one on me, as well as you. He's been working for me for a few months, nothing much more than some little collection errands. He must've got wind that I had stuff coming to town. He told me while I was in the pool that you called. He answered my cell, took your call I guess, then told me that you had phoned in from Florida and wouldn't be in Vegas until next Tuesday. The little twirp must've swiped my phone and decided to double-deal with you last night. I can't *believe* that dumb sucker had enough brains to dream up a scam like that! And how he ever figured he could get away with it and live just blows my mind."

After a moment, a worried Oscar responded, silently banging his clenched fist on the lavatory as he groped for a cool retort. "Nice tale, Gabe. Did you spend all night coming up with it?"

"Hey, jerk! Don't press your luck! You're in *my* town now. Let's both back off a little bit and think this thing through. I want no trouble with you. I either want my money back, or the coke you brought me. I've got no reason to ice you. I more than double my money doling out the admittedly good stuff you bring me. If possible, I'd like to keep it going. If you and I could just sit down and sort this out, I think we could get it behind us. What you did to that idiot Billy, I couldn't care less. And I have no idea who this Earl guy you said you wasted was either. Where'd you stash them?"

"Lake Mead," Oscar quickly lied.

"Lake *Mead!?* Those two good ol' boys will have lots of other fishes to play with, that's for sure. All right, Cuban. Let's pick up our deal just as if this never happened. OK?"

"I dunno, Gabe. That was some shock I got, when *your* people were ready to pop me. Give me a couple days. You call me."

"Then you *will* be staying around our town a while," Gabe replied. "You *won't* be pulling out on me and doing something really, *really* dumb. Like leaving with my money. Something Billy C. might try."

"I'm not a thief, Gabe. I'm not a sucker either. Let's cool it, man. I will await your call in a day or two."

"All right, a*migo*. Then I don't need to have any local employees with no consciences and lots of contacts to come looking for you. *Comprende*?" Gabe paused, then added just before disconnecting. "I can, you know. Please believe it."

M.K. Arnez slowly pulled the bathroom door she had cracked open back to the closed position. Her hands were shaking when she lay back on the bed and waited for her husband to rejoin her.

IT WAS three p.m. when Brad pulled the rental through the Desert King Golf Club entrance and parked by the pro shop. He reached behind him, lifted a bag containing a camera, notebook, pens and tape recorder, got out and walked through the shop's doors.

"Here come th' man," Struts said. "Sit down, friend."

"Hi there, Brad," Cardenas greeted.

"Sure appreciate this, men. Took a little getting used to, being sorta snubbed by Treb," Brad said, as he set up the recorder and placed the microphone in the center of the table.

"Maybe after we git goin' here, you gonna sort of understand just why our guy is gun shy when it comes ta talkin' to press folks," Struts said.

"OK. So I understand that Struts has only known Treb since caddying for him at Boise and then Napa, in the only two tournaments he's played on the senior circuit. Right?"

"They call it Champions Tour now," Cardenas corrected. "But that's right. It was the senior circuit then, even though Treb was super-senior age, at 67. Of course, Treb couldn't qualify for *that* gravy train, before it ran out. Strictly for sixty and above *with* past credentials, like winning, and you could claim fifteen thousand from Mastercard on top of the little dribble you could expect in the main dance, playing against Hale Irwin and Bruce Fleischer, Fuzzy Zoeller and Tom Kite, and some of those hot shots who weren't too far past fifty. Not flat bellies, of course. But not flab bellies either.

"I came out to Boise for the last two rounds, when Treb was really hot. That's where I met Struts, eighteen or so months ago. He can tell you about the tournament and some of the *caca* that went on out there. Me and Treb, we've been friends since the first grade. I can fill in on his early life, more or less."

"Great!" Brad said, taking one last glance at the tape to make sure it was going. "Then let's start with you, Mike, and keep the life of Trebor Maple in time-proper context. What was it like, growing up in Brownsville, Texas?"

"Pretty good. Back in the forties, we hung out all the time. Got through the war years, then into junior high. My daddy worked on a shrimp boat. Treb's did jobs on the docks of what would become the Port of Brownsville. That was before they dug a channel several miles from Point Isabel inland to just east of Brownsville. Neither of us had what you could call a classic dad. I guess that's why we became close. It wasn't unheard of for a gringo kid to run with a Latino, there on the border. But it wasn't commonplace either. We had another close pal who buddied with us. Al Cisneros grew up to make something out of himself. He was the port director for many years, during the sixties and seventies. Went to the same church as Treb. Presbyterian, before Treb drifted away.

"He used to spend his summers in Abilene, more'n 500 miles to the north and west. He'd catch MoPac, go through San Antonio and up to Dallas, then west to Abilene and his grandmother's. I went with him one summer, when we were fourteen. I liked West Texas.

"Anyway, it was in Abilene where Treb learned to play golf. Must've been 1946 or so. He got hooked up with some guys who worked as caddies for a pro named Morgan Hampton, at the Abilene Country Club. Across the fence, south of town, was Willow Crest, a muny layout run by W. O. Maxwell. He had twin boys not much older'n us, Billy and Bobby. They were top regional amateurs in their teens. Billy would win the U.S. Amateur in the early fifties, then become a longtime touring pro who won some money. He was a pioneer on the senior tour. Billy wound up co-owning a great little green fee course outside Jacksonville, Florida. Bobby played some pro golf, but mostly worked as a teaching and club pro around the Dallas-Fort Worth area, and in West Texas. He also spent a couple years outside New York City as a teacher.

"Anyway, Treb got a lot of learning done when he was twelve or thirteen. He and the Abilene kids he ran around with got to play Mondays, caddy day, at the club. Then they played across the fence at Willow Crest for little or nothing, Tuesdays through Fridays, when they didn't have caddy jobs at the club.

"Hampton, the country club pro, gave Treb some lessons and helped him put together a rag-tag set of clubs. When I came up with Treb in '49, Hampton did the same for me. Now, that was kinda unusual for West Texas—a Mexican kid who got to know some gringos and pretty much was accepted. Anyway, that summer was really special. We got to caddy in the club's big July 4th Invitational. Championship flight of sixty-four players from all over the state. Dick Jennings. Dick Martin, Charlie Brownfield, Ed Hopkins, Don January, who like the Maxwells played there as a teenager. Lee Pinkston, who used Treb regularly to tote his bag. The Abilene people turned out in huge galleries. The guys who didn't get eliminated played quarterfinal and semifinal matches, or 36 holes, on Saturday, then a 36-hole title final on Sunday. Even though the Invitational was amateur, it was our first brush with big-time golf."

Mike laughed. "We also learned some p-r-e-t-t-y salty lingo there. Stayed with us down through the years, until Treb saw the light and insisted I see it too. There was this guy from Fort Worth. Good player. Said he knew

Ben Hogan and Byron Nelson as kids, though I don't remember *his* name. He was about forty, forty-five. Wore a Sammy Snead straw hat and dark glasses. Didn't have a thumb and little finger on his right hand. He could play though. And could he cuss!"

MIKE TOLD how he, Treb and Al Cisneros made the Brownsville High golf team as sophomores. "Wasn't a great program. If you didn't play football, you weren't much. But we had a lot of fun. Played mostly at the Fort Brown nine-holer, but got on Brownsville Country Club every now and then. Mr. Tatum, our non-playing math teacher, was our sponsor. We took trips up to Corpus Christi, Alice and even San Antonio to play in big high school tournaments. Then we played district matches at Harlingen, McAllen, Edinburg, Weslaco and Raymondville down in the Valley."

"Valley?"

"Rio Grande Valley. Where we lived, Brad. You didn't—"

"Oh yeah. I know now. So, were you guys hot-shots?"

"We could play a little. Al and Treb in the mid- to upper-seventies half the time. I was pretty steady in the low eighties. Treb used to be a whiz in practice matches. He could shoot in the sixties now and then. But when it came time to play another school or in a big tournament, he usually screwed it up."

"You mean, he choked?"

"Well, I guess that's what he'd call it if he were sitting here. I guess it was true. He'd win a match in impressive style every now and then though. And he actually won a tournament one year, at Alice. Hey, I mean't to ask you. Treb said you met a guy named Baxter Randall out here the other day."

"Yep. Said he knew Treb."

"They used to hate each other, when we were kids. Mainly because of me. Bax has been a golf bum all his life. He played some pro tourneys in the 1960s. Made a few cuts. Senior tour came around, and he tried that off and on up until a couple years ago, as a Monday qualifier."

"Bax was a hustler. He was a cheater too. I know. I was paired with him at Meadowbrook in east Fort Worth, back in February of 1952. I was the only Mexican kid in this huge high school tournament. I was fifth man on the Brownsville team. Being a border town, the team was integrated. Man, I was scared! Treb always looked after me when we were out among the gringos, but he couldn't help me that Saturday, since we weren't paired together."

"What happened?"

"I played like I had crap dripping off my grips. We started on the back nine. Number 10, a four-par that went south, had out of bounds that cut in from the right. You had to hit your drive over a part of OB if you wanted to reach the center of the fairway. My first hole, and I proceeded to slice not one, but TWO shots over the fence. Took a *nine!*

"Well, it didn't get much better. By the turn, I was lucky to have shot 46 and figured I wouldn't break 90, a supreme embarrassment. We were waiting on number 2's tee box—two was our 11th hole, remember—and Bax, who played for a Corpus Christi school, started talking about how we all needed some help. Two was a three-par, where they just sort of laid a green on the side of a hill across a little valley and creek, one-thirty away. Bax had choked like a baby, three-putted maybe four times and shot 43 going out. Our third player, whose name I've forgotten, had a 44. Our coaches had all checked our cards at the turn, so they knew we were dog meat."

Randall, Mike recalled, said something to the effect that they could shave a couple strokes off their back nines and wind up if not respectable, at least passable.

"What do you mean?" the other player, from College Station, asked.

"'I mean, you're keeping my score, I'm keeping Chico's'—he called me Chico from start to finish—'I have Chico's and he has yours. Let's just overlook most of the bogeys from here on in, and for sure no doubles or triples like the first nine. What's it gonna hurt? Not any of us is going to be beating many guys. We're alternates, so we can't help our team. We're just saving ourselves some grief."

"Hey," College Station said, "I don't see the harm. I'm for it."

"What about you, Chico?" Bax asked.

"Count me out," I replied.

"Why?"

"Just count me out, OK?"

"Well," Mike continued with his story, "We got in without talking much to each other, or at least they to me, and I shot 45. A 91! Bax and the other guy sort of laughed and joked, but they didn't do much better. I gave the guy his card that I signed, and Bax gave me mine. He was smiling. I signed it, and I swear I don't remember looking at the total. I was sick of golf. I just wanted off the course, *fast!* 'I'll turn 'em in, since I'm heading that way,' Bax said. So I went off to sit in a corner somewhere and lick my wounds. Treb had already finished. I hated to see him. I was so ashamed. Pretty soon, he and Coach Tatum came running up. 'Good round son,' coach said. 'Atta boy, Mike,' my best friend added.

"'What're you talking about?' I asked. 'I didn't break—'"

"'Lousy first nine on the back side, right,' Treb said, laughing. 'But look at that comeback! A 38! Eighty-four ain't bad. Hell, I shot 81!'"

"WELL," MIKE said, as he, Struts and Brad sat in the pro shop grill, "I walked up to the big board and there it was. Bax had shaved seven shots off my last nine. He even gave me a *birdie* on six! I maybe hit two greens in regulation, and three-putted one of 'em. Anyway, I stared at the damned board and didn't know what to do. Al came over and slapped me on the back. Couple other teammates and players from other schools I had met congratulated me. Then here comes Bax, and he slips up next to me and whispers—I'll never forget his words—he whispers, 'Don't say a thing, Mex! Not a shittin' word!'

"So I didn't, until we got back to Brownsville and I couldn't take my throbbing conscience anymore. I cried like a baby and told Treb what happened. He got real mad, not at me but at Bax. Said he'd tell him off the next tournament they played in together. And he did too. Treb said I should forget it, that it wasn't my fault. I dunno. To this day, I wonder if I *really* didn't look at my total before Bax turned in the card, or just blocked it out of my mind. At any rate, I never was a good tournament player. Never have been. Maybe I never would've. But for sure, I've never forgotten Meadowbrook. Low point of my life, just about."

"Bax, he got a stone fer a heart," Struts said. "I toted for him a couple times, back in th' early sixties and 'bout thirty-five years afore I ever knowed there wuz a Mike Cardenas. Bax was a shitass then. I can remember three or four times when he pulled somethin' on the course—in a PGA tournament, mind you. You know. A little foot wedge from behind a tree, when you're out there with just a threesome, and no gallery anywhere. Or ground a club in a trap and not call it on hisself. I even saw him palm a ball and drop it, when he wuz lost in knee-high rough."

"He seemed real curious about Treb," Brad offered.

"Well, Treb got back at him real good. At Boise, fer goodness sakes," Struts said. "That ol' boy come around *my* man now, an' I'll cold-cock him m'self!"

"ANYWAY, AFTER we graduated from high school, Treb and I looked around somewhere to maybe play in college," Cardenas continued. "Weren't many golf scholarships back in '53, let me tell you. But Treb heard about Texas Tech maybe wanting to upgrade its program. The athletic director, Dewitt Weaver—"

"Didn't he play on tour? And win some in senior golf?"

"Nah. That was his kid, Dewitt Jr. Senior was head football coach as well as AD at Tech. That summer of '53, Morgan Hampton told Treb that Weaver wanted to get Tech into the Southwest Conference, and he was out to upgrade all the programs. He had a fantastic football team coming up that fall. Bobby Cavazos, a Latino bless him, would be Tech's first bona fide all-American. Walter Bryan, better known as Jo Jo, was a great two-way halfback. He played pro for the Colts along with Johnny Unitas and Alan The Horse Ameche a couple seasons.

"Tech already had a cracker-jack basketball program under head coach Polk Robison. They wanted all sports—men's, of course; back then nobody cared a hoot for the gals—all sports upgraded from the Border Conference level to the SWC. A pro who had been at Abilene during the war, Warren Cantrell, had just designed and built a new layout north of Lubbock. Hillcrest Country Club. Hampton told us about Cantrell's being tapped to take over Tech's golfers. He made a call, then turned us over to Cantrell.

"Coach said no scholarships until 1954-55, but we were welcome to try out on our own. He'd be having tryouts in the spring of '54.

"Treb's father by now was dead. His mom and grandmother in Abilene had enough money put away to get Treb started. My folks had little or nothing. Cantrell, upon Morgan's recommendation, said I could work in his pro shop. So we were off to Texas Tech, just under 700 miles northwest of Brownsville. Cantrell, incidentally, headed the PGA around 1960, when club pros and the touring guys were in the same bag. Cantrell had a lot to do with promoting TV golf coverage. A real interesting guy.

"Anyway, we were late getting into a dorm, so we didn't room together. But we did get in the same one—Bledsoe Hall. Treb lucked out and got in a room with C.R. Black, a guy he had gotten to know in Abilene, as a kid. Black was a brain with that great charisma. You know, the kind guys like to be around and the kind girls just adore. He wound up being executive vice president of Texaco Inc. before he retired. Couple years later, Black was named to the Tech Board of Regents. A year after that, he was elected president. I had a roomie the floor below them from Grand Prairie. Ed Harries. A real nice fella.

"Anyway, in the spring of '54, Treb qualified as number one on the Tech golf varsity. I took some classes, worked for Cantrell, and played as an alternate. The fifth man again. We got some great trips out of that deal. Especially to Tucson for the Border Conference championship.

"But what looked to be the start of something big for Treb fizzled in Arizona. Cantrell made the team re-qualify in a practice round at the old Tucson Country Club, probably the best course we'd ever played. Tough too. We weren't used to sand traps. Anyway, Treb choked big time. Couldn't even beat *me.* Our number one sat on the sidelines while I shot 82-78 and, if you could believe it, was the second best Tech had to offer. We finished sixth in conference, and Treb began to *believe* he was a choker.

"So did Cantrell, I guess. Treb spent half the summer of '54 in Abilene, 'cause that's all the time he could stay away from Clarice. He played in some tournaments around there. A hot-shot high school sophomore was winning one out of every two, it seemed. His name was Charles Coody. Yep. The same guy who won the Masters thirty-five years ago. Anyway, Treb almost beat him in the quarterfinals of a little tourney in Anson, a town just outside Abilene. Though Treb lost, one-up, he got some good ink from the Abilene paper. I made sure Cantrell got clippings, and Treb called him about maybe landing a scholarship. But nope. Cantrell had recruited a team of freshmen who wound up making him look *very* good. John Paul Cain, John Farquar and Don Kaplan led Tech to its first Southwest Conference championship in *any* sport, four years later."

"So, Treb quit Tech?" Brad asked.

"No. I did. I hung around Hillcrest for a couple years, then went to the Army. As a sophomore, Treb continued to *try* to be the scholar, but when he and Clarice—that was his high school sweetheart back in Brownsville— when their hot and heavy romance couldn't survive her going to college a year after us, he just went to pot. Drank a lot, screwed up in classes. I think he had four majors in four and a half years, and still lacked more than a year to graduate in any of them, when Tech gave up on him. He went downhill in the fast lane. I never thought high school romances would do that to you. Didn't me.

"I guess what hurt him the most was, Clarice landed with a guy Treb didn't much care for. A guy from Brownsville who went to the University of Texas the same time she did. For a couple years after that, maybe three— right before she married this guy—she and Treb would wind up now and then having one last fling, and he'd fall hopelessly in love all over again. Then it'd fizzle again. Drove my buddy crazy out of his gourd, I tell you. And I won't, any more. What you get about Clarice, you get from the man himself.

"Anyway, he was a six-month soldier about 1958 or '59, while I was serving my third year and last year with Uncle Sammy in France. He and I tried to run a green fee course just outside Corpus for a year. The fellow backing the thing lost a lot of money, and pulled the plug. While I stayed there trying to revive the little nine-holer, Treb took an assistant pro's job in Wichita Falls, at Weeks Park Municipal. He met Louise there and married her, then wound up back in Brownsville. So did I. Married a girl from Matamoros, across the river, got burned on that, and worked in golf shops with Treb off and on around the tip of Texas."

"Did you ever get married again?" Brad wanted to know.

"Nope. Once was enough for me. I have a lady friend in Vegas these days and we're pretty thick. But I've had several of those romances since 1970, and none has come close to taking yet."

"We got Treb out of Tech, and into the club golf pro line of work. But we've missed something big. His year or whatever with Buddy Holly."

"Like I say, that came in '57 and I was out of the loop," Mike answered. "Ask our guy himself about that. Pretty interesting story too."

"SO, STRUTS, tell me about Treb and the senior tour," Brad said, after the three had come back from taking a break. Brad was sipping a gin and tonic, and had bought the other two soft drinks that they preferred.

The story Struts told was the stuff Hollywood sports movies were made of, fifty years ago. At least on the surface. Struts had a way with narrative, a knack for fleshing out details, and Brad loved it. He continually checked his tape recorder, and soon was working on his second two-hour spool covering his interview with the two men.

Struthers told how he had walked up to Maple almost two years before in the parking lot at the course just outside Boise. He asked if Treb needed a caddy, half hoping the unfamiliar Monday qualifier would say no so Struts could hop in his well-worn '88 Cadillac and head for Houston.

But Treb hired him, his dog-eared shot yardage notebook and a large frame that begged for the caddy to get to use the cart, instead of the player riding it while the caddy lugged the clubs behind. It was the first decision Treb made in their association, and Struts loved him for it right away.

They played a practice round on Sunday, and Struts was impressed with this 67-year-old guy who could still manage enough clubhead speed to at least stay within shouting distance of the 50- and 55-year-old fading stars who had joined the senior tour.

Monday qualifiers were a hapless lot. Either they showed up out of habit, not believing for an instant that they could get one of the handful of spots in the 54-hold tournament. Or they were basket cases in the head, realizing that for eighteen holes, their fate and the chance at a sustaining check hinged on one or two 24-inch putts, a bad bounce that might kick their Titleist—the ball of choice, then as now—kick it into a bunker or water hazard, a damnable tree limb that waited to bat the ball into knee-deep rough, or maybe a fat wedge on the eighteenth that turned making it to the regular medal play tournament into missing by a single stroke.

"In other words, almost all these guys lived on th' dark side," Struts explained. "They wuz eaten up by negatives each time they faced a tricky situation. 'Specially on th' greens."

Treb was different, and Mike made the point here that it had come about "when Treb found Jesus, back in the late '80s. He quit worrying, something he had held the patent on all his life, and all of sudden, for the first time ever, he could play to his potential.

"He used to tell me that when golf suddenly wasn't all-consuming, when he could play and not worry about what the ball would do or how the bets stood, he got *really* good. So, at the darkest shade of twilight of his potential for playing professionally, something he always wanted to have tried, he tried. He packed up and headed for Boise. I wanted to go with him to caddy, but I was tied up. Great thing, as it turned out. It brought Struts into the mix."

Struts talked about Treb birdying the first hole in the Monday qualifier, "an' I suddenly tole myself, whoa! We got somethin' goin' on here!"

Treb was all fairways and greens that Monday. His putting speed was perfect. He could count on knocking every long birdie effort to the hole, but never more than two or three feet past. And his old-fashioned Zebra was stroking those short ones in the back.

WHILE TREB was relaxed and in a rare zone, his two qualifying partners were scrambling and dying with every missed shot. The target score was a three-under 69. A lot of California seniors had come over to try to get in, while honing their games for the Transamerica in Napa the following week. Then his only poor drive of the day at the 593-yard ninth set up leaving Treb's third shot of 170 yards uphill on the par five. Water parallel on the left, Struts explained in his inimitable vernacular, with water in front of the green. It looked to Struts as if maybe the glory train might be about ready to derail.

"But he took out his trusty seven-wood, put his patented little draw on it, and knocked his little sissy Top Flight woman's ball nine feet past the pin. His down-hiller with a cup and a half break to th' right caught the left part of the hole, and *dropped!* My man done turned a bogey into a birdie an' we wuz on our way."

One of the two playing with Maple, Struts said with a grin, was none other than Baxter Randall.

Pat Higgins, the third member of the group, was settling in for a respectable one or two over round as they strode up the seventeenth, a 430-yard par four that long-driving Higgins had reached comfortably in two. Respectable, but no cigar on getting to play Friday. Meanwhile, Treb had already birdied three on the back side, versus failing to get up and down from a bunker on the par three fifteenth for his only bogey of the day. When he laced his five-iron onto the seventeenth green, the way he was putting put him in great shape.

"Th' zone ol' Treb wuz in, weren't no way that boy wuz gonna bogey eighteen," Struts said. "He had been center cut all th' way."

"I'd like to track down that dummy talking head who dreamed up that center cut junk, and kick his no-good butt," Mike grumbled.

Meanwhile, Bax Randall was an enigma, Struts said. He had holed out twice amid a roller-coaster round, and had turned in some miraculous par-saving putts. Randall had struggled to get himself to three-under, but he overshot the seventeenth green and stared at a scary bunker shot downhill toward the water. He could stand to bogey, since in an unusual setup number 18 was an easy par five birdied more often than not by the old pros.

Struts said he and Treb were toward the back of the green, to the side, already lining up Treb's putt. Higgins was to their right, farther still from Randall. Bax elected to blast with an L-wedge, which he took back haltingly, then stopped the swing a foot or so past the ball. It popped up, then went sideways to the left in midair.

"In other words, he done hit his ball twice," Struts said. "I asked my man, did he see that? Treb said yes. Then them two strokes on top o' what now seemed like a cinch bogey would've done shot that motor mouth outta this thing."

When the hole was finished, Treb and Higgins had parred, and Randall had carded a tournament-ending double bogey. But as they walked to the eighteenth tee, Randall mumbled to Higgins "who wuz keepin' his card, 'boy that bogey didn't help me none. Now I *gotta* birdie eighteen!'"

Treb watched Higgins write Bax's score as a five, and he didn't hesitate in challenging Randall, Struts related. "Bax, you hit twice coming out of the trap, didn't you?" "Hell no!" Bax shot back. "Then how did you wind up left of the flag some twenty feet?" "Cause I hit a bad shot, Maple. You saying something else? What about it, Pat? You see me hit it twice?"

Higgins said he hadn't been watching that closely, but he *had* been surprised at how far left Bax's ball had wound up. There was no TV coverage, so that option at checking things out was moot. "Honey, you see me hit my ball twice?" Randall cooed to the woman volunteer who was charting their shots. "She wuzn't 'bout ta git into what she perceived to be th' makins' of a pissin' match betwixt a pair o' skunks," Struts said. "So she jus' shook her head and walked away. Real fast."

"Now, any more questions, hot shot?" Struts said Randall demanded of Treb. "Bax, you know what you did," Maple responded. "If you keep that five and birdie here, you're going to knock somebody out of the tournament who deserves to qualify. You don't."

"So what you gonna do about it?" Randall shot back.

Treb stared at Randall, and slowly shook his head. "It's not what I'm going to do," Struts said Treb replied, just as calmly as you please. "It's up to you. Call the penalty shot on yourself, and sleep well tonight. Or don't, and you might as well be back at Meadowbrook in Fort Worth fifty years ago, with nowhere to go the rest of your life in golf—again—but down the tubes."

Randall went ballistic, Struts related. He refused to call the penalty shot on himself. All he needed was a straight drive and a long-iron second, and he'd be on the tight, downhill par five eighteenth's green. Then two putts would put him back to three under, and more than likely in the tournament. Or at least in a playoff for the last opening.

However, Bax duck-hooked his drive, whacked out of rough to about an eight-iron from the green to give himself at least a chance, but then chili-dipped from there, overshot the green in four, and eventually took a double-bogey seven on the Caldwell Golf and Racquet Club's easiest hole.

"He fumed off the course, mad as a rattler in a burlap bag. Whispered somethin' ta Treb, who later tole me it was, 'You gonna regret this, shitass!' An' he wuz off to Napa, where he'd shoot 78 on Monday qualifying to miss bein' in *that* field by eleven strokes. We ain't heared of or seen hide nor hair o' that cat since you said he talked to you th' other day."

STRUTS SAID the rest of the Boise tournament was a storybook. Treb shot the low round in the Thursday pro-am, then opened with a bogey-less 67 on Friday to share the lead with Joey Beale, an established ten-time winner on the senior circuit. The press got interested, and grilled Maple in depth after the round.

"That's where our little ol' life together started getting' controversial," Struthers explained. "Here wuz this 67-year-old pro nobody ever heared 'bout before, leadin' a senior event. He had ta keep explainin' that his game just came together late in life. Finally, one o' th' scribes asked him how he looked so comfortable out there, playin' in his first event and not even comin' close to a bogey.

"Well, Treb never hesitated. 'My life turned around when I was reborn in Christ, about twelve years ago,' my man says. I was in th' back, watchin' our clubs and figurin' I done latched me onto a winner. I cringed a little. Not that I wuz anti-God back then. I jus' knew th' importance o' separation of church 'n' self, so fer as th' golfin' public wuz concerned.

"I done knowed lots o' born-again Christians on both tours. Golf's a lonely existence. As ol' Will McNeil done tole me, when I toted his bag to a second place at Colonial, in th' twilight o' his regular tour days, 'Struts, th' cruelty of this game is astounding. It turns on you when you think you've finally figured it out. You can't take drugs, 'cause they'll leave you uncoordinated. Same with booze. You can drink yerself ta sleep th' night before, but you show up on number one tee looped, an' you ain't gonna break 80. It's mighty lonely out there, even if you and a sharp caddy have a good…good…what's th' word, Mike?"

"Rapport," Cardenas said.

"Right. Rap-port. Pretty soon, many pros turn ta God, fer survival and not jus' prayin' an' do-goodin' to be winners, like a few attempt. God 'n' golf done got *them* folks figured out. You think God's gonna be fooled? An' golf is the Big Man's game. He gonna use it on them kinds. Misery awaits.'"

However, Struthers continued, "lots of other pros don't like ya to go public if'n you be a true-blue born-again. Sponsors often don't either. Politically incorrect, ya know? Remember Bernhard Langer when he won th' Masters on Easter Sunday, back in th' late eighties? Said somethin' to th' effect that *this* green jacket was particularly special, 'comin' on th' day my redeemer wuz resurrected.' Beautiful witnessing. But poison fer them's that lurk around, ready ta turn a good ol' boy's honesty into somethin' stupid-sounding an' ugly, while playin' to th' masses.

"Anyhow, Treb explained how he didn't believe God won Boise fer him. That God just made it possible fer Treb to win it fer hisself. But you think some o' those scribes worked that little…little—"

"Disclaimer?" Mike cut in.

"Yeah. Dis-clammer into their stories? Uh-uh. They done already *knowed* how this day was gonna read."

"I researched some of the accounts," Brad acknowledged. "Looks like Treb would've been well-advised to keep his rebirth to himself."

"But he wouldn't. *Nosir.* Ever time a reporter brought up th' Jesus angle, well my man would talk non-stop. That's how all that *caddied by Christ* and *charted by th' Holy Spirit* stuff got goin'.*"

Struts told Brad that his own old ties to God from his childhood were reconstituted, after an evening in a Boise restaurant, talking to Treb. "An' I ain't looked back since.

"Th' rest o' that storybook tournament is history, as they say," Struts continued. "One bogey—a three-putt when he charged a ten-footer downhill fer a birdie, and went by eight—and six birds ta lead by three Saturday, then th' smoothest 64 ya ever did see on Sunday to bring the Caldwell Golf an' Racquet Club ta its knees. The oldest guy ever ta win as a senior; not only that, he done won Boise by six.

"History, except fer somethin' that happened in th' locker room after Saturday's round, somethin' that history never heard about," Struts added. "Treb, he tole me he was by his locker, changin' shoes, when he hears some of th' players talkin' about him over on th' aisle next door. They can't see him. Well, Fred Sheffield, that horse's butt, is tellin' some guys how Treb spooked pore ol' Bax Randall, Fred's longtime buddy, into takin' th' gas comin' down th' stretch in th' Monday qualifier. That he lied sayin' Bax hit his bunker shot twice on th' same swing, and that Higgins—Fred claimed—had backed Bax up on it.

"Couple others brung up th' religious angle, and th' stuff about sponsors. In one o' Treb's press conferences, somebody asked my man if he had sponsors yet. Treb didn't bat an eyelash. Said he didn't believe in 'em except in rare cases, and only then if th' pitch to be made wuz honest. Not bought. Said—an' here wuz th' clincher—said pros wuz sellin' their bags fer sponsor logos, then their hats—almost got th' tours in trouble with th' FCC on that, I think—then their shirt pockets, then their shirt sleeves. Shoot, Treb said. Pretty soon golf pros'd look like stock car drivers, an' wear racin' suits to th' course. Figure how *that* went over with established pros, who as a group pull in tens of millions each year in showin' sponsor logos on camera.

"Well, in no time, in low voices, these five back-stabbers wuz jus' *massacring* my man. Treb tole me he don't know what ta' do. Confront 'em? Slip out and pretend he didn't hear? He starts ta do th' latter, but can't resist stickin' it to 'em. So at th' last second, he turns right 'stead of left, stops, smiles and says, 'Hi guys. Good luck tomorrow. Hear?' Then he walks away, whistlin.'"

"Good for him!" Brad said.

"Yeah. But ya' know what my man said he done went and did? He goes out to his car, bows his head and prays fer *forgiveness,* fer *not* forgivin' that bad-mouthin' fivesome 'stead o' humiliatin' 'em."

"Why, Struts, did he walk away from a renewed career the following week, at Napa?" Brad asked.

"Ya gonna have an exclusive, if ya' ask Brad," Struts replied, scarcely above a whisper. "An' he will tell ya, I wager, if ya ask him 'bout Don Baker."

"Don Baker?" Brad said, scribbling the name in his notebook.

"Don Baker. It's a wild story. An' I'm here ta' tell ya', it *really* happened. Me, if I ever wuz ta backslide, as my Baptist preacher used ta call it when I wuz growin' up in Houston, well th' memory of Mister Don Baker ferever done made that impossible. I'm God's fer *good.* "

"I was in the gallery at Napa, and I'll second ol' Struts here on that," Mike Cardenas added. "What was that gal's name who sang, *I Believe in Angels?* "

"Cristy Lane." Struthers said, with an animated sigh, followed by a fractured tenor mini-version of *Footprints In the Sand* and *One Day at a Time, Sweet Jesus.*

"Yeah. Cristy Lane. Well, I believe too, just like my old pardsie here, if for no other reason than Don Baker."

"I'LL BE sure to ask Maple about Don Baker," Brad agreed. "You know a lot about Louise and Treb, I guess, Mike."

"Sure. From Day One. She was about the prettiest woman I'd ever seen, when Treb brought her an' Gale, her sweet little girl whom he eventually adopted, from Wichita Falls to Brownsville back in 1960. Louise, well she was in a looks class with—aw, what's her name, Struts? Mike Douglas' young chick bride?—

"Catherine Zeta-Jones?"

"Yeah. Catherine whatever. Treb went to work at Fort Brown, then they moved over to Harlingen. He was assistant to Tony Butler at the muny there. I joined 'em pretty soon. Tony made room for me.

"Tony was a prince—*the* prince—among club pros. Used to share rooms and vehicles with Hogan back in the late '30s. Fantastic with the flat stick. Played an exhibition with Bobby Locke, the acknowledged world's best putter of the 1940s, a South African who took his hat off to Butler. Literally. Tony couldn't hit it outta his shadow from the tee though, so he quit the money-poor pre-World War II tour and turned to club professionaling. Had a little girl named Jeannie who could play super too.

"Treb's two sons were born in Harlingen. Our happiest days were there, working with Tony. But when Bill Bass and his high-rolling, free-wheeling promoters took over Brownsville Country Club, turned it into Valley Inn and Country Club, then built two more courses twelve miles to the north at Olmito, well, we got sucked into the excitement.

"It was a great idea, while it lasted. But when the initial housing development sold out, then the oil embargo of the mid-'70s kicked in and left them with their pants down, contractually speaking, the dream development went belly-up.

"We stayed on, Treb at VICC and me at Olmito. We'd work for the new owners in the winters, at the height of tourist season. Then Treb landed a nice, albeit low-paying, summer deal at Cloudcroft, New Mexico. Eight-thousand feet straight up, mind you. One of the highest courses in the world. You could tee it up, with White Sands glistening maybe sixty miles on the horizon to the west, and watch a ball fly an extra fifty or sixty yards, sometimes."

"Cloudcroft. That's where Louise had her accident, isn't it?"

"Near there, yes," Mike replied, then looked at Struts. "Whaddaya think, pard?"

"He said he done trusted us. If he wuz tellin' his life story hisself, he'd trust Brad to do th' right thing. You th' man on thisun, though."

Mike sighed. "OK. Treb and Louise loved each other like crazy. Specially when we were at Harlingen. But as with couples who love hard, they could fight harder than most.

"Treb taught Louise to smoke. Then he had to quit, finally, when a doctor told him with his lungs, he could live without the cigarettes or die with 'em before he was fifty. His call. It took him three tries at cold turkey. Finally made it in, oh, about '76. Thing was, he left poor Louise hooked. She liked the coffin nails, though. Never has wanted to quit.

"When they got married, Treb drank like a fish. He and I used to chug-a-lug Lone Star Beer by the truckload. Then when we hooked up again in the Valley after he got married, well Matamoros and Progresso were just across the Rio. Oso Negro made a pretty good rotgut vodka and gin, and you could buy Mexican tequila real cheap. Fifty cents toll going, a quarter coming back, a customs stamp at the U.S. side and you had the makings of real cheap drunks. He taught Louise to drink. When he swore off the hard stuff, again he left Louise in the lurch. She had a bad stomach and shouldn't have been hoisting a cocktail or two that turned into three or four. or five every night. But you can blame Treb.

"That's another testament to born-again Treb—and yes, living with and watching him and his rebirth, like Struts, had a profound effect on me too. I still have a ways to go to get to Struts' level. But I'm pretty certain I'll *never* lose the magic. Because I've been to the river and watched Treb get baptized by the Spirit. Man, the Word is true.

"Anyway, Treb the souse that he was simply walked away from heavy drinking. Now, he can sip just one of his sissy wine coolers and never want anything else. I've seen him drink a gin and tonic—within the last month, even—enjoy it and not want another. Miraculous, that's what it is."

"But not for Louise, I take it. Especially since her wreck. Tell me what happened," Brad asked.

Mike looked at Struts, who shrugged his shoulders. "Your call again bruther," he said. "I weren't with you all then."

Cardenas again sighed. "OK. Each summer in Cloudcroft, I shared a little place with them, after their kids had grown up and moved away from the Maple battlefield. All but their youngest, that is. And he stayed back in Brownsville with his grandmomma. Finally, I couldn't take their shouting matches anymore. I got my own place, which pretty well made me barely break even each three or four months we'd spend in the New Mexico mountains.

"Their war finally came to a head one Sunday in the late eighties. They awakened with hangovers from the battles and the bottles the night before.

He was slipping out to go help me open the pro shop, he told me early that afternoon. She told him she wouldn't be back till late, that she was going to Ruidoso. The Mescaleros have a casino at their Inn of the Mountain Gods, right where the Apache tribe's reservation begins, just west of Ruidoso and north of Ruidoso Downs.

"I told you that Treb taught his wife how to smoke and drink. Well, add gambling to that. You know that Treb's one heck of a poker player. We used to go Vegas when it was just getting interesting, me playing a little blackjack while he'd scare up a five-card or seven-card stud game. Just like he does today, in hold 'em. It isn't gambling where Treb's concerned. Out of every five sessions with the cards, against *anybody* in a fair game, he'll lose his stake once, more or less break even twice and win twice. Big. As in double or triple his stake, at least. We used to keep books on it, so I know it to be a fact.

"Well, we used to vacation together in Vegas, on golfer's specials that Treb hustled. That's after I married Rita. We'd drive out there in Treb's '59 Caddy, hustle some golf, let the girls have some fun in the sun, and Treb would go to work. We never—and I mean *never*—came back that Treb didn't have a wad of somebody else's money.

"OK. Along the way, Louise got hooked on slot machines. Treb's fault, of course. She never had been exposed to them before, and probably wouldn't have bowed down to them as if the infernal machines were gods, had she not met him. So he taught her to smoke, drink and gamble—but the latter was the one that broke her back. Pretty well literally."

Mike paused, and Brad watched him look again at Struthers. "C'mon. Give!" Brad pleaded.

"Well, that Sunday in Cloudcroft I was talking about. When she told Treb not to wait up, he told her that her love affair with slots was worse than if it were with another man. Something like that, he confided to me months later. And while we're at that point, I would bet *anything* that neither Louise nor Treb *ever* looked twice at anyone else. How, I'll never know, the way they fought. Treb thinks God wanted it like that, even before he got to know God intimately.

"But this particular Sunday, Louise and her gambling got to him. He wasn't playing poker much anymore. Nobody with any sense would sit down at a table with him back in Brownsville, for one thing. Treb and Louise were broke, owed a bundle, and had sunk so low in their marriage that they seemed to be living on each other's blood. He told her like he had a hundred or a thousand times before, that slots over the long haul were a sucker's curse. Only bingo was worse, and *that* was *another* pastime she had developed a liking to, though all on her own.

"So she said she'd go to Ruidoso, play Bingo after lunch thank you *very* much, then hit the slots, if that's the way he felt. She had one credit card with a few hundred left on it, and by dang she was gonna use it *today.* If she lost, *tough!* At least, she'd have fun going busted. His money too? 'T-o-u-g-h *shit,* pal!' she spelled out for him.

"That's what he told me that Sunday afternoon, after I had walked on eggs around Treb, who was seething. And I'll never forget his next words. *Never!*

"'Mike,' my best friend told me, 'if it wasn't for M.J.'—M.J. was their youngest kid, back in Brownsville for the summer with Treb's mother—'if it wasn't for M.J., I'd say we should split. But we can't afford to. And it would kill M.J. Our only hope is if one of us suddenly dies. Then *maybe* the other will survive. *By* herself or himself! I think we've both had it with marriage for a lifetime.'

"Well," Cardenas continued, looking down at his folded hands, "it kinda shocked me. I said something like, 'Aw, you don't mean that.'"

Cardenas paused, then continued, matter of factly. "About two hours later, we get this phone call from a state trooper. Louise blew a tire going through the reservation, about a mile from where New Mexico 244 intersects with US 70. Just south and west of the Inn. She rolled, going about sixty-five, and then slammed head-on into a pine tree. They had her in the Ruidoso hospital ICU, in a coma and with back injuries.

"I drove Treb over there and sat with him for two days. I didn't know what was going on in that mind of his, since he didn't say much. His words from that Sunday afternoon had to be ringing in his mind's ear though. They were in mine, let me tell you.

"Well, Louise came out of the coma three days after the wreck. She hasn't walked since, and she never will, even though she does have *some* feeling in her legs. Two months later, Treb confided to me that he had tried to pray Louise back to health, and was told in no uncertain terms in his mind that where she was, was as good as it was going to get for her. He said there was this bright sun in his head. He couldn't remember a voice coming out of it. But he got the words. And—this will blow your mind—he got the *vision* of an exclamation point!

"That was good enough for Treb. God completed his restructuring of my friend's soul before the year was out. Mine too, by the way. Living with him through all that left its mark. Like Struts says, being with somebody you *know* God lives in does something profound in *you.* Treb has told me that he's never loved Louise more than he does now, even more than the upbeat, wild love-making times in the sixties."

"I don't mean to be just a bit skeptical, but what about Louise?" Bred pointed out. "Forgive me, but has your Holy Spirit *skipped* someone here? Someone pretty integral to this, this *adventure* in salvation?"

"Louise," Struts hastily inserted, "is God's business. She's on *his* timetable, an' neither Mike, or me, or Treb worries that she's out of the creator's loop."

"'She'll be OK,' I've heard Treb say many times," Mike offered, as the three men stood while Brad turned off the tape recorder. 'I put her where she is. When he's ready, Jesus will make it all come out right.'"

"Till that time, you can bet our man will take real good care of her. We done seen too much love come down th' pike twixt him an' his mate to believe anything else," Struts said.

"See you later, Jack," Mike hollered at the assistant pro, as they exited and walked to their cars.

11. The Mysterious Don Baker

About the time Brad, Struts and Mike were just getting started with their interview at the golf course, Treb was arriving at the Fifth Jack. He used the house phone and dialed Amanda's room.

"Come on up," she invited. When he got to the suite's door and was greeted by the young woman, Treb was taken by how much she *really* favored his first love. Mandy was decked out in rolled-up jeans, a man's white shirt, white socks and black loafers. He wondered if she was trying for a fifties' look, and chuckled to himself. She should've looked around for some pedal-pushers, he mused. That's the first thing he thought of, when he remembered Clarice.

"Good to see you, Mr.—"

"Ah-ah!"

"Uh, Treb. C'mon in. I have Brad's other recorder set up on the living room table, and he left me some questions. I *think* I know how to work the tape machine. You want something from the fridge?"

"Nope. I'm fine. You lead the way."

"Actually," she said, as she sat at the table after pulling out one of the other chairs, another nice touch Treb couldn't help but notice, "I'm really looking forward to this. I was a little scared at first—"

"No need for that, my dear."

"Well, it's—it's sort of like *prying,* you know?"

"But that's what reporters do. Pry. Brad will be looking for *anything* that will make a good angle. I've learned *that* much about writers. You and I might not think much about a phrase or a thought, but how he fits it into the flow of his feature could make a trivial sentence important. And," he smiled, "ultimately be embarrassing to me. But we won't know what's on *his* mind until he writes it, will we? So," he added, "fire away when you're ready. I've committed to this."

He dutifully answered biographic queries, such as what it was like to grow up at the tip of Texas—and the U.S.—during the World War II years. Al Cisneros and some of their other pals Mike Cardenas was discussing with Brad. Summers spent in Abilene. His forgettable relationship with an uncaring father. Life with his mother, who had died in the early 1990s.

"When, and how, did you meet Clarice?" Amanda asked, referring to the notes Brad had left with her.

"Let's see. That must've been the fall of 1952, when I was a junior at Brownsville High. She had just moved to town. Her father was a mid-level wheel at Union Carbide, which had a new plant being built where the Port of Brownsville was going in.

"I guess it was one morning at school, when I saw her flitting down the hallway. She opened her locker. I stopped and watched this slender, ever-smiling, dark-haired beauty in a fuzzy pink sweater wearing those sleek-lookin skirts, tailored and well below the knee. She had on loafers with fat white socks, rolled down a notch. Then she was off, carrying her books to her next class.

"I saw her again that day, in the cafeteria. 'I think I'm in love,' I told Mike, and pointed her out. He didn't know her either. After a few days of snooping around, I found out she was dating some football jock, also a sophomore, but nothing serious as yet. Now, I wasn't much with the young ladies. Pretty shy, is what I was. So I backed off until I kept seeing her in the hallway, and realized that I was getting obsessed with her. I'd see her walking with her football player and really *feel* the pangs of jealousy for the first time in my life.

"Finally, some excuse for me to introduce myself came about—I can't remember exactly what it was—and that evening, I got her family's phone number from information, heaved a big sigh and called her up.

"We had a short conversation and then I asked her if she'd like to take in a movie Saturday night. Fridays in the fall were always taken up with football, of course. I figured she'd be seeing her grid stud *that* night, after the game. Well, she surprised me by saying yes.

"I remember it perfectly. We double-dated with Al Cisneros. He was with this real good-looking blonde named Linda. We took our girls to the Grande, the first-run theater in the heart of downtown, just a block or so from the International Bridge."

Treb laughed. "Actually, I guess I fell in love twice that night. First, with Clarice. Then with Cyd Charisse. Like Clarice, she was a brunette. The long-legged dancer from Amarillo was debuting opposite Gene Kelly and Leslie Caron in *An American in Paris*. Great flick. You like Gene Kelly?"

"Yes," Mandy replied. "I have a tape of *Singin' In the Rain* at home. I got it from my grandmother. Not a year goes by that we don't make some microwave popcorn and watch him, Debbie Reynolds, and Donald O'Connor."

"*And* Jean Hagen, don't forget. As the silent screen star whose voice isn't good enough to transition to sound. One of the best comedic performances on film. Ever! A little trivia here, my dear. You remember Debbie Reynolds' ingenue is supposed to dub her voice for the wildly absurd naturalness of Hagen's character. Only in *real* reel life, *Singin'* producers decided Debbie's speaking voice did not mesh with what they wanted. So when we watch Debbie dubbing her voice over Hagen's character for an early film soundtrack, it's not Debbie. Hagen is dubbing her *own* regular speaking voice over her *Singin'* character's; in effect, Hagen is dubbing over Debbie who is portrayed as dubbing over Jean's."

"Whew!" Mandy gushed.

"I fancied myself as a pretty solid film buff in the fifties," Maple said. "Anyway, that night at the Grande Theatre was the beginning of my first real romance. I shared Clarice with the jock for a few weeks. I think he was just trolling around, and pretty soon moved on to other girls. That left Clarice with me. And we fell in love. Seventeen and sixteen, and we were pledging ourselves to one another for all eternity."

"Real hot deal, huh?" Mandy said, smiling a little impishly.

Pretty quickly, she wished she hadn't put it that way. True to his word, once he got started telling the truth, Treb *told* it. All of it, she figured, and soon she wouldn't have believed he had left any of the many edges untouched.

"I was a virgin, if you can believe *that* of a healthy male teenager not slowed by religious or physical constraints, who lived in a border town along the Rio Grande. She was too. I hungered for, lusted after and feared sex with her, with equal passion. Clarice was ripe for finally coming of age in experimental petting. By the spring of '53, we couldn't keep our hands off each other. But we always pulled up short of consummation."

He looked at Amanda, who was doodling on a hotel scratch pad. "This isn't getting too steamy for you, is it?" he asked, grinning.

"No...no. Interesting. Go on."

"No where to go from here, much. At least on the surface. We high school sweethearts stayed true after I graduated and went to Abilene for the summer, then to Tech. She traveled with her parents that summer, anyway. We wrote passionately to each other, resumed our hands-on—if you'll pardon me, my dear—romance in Brownsville the summer after she graduated, before I returned to Tech while she entered the University of Texas at Austin. Our love remained strong, it seemed, via almost daily letters. At least, for a month.

"She used to call me 'Trebby,' and started each of her letters 'Dear Trebby.' I loved the special way she referred to me; but then, I loved *everything* about Clarice.

"Around mid-October, the salutation of a week-late, really boring, no-nothing letter was 'Dear Treb." She signed off with, "As Ever, Clarice." As *ever*? What gives? I thought, even though I feared that I really knew. I called her, and she admitted she was dating another guy.

"Had we ended it there, our little romance would've been just like tens of millions of others. Soon the wounds of the third person out—me, in this case—would've healed. But no. I asked her if I could drive down and talk to her, face to face. She said yes, the following Saturday afternoon. She'd get me a ticket to go with hers in the student section for the UT-Baylor game. I borrowed Jerry Bob Farley's green Ford sports coupe, flew low Saturday morning in the pre-dawn hours to Austin, threw away our tickets to the football game, and drove her to a spot she selected out by Lake Austin.

"That should've tipped me off even more. This must've been *their* necking place. And I was getting the feeling necking was a little too tame a description of what this clown had led *my* darlin' into. I tried to push the envelope myself, that afternoon while the Longhorns were grinding Baylor into Memorial Stadium's turf a few miles away. But you know something? Being a red-bloodied, all-American boy when it came to fantasizing about women and girls, I never had *any* trouble conjuring up images of my making love to them. But *never* a fantasy with Clarice. She was too special. I couldn't even force myself to get it going out there overlooking Lake Austin that Indian summer afternoon, either. I cried, she cried, we did most everything but consummation—I'm sorry Amanda. Am I getting too graphic now?"

"No, no," she coughed. "I...I can take it. I think."

"Anyway, we as much as told each other goodbye that blue day in late October, 1954. I took her back to her dorm. We stood in the street, by Farley's car, still crying and holding on to one another. Then this clown in a 1951 Plymouth comes screeching by, honking and swerving to within a foot of where I was sticking out into traffic. It was her guy. The jerk! Forgive me God."

"You've...you've never seen her since?"

"Oh yeah. Three or four times, actually. Right before she got engaged, she had one of her married girlfriends in Brownsville invite me over, and they gave us the run of the place for an evening. It tore me up. But again, I simply couldn't make love to the love of my life. By then, I had become a rabid skirt-chaser at Tech, drunk *or* sober. So I guess I was fearful of what I might discover, had we...you know."

Mandy coughed again. "Then...then that was it for you two?"

"Not Quite. This guy I knew in Brownsville, a good friend of mine named Tom Griswold, babysat me the night Clarice and Jerk got married in a la-te-da formal Catholic wedding. We drove over to the Las Dos Republicas near the market in Matamoros for margaritas. Then we got Chinese at the Santa Fe and sipped gin and tonic for me and whiskey sours for him. *Then* we stopped at Garcia's before we got to the bridge for a last round of margaritas. Finally, close to midnight, we drove around Brownsville a while.

"He asked me if I was going to be OK. I mumbled yeah or something. Then he laid a bombshell on me. 'Treb,' he said, 'Beck'—that was Becky, his girlfriend, 'Beck told me one of her friends told her that if Trebor showed up at the wedding and Clarice saw him, she'd made up her mind to walk out and call the whole thing off.' I guess that meant she knew she'd not be able to marry Jerk. At least not that night."

"Really!?" Mandy responded, suddenly back in the story with a vengeance. "Just like in *The Graduate*!?"

"That's what he said. I remember looking at my watch in some crazy gesture, then yelling, 'Griz, thanks a lot! They've gone to South Padre or Corpus or somewhere by now to spend their first honeymoon night.' He told me he wasn't about to tell me beforehand, that my poor ol' heart might not survive another graveyard spin into the turf. He talked that way. Griz was a pilot.

"I remember sighing and telling him he was right. Jerk was graduating with a hot business degree and had a promising stock brokerage career ahead of him. I was flat busted. I had screwed up almost four years at Tech. I had jettisoned the idea of maybe becoming a club golf pro, and the big dance—the PGA—was out since I had proved to myself that I couldn't stand the heat to compete. So with nothing else on the table, I decided to give show business a try. That little career move figured to be 100,000 to 1 odds against me, probably shaded on the optimistic end at that. It looked to be time to get on with the rest of my life, to borrow the trite, already overworked phrase which had surfaced somewhere about that time."

"And you did," Mandy said.

"It's pretty much a blur, but I guess I did. Chased women, particularly the pretty ones, over and over; those who would flush me and my beat-up heart into oblivion. Something Freudian there, you figure? Gave up golf for a while, and of all things turned to becoming an actor, or a singer, or both—and finally becoming neither, excluding the Buddy Holly experience, of course. Also, I took a long, long time getting over Clarice. Actually, never did, quite. I used to have nightmares about her and Jerk. She never spoke and she never made eye contact, in my sweat 'n' screamers. I couldn't tell if she was happy, sad or just resigned.

"Then I met Louise, and fell dad-blamed totally in love again. I had virtually flunked out of Tech after four and a half years—I also had changed my major for the fourth time, back to business administration. I dodged the Lebanon crisis by joining the Army Reserves and serving a miserable six months in Fort Chaffee, Arkansas. Before discharge, I got a lead on a beginner's assistant pro job at Weeks Park in Wichita Falls, Texas. Met Louise there. The most beautiful woman I'd ever seen in person, a disclaimer designed to give honesty and my infatuation for Elizabeth Taylor, *circa National Velvet* through *Butterfield* 8. Louise and I got married in '60.

"Around 1961 or '62, the Clarice nightmares slowed steadily to about one a month, then maybe one ever four months. Only in the last couple of years have they picked up again. This time as just plain dreams. No nightmares. But the message is always the same. She never looks at me. Never speaks. Can't tell if Clarice is happy the way her life turned out. It was a life, I was told by a friend of hers a few years back, that gave her a couple kids, a grandkid or two, a huge house in Darien, Connecticut and comforts in life most people can never expect to enjoy.

"My dreams of her are back to maybe once a month—same old song too. No eye contact. No clue as to whether she even knows I still exist, or cares if I do. Just a sweet vision of a girl I once loved, totally disengaged from my life—except she won't stay out of my dreams.

"Who was it who said 'better to have loved and lost, than never loved at all?' That's me. Only, the second time around it took, warts and all. In spite of double-downers threatening to offset our dizzying highs, I couldn't have loved anybody any more than I have Louise, and do today for that matter. But for a brief time when I was a kid, I loved someone else just as much."

"Wow!" Mandy exclaimed.

"See? Now you've got all that garbage on tape. I'm at the mercy of your boyfriend," Treb said, smiling. "The tape still going? OK. Brad, don't use Jerk as the name of Clarice's ultimate main man. It's just my little pet moniker for him, for when he almost ran me over that time at the UT dorm. Just call him James now. Hey, Amanda. Let's take a break. Think I *will* have something from that fridge. Getting all this old spooky stuff off my chest has whetted my thirst."

OSCAR LAY in his bed at New York New York, hand under his head and staring at the ceiling as he blew baby-cigar smoke upward. He tried to remember his conversation with Gabe, attempting to pinpoint just which sentence or phrase Gabe had uttered that now bothered him.

It was something to do with Billy C. and his purported doublecross on Gabe. What didn't compute now, as he lay trying to decide which move should come next?

Gabe had said the phone rang while he was in the pool, and Billy answered the cell, then switched off. He told Gabe it had been The Cuban, that he had been delayed in bringing almost a million dollars in coke until next week. Then, Gabe had surmised to Oscar that Billy must've hatched a plan to rip both him and Oscar off. He would slip out to meet Cuban, make the exchange, kill the Cuban, keep his cocaine and Gabe's money, then head for LA or Denver or Phoenix and live high.

What was it?

Suddenly, Oscar bolted upright.

"What wrong, hon?" a startled Mary Katherine Arnaz asked, as she lay in the adjoining queen-sized bed while reading *Will's War,* a historical novel she had bought when they had driven through West Texas a few days earlier and found it to be a neat page-turner.

"That's IT!" Oscar exclaimed.

"What?"

"If Billy was fooling Gabe into thinking the meeting wouldn't be for several days, then how did he get hold of Gabe's nine hundred grand? Gabe *has* to have known Billy was going to meet me that night. And he *had* to have hatched the plan!"

"*What* plan, sweetie? You're scaring me again!"

"Go back to your book, M.K. You've hardly had your nose out of it since we got here."

That was it! Oscar thought. Billy *was* on orders to kill me and snatch my stuff. Now, does Gabe know that *I* know? He must, after that goof under the gun about Billy intercepting my phone call and coming up with a scam. So what now? Do we high-tail it out of here? If this Gabe guy knows Vegas like I *think* he does, he has connections. He probably has us staked out, in spite of our *not* being on Fremont Street like I told him. If we run, I think they'll follow us and be a lot better prepared for battle than I am. If I hang around, I don't think Gabe will move until he's sure I have the stuff and his cash with me.

In a little while, Oscar decided that his best—and safest—plan of action would be to convince Gabe that he hadn't caught Gabe's phone *faux pas* about Billy and the money. He smiled, realizing his success at counteracting Billy's scheme in a deadly defensive ploy now had given him confidence. That after more than a dozen years of trafficking in drugs, he knew he could kill, quickly and decisively.

Maybe it would be best to wait for Gabe to call his own cellular phone, which lay on the nightstand by Oscar's bed. Wait for the next move.

ACROSS AND up above town, near Summerlin, Gabe sat in his sprawling den decked out in stuffed big game trophies and autographed photos of celebrities. With him was one of his chief lieutenants. They discussed the predicament with the former associate and now adversary known to them only as The Cuban.

"It was stupid, I know. I could've bit my tongue off, right after I said that Billy was going to take my place without my knowing it," he said. "Stupid! *Stupid!* STUPID!"

"Hey boss, don't beat up on yourself. You didn't have time to think of *everything*. We can work it out. We know where th' cat is holed up, an' he probably thinks *we* still think he's at th' Four Queens or someplace downtown. You don't expect he's got th' stuff in his room do you? Hotel safe is out, of course."

"My guess is, it's in that fancy black SUV he drives. Someplace real hard to get to, or else DEA would've had him before now. But then, he might do something plain and ordinary, like have it all stuffed in a locker at Greyhound. If we snatch his car, he knows we're on to him. He grabs a plane for Miami, and he's back on his turf. With friends, whom I've got a hunch will come after us. If we make a date for *another* exchange, I don't know what to expect. He's smart. Getting the drop on Billy that way proved it. So that's chancy."

"You want to know my thoughts, boss? I say let's let it ride a day or so. Give me an' a couple guys time ta go over their room nice and neat and thorough. They won't suspect we've been there. Then you call him up on yer phone, make a date to meet him the next day or two, only we tail him the night before. Find a parking garage or somewhere to surprise 'em, put a .38 magnum up aside his wife's head, if the gal with him *is* his wife, and tell him to give us our coke. Then we will part as pals. Only—"

"Only we snuff them both, once we see the coke. Our cash has to be where ever it is, I figure. Hey, nice idea, Nick."

"That's what you pay me for, boss."

"WHERE WERE we?" Treb asked rhetorically, as they resumed their seats and nursed soft drinks. "Oh yes. Exit Clarice."

"I'm interested in how you got to sing with Buddy Holly. You know, I think my grandmother still has some of the 45s and the LPs you did with him," Mandy said.

"Getting to Buddy requires a pretty extended preliminary."

"Well, I'm ready, if you think the tape recorder is still doing OK. Brad said to make sure every now and then that the little wheels are turning in the window."

"They are. Let's see. I went from bad to horrible grades my first sophomore semester, which paralleled my losing Clarice. I was an engineering student, though I remain at a loss as to why I thought I could ever crack *that* nut. Mechanical engineering, to boot. While I had struggled to just under a one-point grade point average my freshman year—that was on the old basis of three-points are perfect, as opposed to the four-point system they use now—I had sunk to a point-two by the end of my sophomore year, first semester. I recollect that was an F or maybe a WF, that's—"

"Withdrew while failing, yes I know," Mandy interrupted.

"OK. I had a lot of those during my four and a half-year college career. Well, three Ds and a C in English, and I was a semester away from scholastic probation. I was also in Air Force ROTC, and they were not impressed when I had said I hoped to be a pilot.

"Most of my friends I'd made at school, Mike too, were doing OK to super at Tech with the books. Most were pledging or had already pledged fraternities, so that was another exclusion to Mike and me. I decided not to try to beat the freshmen golfers Coach Cantrell had recruited for 1954-55. I hated engineering, so I changed my major to business administration. While engineering had been too tough and not for me, it *had* been adventuresome part of the time. Business was simply boring. Besides, I was making a discovery about myself. I think I had a mild form of attention deficit disorder. I always had made marginal grades in high school. I just never studied. Couldn't stand to. Now, at Tech, I found when I studied, I couldn't retain what I had read. In class, I couldn't remember what the instructor lectured about five minutes later. Even with notes. My mind drifted. Yes, part of the time it was to Clarice. But if not her, or a problem with the current girl, something else. *Anything* else.

"I saw an ad in the school paper that auditions for the Varsity Show would be held at the Student Union Building the following weekend. They were doing *Good News,* the old college-themed Broadway musical, the movie version of which starred Peter Lawford and June Allyson as the romantic leads. I had done a little singing one summer in Abilene, two or three years before, when I got a wild hair and auditioned for Slim Willet and his country stage show at Fair Park Colliseum. I sang a couple of times, doing current Carl Smith and George Morgan hits, then didn't show up for a third, when the producer, entertainer and songwriter—he wrote *Don't Let the Stars Get in Your Eyes*, a big crossover hit in 1952—when Willet finally showed some interest in me.

"Anyway, I auditioned, loved the songs the show had, like *The Best Things in Life are Free,* and was shocked when I got the lead. A pal of mine from the dorm, Dave Pool—no kin of Brad's incidentally; he spelled his last name with no 'e'—Dave landed the comic lead, so this looked to be a big turn-around for ol' Treb. A really great looking and talented young woman, Mary Jo Cappleman, played opposite me in the June Allyson part. I got some super smooching on stage, and we dated for a few weeks, even though this was tough since I had no car. I dated one of the chorus girls after that, another sweetheart named Gladys Bain. Her nickname was The Body. And that she had. Playing Tom in the musical certainly had its perks for a while.

"Anyway, I was thinking I was hot stuff, until the reviews came out. Jack Sheridan, the *Avalanche-Journal* writer, loved Mary Jo. Really loved Dave. Really, *really* loved the show. And hated me. 'Treb Maple was inadequate as Tom, the romantic lead,' he wrote. I remember walking into the SUB the morning after opening night, decked out in my white buckskin shoes, white T-shirt and white baker's pants, figuring I'd be signing autographs. However, nobody would look me in the eye, except smiling troublemakers, so I knew something was wrong. I picked up a copy of the Lubbock paper and read the review, with five hundred pairs of eyes watching me. It was a sobering experience.

"Undaunted, I changed majors again. This time speech and dramatics. I was in school plays, some Shakespeare and dramas, then landed Bernie Dodd, the old William Holden part in *The Country Girl* at Lubbock Little Theatre. Never got to know the guy who played Frank Elgin, the Bing Crosby lead. He *finally* learned his lines by dress rehearsal. He was OK. The star of the show was a former Tech drama stalwart, Joyce Lowe Wilson. She had the Grace Kelly part. More good smooching on stage, by the way.

"Ronald Schulz was our director. He had directed me a few times at Tech, where he was on the faculty. After our run, he told me that I ought to consider maybe trying New York, even though it would be a big crapshoot. I thought about it. Also, my nemesis from *Good News,* Jack Sheridan, had said startlingly nice things about me in his *Country Girl* review.

"Mother's money for school had long since run out. I put myself through Tech for a couple of years playing poker. A good friend I had known during summers back in Abilene went to Tech. Kenneth Thomas taught me cards, advance course. He was *good.* He'd often chew me out in front of the table, telling me how I had misplayed a hand. *After* he had swept the chips to his side, of course.

"I lost my shirt one night, thinking I could stay in a game with Kenneth *and* Doyle Brunson, also known a few years later in this very city as Texas Dolly. I got tapped out pretty big. So, I took a job as a check liner at First National Bank. That's where I met John Pickering, who had the same job. John had seen me in the Varsity Show, and had not been impressed except with the fact that I had a passable baritone voice.

"A year later, a Lubbock rock 'n' roller named Terry Church bought some studio time from Norman Petty. He knew Bill Pickering from the Baptist church both attended, as did Buddy, by the way. Terry wanted vocal background singers with him. Bill asked John whom they could get to complement their two voices, which in natural ranges were first tenor and second tenor. John thought of me. So we drove the hundred miles from Lubbock to Clovis one Sunday afternoon, backed Church—whose stage name was Terry Noland—on a couple of songs he was releasing as 45s. *Ten*

Little Indians was pretty tame stuff, except that KLLL, I believe it was, banned it from its air play in Lubbock for some sort of suggestive element that to this day escapes me. The second song was supposed to be the A-side, something called *Hypnotized*. Only Terry pronounced it 'Hypmotized' in his lyrics, and I vaguely remember that the title was spelled the same way on the record label.

"Nothing happened for a few days. I continued to hang around Wayne's Record Rack, Lubbock's recorded music store of choice during the '50s. Got to know Dee Bowman there. He and two of his brothers sang backup on a sleeper hit in 1953—the Norman Petty Trio doing the old Duke Ellington standard, *Mood Indigo*. Vi Petty, Norman's wife, sang a sultry lead vocal.

"I got to know a lot about Petty, who was producing other hits in his little studio in Clovis. *Party Doll* by Buddy Knox, a radio personality and songwriter who was a student just across the border at West Texas State College in Canyon, was an example. Norman's studio produced a rich, clean sound, enhanced by his experimenting with echo chambers, Dee Bowman told me.

"The Bowmans offered to give me a helping hand as a single. They were going to headline a Kiwanis gig in Brownfield, a little town west of Lubbock, and I could be their 'guest artist.' It was a tragedy of titanic proportions. I sang some ballad I've since purged from my memory. I started in the wrong key, and Jay Bowman on piano spent the entire song frantically searching for the gear to which I had shifted. He never found it. I still remember those shocked faces in the audience as I warbled away, sounding I'm sure like one of Spike Jones' throw-aways."

The door to the suite opened and Brad entered, lugging his briefcase and camera.

"How y'all doing?" he asked, dropping his stuff on the bar and walking to the table.

"My, you sound chipper, and certainly West Texan," Mandy mumbled, however dryly. "It must've gone well with the guys. We're just getting Treb from Tech and Lubbock stages to Norman Petty's recording studio in Clovis, New Mexico."

"Hey! That's my territory. Otherwise, how's it been going with you two?"

"I've enjoyed spending the past—gee, more than three hours? I don't recall you changing the tape, Amanda," Treb noted.

"I did. You were busy talking about Tech. I didn't miss much."

"Is poker still on tonight?" Brad asked.

"Far as I know. Well, I'll let you two get on with your dining plans," Treb said, taking out his cell phone.

"Hey. I have an idea. Why don't we order in, and you and I can wrap up our taping on Buddy? We've got three hours, actually a little over, before we're due at the Adobe. What about it?" Brad asked.

"I've got to pick up Louise, I'm sure," Treb replied as he punched in a number. "Hey Lou. You ready to go home? Um-hum. Having fun? I'm up here at the Fifth Jack with Brad and Amanda. Yeah. So, where are you? Caesars, huh? Oh that's right. The slots tournament. How'd you do? Um, too bad. Maybe next time. Are you about ready? Good. I'll come in and find you. Yeah, I know where that line of machines is located. Be there in forty-five minutes...Love ya. Bye."

"By the way, Struts and Mike said be sure to ask you about Don Baker," Brad remembered. "It had to do with golf."

"*Everything* to do with golf, in Idaho and Napa," Treb replied, looking at his watch and pointing to the tape recorder. "That thing still going? I can tell you about Mr. Don Baker in five or seven minutes, which I have to spare. But no more."

"It's still going," Brad said. "Fire when ready."

"OK. This starts sixty-five or sixty-six years ago in Brownsville. None of this I remember, but it was told to me often by my mother. She said she used to enjoy watching me out the kitchen window, playing in my sand pile with a table knife and spoon I had lifted from the silverware drawer. I would be by myself, but talking a blue streak. She said she asked me one day whom I was speaking to, and I told her Don and Bake. 'Who're they?' she asked. 'My friends. They always stay close to me,' I replied. They went away about the time I hatched my keeper memory. Or I thought they went away, since I no longer saw them.

"But then, many years later, I wondered. Especially about how a kid two or three can come up with the name 'Bake' for an imaginary friend. The only Bake I ever knew was Bake Turner, a great running back in Dewitt Weaver's mid-1950s belly series offense at Tech. Anyway, Mother told me the pretend playmates seemed so real and natural to me.

"I was always accident-prone, especially as a teen-ager. I can recall the time I almost had a killer of a wreck, but something unseen told me to take action a millisecond before plowing into a parked car while doing fifty. Other times I was so drunk, I could've had my throat cut or sunk to the bottom of Laguna Madre. Lots of incidents when I somehow cheated injury, or worse, in spite of stupid mistakes.

"When the Holy Spirit took over my soul for good twelve or so years ago, I got the weird feeling that Don and Bake *had* been with me, when I knew them as a toddler *and* when I only sensed a special presence later in life. As a new born-again Christian, I believed I had uncovered my direct

156

connection to God—*through my guardian angels*. No particular reason. I just believed.

"Now, let's fast-forward to Boise. In that Monday qualifying eighteen, I remember seeing this smiling guy hanging around the first tee, and following us for a few holes. Wore a red baseball cap with *John 3:16* stenciled in over the visor. Had a yellow golf shirt, rather garish red-and-yellow striped walking shorts, white sneakers and socks that came up just below the knee, and he wore dark glasses. He smiled and applauded when I scorched a long and straight drive for an old fart—sorry about that, Amanda—an old guy on number one. I nodded at him.

"Two or three holes later, I ran in a ten- or twelve-footer to save par. Struts picked up my ball, tossed it to me and as I turned to walk off the green, I saw this same guy. Smiling, nodding. It seemed strange, since we didn't have a gallery of *any* kind that morning. I figured Red Cap must be following Bax or the other player.

"Well, he's right there with us on Friday, all the way. Smiling and nodding. Not clapping this time. Not yelling. He's looking at me all the while. And I begin to notice a glow about him."

"Glow!?" Brad asked, as Mandy pulled her chair closer to the table and stared into Treb's face.

"A glow. 'You see that guy over there?' I asked Struts. By now, keep in mind, he and I had had a long talk about God and Jesus and things I had found out about myself, through them and the Holy Spirit as one. Well, Struts says yeah, he sees him. 'Does he glow?' I asked Struts, who stops in his tracks in the twelfth fairway and stares at me. 'Glow?' he asks. 'Yeah. Glow.' 'Boss, he does act kinda funny all right. But *glow*? Don't see it.'

"Well, same thing happens next day. And Sunday, when by now we have a pretty big gallery following us. 'Hey Treb,' Struts says, when things are really going our way that final round. 'I think you is right. That cat in th' red hat *do* have kinda glow 'bout him! How come nobody *else* but us know it though?'

"I told him I had no idea. And in the excitement of the win, we didn't see him again. Until," Treb continued, "the next week in Napa. First round, and there he is.

"I had to find out about our smiling friend, who if you can believe it was wearing the *same* hat, shirt and striped pants he had worn *every* day at Boise. After the first round, when I got the lead with a bogey-less 64, I walked straight to the guy and introduced myself to him, even before I went to the scorer's table.

"'Hello,' he said, in this soft and beautiful yet somehow undeniably manly voice. 'I'm Don Baker. And I admire your playing. Especially the way you handle yourself in the interviews, even though you're not getting much help communicating your feelings because of the reporters. But you *are* getting through, to a lot of people. We appreciate it.'"

"'We?' I asked him. 'Somebody here with you?' 'Of course,' he replied. 'Keep up the good work.'

"Well, next morning the wire services and TV were full of this connecting with God and golf, continuing what had gone on in Idaho and intensifying it, since I broke out of the gates at Napa full speed. This, despite my efforts to explain God's presence in my life as it really was, an enabler and not a puppeteer. I felt wretched. Struts did too.

"The second day at Napa, I played with Jay McKay, one of the guys on tour who always attended the Sunday services several of the pros held themselves and open their own each week, since they'd be playing that day. I had joined them before the final round in Boise.

"Anyway, Jay was sympathetic when I had explained how my answers to the press were tainted or out of context, when they came back at me in print. But he was clearly bothered, like the rest of the seniors it seemed, that I kept answering *every* query thrown my way, and didn't seem to *think* before I spoke.

"I remember telling Struts I couldn't stand much more of this, that my relationship with God far outweighed my sudden stardom in pro golf. He could give me yardage down to the inch, and even club me if I ever asked him, which I seldom did. But Struts didn't quite know what to tell me regarding *this* situation outside my scorecard.

"By the turn the second day at Napa, I had upped my lead to six shots," Treb continued, glancing at his watch and obviously noting that he had been at it almost ten minutes. Undaunted, he ploughed on. "I was standing on ten tee, waiting for the group ahead of us that had slowed, waiting for the threesome ahead of *them*. All of a sudden, I saw Don Baker smiling and nodding near the ropes, maybe ten feet ahead of the tee markers. Don Baker! It suddenly struck me. Could this be *my* Don and Bake, in one guardian angel? I walked over to stand by him, while McKay looked kind of shocked and Paul Sheffield, who was in third place and having his best tournament in years, scowled.

"'Don,' I said, not asking him who he was or anything, 'This is no good.' 'What do you mean?' Don asked. 'This tournament. This new life. Just when I want to witness, to tell how much God means to me, to'—

"'To *brag*, Treb?' Baker responded, ever smiling. 'About being one of God's chosen?' 'You think that's it?' I asked. 'Doesn't matter, Treb. You've done a lot of good these last eleven days. Good you might not be aware of. Those who make fun or light of you and your relationship with God, they don't count. At least, not yet. Others you don't know about have caught on.'

"'But it's still no good, is it? I can't answer any more dumb questions about what they claim the Holy Spirit tells me to do, hit the nine wood instead of the six iron, or stuff like that.

"'Then walk away from all this, if you think you're going to do God a disservice. If you *think* you can live without your newly discovered limelight, that is.'

"Well, that sort of floored me," Treb told Brad and Mandy. "I relayed to Struts what Don Baker had told me, as we walked up the tenth fairway. Then, it hit me. I *knew* what I had to do. McKay had scolded me mildly about talking to a spectator at the ropes during competition, and Sheffield whined that he was going to the players' committee about me. So when I got to the green, I just picked up my little ol' Top Flight Women's 2000, numbered three. No spot. Just put it in my pocket.

"'Maple, you stupid ass, that'll cost you!' Sheffield growled. McKay asked me if I knew what I was doing. I told them yes, I'd had enough fun with pro golf to last me the rest of my life, and 'You guys play hard now. Hear? Good luck! Let's go home, Struts.'

"Sheffield's voice was pretty loud. 'Treb Maple, you'll never play *our* game! You know that!' I turned and smiled. 'I know, Paul. Now maybe *you* can win one.' I regretted that last remark. Or actually *kind* of, if you want to know the truth.

"Anyway, Struts and I head for the cart path and off the course, while the gallery buzzes with puzzlement. He pulls on my sleeve and points up in the crowd, to a smiling and nodding man in a red hat, yellow shirt and red and yellow pants. I take off my hat, walk over to him and give him my ball. 'Thanks for everything,' I told Don Baker. 'And I do mean *everything.*' 'Why Treb, it's been my pleasure.' '*All* these years?' I ask him. He just smiles. Real big. I turn to Struts who has heard the whole thing; we look at each other a second or two, and when we both turn back to Don Baker, he's gone. Simply not there anymore."

"Oooohhh Treb!' Mandy purred.

"What a story, pro!" Brad added, trying to mask his being skeptical. "Now, what do I do with it?"

"I'm sure you'll do whatever needs getting done," Maple replied.

"And you *are* going to be at the hold-em game tonight, right?" Brad asked.

Treb stood, smiled, and patted Mandy on her right hand. "I wouldn't miss it for the world, Brad."

"Just don't bring Don Baker with you," Brad said, half-laughing, conjuring up a mental image of a hold 'em foe's guardian angel smling and nodding as Treb made bets.

"Y'all have a nice dinner. Hear?" Treb said. Then he strode to the door. "Tell you what," he added, before exiting. "Let's plan on our little taping session up here early tomorrow evening, after I get finished out at the course. I think we've got a full day scheduled. I *know* we have one for tomorrow afternoon. OK? Good. Bye now." And he left.

"Get some good stuff from him, hon?" Brad asked, hoping Mandy had warmed up to him at least a little. She didn't show it though.

"He was nice. And I had fun," she said, then walked to her bedroom and shut the door.

"You want to grab a bite?" Brad said, standing outside her door.

"Go ahead. I'll do something. I might even call M.K., since you'll be out playing cards."

"I don't *have* to, you know," he said, not believing she would believe him.

"Keep your plans, Brad."

12. Hold 'Em Is No Game for Cowards, Dummies

Treb pulled his five-year-old Cadillac around Caesar's horseshoe drive and found a handicap spot. He got out and waved at the doorman who was eyeing him casually.

"Picking up a handicapped lady in a wheelchair," Maple hollered, and got a smile and a wave in return. He walked into the ornate, sprawling casino and knew exactly where to go. Sure enough, there was his wife, idly feeding only a quarter at a time into a red, white and blue slot machine designed to resemble July 4th fireworks amid flag bunting.

"Hey! How's my girl?" he greeted.

She turned responded with a lackadaisical "Hi." She cashed in and scooped out a small handful of quarters, reaching under the hopper and scraping around, making sure one of the coins hadn't got stuck.

"Sorry you didn't win," he said.

"No big deal." She backed up her motorized chair, turned it a hundred and eighty degrees on a dime and shifted to forward. "You out front?"

"Right. Need to use the restroom before we head home?"

"Nah. Just been."

He walked alongside her as they headed for the entrance. "I marvel at how well you do, Lou. I'm proud of you."

"I'll bet! If I didn't learn to do for myself, I'd either be down here drowning in my own pee or stuck in my bedroom back home, watching Bob Barker or *ER* and *Law and Order* reruns on TV, a prospect that chills my blood."

They went through the open door and got on the escalator-like moving sidewalk.

"All the same, I'm proud of you. Any time you want me to stay home with you, all you've got to do is ask. You know that. Right?"

"I know…I know, Treb," she sighed.

They got to the Cadillac and he unlocked the door, then stepped back when she waved off his proffered hand, as she always did. Once she had laboriously maneuvered herself into the front seat and buckled up, he pushed the wheelchair to the back of the vehicle and groaned as he hefted it to a carry-all that was hooked under the back bumper.

They drove home mostly in silence. "Home" was a well-kept, 1950s ranch-style triplex, half of which he paid for with his winnings at Boise. They lived comfortably in one of the two-bedroom apartments, complete with a small garden yard in back that included a hot tub and a barbecue grill.

Their one-bedroom unit housed Louise's sister, who usually taxied Louise around town when Treb gave lessons or played poker on those rare nights when she did get out. Billie was a permanent, and very welcome, non-paying guest. The other two-bedroom apartment was rented out, proceeds from which made regular payments and paid taxes on the whole complex. Treb had taken a balloon note on what hadn't been covered by his down payment. If his seniors' lessons kept up the pace of the past year, he'd have the note paid off soon.

His healthy poker winnings were deposited into a joint brokerage account with Morgan Stanley. Both drew Social Security and had Medicare, and Treb had supplemental policies for both him and his wife.

Their biggest overhead was Louise's daily gambling. Though she almost always played only for quarters at a time, figured annually her net losses amounted to more than a thousand dollars a month.

They went inside, where Treb's sister-in-law was putting the finishing touches on beef stroganoff with mashed potatoes, green beans and garden salad.

"Hi, Billie," Treb greeted. "Something smells *purty durn* good around here."

"Be ready in fifteen minutes."

"Excellent! I'll help Louise change into something else and we'll be with you."

"Want a drink?"

"Don't think so. It's my poker night, y'know."

"I'll damn well have one," Louise growled. "Jack Daniels Black Label with just a *little* Ozarka natural spring water."

"Comin' up," Billie said, as Treb followed his wife into her bedroom. Treb had taken over the guest room months before, but he did bunk with Louise from time to time, usually when she felt weak and needed help on nighttime bathroom usage, or when one of the kids and their families visited.

When he closed the door, he gazed at Louise sitting at her mirror, staring at herself. He started to say something, then noticed her crying.

"Hon, what's the matter?" he asked softly, looking over her shoulder at her image in the mirror.

"I...I'm tired, Treb."

"I can imagine."

"No. Not just for today. I'm simply *tired* of going on. Living like this is crappy."

He grabbed the armrests of her wheelchair and turned her to face him, then gently rested his forehead on hers.

"Hey, sweetheart. You've been doing *so* well. We haven't come up with *this* stuff in quite a while. Something happen today?"

She sighed, wiping tears with her arm. "It's just so...so endlessly *nothing!* I've turned into a real bitch. No, don't say it. I have and I know it and you know it and so do Billie and the guys and the only friends we have together, the Leventhals. And don't say I can change either! This is *me!* This is what I have become!"

He kneeled by her and looked into her still-beautiful eyes, and the face that still took his breath away. "Lou, I haven't done enough for you—"

"Oh, *please* don't go there! *Nobody* could ask for more than you give me. Sure, I still resent that it took my wreck to bring it out in you, and this...this religious fervor that was born in you simultaneously with my just about killing myself. Just when we end twenty years of fighting—a third of our life together—I'm stuck in a wheelchair! It's just not fair. You tiptoe around God in my presence, because you don't want to hear me badmouth him. I know!"

His wife had keen insight, Treb consistently reminded himself. She was disarming when it came his trying to faith-witness to his wife.

"What can I do for you? Right *now*?" he asked, leaning over and kissing her lightly, first on her wet cheeks and then her lips. "I'll call the Adobe and tell them I won't be in tonight."

"No," she sighed. "I don't *want* that. Besides," she added with a sardonic little laugh, "you never can tell when we'll need the money. You *always* bring some home. I rarely do. I'd like to quit slots. I'm so weary of those clanging reminders that I've got a serious addiction. But what would I do? I'm *afraid* to try to quit."

Her admitting her problem disarmed him. He reached for the phone next to her bed. "Let me have Streater. Yes, the poker pit boss," he asked.

"Hang up, Treb! I *mean* it!" Louise ordered, and he smiled while shaking his head. "Please!" she pleaded, and began to cry again. So he hung up.

"I just don't know what to do," he said. "I pray for you. Morning *and* night. But that's—"

"Treb, I'm going to be honest. I pray too. I *know* you find that difficult to believe. But I *do.*" She reached up and brought his lips to hers, kissing him almost passionately for the first time in at least five years. His tongue responded to hers once the shock subsided. "One of these days, God and I will have our own thing going, just like you and he have now. Living with you and seeing the day-night, black-white change Jesus has had with your life *can't* have not had an effect on me." She sighed, and backed her chair from the dressing table built for her handicapped height. "It'll just take time. OK? Promise me you'll be patient."

Treb kissed the top of her head. "You got me, babe, to paraphrase Sonny and Cher. *Ferever!* Just talk to me once in a while. Tell me what I need to know, or do. All right?"

She sighed and smiled, looking back at him. "You've never understood a woman's need, her *right,* to have a crying jag now and then. This one's over. Actually, it felt pretty good. I don't need to change clothes. Let's go eat."

BRAD ENTERED the card room at the Adobe Casino and strode to the table where he understood a weekly game that included Trebor Maple would be held.

"You still have me reserved for nine o'clock?" he asked Streater, the pit boss.

"Name?"

"Brad Poole."

"Oh yeah. Treb's friend. Here's the place, all right. Have a seat."

There were five or six openings on the nine-place oval table, not counting the actual dealer who was setting up at the near end. "Does Treb have a regular place?" Brad asked.

"Yep. Third player, or behind the big blind, to start," Streater said, observing the younger West Texan as he looked for the white porcelain disk called the button. He found it and counted three places to the left of where the game would begin, with an assumed dealer who actually would be a player. The official dealer was a casino employee. "You th' second guy who wanted to know where th' pro sits."

"Here, then," Brad mused, half to himself, before looking at Streater and asking, "Mind if I take fourth chair?"

"Be my guest."

Brad sat and continued, "Wonder who the other person was—"

He stopped in mid-sentence, when he looked across the table to where Baxter Randall was sitting, ruffling the several thousand in chips he had just bought. Randall smiled. "That's right. Me. I wanted to be where I could watch 'Pro,' as they call your precious Mr. Maple around here. And he could watch me. Want an up 'n' up game, ya' know."

Streater overheard, as Treb came through the double doors and headed for his usual chair. "Friend, we handle *all* the action here. You'll get a fair game, if that's what you're referring to. Calvin here will deal th' cards, and he's our best," the pit boss said, matter of factly.

Baxter watched Maple approach the table. "Meant nothing by it, friend," he purred.

"Good. I don't want to get th' feeling that there's gonna be even the *hint* of trouble at this table tonight. Elsewise I'll kick th' perpetrator, real or suspected, right *outta* here on his ass. Got me?"

"Loud and clear," Randall said, as Treb took his seat and noticed who would be sitting directly opposite him. He smiled.

"Why, Baxter Randall. Heard you were in town. What a coincidence to find you directly across from me at a poker table, with all there is to do in our fair city."

"Hi Treb. It's been a long, long time, hasn't it?"

"Well, let's see now. You referring to when we last sat at a poker table? Big night for me, I recall. Or when we last saw each other? Not that long, has it been? Believe it was eighteen green at Caldwell Golf and Racquet Club, not even two years ago. You were trying to qualify for the Boise senior tournament. Missed it by a shot, as I again recall. Too bad."

Baxter stared at his chips. "I missed qualifying because of what you might call a technicality. I got *needled* into missing, is how it was."

"What a shame," Treb said, momentarily hating himself for clucking his tongue to his cheek. "Well, gamesmanship does happen. You ought to know. A guy's gotta be prepared to overcome it, if he *feels* he's getting worked over. I still follow the seniors—*both* tours actually, not to mention the ladies; I love that Annika Sorenstam—I keep up through the Golf Channel and our fine local newspaper, the *Las Vegas Sun*. Don't recall seeing your name in the agate scoreboard listings for a long time. You still trying to qualify on Mondays?"

"Still trying, Treb. That's the one thing I *ain't*—a quitter!"

"Good for you, Bax!"

"We gonna play cards at this table or we gonna play fantasy golf?" Streater barked as the rest of the nine players—one of them a sixtyish woman—took their places, and Brad silently licked his chops in anticipation of a bonus to his pursuit of a feature story.

"HELLO, MANDY," Mary Katherine Arnaz said, speaking into her room phone at New York New York.

"Oh hi, M.K. How're you doing?"

"Fine. I was just wondering. What if I came over and took you out to eat?"

"Oh, I'm sorry. I ordered room service not twenty minutes ago. Wish I had known you weren't busy. I'm on my own tonight. Brad's down the street, playing poker with Treb."

"Is he *that* good?" M.K. wanted to know. "I mean, to play casino cards?"

"He's experienced," Mandy replied. "He's confident he can take care of himself. He hopes to work the game into his feature somehow."

"Well, I'm disappointed we're not getting together. It'd be just you and me. Oscar doesn't feel like getting out."

"Would you want to come over and visit? I'd go to your hotel, since the rental car is here. But I'm not that confident in this kind of traffic."

"Sure. I'd love to drop in on you. I haven't been to the Fifth Jack in a long time."

"Then come on over. I'll have eaten, and if you want, I'll order again and have something for you when you get here."

"No, no. Vegas does something to my clock. I'll snack on the way over, and probably eat a meal after midnight. One of the buffets, you know. Expect me in about thirty or thirty-five minutes. Your room number is...Um hum. Got it. I'll just come on up. See you then."

She hung up and headed for the bathroom, grabbing a pair of beige slacks and a cream-colored blouse. "You sure you don't want to go with me, hon?" M.K. asked her husband, who still showed that he was slightly younger than she, a furrowed brow notwithstanding.

"Huh? No, I'm not too keen on getting out. My, uh, business deal is still on hold. I better hang around here. Do me a favor, will you? Don't use the Navigator. Take a taxi." He didn't tell his wife, but he had paid to have the car watched around the clock, when it was parked in the garage.

After she had dressed, Mary Katherine Arnaz kissed her brooding mate goodbye and headed for the lobby. She didn't notice when a dark-complexioned man, about thirty, put down his newspaper and followed her out. She didn't see behind her when she left in her cab and a black Chrysler Imperial picked up the man and followed her cab down the strip, to the expressway and over to the Fifth Jack, downtown. She paid no notice to the man exiting the Chrysler just after she paid her cabbie, then going through the hotel entrance behind her.

Two hours later, following what M.K. felt had been the first positive visit in years that she had enjoyed with her daughter, she never noticed the same surreptitious companion and his ride, escorting her back to her hotel.

Mary Katherine couldn't help but continue to worry when she found Oscar as she had left him—lying on his bed, smoking little cigars and occasionally glancing at the cellular phone he kept beside his bed.

TWO HOURS into the game at Adobe, Brad guessed without committing the unpardonable bush league play of counting his chips that he was within maybe a hundred dollars of being even, one way or the other. Two of the original nine players had folded their tents and left, leaving behind probably five thousand, total. They had been replaced by two more men. So far, the big winner had been the lady. She was from New Jersey and obviously had been around hold 'em for quite some time. She was up by several thousand, and she could play.

Treb had been conservative. Brad wondered how someone could be so patient, escaping betting early on most of the hands except when sitting in one of the blinds, the coming-out positions. Still, the one hand in approximately fifteen he *did* play had put him a good five-hundred dollars in the black.

Brad had decided against going out of his way to go head-to-head with Treb, who was known by most of the players. That would come, sooner or later. It was more fun, watching Bax Randall attempt to maneuver into gaming position with Maple. Once, Treb had tried to buy a pot but got out before he lost too much. Randall had made a show of turning over his cards, displaying what three of five flop cards had indicated could be an ace-high heart flush, but ended up actually being a successful bluff. He had taken a big chance, and had won. In the two hours thus far, that hand had been his lone shining moment.

"The game remains Texas hold 'em, $10-$20 limits. Pro Maple is on the button. With $5 from our visitor from Salt Lake City, our small blind, the pot is right. Pocket cards comin' up men—and my lady—so pay attention," barked Calvin, the young casino dealer. Normally such a narrative wasn't given. It showed the time of evening and a little shake-up from the boredom of a pretty tame game thus far.

Treb peeked at his two down cards and as usual, his face was expressionless. He had a pair of kings—the spade and the diamond—to begin. His being on the button—or the dealer in theory only—all eight men would bet before him.

The obligatory five-buck chip from the small blind was followed by a ten from the big blind. Usually at this point, four or five players escape from potential trash cards down—no pairs, no Ace-King, Ace-Jack, King-Queen, no like-suited cards—but the Adobe dealer perked up when he saw no folds, up to Treb. With a ten-dollar raise from Ms. New Jersey at one of the middle positions, he called the twenty-five dollars and raised another ten. The small blind to his left relinquished his original five-dollar opening in lieu of facing thirty to stay, and tossed in his cards. Everyone else called Treb.

The first street, or the first of five up-cards that comprise the flop, was the two of clubs. Exposed flop cards are community cards that all players may use to put together with, if possible and usually hopefully, their pocket cards of hidden value. A groan or two went up from the players. The big blind bet ten dollars, and lost only one player around to Treb, who only called. Baxter looked up and smiled, Brad noticed. He knew that the easy-to-read Randall was figuring Treb had raised the raise earlier in order to chase potentially makeable hands.

Second street, the second of the flops, produced the nine of hearts. A shuffling of feet and nervous movement of hands indicated it would be decision-making time for some of the players. Two-fifths of the exposed cards showed to be about as poor as possible. It was time for someone with good cards—a high pair, or perhaps two clubs or hearts—to emerge, attempting to chase still more players who might be hoping to make a hand out of little or nothing, so long as it came cheap. Two checks, including Brad, were followed by Randall's ten-dollar bet, the maximum at this level, with no more folds. Although Treb knew his stock just got better, he only called the ten. One of the checks to his left called, the other folded. Despite only ten dollars due, Brad decided that trying to draw out to the ignorant end of a straight wasn't worth even that. He also folded.

Third street exposed the king of hearts. Betting interest increased, including a raise by the smiling Baxter Randall, followed by another by the player to Treb's right. Despite having a well-concealed three kings, with no ace on board and not much in the way of anyone near ready to put together a viable run at a straight or flush, Treb only called thirty dollars!

The limit at the fourth street would go up to twenty dollars. Out on the green felt came the three of diamonds. More groans, as interest among the kibitzers keened up. Ms. New Jersey made a face when the max twenty was passed to her, and she folded. Bax raised twenty. Treb quickly raised twenty more.

Brad looked at the flop cards and could see the possibility of a king-high straight open only inside, unless the players were foolish enough to try to for a straight at the ignorant end, if they had a four-five in the pocket. There was a slight gasp from the spectators when Bax raised twenty, chasing the last of the players except for Treb, who took no time in raising again.

The best pot of the night was flooded with red, white and blue chips, and a couple of blacks and a yellow that had come into the game to make change while multi-raises were being called.

The dealer burned a card, then flipped up the seven of spades. Brad was watching first one and then the other player, quickly scanning them from the corners of his eyes. While Treb showed no emotion, Brad noted the hint of a smile from Bax. Had the guy really been drawing to inside straight? Apparently not. He was wanting to go head to head with Treb, that was certain. And he had trapped himself into investing a lot to try and chase the rest of the players from a seemingly nothing hand.

"I bet twenty," Bax said, smiling.

"Call, and raise twenty," Treb responded, tossing two blue chips to the large pile.

"Raise the max," Bax countered, still smiling.

"Raise."

At this point, Brad felt he knew what was going down. Neither player could have a straight or flush. No pairs were exposed in the five-card flop, so a full house was out. Betting indicated that one, or both, had three of a kind. Brad had watched what pocket cards had been carelessly exposed, when the other players folded, and could recall seeing a two and a three, and—he thought—a nine. No kings or queens. But he had glimpsed less than half of the folded pockets.

Two kings down by either man was the nuts—a hand that could not be beat, using the king of hearts in the flop to make trips. Treb didn't figure for that, since he had checked early-on, when the obvious play would have been to try and chase as many into folding as he could. Two queens would be nice, but beatable. More so, in proportion, would be concealed pairs down the line from nine to three to two that might make three of a kind.

As the two men took time out from their raising so Bax could do a quick perfunctory study of his pocket, Brad mused on who actually had what. This was the trouble in a limit game with just two players left. It was difficult to chase somebody since he could always halt the wagering by just calling. At this stage, with an obvious nut-hand looming as a possibility, the one without it would be foolish to continue raising. Then Brad smiled. That had to be Bax, whose twin stacks of chips starting the hand had dwindled considerably. On the other hand, if Treb were trying to buy the hand, he had to believe that either Bax had the nut, or if not, he could call at any time and force Treb to show.

Brad felt himself smile. He *had* it figured. Bax had two queens in the pocket, and Brad two kings, despite his early conservative betting which, if so, would've fooled Bax into believing kings down was not in the cards for Maple.

"Mr. Randall?" the casino dealer asked.

"Twenty more," Bax hissed, no longer a hint of a smile on his face.

"And twenty," Treb calmly replied.

"CALL, *damn it*!" Bax came back loudly, ignoring the scowl from the pit boss. "I got trip queens!"

To his credit, Brad thought, Treb didn't milk the moment. He quickly turned over his two hidden kings.

"The pro wins, with three kings," Calvin the casino dealer exclaimed, not without some excitement.

"Too bad, Bax," Brad said. "Nice hand. Almost worked."

Treb was silent as he pulled probably four-thousand dollars in chips to his place at the table.

"No damn *shit*!" Bax mumbled. "I'm cashing in."

"Good move, unless you're prepared to buy in for more. No? Good evening sir," Streater chirped. "Come back to see us. Hear?"

Bax put maybe two hundred in whites, reds and a single blue in his coat pocket. He kept two other blues—forty dollars—in his right hand. He stared at the Calvin the casino dealer a few seconds, then wryly grinned as he put them in his pocket, too. "Little bit over-excited there at th' end of that last hand, friend," he said. "*That* cost you a tip of forty bucks." He stood and walked away.

"Have a nice evening. Sleep well," Calvin called out.

"Well played," Brad complemented the man to his right, the table's new leading winner. "You set it up nicely."

"Not really that much," Treb replied. "Just very poorly played by the loser."

A NEW appreciation of the man he had come to see in Las Vegas took hold of Brad. It was enhanced just before one a.m.

More than half of the original nine had left the table, including Ms. New Jersey who exited probably two thousand ahead, explaining, "I gotta get up early and play Desert Inn as Dolly's partner; wish I had you, Treb."

He thanked her, stifling a yawn. "You're a good player, m'am," he said, the true Texas gentleman. "Play well. Hear? Tell Dolly I said hi."

The flop came up nine of hearts, jack of diamonds and queen of spades. Betting had begun not overly enthusiastic after pocket cards were dealt. Treb checked, and Brad bet ten. Then came a call, a fold, then a raise and finally another raise by Treb, even though he had opened the round by checking!

The possibility of a straight, or on the outside two pair and at least one of those a face card, loomed. But Treb's well-deserved reputation had most of the players fearing the worst.

Since Bax had left, Brad had won two nice hands and was comfortably, though not wildly, ahead for the night. He decided to stay with Treb and see what lesson he might learn from this formidable foe. His outside down card was a king.

Fourth street was the four of hearts. Not good news if someone had been nursing a couple of same-suited cards in his pocket. It certainly didn't help Brad's hand, which still included a jack and stood as four to a straight, open on both ends. But he not only had to stay, not having a feel at all for Treb's holdings, he felt obligated to bet. Sure enough, he chased a couple more players. And another left after Treb raised him.

The fifth up card, or the River, did nothing for Brad. It was the seven of clubs. All he could do was call Treb's twenty, to keep him honest since no one else was in.

Treb had a jack and nine in the pocket, so he won with what turned out to be a mediocre two pair. But his check-raise, Brad surmised, had demoralized enough of the other eight players that they turned down chances at trips, a higher two pair or even a flush, early on.

"Want a drink? I'm buying," Treb asked Brad after they had cashed in.

"Sure. If you don't mind my asking, how'd you come out?"

"One of my better evenings in the past couple of months, actually," Maple replied as they sat at the bar.

"You could've fooled me."

"How's that?" Treb asked.

"You got a real, live-wire hang-dog look on your face, Treb."

Maple swished his club soda around the ice cubes in his glass a moment or two, then shrugged. "Two things. One, my wife was particularly down earlier this evening, and that always puts me in a blue funk. Two, I love competition at cards, and I think it keeps me on my toes, age-wise. Be assured, Mr. Poole, your day is coming. The golf swing begins to decelerate at an alarming rate when your clubhead speed goes the natural way, which is down the tubes. And your mind goes, sooner or later. You need to keep it active and alert as possible. Texas hold 'em is the supreme test of all games of poker. It could add a few years to the normal decline within the gray matter, *if* you can stay with it.

"However, what I experienced tonight was *not* fun. Nor was it healthy."

"You mean, waxing ol' Baxter Randall's twat? He had it coming!"

"Be that as it may, my young friend, I got no kick out of it. I showed myself to me to be cunning and calculating to a fault, and not a little insultingly condescending to a fellow human being, irregardless of how he might have treated *me* in the past. Or tonight, for that matter."

He heaved a sigh, then continued. "No one can be *like* Christ, but I have accepted the pledge within myself to be as *Christlike* as I can. Competing is fun. But it can be bitterly disappointing, when you win as I did tonight. Much more of what I felt shortly after the key hands this evening, and I'll just have to give it up."

"If you say so, but *I* say, *what a waste!*" Brad muttered.

"No, I'll give it up gladly. And never look back. Just like the tour." Treb signaled for the check. "OK, so you and I will sit down over hamburgers at Desert King tomorrow noon? Or more realistically, in about ten hours?" He looked at his watch. "Hey, I've got to get going!"

"I'll look forward to it, Treb" Brad answered, ignoring that Maple earlier had suggested a different time.

171

"Why don't you just let me start from the beginning with Buddy Holly and keep yapping until I get through? There actually won't be much, except what there is will be new stuff for your readers. OK? We'll still have time for any questions you might have."

"See you then, Treb. Tomorrow noon at the course. Right?"

"Um-hum. By the way, Brad. You're a good hold 'em player. But my advice while you're in Vegas would be to stay with the kind of game we had tonight. Don't let any of those Fifth Jack high-rollers sucker you in on a fifty or hundred-dollar game. I think I know your resources, and I figure you have no business slapping fifteen or so thousand on a table. Those sharks will just bet you into oblivion. Keep in mind, they often swim in pairs."

"Good advice, and I'll take it," Brad promised, a pledge he had no intention of keeping. Not with Tornado Thornton's seed money still in his grasp, while the casino manager was in Atlantic City.

Brad figured he'd make his play for a big payday the following night.

13. Buddy Holly and The Picks

"Want fries with your cheeseburger?" Treb Maple asked Brad Poole as they set up their lunchtime interview at the golf course grill.

"Fries for me," Brad answered.

"One with fries and onions, one with chips and no onions, Sondra, both with cheese. And two iced teas. Large," Treb told the waitress/cook.

Early on, Brad knew that he would have no trouble putting this little known but important part of early rock 'n' roll history into narrative. The hour went quickly. To help him remember names, dates and titles, Treb had brought along and often read from a small booklet titled, *Buddy Holly and the Picks—Rock 'n' Roll's Best-Kept Secret.* He and John Pickering had co-written the booklet in 1984, to include in LPs of the first of two compilations Pickering produced, reuniting Maple with the two brothers in overdubbing early Holly songs. Most had been old Decca throw-aways or later Crickets and Holly songs that had failed to gain a public following.

A couple were classics that John, who composed all the 1984 as well as subsequent arrangements, had insisted on including, against the wishes of Maple. One of those was *Peggy Sue,* and loyal Holly fans generally were critical of the venture. Another, *True Love Ways,* proved to be perhaps the best ballad the Picks ever did with Holly, 1950s *or* 1980s sessions. But the public never gained access when MCA pulled out of the venture. This left John fending for himself and releasing on his own the LP, tapes and a subsequent recording session, since Treb wanted no part of the financing. He had agreed only to splitting a fixed royalty percentage three ways, as they had always agreed to do, but had never had the chance.

Bill, the best voice of the three in the fifties, struggled with what a stroke-ravaged mind and coordination had left him. He died a year after the session. In a later return to Soundmasters Studio, Treb and John overdubbed background vocals as a baritone-first tenor duet, then John added his now-deceased brother's second tenor part in yet another overdubbing session.

"John paid for and got backing to produce the compilations," Treb said. "You can still buy some of them in record outlets in Europe and Japan. But mostly, John advertises, answers queries and sells from the internet—www.buddyhollyandthepicks.com—or just visits via e-mail at jpickering4@houston.rr.com"

The tape recorder picked up every word. And Brad just sat back, listening to Trebor Maple tell about his and co-Picks Bill and John Pickering's contribution to the Holly legend during the summer and fall of 1957.

As he listened, Brad wasted no time putting together in his mind the beginnings of a narrative that would become the heart of his planned feature article. Maybe even a book.

THE EARLY world of rock 'n' roll had been littered with hastily forgottens; those performers who had hit quickly, then took express trips to permanent obscurity. Nervous Norvous (*Transfusion*) comes to mind, as do Nino and the Ebb Tides (*Franny Franny*), Patience and Prudence (*Tonight You Belong to Me*), Rosie and the Originals (*Angel Baby*), John D. Loudermilk (*Language of Love*), and Paul and Paula (*Hey Paula*). Even Kenneth Copeland had enjoyed a stand-alone teeny-bopper hit in 1957 (*Pledge of Love*), but a huge following as a TV evangelist years later kept him far from becoming obscure.

Copeland had lived in Abilene as an adolescent, and Treb, a year older, had known him briefly during summers.

What these quickly-disappearing young recording artists had been blessed with were quick hits. What cursed their flamed-out careers was nothing worthwhile with which to follow.

Buddy was better off, but only temporarily. *That'll Be the Day,* written by him and Crickets drunmmer Jerry (J.I.) Allison, was strictly a Crickets hit. Two months later, on a companion label thanks to a bit of managerial chicanery by their manager-producer, Norman Petty, *Peggy Sue* introduced the world to Buddy Holly, a world that quickly figured out the same guy was featured vocalist on both records. The Crickets seemingly were a vocal group that sang and played with Buddy. However, with one exception involving Niki Sullivan, they were not singers.

Two big hits in a period of three or so months, and no place to go. Buddy, Allison, young 17-year-old standup bass player Joe B. Mauldin, and rhythm guitar Niki Sullivan were quickly on the road, doing one-nighters.

Petty and his wife, Vi, had all but abandoned their modest regional enterprise of playing for dances in Lubbock, Amarillo and elsewhere along the Texas-New Mexico border. They had a medium-sized truck that would be in the U-Haul and Ryder class today, since Vi—who gave up a promising career as a concert pianist to marry Norman—and her husband, who played organ by ear, often took their instruments to dance gigs. Norman almost always. The third member of the Norman Petty Trio, bassist Jack Vaughan, was a part of the early Petty Recording Studio crowd. A part of his name gained lasting fame when Norman called his record label that put out *Mood Indigo*, and later his publishing company that would become a multi-million dollar gold mine, Nor-Va-Jak, though in the early going it was handled by established music publisher Peer Southern, which wound up owning a piece of *That'll Be the Day*. "I guess Nor-Vi-Jak didn't do much for him," Treb said of Petty. "But then, Vi's full name was Violet Ann. So there. All of this, understand, is the third-hand memory stuff of an insignificant cog in the rapidly expanding Clovis operation.

"Anyway, they became too busy in the Clovis studio Norman had built, much of it by himself on property his father owned next to the elder Petty's auto repair garage, to keep the trio on the road. Also, they had just recorded an instrumental that Norman had composed. It showed promise. *Almost Paradise* would be picked up and covered by hot pop pianist Roger Williams. The Norman Petty Trio truck came in handy though, when Petty caught up with the Crickets at an Air Base in Oklahoma, where they were appearing at its Officers Club. He had scraped up several songs songwriting wannabes had offered to him, and found other obscure tunes, and the Crickets and Buddy recorded them. No vocals other than Buddy's lead. Only Sullivan of the four Crickets had done, and actually could do, passably, any singing. Petty had used his trio's truck to bring recording equipment to the Oklahoma session, on the fly.

"BACK IN Clovis, that large stucco two-story building next to the studio housed an apartment where Norman and Vi lived upstairs. Never far out of sight was Norma Jean Berry, who had grown up in Clovis with the Pettys. She'd slip in and out of the studio. I got the idea early on that Norma Jean was a glorified housekeeper. But she never did any housework that I could see. She was just sort of always there. But that was then, the summer of '57. Ellis Amburn's 1995 book, *Buddy Holly a Biography,* publicly exposed the trio as Norman being gay, Vi bisexual, and Norma Jean a lesbian.

"We heard whispered suspicions about this, when we worked extensively at the studio for three or four months," Treb told Brad as an aside to his and Pickering's booklet, while Brad hung on every word. "Not from Buddy and the guys, as I recall. Some people who came and went. Bill had his suspicions too.

"Norman never made a pass at any of us, and that would've included Bill, who was by far the best-looking of the three of us. But Bill had known Norman and Vi from when his and John's family lived and performed gospel on a radio show in Clovis, in the early forties. Norman was a very secretive guy. He would've checked any advances on Bill here, since Bill was a ladies man and possessed a big mouth.

Years later, when author Ellis Amburn wrote in his *Buddy Holly a Biography* that Cricket Niki Sullivan had confirmed that one night, during a busy recording session, Buddy told him Vi.had crooked her finger to him, taken him upstairs to her and Norman's apartment, and bedded him."

Treb told Brad that he had always wondered about a situation in which he had found himself, and he figured he knew to what session Sullivan was referring.

"It was the Sherry Davis session—*Broken Promises*—I'm sure. There was a lull. The business end of the studio was up front, and there was a little apartment in the rear. In the middle was a restroom and a kitchenette. I went back there to scavenge a snack. Vi was whacking away at something, a tomato I think, and I said, 'Well, it seems to be going well tonight, doesn't it?' Just making conversation.

"Vi continued attacking the vegetable with a knife, and I could tell she was in no mood for small talk. So I started to walk away."

"I'll tell you one thing for sure," she fairly hissed, stopping me, "Mr. Norman Petty better watch *his* step! I *promise* you that! All...*whack!*...all of this is getting *way* out of hand."

"I said something pithy, like "um," and left her to her tomato mutilating. Forty years later, when I read Amburn's book, I could just *see* Vi chasing down Holly and having her way with him. It was a lively session, and a dozen of us were coming and going to and from the studio, all the time."

Treb's candor sort of caught Brad Poole off guard here, but he liked it. More spice sent him to his notepad, to back up the tape that was humming along, out there in a cool snack bar located in the southern Nevada desert.

"What about those dressing room sex orgies Amburn wrote about, involving Little Richard and Buddy, among others?" Brad asked Treb.

"I have no idea. Niki Sullivan disputed the really weird version Little Richard told of, in *The Quasar of Rock*. I'd back Niki all the way. That other junk was real, *real* ugly. Not Buddy."

"THE ONE thing I remember best about Norman was, he was a neat and cleanliness freak," Treb said, coming back to Petty's sexuality. It was summer; air conditioning was not the best and we would get pretty ripe, especially on long sessions that might last ten hours with hardly a stop. Norman would be at the controls, suddenly disappear, then return fifteen minutes later clean and freshly clothed, and smelling almost perfumed. This happened maybe six or eight times a day.

"Vi was strange. Beautiful, but strange. I had a tiny crush on her, mainly from her sultry treatment on *Mood Indigo*. When we spent the night in Clovis doing our first background dubbed-in singing behind Buddy and the instrumental Crickets, John stayed at Bill's. The older Pickering brother was back in Clovis, working as DJ for radio station KICA. I recall sleeping in the little one-room apartment at the back of the studio, and waking up in the wee hours. Vi was outside my sliding glass door, flashlight in hand, burying something under a cedar tree. I went back to sleep and told John about it next day."

"I've seen it too," he said. "She's burying *cats!* And look closely. You'll see little crosses made of popcicle sticks all over the place. Every gravesite contains a deceased cat. No telling what feline diseases run rampant through the garage."

The echo chamber—that was the deserted large workroom of Norman's recently deceased father's garage next door—was full of cats. Vi would find a stray, throw it in with dozens of others, and keep them fed.

The Crickets had helped Norman install speakers at one end of the garage, and microphones at the other, to make the echo effect that was remarkable. Especially for a home-made fixture, Treb said. A young arranger in Los Angeles Phil Spector aspired to be a record producer. He once told an interviewer that his "Wall of Sound" was inspired by Norman Petty's Clovis sound. Particularly what the "Crickets" (actually the Picks, both as arrangers and vocalists) did on Holly songs such as *Oh Boy!*.

Anyway, here Buddy and Norman and the three Crickets stood. A monster first hit, but with no place to go. *Peggy Sue,* Buddy's debut as a solo artist, was still in the planning stages. What Norman had recorded in Oklahoma, by and large, literally screamed for some punch. Some pizazz. Norman had to know, as they treadded water in this initial stage, that none would do for a followup to either a Crickets or a Buddy Holly first hit. Buddy sure did. He later would convey to John that he had been very worried during playbacks in Oklahoma.

Bill Pickering, meanwhile, was behaving himself in Clovis. An alcoholic of the first magnitude most of his life, he was an excellent radio announcer and DJ when sober. But just a sip of gin would send him off like a rocket. Treb had discovered this earlier, one night in Lubbock.

Bill, 29, had enticed Treb, 22, into double-dating with him. Bill had a bevy of attractive but usually strange women on the string. He had picked a single mom, an Italian war bride deserted by her GI husband once they came to the states from his overseas duty. She couldn't get a babysitter though, so Bill left Bob at her tiny two-bedroom house, two small children not anywhere near ready for bed, and drove off with his date for unknown destinations.

"Wanna drink?" Bill had asked Treb, taking a pint of gin from the glove box before they got to the really sweet Italian lady's place. It took Treb by surprise, since John had warned of Bill's addiction to alcohol, now thankfully in remission from crazy-mean binges. Treb drank regularly, sometimes heavily though almost always controlled, but this time he declined, got out of Bill's car and spent most of the evening with his blind date.

Bill came back a while after midnight, three sheets to the wind. Treb drove him to Treb's apartment and muscled Bill inside. Bill proceeded to try to tear the place apart, acting like a wild animal suddenly caged. Treb called John to come quickly. John arrived, staring daggers through Treb. "I didn't know this was happening. Honest," Treb said, defending himself.

"Help me get him to Mother's house," John ordered. It was a job, but they managed. Mrs. Pickering lived near downtown, in an old part of Lubbock and not far from where Buddy's parents had their modest home.

Bill broke running as soon as the car door opened. Treb chased him down while John grabbed a rope from the trunk of the car. They wrestled Bill to the ground and tied him to a tree. He began howling like a wounded wolf, and lights quickly popped on around the neighborhood.

"Let's loosen the ropes and try to gag him," Treb suggested. Somehow, Bill got free and ran to John's car. He jumped in, found the key ready, started the car and drove down the street, going from one side to the other, switching sides each time he rammed into a curb.

"Go on. Kill yourself!" John shouted after the careening car. "I don't care anymore. I'm tired, Bill! Dead tired!"

Next day, Treb went to the Lubbock Police Station and bailed Bill out. He had been apprehended by a patrol car only a few blocks from where Bill and Treb sat on the ground, dismayed. Bill knew better than to ask his brother for help. A week later, Treb got a Sunday morning call at dawn. "Come get me!" Bill pleaded. Treb got the address of a ramshackle motel, and Bill was waiting at the screen door of one of the rooms, a horrified young woman behind him pleading, "Get him *out* of here. Please!" No telling what had gone on there. Bill obviously had been drunk out of his mind, but was slowly and somberly sobering up.

John finally convinced Bill that the Picks, who had just applied backup vocals to *Oh Boy!,* were on the cusp of something potentially big. So, Bill seemingly got his life back. He wanted a career in music too.

GOING BACK to March, 1957, Treb related to Brad via the booklet, Norman Petty had watched and listened as Bill Pickering, 29, his younger brother John, 23, and Treb, 22, did vocal background for Terry Noland— two sides during a Sunday afternoon session.

Petty's enterprise usually worked best at night, in the wee hours, when huge trucks or a train were less likely to rumble by and be picked up on tape in the not-completely-soundproof studio.

The session was long and tiring, but it turned out well. Bill and John would take the rough edges off the arrangement they crafted for background voices, then devise the baritone part for Treb. Bill, often fighting not to lose his patience with Maple, would hum his part over and over until Treb had it. Then they'd go for a take.

Treb's lack of expertise attempting to match the Pickerings and other musicians at the studio, often including Buddy and the Crickets doing *pro bono* work as instrumentalists for their manager, cast Maple in a condescended light. Though they would go out and have hamburgers together in early morning hours, after an all-night session, Treb never felt accepted by Buddy and the Crickets, or musicians such as outstanding bassist George Atwood, formerly on the road with young Mel Torme. Years later, however, Atwood would become a close friend of Treb's.

The Pickerings, as well as Norman and to a lesser degree Vi, realized the Picks were emerging with a unique, very easy to listen to pop sound. The blend to their voices complemented the Pickerings' excellent arrangements.

Norman approached the Picks through Bill to "do me a little favor" and spend a Saturday—July 12, 1957 to be exact—doing background vocals in a recording session, so Treb and John made the hundred-mile drive from Lubbock and found Bill waiting at the studio.

"We tried to back up a 14-year-old girl from Dallas," John recalled, in the booklet from which Treb read to Brad. "She sang well enough, but when she got to the same measure in the last song in her session, her A-side, each time she developed a mental block. We never were able to finish the session.

"After she left and the studio cleared of all the musicians, Norman asked for "one more little favor."

"Sure," Bill replied.

Petty set up a single microphone near the east wall of the studio and played *Oh Boy!* which Holly and the instrumental Crickets had recorded on the run. "Could you make that a Crickets sound?"

"No problem, Norman," Bill said.

"How much would you charge me?" Petty asked.

"Nothing," Bill replied, while John nodded with a smile and Trebor just stood there, dumbfounded. "Play it again, Norman."

"He ran the tape about ten times before Bill and I had the background arrangement worked out," John wrote in his and Treb's booklet. "Then, for about five run-throughs, Bill sang Treb's part with him. Treb's voice was more in Buddy's range, so usually he was covering Buddy. That helped Treb. Next, we rehearsed the tape about five times more, with Bill wearing headphones. Treb and I felt more comfortable singing along with the small speakers in the studio, turned down low enough to prevent any feedback.

"Bill was always clowning around. He put in that high-pitched rebel yell on the bridge during one run-through. We thought Norman would let it pass as just another bit of horsing around by Bill, but he smiled and told us to leave it in. So we did."

And so came about the signature part of the upbeat song that would serve as Holly's bridge between obscurity and certain stardom. And eventually, rock 'n' roll hall of fame status. Buddy and the Crickets, of course, and deservedly so. But not the Picks. Treb, John and Bill's lone claim to recognized achievement was being named to the little-known Rockabilly Hall of Fame in the 1990s.

At any rate, *Oh Boy!* took off when released in October. It anchored *The Chirping Crickets* album that emerged then too, with the Picks backgrounding on nine of the 12 songs. Included were the ultimately charted singles *Maybe Baby* and *Tell Me How*. Treb told Brad that his favorite among the throw-away songs was *An Empty Coke and a Broken Date*, a real teeny-bop weeper. "For the first time, I could hear myself apart from John and Bill, doubling Buddy." The song was written by Roy Orbison.

ON A hot day in August, 1957, in the tiny six-by-eight foot control room at Norman's studio, a group of very interested people prepared to listen to a playback of the final tape version of *Oh Boy!,* which Buddy and the band hadn't heard yet.

Besides Norman at the controls were Buddy, the three Crickets and the three Picks.

The Crickets were dressed almost identically, in faded blue jeans and white T shirts, and wearing penny loafers. Buddy was wearing the same attire, except for natural-leather Indian moccasins on his feet. Chances were, he had made them himself.

The sudden stars seemed unaffected by their rise to fame. Allison was a bashful sort, according to Pickering's assessment. Joe B. was "a great joker, the youngest and shortest who was still very much a teenager. Niki was outgoing and friendly, the same as now."

By this time, the Picks had become Norman's in-house backups for all sessions. Petty was enjoying a bountiful summer. Money from the Crickets' enterprises was beginning to roll in, and only he had the key to *that* bank. Mitch Miller, the A&R genius at Columbia Records, had taken note and verbally contracted to try the Picks as a new pop recording act. Miller was said to loathe rock 'n' roll and was fighting an uphill battle to keep it off the Columbia label. Also, he had made a deal with Petty to produce a "south of the border" instrumental album that would include Norman on organ, Vi on piano and George Atwood on bass. Roy Orbison, tiring of Sun Records' facilities, was beginning to experiment with the Clovis sound.

Sherry Davis, a fantastic talent with the Big D Jamboree in Dallas, had been brought to Norman's studio to record a 45 that would include two ballads—*Humble Heart* and, on the A-side, *Broken Promises.*

Sherry was pretty, and had a well-schooled alto voice. Again, Treb developed a temporary crush. The Crickets supplied the instruments, including a fantastic lead guitar by Buddy on his Fender Stratocaster. The two songs were perfect, but her little-known label, Fashion Records, was not. At least, not for a venture so promising as this. *Broken Promises* never made it past regional hit status. The Picks' best vocal arrangement ever for a live session was an integral part of the well-produced record. Petty had increased their input until the trio actually sounded like a quartet, with Sherry singing lead.

THE SUPER summer heightened in excitement when the Picks, Buddy and the Crickets crowded in to hear Norman debut *Oh Boy!*

Buddy listened intently until the all the "dum-de-dum-dum—oh boys" had faded. Then he beamed.

"You guys *did* it!" he exclaimed, going to each of the Picks and shaking his hand—the only time all summer, in hours and hours of recording and rehearsal time, he had given even the slightest notice that Treb existed. To Buddy, Maple had been the bumbling, stumbling and often off-key foulup of the several sessions they had worked together. Now, Holly—who had liked John and idolized Bill, from their days as members of the same Baptist church in Lubbock—was ecstatic and animated.

"You guys were great. Really *great!* When we first recorded it, I didn't know," Holly said. "Now I do. We got ourselves *another* hit!" Later in the year, he would confide to an interviewer that he liked *Oh Boy!* more than his signature song, *That'll Be the Day.*

"That's as good as anything Pat Boone ever did," John Pickering offered, after *Oh Boy!* had been played again.

"Pat BOONE!?" Buddy shot back. "Man, Pat Boone ought to be standing in the background, doing doo-wahs!"

John pretended to take offense. "Thanks a LOT, Buddy."

The rest of the room erupted into laughter. All except Holly. He was concerned that his remark, intended to put down Boone, had been misinterpreted by the Picks.

"Hey man," he said, "I didn't mean it that way. I meant Boone ought to be backing up *all* of us here."

"I knew what he meant," John said. "I was just needling him a little. Besides, I *liked* Pat Boone. A lot."

From that time on, around the studio the Picks were dubbed The Doo-Wah Boys.

Soon after *Oh Boy!* was released, Buddy and the Crickets were booked on *The Ed Sullivan Show,* or *Toast of the Town* as it was officially called. Whereas their first appearance with *That'll Be the Day* featured Buddy's stand-alone strength, even though the record had the Tolletts on background vocal, Norman had produced *Oh Boy!* in such a manner that the backups were more integral to its success. Buddy, in particular, worried that he'd be 'stuck up there on stage naked,' as he later put it to John. So, it was decided to take the Picks to New York. The Crickets were not excited about sharing camera time with three guys who suddenly sounded just like the Crickets did, on the record. So Norman decided the Picks would sing off camera.

Curiously, American audiences who saw Buddy and the Crickets never seemed to mind that half the songs they sang didn't sound like the record; i.e. didn't have vocal background. It wouldn't be until their tour of England that fans began wondering—then demanding—to know what was going on here. They found out, thanks to John Beecher. So to this day, the Picks are virtually unknown in America, in reference to Holly. But England's more loyal fans are quite familiar with them.

Anyway, Petty told the Picks to pack, that he had their tickets. He had worked a deal, he said, where Sullivan wouldn't be out any more money, that the Picks off-camera came as a package deal with the Crickets. They would take off from Amarillo Friday before air date. John, Bill and Treb were more than willing to work for no pay, so long as their airline ticket to the Big Apple was paid.

Then, disappointment riddled the Picks' euphoria. They came to the studio a week or so prior to "the big shew," and Norman had a telegram from Sullivan to show them. "Don't bring the other boys unless they belong to the union," Sullivan said.

"We're making money, but we can't afford that. Not yet," penny-pinching Petty told the Picks with a frown. It would cost about five-hundred dollars apiece, he claimed. None of the Picks could afford it either. Buddy was disappointed as much as they, Treb told Brad.

A WEEK after *Oh Boy!* had been recorded earlier in the year, the Picks were to get their big break. Payback for all the work they had done for Petty in general, and Holly in particular, without receiving a single dime. In fact, the only time after dozens of sessions that they *did* get paid, it was for the first—Terry Noland's two songs. However, Terry Noland—or actually

Terry Church—was *really* slow-pay. Each of the Picks was to get thirty dollars. Bill finally collected for all three, late in the summer or perhaps the next fall or winter. Maple never got his thirty bucks. The last time he tried was in 1960, with a call to Bill to see if he'd send a check.

"Oh sure. You bet." But Bill died before he could carry out his promise. Twenty-four years later, he took Treb's thirty bucks to his grave.

Anyway, the Picks would record two songs which would be their debut on Columbia. Norman had just composed an instrumental, a *Bolero*-beat piece called *Moondreams.* He hadn't even written the lyrics yet. "I've got them in my head," he explained. The B-side would be a rather upbeat ballad by Niki Sullivan called *Look to the Future,* which they sang in unison.

This was a major crossroads for the trio. John was graduating from Tech in August with a degree in petroleum geology. He had a job offer from Humble Exploration, the same company that later would be Enco and then Exxon. He was marrying Vicky Billington in a few days and had to reach a decision about either music, or sniffing out well locations in the oil patch. Treb was flunking out at Tech and the Army was waiting to snatch him up for two years. A retreat to the Army Reserves and a six-month active duty obligation looked to be his best bet as a bail-out.

However, Bill would make all decisions moot points.

JOHN AND Treb finished work at the bank and headed to Clovis in John's car. They were in great spirits. Until, that is, they tuned in to KICA along about Farwell, Texas, to listen to Bill's DJ show from Clovis.

"Sounds good, doesn't he?" John said.

"Um-hum," Treb casually agreed.

A Percy Faith instrumental ended, and Bill came on with his usual slick chatter and banter.

Suddenly, the interior of John's car seemed icy cold. Neither man said anything until Treb half-whispered, half-whined, "John, did...did Bill just say, on the *air,* 'And that was Pussy Face with *Swedish Rhapsody?*'"

"Treb, it sure *sounded* like that to me."

They picked Bill up at the radio station, drunk as a skunk all right. There was nothing to do but head for the studio and hope for the best. Treb recalled—though Pickering disagrees—that this was the night Buddy was finishing *Peggy Sue* and *Everyday.* At any rate, John had Bill in the little bedroom at the back of the studio. Treb watched Norman and Buddy put the finishing touches on the classic recordings. *Everyday* was last. Rock 'n' roll history insists that Vi Petty played the celesta on the bridge, but Treb was sure he watched Norman overdub the little music box which he had built himself.

He would start the tape, then run though the little entrance alcove and into the studio to the east wall, behind the organ, to bang out the celesta's keys.

"John could be right," Treb told Brad. "I was in a daze, worrying about what was happening with Bill in the back. Maybe this was another night. But I sure remember watching Norman play the celesta."

Norman finished, took a short break, discovered Bill's condition and told John and Treb that their session would be postponed. So they took Bill home, got him to bed, and began the long drive back to Lubbock, all of a sudden wondering what was happening with their aspirations to become the next Four Aces, Ames Brothers or Four Lads.

About the time they were reaching Muleshoe, just short of midway to Lubbock, Bill had snuck back into the studio and was tearing up the place. Bassist George Atwood, at six-four and 350 pounds, was a mountain of a man. When Bill began chasing Vi all over the studio while laughing lasciviously, Atwood had picked up Bill in a bear hug, carried him outside and dumped him at the curb. Everybody went back inside and the studio's doors were locked. A truck driver came by and carted Bill to his apartment.

Norman called Treb and John to the studio the following weekend and gave them the word. "I'll take *you* and I'll take *you* and try to do something, but Bill is out! *Period!*" he told the two, pointing with emphasis at each.

That clinched decision time for John. He told Humble he would come on board. Treb had already decided to join the Army Reserves, going in as a Specialist Fourth Class, since he had two years of Air Force ROTC at Tech. As a footnote to that experience, Maple ultimately would be honorably discharged from six months active duty and five and a half years in the reserves as a Private First Class.

In other words, he managed to go *down* one rank in *six* years.

A contrite Bill Pickering was best man at John's wedding. Treb served as an usher. John serenaded Vicky after they exchanged vows and just before they exited during their processional. John had borrowed money from his grandmother to get married and finance the trip to Corpus Christi, Texas, where he would join Humble.

NORMAN, EVER the money man, contacted Treb while John and Vicky were on their abbreviated honeymoon. Mitch Miller had been interested in signing the Picks, but when told that Bill had this problem, he said Columbia would release only one 45 and see how it went. Petty, acting as the Picks' manager, agreed and offered to supply the trio as backup for a rockabilly singer from Portales, New Mexico. Rick Tucker would become Miller's first foray into R&R, sight and obviously sound unseen and unheard. The Picks would get label credit, much like the Four Lads had when they backed Johnny Ray on Columbia's 1951 blockbuster, *Cry.*

John now was some 650 miles from Clovis. Treb knew a tenor at Tech, and recruited Ross Cass to sing John's parts, for free. Again, Bill did all the arranging for background voices.

Tucker had two songs to record, *Don't Do Me This Way* and the infamous *Patty Baby.* Buddy and the Crickets were back in town, so Norman pressed them into unpaid service as musicians. Vi, these days in a really nasty mood when she was around her husband in the studio, played a mean piano. The studio was full.

It got even fuller when they recorded *Patty Baby.* During taping of the first song, Roy Orbison had tooled his white Cadillac or Imperial or something fan-tailed into the studio's parking lot. He had just married Claudette, a 17-year-old girl a week before. She sat in Norman's control booth.

"I was standing at one mike with Bill and Ross," Treb recalled. "Not three feet from me was Buddy, who sat with his stratocaster on which he was playing lead guitar. Out of the corner of my eye I saw Buddy idly strum, glance up through the glass twenty feet away at Orbison, then look down again and strum. Roy occasionally would peer into the studio and set his eyes on Buddy, then quickly look away."

Roy, from Wink and Odessa in West Texas, became a regional hit before Buddy. Now Buddy was tall hog at the performing trough in those dozen or so counties, with *That'll Be the Day,* an even bigger hit than anything by Orbison up to then. Treb got excited. "I sensed a turf war was about to erupt, as if a young Hereford bull had been dropped off to service a herd 'owned' by an Angus bull. I had witnessed such a battle as a kid. Didn't matter if the Angus didn't have horns like the Hereford. This was *his* turf, to be defended till the bitter end."

Pretty soon, there went Roy out to his car, Treb said. He returned with his guitar case. "He comes into the main studio, smiles and chats in whispers to Buddy, then pulls up a chair and sits facing Buddy. Two future rock 'n' roll legends, knee to knee, then shared lead guitar in a performance that had to be seen and heard to be believed. Awesome."

"Tucker tried to get their autographs afterwards but Norman told him no. Nothing must *ever* be said about Sun's superstar and Brunswick's big gun serving as studio musicians on a Columbia record. Still, Tucker, who was supposed to be the man of this particular hour, remained starstruck for the rest of the session."

NORMAN'S FORGIVENESS of Bill included scheduling another taping of *Moondreams* and *Look to the Future,* since Columbia Records' Mitch Miller had OK'd a trial balloon for these voices he seemed to like, very much. At least together.

John left Corpus Christi after work on a Friday in early October. He drove straight through, left Vicky at her parents' house, and met Treb and Bill at the studio late the following Saturday afternoon. Norman had pre-recorded either George Atwood or Jack Vaughan on bass, Vi on piano and himself on a very intrusive organ. He sat at his console in the control room and for the first time, whacked out lyrics to Moondreams on his typewriter. This took maybe fifteen minutes.

By now, the trio was proficient at overdubbing. They whipped through Sullivan's *Look to the Future,* then took less than two hours to do the A-side, Norman's *Moondreams.* Norman gave each Pick a check "for expenses"—about $45 to Bill and Treb, and $60 to John—to cover their previous trip to Clovis to record *Oh Boy!.* It was the only money that would ever pass from Petty to the Picks. Ever.

Cashbox Magazine gave the record a lukewarm "B" reception. However, *Moondreams* did receive a good bit of air play nationwide. Of course, no connection to Buddy Holly could ever be allowed. That certainly hurt any public relations potential.

But the killer blow was the bad-boy Pick. An uncle of the elder Pickering brother once dubbed him as "Wild Bill from Vinegar Hill, never worked and never will." About a month after the release of *Moondreams,* Wild Bill started swishing down a half-pint of gin. He called information in New York City, got the number of Columbia Records, told the switchboard he was a member of one of Mitch Miller's recording acts, and somehow got put through to Miller's office. Bill proceeded to read him the riot act, ordering him to "get out there and push our record, like you're supposed to do!"

Miller called Petty and reported the intrusion, and said he was pulling the plug on the Picks and their record. And he did. It wasn't going to make it, anyway, he said. *Adios,* Columbia deal. One of those came along for maybe one in every one million singing acts.

In a few weeks, after watching the mail each day—according to George Atwood, who knew a Columbia secretary—and asking "anything from Clovis?", Mitch Miller also jettisoned his deal for an album by the Norman Petty Trio.

Norman could not have cared less. He had found his life's work, and as talented as he was, it would not be as a performer. He had Buddy and the Crickets under management, and their handshake contract had been turned into something more legally substantial. Basically, they were equal partners in Crickets stuff, recording and performances. Later, when Buddy's parallel solo career developed, the two of them shared fifty-fifty. And Norman retained control of *all* money coming in.

Also, hopeful rock 'n' rollers from Dallas to Albuquerque were flocking to Clovis, begging for a break. Ten percent? Twenty? Nah, Treb said. *Fifty* percent if you wanted Norman's help.

Treb said the Picks never had a written agreement with Petty, which used to puzzle Maple, given Petty's perfectionist attitude. Then he put two and two together and figured *he* had Norman figured out.

"After we finished recording *Moondreams*, we sat around Norman's control room for a while. Pretty soon he said, 'OK, let's talk money. I'll offer you guys the same deal I have with the boys.' He meant Buddy and the Crickets of ocurse. 'We split *everything* fifty-fifty.' I spoke up quickly and asked, 'You mean, we each get twenty-five percent?' Norman looked at me in a cold, calculating manner and replied, 'No. Fifty-fifty. I get fifty percent and you three split the other fifty percent. I'll leave you guys alone now, and close the door. Talk it over, and if we've got a deal, I'll fly to New York with the tapes next Monday.'

"Well, Bill said something like, 'Gee, I dunno. That seems awfully steep for us to hand over to Norman.' John was stunned. We knew Norman was lying, that he and Buddy and the three Crickets were equal partners. They had told us so. Then ol' Treb, the genius businessman, said, 'Hey, guys. *Sure* we say OK. We're not signing anything, are we? I don't really think *Moondreams* is gonna do anything real great. But I think Mitch Miller likes us. Let's get this record out, then let's *dump* Norman. We can always say we were just obligated to this first record. After that, if he wanted to manage and produce us, fine. He'd get the usual ten percent, and maybe five more for bookings.' So we agreed, and waved Norman back in.

"Later that evening, when Bill and I were driving back to Lubbock in my '53 Chevy coupe, a bolt out of the blue just about fried my brain. 'Hey Bill, what if Norman left a mike open in the control booth, and was out there in the studio, listening to us. To me, in particular. Or even, what if he had his tape recorder running?' Bill just shook his head and said, 'Y'know, I wouldn't put it past him.'

"To this day," Treb told Brad, "I believe that's what happened. Norman wasn't *that* trusting; to let us get by with just a verbal handshake.

SONNY WEST was a promising 19-year-old singer-songwriter from the Texas Panhandle. He had brought Norman *Oh Boy!* and Petty had put it into his Nor Va Jak stable, through Southern Publishing. Sonny, who had written the song, wanted it to be *his* breakout record as a performer. Norman told

187

him OK. Another new Petty wrinkle the summer of '57 was to insist on listing himself as co-songwriter, "if I have anything at all to do with producing the music," which could *always* be anything at all for someone at the controls, such as lowering the key for *That'll Be the Day.* So, Norman would participate as song publisher, then enjoy a double-dip at the money well as co-writer. Young, usually poor people could not look past next week, when it came to career moves. But Norman had to know that, from royalties via radio and other performers' play as well as record royalties, he was in charge of a future gold mine.

"I was dumb, dumb, dumb, just a kid," Sonny West told Treb late in both their lives. He had a friend who also wanted to be a songwriter. Bill Tilghman was unpublished, so when Petty picked up *Oh Boy!,* West said Tilghman begged him to let him be listed as co-writer, to allow him access to established songwriter status. Tilghman promised that he'd return the favor, that they would become a songwriting duo. Later, they would actually co-write another big Holly hit, *Rave On.*

So here was West, learning the ropes in which many others would become entangled in Clovis. He thought *Oh Boy!* was to be his performance vehicle, and was never told by Petty—also *his* manager—that Buddy and the Crickets (using the Picks' voices) were premiering the now-classic R&R song. Not until it had been recorded and released. West had given up half his songwriting credit to help a friend. And both of them were cut to a third when Petty insisted on adding his name to theirs.

"He never did a thing, not *one* thing, that could be construed as helping write the song," West said, although he added that he "was just blown away" when he heard Buddy and the Picks sing his first effort, and the Crickets play it. "It was great. It's just that I would've liked to have had a chance to do my *own* song, first."

West managed to get a contract as a singer with Atlantic Records, Treb said, but it never amounted to anything. "I even lost some jobs because I was under that contract," Treb said West told him. "I still remember the part at the end, which read something like, *all monies which will be due to Mr. West will be paid directly to Norman Petty, in which case Mr. West will have been considered paid in full.* Yep. I was dumb, dumb, *dumb!*"

The difference in songwriting royalties over the years for West had to be losing tens of thousands of dollars. "But I made up some of that with Tilghman and *Rave On,*" West added. "For a while there, until the Buddy Holly movie came out, I was making more on it than I was *Oh Boy!*

WERE PETTY alive today, he might argue that his part in writing *Oh Boy!* was in the production and, in particular, the background arrangement.

Before his death, and after the horrible film *The Buddy Holly Story* sent fans of Buddy's from all over the world scurrying to Lubbock and Clovis to pay homage, Petty used to enjoy conducting tours of the old studio, now closed since he had moved his record-producing facility to a movie theatre he converted into a studio in the 1960s.

During these tours, a highlight would be Petty explaining how he could take a seemingly listless song and turn it in to gold, via overdubbing. He used *Oh Boy!* as his prime example, ignoring the truth, that Bill and John were the *only* ones ever to arrange Picks vocals. Petty's role was to just say either yes or no to each of the Pickerings' innovative elements. And, in truth, one could argue that perhaps *this* constituted some sort of artistic involvement. After Petty died in 1984, Vi Petty would conduct the same type of studio tour, extolling the genius of her late husband in a like manner. If the Picks—probably closer to anyone other than Phil Spector himself in the evolution of the "Wall of Sound," even though by accident—were ever mentioned in these before she died, it was as an aside. A small footnote.

In a way, Norman Petty *was* a genius, Treb told Brad. His home-made studio, a perfectionist's way with recording talent, how he could get the most out of seemingly the very least, and above all, how he had an ear for talent, were genius-like features.

But the darker sides to his personality began turning the Camelot in Clovis into failure, shortly after that storied summer of 1957. Buddy got married to Maria Elena, against the wishes of Norman, who had assumed near-parental attitudes with the Crickets. He had an even tighter hold on their money, Bill was told, when Bill again began working around the studio—thrice forgiven by Petty. Norman either caught Buddy and the Crickets jumping up and down on a hotel bed, tossing currency bills including hundreds around like play money, shortly after their victorious appearance at the Apollo Theatre, or he heard about it. Over and over, he used this bit of horseplay as a reason for forbidding the Crickets access to more than a token of their money at a time.

This caused Niki Sullivan to leave the group, when his father accompanied him to Clovis for an accounting that they were unable to get.

After Buddy's marriage, he and the Crickets began drifting apart. Allison and Mauldin tried different sidemen, and returned to Clovis to record on their own. Meanwhile, Buddy was in the process of severing ties with Norman and was recording in New York. His actions, it was reported, led Petty to angrily tell one of the Crickets, "Let him try! I'll starve him out!"

Buddy was threatening legal action to get to what he claimed was considerable money owed him. After Buddy's death Feb. 3, 1959, L.O. Holley, Buddy's father, was trying to manage up and coming acts from around Lubbock. The different spelling of the family name was due to Buddy's contract with Coral inadvertently dropping the second "e", and Buddy simply going along with the change.

Other legal action was aimed at Petty. Charlie Phillips had recorded his song *Sugartime* in Clovis, with a studio musician named Buddy Holly filling in on guitar and good ol' Billy Wayne Pickering on background vocals. The song was covered by the McGuire Sisters, one of pop music's big acts of the day, and that one became a huge hit. The opening two bars of the song, however, sounded exactly like an old gospel song that went, *Tell 'em on the highways, tell 'em on the byways, tell 'em that I'll be there.* That song, however, was not in the public domain. Norman, as publisher and, ironically, as pseudo co-writer, faced answering a plagiarism suit. Before his death, Bill recalled Petty phoning him and pumping him to remember some incident in Nor Va Jak Studios during the recording of Phillips' version that would prove the music actually was composed in Clovis, regardless of the "coincidental" duplication of portions of the old gospel song. "He kept on and on, telling me I had to get ready to testify in his behalf," Bill told Treb in 1984. "I said I'd try, if he needed me to. But I think they settled the thing out of court."

Despite the continuing feud with Petty, particularly involving Maria Elena Holly, Mr. Holley was using Norman's facilities. And one of his clients who never quite made it—again—was none other than Bill Pickering. "He even enjoyed thinking of himself as a crackerjack songwriter, though he seldom got past titles," Treb recalled. "An example was one he wanted to call *Shake Hands With My Heart.* But could that cat vocalize! Especially in the upper register."

At the request of Buddy's Lubbock family, Bill would sing two Baptist hymns during Buddy's funeral."

Both Pickerings got to know Maria Elena fairly well, particularly John. Treb said he didn't meet Buddy's widow until they had lunch together in mid-1999. "We told each other stories about Norman Petty," Treb said. "She loved it."

Before the fatal plane crash, Buddy was using other musicians, this time experienced studio professionals in New York. His traveling musicans were billed as the Crickets too. And they usually could sing. He had taken young Waylon Jennings, a Plainview, Texas DJ and a good friend of Bill Pickering's, under his wing. Waylon played bass and sang backup, taking Treb's part on the Cricket songs the Picks had done. It is said that Buddy was on the low-paying Winter Dance Party tour because he was broke, with tens of thousands of dollars belonging to him lying unattainable in a Clovis bank.

Buddy had decided that he wanted to produce music, and was intending to build a state of the art studio in his hometown of Lubbock. George Atwood, the bass player, was in possession of preliminary blueprints of the venture when Buddy's plane crashed outside Clear Lake, Iowa. Atwood was going to be a part of the studio's administrative as well as artistic teams. Waylon was going to be handled personally by Holly.

"When was the last time you saw Buddy? Visited with him?" Brad Poole asked Treb.

"I had been to Clovis for something. I think I had taken my current girlfriend at Tech, a really sweet sophomore named Judy Schreider, over there to show her the studio and listen to tapes. Norman asked me if I would drop by Buddy's parents and leave off a dub, a preliminary cut of a recording, for Holly.

"This was when he and the guys—at least, Jerry Allison and Joe B. Mauldin—had returned from a big tour. They had stopped off in Dallas, and bought motorcycles, then drove them to Lubbock to be received, for the first time with anything approaching the fame they were getting most everywhere else."

"Buddy's in his room. Go on back," Treb said Mrs. Holley told him. "I walked in and there was Buddy, acting like Marlon Brando from *The Wild One*. He had black motorcycle boots on, over tailored Levis. He wore a black leather jacket over a white T-shirt. Buddy was slowly combing his coal-black hair. He wasn't wearing his horned-rim glasses at the moment. He looked at me in his mirror and nodded.

"'I've got a dub Norman wanted you to hear,' I said. 'Um…thanks,' he replied. 'So, things are really hopping, what?' I observed, searching for a little conversation. Maybe even a smile.

"I got neither. Buddy nodded, still looking at me in his mirror. 'Well, see you around, Buddy,' I said. He nodded, and I left, clearly having been put in my place by a superstar. If I ever meet my ol' rock 'n' roll pal at the River Jordan, I'll ask him if he remembers the day when a kind five or seven words and a two-second smile to somebody who had done right by him would've been too much to ask.

"In all fairness," Treb added, "Buddy probably heard about my assessment of the popular music scene, *circa* 1957. I had told somebody at the studio, about the time *That'll Be the Day* first charted in the Top 20, that 'when Elvis goes to the Army, he's through. So will be rock 'n' roll. And Buddy Holly will be just another one-hit wonder.'

"I'm pretty sure Norman Petty heard me. The tattle-tale!"

"I CALLED Norman in 1958, during leave from my short stint with the reserves," Treb told Brad. "I asked him if he owed me any money from *Moondreams,* and he said no."

Petty told him that "Columbia sold around 35,000 copies, but after studio and musicians fees, your and John's and Bill's royalties didn't have anything left. In fact, they came up a little short. I can send you a statement, if you'd like. I'm in the middle of a session right now, though, recording the Fireballs." That New Mexico group would become Petty's last claim to production and managerial fame.

Treb told Petty no, don't send any statement, that this "pretty well closes the books on him and me. I wished him good luck, and I seem to remember he wished me the same, although I couldn't swear to that. The books we were closing included at least twenty round trips between Lubbock and Clovis, in my car alone; vocal background singing on more than fifty songs, all but a couple on Petty's request; no pay for any of them, although Petty received money covering 'studio and musicians fees' in our names. In return for our work and time and—at least in the case of the Pickerings—considerable talent, we were to get a recording contract of our own.

"Again, in Norman's patented way of dealing with people, I suppose he might consider his part of the bargain as having been kept.

"But you know, as I rang off from talking to Norman, I couldn't help but recall that October 4, 1957 evening after we recorded *Moondreams.* When Norman left us in his office to talk over his offer to manage and produce us under conditions which even Shakespeare's Shylock would've been embarrassed to admit to.

"I could almost hear Norman saying to himself as he stiffed me that final time. "There, stuff that in your pipe and smoke it, Maple. Try to outfox *me,* eh fella? Ha!"

Maple had one more meeting with Petty, almost thirty years later. That was in a Lubbock hospital, a month before Norman died it 1984. Bill Pickering was living with his mother in Lubbock, and John's first *Buddy Holly and the Picks* compilation album was about to be pressed. John wanted Treb to interview Norman, to ask some "really tough questions," if he didn't give us his blessings on John's project, Treb said.

"I took a tape recorder. Norman was a shell of his former self. The leukemia had drained him so, he couldn't move. His voice was weak. He lay there, smiling, even laughing softly as Bill and I broke the ice with some humorous recollections of the summer of '57.

"I asked him about the celesta being played on *Everyday.* Was it he or Vi at the keyboard? That I remembered seeing him doing the bridge, in a one-man overdub.

"Vi believes she played the celesta, and she's told interviewers that for years," Petty replied softly, smiling. "I'm not about to say otherwise, at this juncture."

"I told him we were wanting to get some comments from him for a booklet John and I were writing, to go with the LP," Treb told Brad. "He wished us good luck. I could imagine the man's suffering during the past eighteen or so months. This former colleague whom I had grown to consider an enemy over the years. Then I shut off my little tape recorder, and began suggesting to Bill that we ought to be going. Bill, bless his heart, had told me earlier that sure, he could set up a hospital interview. 'Norman looks great! I think he's gonna be OK.'

"Somewhere in the conversation, Norman told me that he was at peace with God. This was before my Christian rebirth, so I didn't comment, one way or another, except to think about all the many people Norman's money-hungry ways had hurt; perhaps even killed, in Buddy's case. How many dreams he had not respected enough to give a fair shake."

Treb paused, looked at his watch and said, "I gotta go. My man's waiting for us out there. Here comes Struts just a-huffing, ready to pull me out to the practice tee by my ear."

He stood. "One last thing. Looking back, I think Norman Petty *was* at peace with his maker. The last words I ever heard him speak were: 'Trebor, if you write a book about me, be kind.'

"He gave me a little smile, and Bill and I left," Maple said, turning and walking away. After a few feet, he turned back to face Brad. "You know, when I left that hospital room and waved one last time, I now remember that Norman Petty *did* have a glow about him."

Treb resumed his trek to the door, then added over his shoulder, "a *little-bitty* glow, but a glow all the same."

14. A Night of Death…and Life

That evening, using the PIN he had stumbled onto, and taking advantage of the continued absence of casino manager Rick Conti, Brad had little trouble drawing fifteen thousand dollars in a letter of credit for the casino's poker pit boss. He had intended to find a place at a $50/$100 hold 'em table, in the Fifth Jack's restricted poker room.

"Welcome!" the pit boss greeted, as Brad handed him the letter of credit. "You're all set up at table two. Right this way."

He was introduced to the four players who had checked in ahead of him. Within fifteen minutes, the table had filled out to nine. It was a more businesslike, less talkative group, he noted, than he had enjoyed playing against at the Adobe. That game had been the most he'd ever played for, except when he lost the infamous bundle at Midland that had cost him his marriage. Tonight, he was in a different league. If this had been baseball, he mused, he would've gone from AA at the Adobe, to AAA ball. The World Series of Poker was the majors.

All of a sudden, Brad felt a cold chill run up his spine. He *had* to dismiss *this* reaction to the pressure of the game that was about to start. Hold 'em had no place for sweat and fearful precaution in its participants.

But as he stared at his stack of chips, while the casino dealer asked for a cut of the cards and then burned one and began dealing the first pocket cards, Poole knew he had placed himself in harm's way. He couldn't cover losing fifteen grand. And he didn't want to lose his job, a dismissal which if Tornado Thornton did what would seem fitting, would carry an indictment that would prevent him from getting a corresponding job again *anywhere* in the newspaper business.

He could walk away after a hand or two and breathe easy, while missing on an opportunity to maybe double his stake, or more. Or he could stay, and take the biggest chance of his life.

He stayed…sad to say.

An hour into the game, with Brad down a couple thousand, it dawned on him that he might be sitting between two players whom he suspected of being in cahoots. They were crafty, all right. But their check-raise and chase everybody but one guy with an obviously good set of pocket cards was difficult to mask. By fourth street, the two guys whom Brad suspected had squeezed the guy with continual raises bookending his calls, until he lost confidence. He stayed to see his river card, then faced the same blood-letting ritual. He folded, and left the game with what appeared to be less than a thousand of his stake.

When Brad was dealt the Ace-Queen of diamonds eight or nine hands later, he decided to see the flop. Up came two treys flanking the King of diamonds, one of the threes being the diamond. He had four to an ace-high flush, and almost a fifty-fifty chance of making his flush. He bet fifty, got bumped fifty by one of his two suspected twin sharks, called the fifty, then got raised by the other suspect, with his obvious suspect partner raising *him*. It was a costly round of betting, but Brad had to stay. Two of the four community cards on the table were spades. Two others were diamonds. He doubted either of the two big-bettors had the Ace-king of spades in *his* pocket, but he hoped one did, since Brad had the ace-king-*queen* high working in diamonds.

The two exposed threes posed another problem. A trey and, say, a king down in one of the hands would be the nuts—a killing full house—unless a *couple* of threes hidden produced the ultimate nuts—four of a kind.

The two let Brad stay, finally ending their continual raises, while the pit boss looked on with increasing interest. If he caught one of them with a junk hand, they undoubtedly would be asked to leave. Once, as with against the now-departed player, could be a coincidence. Twice? There'd be a smell of fish in the air.

Still, Brad had been waiting for a good hand, and if he made his diamond flush, if he were battling a spade flush, he'd win!

Sure enough, the six of diamonds was the river card. He had his flush. It was possible, with three diamonds showing, one of the two had a diamond flush too. But it would come in second to Brad, not one but three ways.

Unless the two threes worked in with a well-hidden full house or four of a kind, Brad had a winner. He *had* to stay!

There had been only the three of them in the game since the flop, and Brad's check followed by a bet, then a raise, his check, then a raise, set the tenor of the final round of betting.

The pit boss got up and walked around behind one of Brad's foes. The guy quit peeking at his pocket cards. The thought came to Brad that perhaps *neither* of these two partners have a winning hand, and knew it. They might be *bluffing* a squeeze, since Brad's unaccustomed tight style of play may have tipped them off that he'd run.

He was committed to stay, though he glanced with worry at his stack and figured he was down to less than two thousand. With the pit boss looking on, one of the two big-bettors *had* to fold soon. Only one of them could possibly beat him.

The man to his right studied the latest raise of a hundred, the limit doubled since they were now in the final "river" phase of betting. After a last peek at his pocket—the pit boss had drifted over to behind his suspected partner—he sighed and said, "Tex, I got a hunch we both got diamonds, but the big-uns are all out. I gotta holler calf rope."

He picked up his two cards, kept them face down, and threw them casually into a stack that the casino dealer was collecting.

Brad called the hundred, and his adversary across from him nonchalantly flipped his pocket.

"The man has threes over sixes, full," the dealer announced. Brad's hands shook as he turned over his ace-queen diamonds.

"Good hand, Tex," the winner cooed with a condescending smile. "Sorry." He raked in the biggest pot of the night, and let the pit boss take out the house's cut.

Brad sat silent, pondering his position. With less than fifteen hundred of his stake on the table, he could draw a few pockets, perhaps up to six or eight, and hope for another golden twosome to which to draw. With a call to the casino office, the boss could approve Brad for the rest of Thornton's so-called protected money. But if Brad got caught in the vicious vice he suspected he'd been witnessing, he wouldn't last long enough to draw out to it.

"Gentlemen, it's been interesting," Brad casually said, putting his chips in his pocket and standing. "Believe I've had it for the night."

"Aw, hate to see that," said one of the suspected sharks, as the pit boss looked at Brad and gave him a sad and apologetic nod.

Brad took a complimentary gin and tonic, drank it down and grabbed the other drink the scantily clad waitress had on her trey for somebody else at another table. He tossed it down too, even though he hated scotch. Then he left the room.

He lingered around the blackjack area and idly watched the action. When he spied the young woman with whom he'd played earlier in the week, he took his chips to her table and sat mentally idle, playing two hands at a time for fifty apiece. He had that sickly bile taste in his mouth. What was he going to do?

Certainly not win more than thirteen thousand back by playing blackjack, that was for sure. Two hours later, to add insult to the evening's misery, he stayed on sixteen when she had a six showing. She flipped over an ace and casually announced, "Seventeen. Dealer has to stay. Pay eighteen."

Brad had a hundred-dollar chip left from his original fifteen thousand poker stake. He gave a sardonic chuckle, trying to remember the last time he had lost fourteen hundred dollars on blackjack He couldn't. Brad flipped the chip to his pretty opponent, remembering that he hadn't tipped the hold 'em dealer. *Tough!*

"Thanks. Sorry the cards were against you tonight," she said as he stood.

"You have no idea," he replied. Then he went up to his and Mandy's room and climbed straight into bed, without so much as looking in on his companion.

OSCAR AND M.K. drove to the Black Rock Ranch earlier in the evening, Oscar taking Gabe's cellular with him. He even took the phone to the bathroom with him these days. He pulled the Navigator behind the deserted house and to the side of the darkened barn, cut the engine and sat in the dark with his wife.

"Now, what are we doing way out here in the boonies, hon?" M.K. asked.

He had his hand on his chin, staring into the darkness at the closed barn door. "All I want you to do is drop me off, if everything is clear," he said. "Then you drive back to the hotel and wait for me. OK? That's all there is to it."

"But how're *you* going to get back?"

"I'm...I'm going to meet somebody. We'll do a little business, patch a fence or two, and I'll see you in two hours."

She shuddered. "Oh, Oscar, I'm scared! Something's wrong, isn't it? Tell me!"

"Nothing's wrong that can't be fixed, and that's what I intend to do tonight. I'll get a ride back in. Don't worry," he said, then added testily, "Hear? Now, let me think. OK?"

She remained quiet while he continued to stare into the darkness. Finally, he made a show of looking at his watch, unbuckling his seat belt and climbing out of the Lincoln SUV.

"All right, M.K. You head on back now. I'll see you in two hours. Three at the most."

"Hon, be careful!"

"I will. Go on now."

She drove off. When she got to the Interstate, she turned left on the access road and headed back toward the bright lights of Las Vegas, unaware of a Black Chrysler Imperial that had emerged from the darkness and fallen in behind her.

Back at the ranch, Oscar closed the barn door behind him, and flipped on the florescent lights overhead. He put on the pair of surgical gloves he had brought with him, popped the trunk to Billy C.'s Cadillac, checked to make sure no blood stains showed, closed it and walked around to the passenger side. He opened the door, took a cloth and wiped where he had sat, then wiped the driver's side for when he had driven the car back to the barn from the cistern. Confident he had cleaned up any fingerprints, he shut off the lights, backed the Caddy out of the barn, closed it up, and drove slowly back to the Interstate. It was taking a chance, but Oscar did not want to leave Billy C.'s car untended, so close to two bodies.

Oscar figured no one would've filed a stolen car complaint except possibly Gabe, and he wouldn't dare. So he shouldn't be stopped. He had thought about leaving the Cadillac at Trucker's Haven, but only for a few seconds. When the car would finally be checked and its ownership verified, a waitress or the cashier at the truck stop might remember Billy C., and the dark-complexioned, Latin-looking guy with a ponytail who met him there. Oscar swore, then promised himself that he was going to get a *regular* haircut somewhere on the road, after they left Vegas.

He drove carefully back into town and thought of a busy parking lot where he might pull in unnoticed, and the Cadillac might remain there likewise for days. Certainly not New York New York. Then he remembered seeing a large Best Western not far from downtown, just off the expressway. Several eighteen-wheelers were always parked in back, along with a few autos. He drove there, pulled the Cadillac to the back and picked a spot that looked as if someone might leave a car if he were to be out of town a few days.

He quietly got out of Billy C.'s Cadillac, left the keys in the ignition and locked all the doors, took off his gloves and stuffed them in his pocket, and staying close to the shadows walked from the parking lot and across the access road. He hiked for about half a mile, ambled unobtrusively into a 7-11, and called a cab.

"MGM Grand," he told the driver who picked him up. He could take another hike, cross under the freeway, and walk to their hotel. He smiled. He needed exercise tonight, if he were to ever fall asleep. Oscar sat in the back seat, going over everything to make sure he hadn't forgot anything, then reacted with a start when Gabe's phone rang in his coat pocket.

"Hello," Oscar responded quietly, checking out the disinterested driver.

"Cuban!" Gabe greeted. "*Que paso?*"

"OK. What's up?"

"We need to get together, don't we? Get this silly business behind us. I don't know how Billy could've got things so screwed up. But frankly, I'm glad he's out of my hair. Now, how about day after tomorrow? Maybe 10 p.m.?"

"I think my wife has dinner plans, and that might make it unwieldy...No, that's tomorrow night. Yeah, forty-eight hours will be OK."

"You still staying downtown?"

"Yep."

"Wonderful! I'll phone you at 2 p.m. on the dot that day, on where and how," Gabe instructed. "Give you time to check the lay of the land, if you don't trust me. Heh-heh. Expect my call. *Adios, amigo.*"

While Oscar breathed a sigh of relief, sensing no sign of suspicion in Gabe's voice or conversation, Gabe clicked off his standby cell phone and smiled.

"Cuban…Cuban," he said, chuckling out loud. "I wanted *so* much to tell you that my guys with nasty mean streaks have just returned. That they enjoyed following you and your wife—Mr. and Mrs. Oscar Arnaz, we have discovered—out to some dump called the Black Rock Ranch. And then escorting your wife back to New York New York. You'd have pissed all over your frigging brown ass. But that will come, *mi amigo.* That will come. *Tomorrow* night. You have just about twenty-four hours left on this earth, Oscar Arnaz. Not forty-eight."

TREB HAD spent the evening lying on Louise's bed and reading, after failing to draw her into any meaningful dialogue. Around ten, he yawned and stood up. "Think I'll head on to bed, doll. Can I get you anything first?"

"I believe Sis poured some natural spring water from the gallon jug into an Ozarka liter bottle earlier this evening. It's in the refrigerator. You could get that for me."

"Sure. Oh…by the way. Little Amanda called—"

"Your girlfriend?" Louise said, looking up from her book with a wry grin."

"Anyway, Amanda called me at Desert King during the noon hour. She said her mother and her step-father want to take us out to eat tomorrow evening. Something about Oscar wanting to pump me to let him play with me Sunday. I didn't commit to that, but Amanda did seem anxious—she mentioned wanting to get to know you better—so I confirmed, reserving the right to cancel for you if you didn't feel up to it by tomorrow afternoon. She asked if Mike and Struts would come, and they're all for a free dinner at the Fourth Street. The new place out toward McCarren. They have a casino upstairs and, downstairs, a great place to eat, or so I've heard. Especially for seafood. She said they'd wait for us in the parking garage, but if we get there before them, to go on inside. Hope you don't mind. I *did* make sure you had a firm escape hatch."

"No, that's fine. I'm curious about that whole extended family. The guy with the ponytail and his chatty wife, ol' brooding Brad and your girlfriend. And it's been a few weeks since I've seen the guys." She laughed. "Like Struts probably said, who are *we* to turn down a free meal at a posh new place we've not been to yet?"

199

He left and returned shortly with the plastic bottle, just as the phone rang. He picked it up on Louise's nightstand, as he handed her the water.

"Hello...oh hi, Missy. No, Louise is reading, but I'm heading off to my room to sack out. You guys OK?...*What!?* No! Oh babe, I'm *so* sorry! What does the doctor say? Um-hum. Aw, no! Josh didn't seem *that* bad the other night. You're at the hospital, right? I'm on my way...No, no! No problem. I want to be there."

"It's Josh, right?" Louise asked quietly, putting down her book.

Treb nodded. "Looks like the beginning of the end. His doctor had already told Missy that there would never be any improvement. Now, a steady deterioration of his lungs has set in, coupled with very labored breathing. This will continue until he just can't muster the strength do draw a breath anymore. Could be a couple days, could be a week. Maybe two. Regardless, he warned her that Josh will *not* get better, or stay the same for that matter."

A tear rolled down Louise's cheek. "I'm...I'm so sorry. I know how much you love that old coot!" she said, of a man about five years her junior.

Treb leaned over and kissed her cheek. He was crying softly. "You do too, Lou. You do too. You don't fool me."

"Don't stay all night, Treb, if you've got to be at the course in the morning," she said.

As he walked out to his aged Cadillac, Treb realized that this had just been the first time in months—in maybe over a year—that his wife had seemed concerned about him in *any* form or fashion. It pleased him.

TREB KISSED Missy on her cheek as he quietly entered the hospital room Josh shared with a likewise old guy who was sleeping, his back turned to them. Treb smiled, walked over to Josh and peered into his friend's face through the oxygen tent. But Leventhal was sleeping, obviously with great discomfort. Maple put his arm around Missy's shoulder and pointed to the hallway.

"What can I do for you?" he asked his close friend's wife.

"Oh Treb. Nothing I can think of. Your being here is enough. I want Josh to wake up just long enough to see you. That's all. Don't worry. He wakes up every few minutes, gasps for oxygen, then slips off again. I think he hears most of what's said in the room though. He just doesn't have the strength to react to it."

"I've got two jobs tomorrow, but I'll drop by and look in on you." He wrote down his cell phone number. "Here. Call me at *any* time, and I'll be on my way. Have you phoned your daughter?"

Missy nodded. Treb led her back inside. He stood for a time at Josh's bedside, until she whispered to him that she wanted him to go home and get to sleep. So Treb reached down and patted Josh's tortured hand, where some hospital staffer had obviously suffered difficulty finding a vein for the IV.

At Treb's touch, Josh opened his eyes wide. He seemed unable to smile or frown. But he did manage to ever so slowly nod his head, just once. Then he was asleep again.

Treb went home, the tears rolling down his face as he drove. *God,* he thought, *why didn't I do a better job witnessing to Josh? Forgive me. I've let you down. I've let my friend down. He could have been saved, with the right person witnessing to him.*

Then Trebor Maple breathed a sigh of relief. "Hey. Who's to say he *hasn't* been saved already?" he said aloud, wiping each cheek as he stared down the expressway. "That's *your* call. I'm praying for Josh Leventhal *now,* his body *and* his soul, as I ask forgiveness for my shortcomings as a lowly foot soldier in your army of faith. One who's been asleep at his post. Again, forgive me."

TREB, STRUTS and Mike were just finishing their burgers with their a.m. client, a guy from Tennessee. "I don't know how to thank you, Treb," he was saying, as Brad walked into the Desert King pro shop and paused at the counter. "You can't imagine how this is gonna help me, when I get back home. It's just so *clear,* the way you put it."

"Dave, it's been my experience that talk is cheap. Just a little more so than only showing someone how it's done. The big thing for you to concentrate on is to practice...*practice!*...PRACTICE! If you want the past four hours to pay a lasting, measurable dividend, then set your goal to hit 500 range balls a week, going over at least once a month the tapes Mike here is going to send you. And remember—*always* work on the hard stuff the most. If you get to hitting your driver the best, start working the *least* with it. If you stink pitching and chipping, start and finish each session with them, no matter how much fun it is to go out and bust the driver."

The man called Dave stood, and shook hands all around. "You guys are the greatest! I thank you, heah? Promised th' little lady I'd be back by two. I will see you again, I hope."

"Tell your friends to check us out, next time they come to Vegas," Mike hawked as Dave began walking for the door.

"I will. You can count on it." And Dave left.

"Shameless, my com-PADRE," Struts chortled. *"Shameless.* Hey! Lookie over there. It's our reporter pal."

Treb turned in his chair. "Brad? C'mon over."

"Hey guys. I just *happened* to be in your neighborhood, and thought I'd pop in and say hello."

"Well, hello...and g'bye to Struts and me," Cardenas said. "I see a guy who has 'well-heeled and stuck with a slice' stamped across his forehead, wandering around out there with a new pair of soft-spike Footjoys on, as if he were looking for somebody. Must be our afternoon client. We'll go out there and get him set up. You got fifteen minutes before we need you, boss."

Treb sighed. "I told you not to call me boss," he monotoned. "Sit down, Brad. Have a cool one on me. And Struts. Thanks. I mean it."

"Hey! No problem. Everbody needs a little helpful hint now an' again...boss," Struts replied, as he waddled along after Cardenas.

Before they had begun the morning session, Treb had told his partners about Josh, whom they all liked. He bemoaned the fact that he feared he had not done right by his friend's soul.

"You still got time, y'know," Struts had told him. "Ain't no angel o' death callin' on ol' Josh yet. If you don' mind me sayin' so, maybe you outta think 'bout changin' y'all's *modus operandi*," Struts said, causing both Mike and Treb to have laughed.

"Been reading again, *compadre*?" Cardenas had asked.

"Nope. Done got it from *CSI* th' other night."

"In what context are you speaking?" Treb had asked, haughtily.

"You don' wanna hear it, boss."

"Yes I do, and *don't* call me boss! Speak your mind."

"Well, don' get mad at me now, but you always talkin' about lettin' folks find their *own* ways to th' lord, that you figger yore role in this salvation business is ta just *be* there. As if standin' aroun' lookin' like *'gee whiz...I done been saved, world. An' I didn't have ta do nothin' ta git that way. God done reached down an' plucked my soul like a daffy-o-dill. So here 'tis. Don' ask questions. Jes BE like me!"*

Treb had paused, first acting a little hurt, but soon appreciative. "You think I'm that way, Struts?"

"What does *you* think? An' don't say you find findin' God ta bein' a private thing. I been readin' bout what if Paul hadn't been *poundin'* them Roman guards what got shackled to his leg, poundin' with th' word o' God. What if th' Apostle had jes gone along, smilin' and pattin' 'em on their haids, an' *golly but you boys ought ta give Jesus a try. But don' strain yerselfs any. Hear? I'm so golly-gee happy, maybe you kin be too. An' is that a angel over there? See how he done glowed?* Well, ol' Pablo done that, they jes might not've been Christ in Rome when we *really* needed him there."

Clearly, Struts had struck a nerve. He had waited for a confrontation with the man whom he had grown to look up to, more than anyone he'd ever known. And he had regretted being so frank. He was about to apologize when Treb broke a two-minute period of silence.

"You know, my friend, I think you're right. I'm a gutless wonder when it comes to witnessing for God."

"Hey boss. I done *never* called you gutless. It's jes that I think ya needs be a mite more proactive. Thas' all."

"No, gutless fits, pal," Treb had said. "And you know something? You talk like a homeboy hiding out behind street lingo. But you, Mr. Struthers, are one of the wisest, most insightful people I've ever met. I thank you for what you've just done."

"Hey, maybe I done laid it on a *leetle* bit too thick—"

"And maybe you've been a messenger from God, swatting me back up on my feet. Thank you again, Brother in Christ," Treb had said.

AS HE watched his two associates go out the pro shop door, Treb turned to Brad and observed, "Friends like those two guys hardly ever come in pairs for one person. They're rare enough to find just *one* at a time. I am truly blessed. Now, what're you doing out here? I understand we'll be dining with you all and the Arnazes tonight."

"So I found out, just this morning, when I bumped into my girlfriend, however briefly."

"Trouble in lover's paradise?" Treb teased, eliciting a shrug from Brad. "What *are* you doing here, then. It's a long drive out."

"Just wanted to get away from town, Treb. Maybe talk to you a second."

"People who come to Vegas for action and excitement need to learn that three days is neat, but four ceases to be a treat. Shoot, son. I've got a good ten minutes yet."

Brad sighed. "I shouldn't be crying on your shoulder, but I feel rotten. I just want to unload on somebody, I guess. I'm too ashamed to tell Mandy. You warned me, and I didn't—"

"You threw in with the big boys, Brad?"

"Um hum. At the Jack."

"How much, Brad?"

"Uh, fifteen grand."

Treb whistled. "Where'd you get *that* kind of stake, Poole?"

So Brad told him. Told him about the deal he had with his publisher. About how he stumbled onto a way to tap into the reserves that were supposed to be off-limits to him. About how his moderate success in the relatively little game at the Adobe had ratcheted up his confidence.

"So, what're you going to do?"

"Well, I'm gonna go back and face the music. You and the guys have given me some great stuff, stuff I can turn into fantastic copy. And you can count on me telling it straight. Maybe that'll bail me out, especially if we win an APME—"

"APME?"

"APME. Stands for The Associated Press Managing Editors. Big deal in Texas among newspapers. Highly competitive. If we can get their award for best series next March, I *may* be able to save my butt. Plus, I'm not *completely* tapped out. Mandy and I have about five thousand in our safe, almost half of which she won when I suspect she got a helping hand from the Fifth Jack's eye in the sky. Most of the rest came from the other night, when I played with you and decided I was gonna whip Las Vegas to a pulp."

"So actually you've still got almost half of your boss' money. Right?"

"Right. About eight thousand, five hundred. I'm thinking I could go back to the Adobe and the game we played the other night. You said I was good—"

"I said you were good the *other* night. Now, hold 'em's got you on the run. Rather than going over there free and easy like before, not playing on your own money, now *you'd* be on the ropes. Feeling like you *had* to win. In that situation, I can virtually *guarantee* you stupid misplays and choked betting. Not only will you *not* win twelve grand in three or four nights. You'll lose the rest of your money. Probably in just one. When's Conti coming back?"

"I have no idea," Brad replied.

"Tell me about these two good ol' boys whom you think sucker-punched you."

Brad described the two, and Treb said he thought he knew who they were. "Who was running your game?" Brad told him the guy had a thin moustache and dark hair, and appeared to be Mediterranean. "OK. That'd be Roberto."

"That's right. I remember now. Roberto de something-or-the-other."

"I gotta go to work, Brad. Two things—one, stay away from hold 'em. If you feel you just *have* to gamble, play the cotton-pickin' nickel poker slots! Two, give me a little while. I can't promise anything. But I can make a call or two."

"Hey, I didn't come out here to beg you—"

"I know you didn't. Just give me a little time. Our boys probably made a killing that night. If I ask them *real* nice, like I won't squeal all over town on them after I talk to Beto, I *might* be able to get a couple or three thousand back. And when he returns, I'll work on Rick to cut you some slack, and not tell your Cyclone—"

"Uh, Tornado."

"Whatever. He'll do us a favor and see what we might come up with. By the way. Mike's got an Explorer. Let's plan on picking you and Amanda up around eight-thirty. I think Louise will be going with us. So she and I will lead the way in my car, since it carries her chair. The rest of you follow us, and we'll meet the Arnazes at the Fourth Street. No sense in all of us taking separate cars all the way out there.

"Sounds great. I'll tell Amanda. We'll meet you downstairs."

"Or I'll come up and get you. I'll call you and tell you which. OK?"

Brad smiled. "Thanks Treb."

"Sally, I'm leaving you twenty-five. That cover it all, including this gentleman's *cerveza?*

"I'll owe you seven bucks, Treb," the waitress, cook and bottle-washer called back.

"Nope, let's call it even at twenty-five." And Treb walked to the door, then headed for the practice tee.

MAPLE CALLED Brad from downstairs to tell him they had arrived. When Poole offered to join them shortly, with Amanda, Treb said no. "I'll come up by myself. I have something for you."

Could it be? Could it be some of my money? Brad asked himself, feeling a surge of anticipatory excitement. *Please, let it be two thousand,* he continued, with a scattershot, unaddressed, sort-of prayer. *Just two thousand. I can figure out how to explain the rest.* He had already been rehearsing what to tell Thornton. He'd simply spout the truth, or maybe about half of it. He hadn't told Mandy yet. Why spoil her night out on the town? But he *would* tell her. The whole nine yards—more or less.

"Mandy, Treb's on his way up," he called to the closed bedroom door, next to his which was still open. "You about ready?"

"Two minutes, Brad."

A soft knock on the door was answered by Brad. Treb stepped in and replied "Good!" when Brad told him Mandy would be just a minute or so more.

"Here," Treb said, giving Brad a plastic grocery sack. "No apologies, no sermon, no explanations, no thanks. I'm going to *hopefully* figure you've learned a valuable lesson. I'm glad you came to me, even though you were *real* stupid, what you did."

Brad took the sack, which rattled instead of crinkling. He was expecting—or at least hoping for—hard cash. He peeked in and saw a sack full of poker chips. Chips from the Fifth Jack's casino.

"What—!?"

"There's exactly ten thousand worth in that sack. I just bought 'em downstairs. About three hours ago, I talked to your buddies from last night. They weren't threatened. I'm no good at that. But they know people who know me. They also enjoy hustling on the golf course now and then. Without saying much of anything, I explained to them that you had made a mistake a lot of folks who come to Vegas make. That I gave Beto a call and found out together, the two of them must've pocketed close to fifty thousand last night. That I would consider it a *distinct* honor if they'd return about nine or ten grand to me, so's I could save a guy's rear end from the shredding machine. And I'd consider it a privilege hooking up with them three Sundays from now, at Desert King, so maybe they could get that back. It'd be a hundred-dollar skins game, handicaps working with me playing to a zero, and a best-ball scratch match between me and a partner of *their* choosing, from a list I'd submit, versus the two of them. Thousand-dollar Nassau, press when you have the nerve."

"Wow!" Brad exclaimed, as he headed for the closet where the safe was. He opened it, tossed in the bag of chips, and continued: "I'll take these down in the morning and fix up Thornton's account. He expects to lose a couple grand, so this is my *salvation!*"

"I only wish," Treb said with a sigh. "Maybe next time."

"Treb, you don't know what this means to me. Actually, this'll put me five hundred in the black, after settling with the office tomorrow. But it sounds as if you've made a bad bet. I hope you don't lose this much back to them, out of *your* pocket."

He smiled as Amanda came swishing through her bedroom door wearing a light blue satin cocktail dress and acting just like Maple remembered Loretta Young on TV, back when he was a kid in high school and then at Tech. As if Amanda would know whom Loretta Young was. Or Brad for that matter. Naturally, she looked just like Clarice.

"Don't worry, Brad. My five choices for the partnership list—and our friends will look over their handicaps closely, you can be assured—my choices are all over sixty. I know them. They like to play and they like to bet. I know their games, particularly on the greens, facing five-foot have-to-have putts. Your two pals are in their forties. Our spot will be, we get to hit off the white tees. About fifty-nine hundred yards' worth. They must hit from the blues, or some five hundred more. All I want is to get away with a few hundred in skins in my pocket, and maybe a bet or two on the matches for my partner. However, if your guys don't *behave,* I may change my mind. I may take another big chunk out of their so-called winnings from last night. You look lovely, Amanda. Doesn't she, Brad?"

"As always," he chirped.

"Why thank you, kind sirs," Mandy acknowledged, smiling as usual as she let Brad slip a light coat around her shoulders while she picked up her shawl and draped it over her left arm. "What were you two talking about?"

"Nothing, really. Just about golf," Brad said.

"Oh Brad. By the way. I spent—can you believe it?—four *hundred* dollars on this dress this afternoon. I did like you said. I took it out of the safe."

Treb laughed as Brad smiled and facetiously moaned, "Oh well. Easy come, easy go. Nah! I'm glad you did, Mandy."

"Hey Brad," Maple said, still laughing, "I can tell you about a place where you can have a *great* evening for two, on just a hundred bucks. However, it's a long drive from here to Bone Dry Gulch, Nevada."

And they left, going to the garage where Louise was waiting in Treb's car and Struts and Mike were parked just behind.

"I'll pile in with the guys," Brad said. "Mandy, you go with the Maples."

"Wonderful," she replied.

"Then we're off," Treb said, helping Mandy in the back seat.

OSCAR ARNAZ pulled his Navigator into the Fourth Street's parking garage. He found no empty places on the first floor, nor the second. Nor did he see either of the two autos Brad had described by phone an hour before. "Looks like we've beaten them here," he said, continually attempting to keep tomorrow night's date with Gabe from monopolizing his mind.

He turned a hundred and eighty degrees and proceeded up the ramp. "Well, looks like we'll just start a new floor," Mary Katherine said, eyeing the deserted tier. "Oh look! Two cars coming up behind us. I'll bet it's them. Perfect timing."

Oscar glanced in his side mirrors. All he could see were two vehicles' headlights. He continued climbing. When his Lincoln leveled, he drove to the nearest marked parking spot and killed the engine, along with his lights. He and M.K. opened their doors as a car pulled in beside him. *That's no Cadillac. Or an Explorer,* Arnaz noted to himself, while feeling a chill as he saw both front doors open on a light gold Lexus.

"Why, hello, Mr. and Mrs. Arnaz," the man Oscar had known only as Gabe for five years said, a phony lilt to his voice.

Oscar looked behind, hoping to see one of their friends' cars coming. But it was a black or navy blue Chrysler Imperial. And it had stopped halfway up the ramp.

"Blocking th' frigging way," Oscar muttered.

"What?...who?...HELP, Oscar!...*Help!*" M.K. screamed, as the man with Gabe grabbed her around her neck, from behind, and pointed a pistol to her temple.

"OK. Here's how it is, my Cuban Oscar Arnaz *dipshit* friend," Gabe hissed. "Get that hidden vault of yours open. Pronto! *Comprende?* There better be both my money *and* your coke in there, or the little lady here is in *mucho* trouble. About like you'll be too, in a couple seconds more."

M.K. gagged and choked, more from horror and shock than the hold around her neck, or so it sounded to Oscar. "OK...OK...You got it, Gabe. I gotta get under the Navigator—"

"You ain't doin' nothin' of the kind, *muchacho!*"

"Then we aren't going to get anywhere. I figure your people have managed to take a look inside the Lincoln. I told you, didn't I, that there's a trigger I have to disengage underneath, to pop the vault under the rear seat?"

"Fine, pal," Gabe responded. "Gimme your keys. We'll take it away, and one way or another pop it open like a tin can. As for you two, now?" He had a pistol out, pointing it at Oscar.

"Uh, boss, I don't think we got time for any of this. Let th' Cuban do it, and then let's scram," the man holding M.K. said, as Treb's Cadillac honked at the seemingly stranded Chrysler, with Mike's Explorer close behind.

Gabe sized up the situation and ordered Oscar to "get it on, and no stupid moves or you and your wife will exit this world, hand in hand!"

Oscar wondered what to do. He knew that by now, Gabe was not about to let them live. And what of the two or three hoods in the Chrysler? Would they shoot to kill their dinner companions? He decided surprise was his only chance—*their* only chance, maybe all of them. He dropped to the garage's floor an scooted under the Navigator. He tried to remember just how he'd worked it so slick on Billy C. In twenty seconds, during which he heard a car door slam and Trebor Maple speak to somebody, he had his hand on his pistol. The safety was off.

"There!" he said, pushing himself from under the Navigator. "Won't be but a minute now. You *are* gonna play this hand straight, aren't you Gabe?"

:"Straight as a dog's hind leg, as they say, *compadre*. Heh!...Hey!"

Oscar grabbed his flabby adversary by his arm holding the pistol, which flew from Gabe's hand. Gabe dropped to his knees and screamed, "Shoot the bastard. *NOW!*"

"HI, FRIEND," Treb asked, as the front windows on the Chrysler motored down. "Having problems?"

"Stalled," a voice came from the darkness.

"Can we help?"

"Nah! I just called inside, askin' for assistance. They'll be here in a minute. Why don't you tell the other car that both of you need to back on down? I bet there's a couple parking places out front."

Treb motioned to Mike with a shrug, and watched his window come down. Then he confronted the driver in the Chrysler. "Funny. Your car was running a couple seconds ago, when I got out of mine—"

They all heard M.K. scream, then the 'pop-pop-pop" of small arms fire. By now, Mike and Struts had walked up beside Maple, and two men emerged from the Imperial.

"Shudda 'got' when I told you to 'git,' dumbass," the driver hissed, brandishing what Treb figured was an AK-47. Mike was by Treb in a flash, tackling the driver, who quickly squeezed off a few rounds as he went crashing to the ramp. Struts caught the rear-seat thug in the groin with a kick from his meaty right leg, a ham hock of an arm bashing the guy over his head. Struts picked up the thug's pistol and pointed it at a man in the front seat, who was pointing a gun back at Struts.

"Mexican standoff, huh?" a grinning Struts said. "I count one-two-three an' let's jus' see. One...two..." Struts was very surprised when *that* goodfella dropped his pistol and put his hands on his head. "Now, outta there, asshole!" Struts ordered, with John Wayne-like authority, again coming as a shock to him.

Mike had the man's AK-47 in his grasp, and he slid down the car to sit in a slouch beside the prostrate form of his foe. Treb, who had frozen before the action-dazzled scene, could see a pool of blood that had already formed between the two figures.

"Mike—?"

"Guy must've shot himself...when I hit him, Treb. I think...I think he's bought it. And Treb...Treb...I'm hit!"

Maple rushed to his friend and knelt by his side, as he heard footsteps from below. He looked up and saw a uniformed man running toward them. "Security? Hurry! There's been a shooting here," Treb called out. "Be careful! Call the police! And ambulances!"

A scream echoed through the garage from above the ramp.

"Mother!?" Mandy yelled, vaguely aware that something she just said didn't sound right, but not able to grasp that she had *never* addressed M.K. in such a fashion, at least since early childhood. She ran up the ramp and fell in a heap when another shot rang out. The security guard yelled through the semi-darkness, "Drop it!" as he pointed his sidearm. Gabe did. Startled by Mandy's footsteps and seeing only the blur of a figure coming at him, through eyes clouded by the stress of dying, he had fired out of instinct. It was his final act as a living being.

Brad had jumped from the Explorer when the initial shock had worn off, and ran to cradle Mandy to his chest. Her blood soon was discoloring his shirt.

Struts slowly walked to the third floor with the security guard, who still had his weapon drawn. They found Mary Katherine Arnaz kneeling and sobbing by the body of her husband."

"Damn!" the guard uttered, shining his light first on the body of Oscar, then on that of Gabe, whose eyes were frozen in a death stare.

"Here's a-nothern," Struts called out, peering down at Gabe's henchman as if he were a dead animal. Which he was, in a manner of speaking.

Soon sirens shattered the crisp desert night air. Treb walked dazed among the carnage, after a still-conscious Miguel Cardenas had been loaded onto an ambulance and rushed away.

"You know what brought all this mess on?" a Las Vegas policeman asked Maple, while a state trooper who had been on patrol nearby walked amid the blood-splattered scene.

"I have no idea," Treb replied. "Excuse me, please." He walked to Brad, who was standing by a stretcher that had Mandy's unconscious form strapped to it. "Brad..."

"I...I don't know," Poole answered. "She's breathing. That's all there is, for now. I'm riding with her to the hospital. She...she seems to have been shot in the stomach. That's...scary, isn't it, Treb?"

"Not necessarily," Maple replied, since he knew absolutely nothing else to say. Then he turned and quickly sped to the passenger side of his Cadillac, two more policemen and what appeared to be a detective now in charge close behind. He had completely forgotten about Louise during the turmoil. Treb threw open the door and grabbed her shoulders.

"Lou...?"

She just sat there, rocking back and forth, her eyes wide with fright.

"Oh honey, honey. You want out? Want me to get your chair?"

She shook her head in rapid little movements.

"Mandy?" she whimpered.

"I dunno. I just dunno right now," he said, watching two officers hold a limp M.K. upright as they guided her down the ramp. She was bleeding from her left arm.

"Just a flesh wound, I think," one said to a third officer walking up to meet them. "Three corpses left back of us."

"Two more down here, with two seriously wounded—a male, elderly, and a young female en route to the hospital."

"Got another ambulance here? I think we ought to send this lady there too."

"One's on the way. She's pretty shook up. Thinks somebody must've mistaken them for someone else. One of the deceased is her husband."

Treb and Struts waited behind, telling the investigators all they could. Which was not much.

"You're Treb Maple, the golfer, aren't you?" One of them asked Treb, who nodded.

"The black guy over there?"

"He's my friend, Carl Struthers, and a hero in all this business. So's my other friend, Miguel Cardenas, the first one you all took away in an ambulance. I really need to get to the hospital and see how he's doing. The young lady too."

"Mr. Maple, how well do you know these folks?"

"Just met them, a couple or three days ago."

"One of the perps from this Imperial here is OK. He's not saying nothing though."

"Hold on to him, officer. I approached this car, and apparently it was blocking our way to the next tier, where the other two vehicles were. He *knows* something, for sure. This Chrysler was in on whatever was happening. And that guy was in the front passenger seat. This I know."

"The reason I ask, this has the look of a drug deal gone bad. Would you know a*nything* that would lead credence to this proposition?"

"Nothing whatsoever."

"What about the lady in the Cadillac? She been out and around any of this?"

Treb shook his head. "My wife. She's partially paralyzed. Is there a way we can do this at the hospital? I *really* need to check on my friend. And the young lady. Amanda Scott is her name."

"Sure. We'll follow you."

Struts had remained quiet through the inquiry. He nodded when Treb asked if he could drive Mike's Ford to the hospital.

"YOUR FRIEND just died," the young ER doctor told Treb casually. "His wound severed an artery in his leg. We just couldn't save him. He bled too quickly. The twenty minutes it took the ambulance to get here were crucial."

Treb buried his face in his hands while Struts banged his backside back and forth against the wall. "No no no no, Mike. *No!*" the big man moaned.

"Can we see him please?" Treb asked.

"Sure. Take your time."

Treb walked down the hall to where Louise sat in her wheelchair. He whispered the bad news to her. She gasped, then sobbed. He led her chair back to Struts. Treb put his arm around his friend's shoulder and the three stepped behind the screen and into the cubical where Mike's body lay. Struts simply lost it as he bent over and kissed his friend's cheek. Louise held Strut's hand, and touched Mike's. Treb brushed a lock of Mike's gray-black hair from his closed eyes.

"Greater love has no one than this, that he lay down his life for his friends," Treb quoted Jesus, in an unwavering voice. Then he added, "Go, and fly with the angels, my dear friend."

"John 15:13," Struts said, then added, "Who we gotta call?"

"No one. His ex-wife lives somewhere in Mexico, down around Valles in San Luis Potosi, last time I heard. That was a good twenty years ago," Treb said. "He had a sister back in Brownsville, but she died a couple years back. I'm sure he has cousins, but I have no idea whom or where. We're all he's got, I guess. I'll tell the hospital that I'll be responsible for the body. We'll get a funeral home here to handle the…things. I'll have them send a notice to the *Brownsville Herald*. You think we ought to take him back there to be buried?"

"I think you ought to do it here," Louise said laborously, finally speaking in a sentence. "Or the nearest place out by Desert King we can find. The year or so you all have been there has been the happiest time of his life. At least, for as long as I've known him."

Treb turned Louise over to Struts, who took her home in Treb's car. He gave Treb the keys to Mike's Explorer. Treb stayed around and finished talking to the police. Then he went up a floor to ICU, where Brad and M.K. were waiting to hear something about Mandy.

M.K. was quiet, sitting in a chair next to the soft drink machine.

"Mandy's resting, pretty well doped up and out of it," Brad told Treb. "A bone specialist was called in. He said it was a minor miracle. The slug, a .9 mm, entered through her abdomen and missed an artery by a quarter inch. The bad news was, it shattered the socket in which her right hipbone rests. He said she'll have several months of rehab, followed by replacement of her hip."

"Mary Katherine, can I do something for you?" Treb asked. She shook her head. "The police are asking a lot of questions. Do you know *anything* about what happened?"

She stared straight ahead. "Like I told the cops, we pulled in to park, looked back and thought you were behind us, then we got out. Only, it wasn't your car. This guy I've never seen took out a gun and grabbed me. Another guy, an older one, put a gun at Oscar's head, and said unless he gave him his money, he'd have the other guy kill me. Oscar tried to do like he said, but they got into a scuffle. The older guy hollered for the other one to shoot Oscar, while he took a shot at me, for some reason. Oscar must've grabbed his gun. He shot the guy holding me, about the same time *that* guy shot...shot my Oscar." Then she began to cry.

Treb stayed with Brad a while, then went downstairs to look in on Josh. A little worse, Missy reported, but still holding on. Treb promised to be back the next day.

TREB FOUND the lead investigator and reported what M.K. had told him.

"Glad she's finally talking" the detective said.

"Hadn't she told you about the same thing?"

"Nope. I'm gonna need to talk to this lady some more. *Quite* a bit more. Evidence at the scene, plus initial fingerprint data show that all three men on the upper tier were armed. So your man was there with a weapon. No permit either, that we can tell. They live in Coral Gables, Florida, apparently. Haven't found out much. We're checking there. We have gone over Arnaz's car extensively. No sign of drugs. But *something* was going down. It sure doesn't seem like routine robbery to me. Yes, we're going to need to chat with Mrs. Arnaz, rather extensively. After we get a report on what the Coral Gables people find out."

TREB WAS was about to leave the hospital when Missy Leventhal caught up with him.

"They're telling me it could...could be tonight, Treb," she said, her voice quivering.

"I'll go up with you," he offered.

"I know what you must be going through, but it would mean *so* much to me. Josh can't move or say anything, or even whisper. But I *know* he hears what's happening. Could you talk to him? Maybe for the last time, Treb? Please?"

"Of course. I really need to, actually," he sighed.

They rushed to Josh's room. An RN was monitoring his vital signs. She shook her head when they entered.

"It won't be long, my dear," she whispered to Missy.

"Treb suddenly realized he was weak in the knees. He pulled a chair up to the bed, held his friend's hand, and began speaking evenly and clearly.

"Josh, I know somewhere in there, you're listening. I just *know* it. We've talked before, but I always did too much listening and too much silly grinning, as you tried to mask a real need to know behind acerbic humor. So let me talk, and you relax. I'm just going to tell you how things are with me.

"First, Christ lived. Died for our sins. Was raised from the dead, as God the father promised. He then left his spirit, the Holy Spirit, behind for each and all of us. He will return from his preordained place beside the creator at the predestined time, as the world measures it. Just as God the father, through the son, has promised. He who believes this will be—is—saved. I didn't believe, not for a long while. But I was literally *shown,* in my soul. This, my friend, to me is undeniably the truth.

"God has no measure of time, not as we know it. The Christ has already returned for those who, like you, have or are about to leave this vale of tears, as Paul called the mess we've made of our earthly home. In the blink of an eye, we can be saved from eternal awareness that we have been separated from God. That is a hell beyond imagination. Only a soul can ever realize the extent of such a horror.

"No one can do better than give up his life for a friend. I lived that this evening, when a friend gave his up for me. No one can live sweeter than casting aside pride, ego, wasted knowledge such as worrying about time-locked concepts such as evolution, the tragedy of being misled, such as by clerics who hide their control-freakishness behind threats and convoluted teachings, or by the likes of TV ministers pronouncing insights on Jesus while lining the pockets of their lives with material payoffs. There, to my mind, are the most dangerous of Satan's con men. Those who seem to embrace Jesus while doing evil's work, forever poisoning the inquisitive minds of those hungering for answers, but knowing these charlatans do not have them. Or those rabbis and priests and the scribe-like whose shallowness is not hidden by their pharasitical love of self.

"Evil lives, just as sure as do the most certain elements of nature. Call it Satan, the Devil, whatever. Evil lives in us, just the same as the potential for good. A life that balances itself between the two is wasted. One that embraces good, through love, cannot be shaken. Its soul cannot die.

"God is a spirit, Josh, whom our spirit discovers by grace and nurtures within us by faith. The spirit in us also surrounds us with beauty. Peace. Love. A knowledge of truth and justice and all the secrets behind the earthly marvels with which we've been allowed to evolve. We are incapable of knowing the true secrets of the universe, and beyond. But once we're allowed to enter the spirit world where time is forever, backwards and forward, we *will* know *all* the secrets in the blinking of an eye.

"Blink, my beloved friend. Blink. Get there before me, and know the truths of the universe. My friend Mike is there already, waiting to help you along. Then you can teach me and Missy and Louise and Struts, and we can stand and worship in the incredibly bright beam of a glow we locked in life cannot imagine exists, a glow that is Christ, who while on earth as the one unique man of all time did not consider equality with the spirit of God something to be grasped. His special Spirit left behind for us, as we still breathe as men and women, is testimony. Our faith is essential."

Josh suddenly gasped, a sound that startled Missy from her state of resignation amid a strange yet comforting euphoria. "Nurse," she screamed. The RN returned, took back the oxygen tent, watched the monitor close in on a straight line, and began the ritual of listening for the final vital signs.

"Look, Treb! He's trying to say something. And my dear God! He's moving his hands!" She rushed to her dying husband's side and listened to his gasping breath slowly leaving his body."

"There! I can hear him, Treb! I can hear him! Listen!"

Maple bent down on the other side of his friend so he could hear. "The...most...beautiful...music...I...ever...heard," Josh whispered. "They...they are *singing* to me! How...I...wish...you...could hear...Oh, how...sweet...the sound!"

"Dear Lord, as we bid our mate and our special friend goodbye, we know our separation will be only for a little while," Treb prayed. "May your angels take him on a journey none of us can imagine, a journey to your blessed side. Amen."

"In Jesus Christ our Savior's name, Amen," Missy added, squeezing a gloriously surprised Treb's hand. He bent over and kissed his friend's cheek. Missy kissed Josh's forehead, and his right hand shot up, as if suddenly it had come back to life. He tapped the place where Treb kissed him, and he tapped three times where Missy's lips had been.

And then his body breathed its last breath.

Treb and Missy embraced. Then they noticed the Leventhals' daughter in the doorway. She had finally arrived, perhaps a little late, perhaps not. She had witnessed the death of her father with a combination of shock and awe.

Treb left mother and daughter quietly, to rejoin his wife at home amid this night of death...and life.

Bob Lapham

Epilogue

Treb, Struts and Louise had Mike Cardenas' services the following Monday. Treb located some cousins—first and second—belonging to his lifelong friend. Several had sent flowers, after reading about the upcoming graveside rites in the *Herald.* None made the long trip to the little cemetery overlooking Lake Mead, however. But none had been expected.

Treb actually tracked down Rita Cardenas, Treb's ex-wife whom he hadn't seen in almost three decades. Now Rita Gonzales, she lived in the small city of Valles, about sixty-five kilometers west of Tampico in central Mexico. Her husband owned part of the San Luis Potosi Distillery. They brewed rum and tequila for Mexican markets. She was apologetic and gave her best to Maple and his wife. She had raised a family of four children with her husband, Jaime.

The services were tasteful. Treb's old pal, Don Cherry, came out and sang a cappella *Streets of Laredo* and *Cool Water,* two cowboy songs that had been favorites of Mike's. A girl singer Cherry knew from the Strip came with him, even though it was an early-morning service. Treb loaned Mike two hymns Treb had requested be sung at his own service which would follow his planned cremation. She sang *Morning Has Broken* and *I Bind My Heart This Tide.*

Treb read from Psalms, First Corinthians and James, then bade his good friend farewell with a two-minute eulogy. Treb was sure Mike appreciated that, seeing as how overt religion, especially Treb's witnessing to clients, always made him uncomfortable.

Louise was particularly moved by the farewell to a man whom she had known for more than forty-three years. She reached up from her wheelchair and sought out Treb's hand. He never relinquished it until time to return to Las Vegas. Struts wept openly throughout.

Treb and Struts stopped by Desert King on the way back, and Struts stayed to make amends with the morning client, who was understanding when it was explained what had happened. The guy was going to be in Vegas for most of the week, and Treb re-scheduled him for two days later. So, it was back to business for them.

Treb had wanted to see Mandy and Brad one more time, so assuming that they would be able to leave North Las Vegas Air Terminal as planned, if Mandy aced her physician's exam, he postponed Monday afternoon's lesson. The guy said the following Saturday morning would be fine.

Louise wanted to see Mandy again, so she told Treb she would accompany him. Struts would drop by, if the timing was right.

It was. All three were there when the ambulance took Mandy to the tarmac and backed up to the King Air Tornado Thornton had hired. Everyone kissed her cheek, and it seemed to have moved her considerably.

Before Brad followed her aboard, he talked to Poole about his plans. He intended to have his feature series ready by mid-December, allowing it to qualify for the APME contest in March. Brad told Treb he bad been doing some outlining while staying with Mandy at the hospital. He felt he might have a book that could follow the series, in which case he'd split any proceeds with Maple. "We would spotlight your connection with Holly, maybe even get his name in the title," Brad said. They shook on it, and Treb said that was all the contract he needed. Actually, he wasn't really interested in doing a book. But now was not the time for negatives.

Asked what his and Mandy's plans were, Brad confessed that she had been non-committal, both just before and since her shooting. "I think if we're to go forward as a couple, it's gonna require us starting over first," Brad said. "We both live by the odds, Treb. My book on Mandy and me is about 65 to 35, against me, I figure. I simply forgot how trusting and fragile she was. While I went right on along with my usual crap, she was expecting total honesty. That's something I have a problem with."

"And you and Christ?" Treb asked.

"OK, Mr. Maple. I'm gonna try and be honest here. I see the same odds—against you. Mainly because I am not sure I can swing it, if Mandy's not with me."

"Maybe it won't be up to you," Treb said with a wry grin.

"Do me a favor," Brad asked, as he climbed the aircraft's stairs. "Promise you'll let me know how your match with the two sharks comes out. What you did for me, well…it was something else. Something to which I was not accustomed."

"Me neither, Brad. Until the world's greatest threesome—God, Jesus and the Holy Spirit—played right through my soul."

MARY KATHERINE Arnaz would be kept in Vegas for another two weeks, at least. The police allowed her to go back to Coral Gables to bury her husband, so long as she had a return ticket. She agreed. While at the service, Desi's two remaining partners grilled her on what happened. All she could tell them was, Desi had said something about still having the coke *and* Gabe's money.

One of the partners said, "Then it must be—"

"Stop! I don't want to know *anything*," she said, then revealed to them that she had hired a lawyer in Las Vegas who was going to go through the police and set up a lie detector test. "If I pass, and I should since I *really* don't know anything, at least anything they could pin down enough to ask me about. Then maybe they'll give up and I'll come home. I'm *pretty* sure Oscar has something hidden somewhere on or under or in *my* Navigator, and it's baffling why the cops can't find it. But I don't want to know!"

"You *will* return to Florida in the Navigator, won't you M.K.?" a partner asked.

"You better believe it. The Lincoln has some kind of special registration, I'm sure. But as far as I'm concerned, it's my late husband's car. *If* there is any cash in it someplace, I expect his partners to find it and give me my inheritance. In other words, *all* of it. If they come up with any powdery substance, the partners can have it, and good riddance! And by the way, I'm leaving a sealed document with this lawyer in Vegas, who I'm to keep in touch with, every two months. If I fail to, and if he finds something funky happened to Oscar's widow, well he's supposed to get in touch with the chief investigator in this case.

"The house in Coral Gables is mine. The joint bank account is mine. Oscar's account in the Cayman Islands is mine. Everybody agree?"

They did.

SHORTLY AFTER Thanksgiving, a retired couple from Baltimore made their first visit to their new acquisition west of Las Vegas. Black Rock Ranch was to be an investment opportunity, and hopefully a retirement home. They were given a tour by Rita Blackwell. She admitted she hadn't been on the small spread "in years." She sold her late husband's property, she said, "because I'd been saving it for my son, Billy Carson, but we had a real bad falling out and I ain't seen him since last January. Probably never will."

The couple pondered their perhaps unwise sight-unseen purchase, even though it came at an attractive price. Paul took a hike around the place while Glenda waited in the dust-incrusted double-wide. Upon rejoining his wife, Paul said, "I found an old home site up a ways. Not promising either. It has a dried out old cistern. Stank to high heaven. Guess a varmint got inside, couldn't get out, and died. Must be real deep. I threw in some large rocks I found lying around, hoping to hear the sound of water. None, though. I think the first thing we ought to do is fill it up with more rocks, so nobody falls in and breaks a leg, then sues us. Remind me to tell the crew that's coming out next week."

Meanwhile, the lone surviving gunman from Gabe's ill-fated gang couldn't be tied to any of the shootings. His lawyer figured his client might have to do a little time, due to his record, but would beat any murder or accessory to murder rap.

THREE WEEKS after Mike's burial, Brad got the following e-mail from Vegas:

Hey, Poole! Treb here. I've taken a crash course in computering and have inherited Mike's laptop. You wanted a rundown on yesterday's little match with your hold 'em pals. Here goes.

They selected a guy who's seventy and has a legitimate 14 handicap. They couldn't have made a worse choice—for them. He hits it 185 down the middle. I think it was in the disco era when he last missed a fairway. He putts like Brad Faxon. He can get up and down from a paved parking lot. You question his handicap? It's accurate—for where he plays, and what tees. Summerlin, next to the back markers. Rarely breaks 85 out there. But can he play a short course like Desert King, from the executive tees! That they feared, so they chose Summerlin instead. Very poor move on their part.

I was going to take it easy on them, until they both came out with some very dumb gamemanship aimed at each of us. Right from the start.

So, we won the original and three presses on the front side, or four thousand apiece. They wised up and quit bumping us on the back, but their front side presses were also made on the 18-hole bets. We won the back, and by 17, we had 'em out on the original and three presses on the 18. Five grand more.

God forgive me! I tried to shame them into pressing on that tough 18th over the canyon and then with water at the green. They wouldn't do it. God forgive me, again! They struggled along, trying for a skin for one of them on the last hole, since everybody but me stroked. From the whites, I had my drive down there in seven-wood territory. Hank—he was my partner—he had a three-wood to the green. Both of our beat-up foes were well back, one with a two-iron and the other having to hit a three-wood.

While going up to our balls, I told Hank—God forgive me yet again!—why didn't he let one of the guys win a skin? It would be tough, since three-wood tanked his approach and two-iron decided he'd just go ahead and lay up, for some reason. He had been choking like a baby for six holes.

Hank, who had 11 skins, thanks to his liberal handicap, said it was against his religion (yes, Brad. I chewed him out). But OK. He pushed his approach in a trap to the right, and would leave his third in the sand with such a so-obvious deliberate miss, it was pathetic.

The guy in the water couldn't do better than six. The other who laid up managed to get on, and would two-putt for a five net four.

Me? I can dump a shot and never be suspected. I came over the top with my seven wood, and put it in the drink pin high to the left.

"Golly!" I swore, where both your pals could hear. "Am I glad you fellas didn't press to get even! Thanks, men!"

Brad, I can safely report to you that your adversaries were pee-ohed!

By the way. How's Mandy? Any change in your status with her?

My best,
Treb.

After Brad got through laughing, he assumed the serious business of responding:

Dear Treb:

How many prayers for forgiveness did I count? Three? Four? I say you're a champ, and I'm going to add that I think your God thinks that too.

Mandy is doing fine. Her grandmother is a caregiver deluxe. I go by most every evening and bring carryout suppers with me. Her doctors here predict complete recovery. But they want to wait a couple months before doing a hip replacement, which they regret having to perform, due to her young age. But both realize she's going to have to have it.

As for her and me, she obviously doesn't love me anymore. She is too nice not to let me hang around. But I can tell. My odds against reconciliation have increased to 85 to 15, I'd say.

Let's keep in touch. I have sworn off poker, by the way.

Your friend forever,
Bradley Poole.

Bob Lapham

About the Author

Bob Lapham is a former award-winning newspaper writer who spent 34 years working mostly as sports editor/writer, news editor or arts and entertainment editor/writer for papers in Brownsville, Harlingen and Abilene, Texas. He retired in 2000 at the age of 65. Lapham is the author of three books of non-fiction.

His first novel, *Meet Me At the River Buddy Holly,* is a story of action, drama and faith, woven around his work as a backup singer for rock 'n' roll legend Buddy Holly in 1957.

He and his wife, Mary, live in Abilene, Texas. They have three grown children and one granddaughter. He plays golf, though he says, "my game now languishes in a state of age-ravaged short-knocking and yipping."

Printed in the United States
1271500001B/267

9 781410 746252